With Than

Valerie Ball my wom   k
wouldn't have devel   it
was m

Barbara Bell Managing Editor of the Experience Publishers
(Canada) for explaining what I needed to improve to become
a published author.

Rosie Brooke my Open University tutor on the Start Writing
Fiction Course.

David Childs of 'Dave in the Doghouse' for the great cover
pictures.
d_e_childs-doghousephotos@yahoo.com

Holly Dixon and Lewis Childs my cover models.

Meryl Scrivener my wife for her patience and opinions on my
writing.

Historical Prologue

In AD 43 the Romans invaded Britain and in the process protected it for 367 years. That was until 410 when Emperor Honorius withdrew all the Roman army from Britain to protect his homeland from barbarian attacks. Because of the Romans' exodus, historians consider this period to be the beginning of the Dark Ages. This was because the Britons had no standing armies, leaving them vulnerable to attack.

During the early 400s Vortigern became King of much of Britain. As he had no army he invited the Saxons under Hengist and Horsa into Britain as mercenaries to help fight the invading Scots and Picts. After marrying Hengist's daughter, Rowena, Vortigern gave the Saxons what is now the county of Kent to live in under their own rule. In 449 the Angles, a German tribe, invaded what we still called East Anglia. Around the year 500 the land of the Angles was shortened to England. The adjacent territories of Wales and Scotland they called Britannium. Then, in 527, the East Saxons took over the area we call Essex; this included the town of London.

The Anglo-Saxon divisions of England were ethnically divided as follows:

- Jutes colonized and ruled in Kent and the Isle of White
- East Saxons ruled Essex.
- South Saxons Sussex
- West Saxons Wessex.
- Angles ruled in East Anglia
- Angles ruled Middle Anglia, also called Mercia
- Angles additionally ruled in Northumberland to the north.

At around the same time, in the fifth century, an Aryan tribe was under attack by the invading forces of Islam. This was far away from Britain in the Himalayan Mountains of the Punjab in India. Not wanting to fight themselves, they recruited surrounding war-like tribes to do it for them. This army, collectively known as the Roma, fought so fiercely they defended the territory successfully for around a hundred years. But in the sixth century the Muslims finally cut off the Roma army from their homeland. The Roma army, including their wives and children, had no choice but to leave India.

After Crossing the Himalayas they travelled via the Silk Road into Western Europe. As they moved across new lands, the Roma didn't attempt to subjugate the other races or appropriate their lands although they were militarily strong enough to do so. Instead they integrated into those societies with many fighting as mercenaries for their hosts. For example, around 1450 AD thousands of Roma warriors fought against the Turks in Wallachia, Romania, in the army of Vlad Dracul, known as Vlad the Impaler or Dracula.

At the end of the eighth century, raids by seaborne Scandinavian pirates began on Britain, especially undefended monastic sites. The beginning of the first Viking Age is considered to have been in 793 when the raiding Norsemen attacked the monastery on Lindisfarne, Holy Island, in Northumbria. These early raids were usually brutal for relatively small-scale thefts of valuables. Later invasions were aimed at finding land where the raiders could settle. By the end of the ninth century there were large-scale settlements and political domination by Scandinavians in various parts of Britain. This included most of the eastern coastal area, where this novel is set.

Alfred the Great, (848 –899) King of Wessex in the south and southwest, fought and reclaimed much of the rest of southern England from the Vikings. Alfred was succeeded by his son Edward the Elder (899-924). Edward and his sister Æthelflæd, widow of the Mercian king, re-conquered the rest of the south of England from the Danes, including Mercia reaching into the midlands. Having reclaimed Essex from the Vikings, Edward the Elder and his men camped at Essex's second biggest town Maldon while having the Witham Burh (Castle) built. Edward later arranged to have an earth-walled Burh constructed at Maldon, in part to house his royal mint. Upon his death, his son Æthelstan (924-939) continued to retake England for the Saxons. Edmund his brother succeeded him (939 to 946.) Then another brother, Edred, from (946 to 955.) Edwy (Eadwig) was next (955-959), followed by Edgar the Peaceable from (959-975). Edgar was succeeded by his eldest son, Edward the Martyr.

However, Edward was murdered, aged sixteen, in 978 at Corfe Castle, Dorset. This may have been on the orders of his stepmother so that her (even younger) son, Edwards's half-brother, Aethelred, could come to power. Aethelred was at some time nicknamed Aethelred the Unred, meaning ill advised. Much later a translator wrongly interpreted Unred as Unready and that has been erroneously used in teaching history.

The period including King Aethelred's reign is considered by historians to be the dawning of the second Viking age. This was very different from the first Viking age in that the raids were on a far larger scale and frequently organised by royal leaders. These huge fleets of longships carried raiders whose objective was to gain massive amounts of valuables by extortion, called Danegeld. This was protection money to leave the Saxons in peace. However, paying this proved to be a waste of silver as with most blackmail incidents; once paid the Vikings kept returning demanding more and in even larger amounts.

Meanwhile the Roma nation, forced from the Punjab in the fifth century, had by the tenth century spent the intervening five hundred years spreading across Europe. The first *written* reports of Roma, in England, were in the early 1500's. However, recent DNA testing has proved that some Roma (now called Romanies) had actually arrived in Britain about five hundred years earlier than the written evidence suggested. For these early Romani visitors to Britain, finding work as Saxon or indeed Viking mercenaries was a logical career choice.

This novel is set in Essex, the land of the East Saxons, commencing in the year 888 AD during the reign of King Aethelred the second.

The North Pole has moved position several times during our planet's past. When the pole was situated at the Yukon it was linked by latitude to several exceptionally sacred sites. These include Machu Picchu, Nanking, Stonehenge, and Mersea Island in Essex, near to Maldon. Because of this, paranormal activity has been endemic in the area of the Essex coast where this novel is set. So the novel's sub-plot includes aspects of Essex's metaphysical past.

I must emphasize that apart from the obvious historical information, this novel is entirely a work of fiction. I do not intend to rewrite history.

Viking Sword Saxon Shield

By

Keith Scrivener

Mirador Publishing
Mirador
Wearne Lane
Langport
Somerset
TA10 9HB

One

Strangulated screeching, like the sound of a beast in agony, stops Eddie in his tracks. With pursuers closing rapidly, there's no way back. He'll have to pass the source of the terrible shrieking.

An enormous black silhouette swoops down towards him, obscuring the full moon's glow. Instinctively Eddie cowers, draws his knife and throws one arm up to deflect the anticipated attack. The screeching fades into a plaintive echo and then is gone.

Eddie smells ozone and seaweed coupled with the dampness and taste of salt spray. He edges forward, sweat running from his brow despite the cold.

A menacing black mass materializes, an unholy wailing emanating from its maw. Startled, Eddie falls down the hardened mud sea wall, rolling towards the shrilly screaming horror. Out of control, he pitches down the bank and crashes into the looming entity. He recoils in revulsion.

But the dark form feels hard, chill and inanimate. Eddie realizes it's just a black scare-goose mock predator kite, fitted with a wind screamer device. He sighs in relief. He guesses that geese flock to this estuary to escape the harsh arctic winters. This is probably intended to divert the hungry birds from devastating the surrounding fields of young crops and drive them towards the local Lord's hunters.

Although this latest perceived threat proves harmless, the original crisis remains; he's still being chased and must hide or outpace his persecutors.

Eddie paused to get his breath back. It was the year AD 888 and his life had changed dramatically in a few months. He'd been with his Romani family, living and working on a Danish farm. That was until Norwegian Vikings had raided the Danes and he had been captured while fishing in the sea. The Norwegians had forced him to help row their Viking longship to England. There he'd been left tied to the longship while his captors pillaged churches and isolated farms.

Initially the Norwegians' raids had been successful until, on one foray, the Saxons ambushed the marauding Norwegians. The Vikings were vastly outnumbered and routed.

Hearing the clamour, Eddie had used a secreted stolen blade to sever his bonds. Then he handed the blade to his fellow Saxon rowing captives before concealing himself in the bushes on the shore to wait for them. He was relying on them to vouch for him with the local Saxons.

However, this was not to be. While the Saxon rowing slaves attempted to release themselves, the Vikings that had escaped being slaughtered returned and prevented their escape. Realizing he would have no help now, Eddie had no other option than to flee alone into the English countryside.

Since then he had been living on his wits, gathering berries and nuts from the woodlands and using a bow and some arrows, appropriated from the Vikings, to kill game for food.

To the local Lord, he was an interloper trespassing and poaching on his territory. Quite understandably, the Saxon leader had sent warriors to capture or kill the intruder.

Late one cold December night, Eddie had been located and pursued by the Saxons. In the light of the full moon Eddie was the one being hunted. Initially, Eddie's Romani guile had served him well… for the present he had outdistanced and outwitted his pursuers.

Eddie listens. The clamour of his pursuers has faded, allowing him leeway to try to find a hiding place. The full moon provides sufficient illumination for his flight but is also likely to make it easier for his pursuers to spot him. However, they are using flaming torches; a choice that Eddie knows will work in his favour, as areas outside the range of their flickering flames will seem dark and impenetrable.

Then nature works against him. Clouds dapple the moonlight, throwing dark shadows in his path. Eddie stumbles on the uneven ground, spraining his ankle. Cursing, he staggers onwards, this new discomfort slowing his progress.

He struggles several miles further across the rough terrain beside the edge of the seawater. His swollen ankle throbs agonizingly. His injury is by now hampering his progress badly. He can hear the pursuers' shouts and the excited barking of their dogs growing louder. They are closing in on him again.

Eddie can now make out the outline of Northey Island, looming like a shadowy castle in the estuary. At the same moment he spots several more flaming torches ahead, moving towards him as a second group of Saxon warriors cut off his escape route. He begins to shake as much with fear as from the cold. Normally he would outwit anyone in the dark across open country. But tonight, hobbling and with the spring tide restricting hiding places by covering the saltings, he is in danger.

There is only one solution. Drain-off lakes had formed behind the estuary wall. They had been swelled by rainfall draining off the waterlogged farmland. Eddie wades in. He sinks, gasping, up to his waist in the freezing brackish water as he breaks through the thin crackling ice that covers its shimmering surface.

To put the dogs off the scent, Eddie splashes through the clinging ooze below the water. At each step, the stench of methane gas liberated from rotting seaweed in the mud assails his nostrils. He's reminded of childhood stink bombs.

There's a coppice next to the estuary wall. Eddie wriggles into it, penetrating the dense branches until he judges that the light from his pursuers' flaming torches will not penetrate the thickly interwoven and sharply spiked blackthorn cover.

Apart from the sharp thorns, this would be a pleasant sanctuary in the summer, but not on this December night with hoarfrost and a force seven north-easterly gale. All night, the unrelenting wind in his face takes his breath away and saps his strength.

As anyone raised in the country knows, dry still cold is no problem; you just wear warmer clothes. However, tonight it is windy and damp, multiplying the energy sapping effects of the cold.

Eddie is grateful for respite from the wind, but his clothes are saturated. He urgently needs to keep moving. Unfortunately his painful ankle won't permit this luxury. He smells Birchwood smoke and longs for the heat of a blazing log fire.

Desperately trying to keep his mind off the bleak conditions, Eddie takes mental stock. He is an expert fighter, Romanies being descended from warrior tribes in the mountains of India. Much of the time on their journey down the Silk Road and through Europe, his tribe had fought as mercenaries for local leaders.

However, being a Romani warrior wouldn't help him as he was vastly outnumbered. Fighting would be suicidal.

Nearby barking interrupts his musing as a group of warriors with hunting dogs passes his hiding place. He decides that the minute it's clear he'll get out of this confined spot and get well away from the place.

Then he realizes he has left a trail of broken ice leading to his camouflaged shelter. All it will take is for one dog to detect where he entered the coppice and his cover will be blown. Again his pursuers turn towards his place of concealment. Eddie's heart is thumping violently but he stays motionless.

He knows he is in real trouble now as his pursuers have fanned out and nearly reached his hideaway. The sensible solution is for him to give up and throw himself on the Saxons' mercy in the hope that, after a beating, he would just be enslaved rather than killed. But he could not rely on clemency. It was more likely the liege lord would have put a bounty on the intruder's head, dead or alive.

He has been to this location a week ago with the Vikings so he knows he is near a causeway between the mainland and the Island.

Whatever he does, he will be killed so, ignoring the almost inevitable consequences, he breaks cover, forcing himself along as fast as his tender ankle will allow.

He is immediately seen. Saxon warriors shout and loose arrows at him. He ducks and the shafts narrowly miss him, peppering the bushes above his head.

Logic tells him to halt as there is no sane option, but he's loath to do the rational thing. He takes his only possible escape route and jinks sideways, plunging into the sea where the causeway to Northey Island begins. He remembers that at low tide the raised pathway is dry and even when partially covered, it is still possible to wade across.

This proves to be a catastrophic miscalculation. Tonight's flood tide is far too high and the water glacially cold. The freezing waters pull at Eddie's clothes with icy fingers. The swirling current sweeps him off his feet. He strikes out frenziedly with his powerful crawl stroke.

Although Eddie is a strong swimmer, today, dressed in sodden winter clothes the task is formidable. Worse still, a powerful rip current boosted by the spring tide sweeps between the island and the mainland. Escalating watery surges gush round both ends of the island, concentrating enormous volumes of water into the confines of the narrow, muddy channel. The water hurls itself against the elevated causeway.

The taste of the brine he's been unable to avoid swallowing makes Eddie physically sick. Soon his arms are barely able to dip through the breakers' assault.

Eddie's entire body is benumbed. His ice-cold legs are like lead dragging him ever downward. What would normally be an easy swim is beyond his capacity in these impossible conditions.

Sensing the warning signs of hypothermia, Eddie realizes with a strange, muted horror that he is not going to make it. He tries one last but ineffectual physical effort before surrendering to the inevitable and sinking below the waves.

He retches as seawater forces itself violently into his nose and mouth. He is drowning. Soon even his retching ceases as he descends into a moribund state. He is vaguely aware of a stream of brilliant white light in the far distance, illuminating the depths of the murky water.

Then total calm, relaxation and blackness.

Two

Seawater drained away from the tidal reaches of the Blackwater Estuary. Only a trickle of freshwater from the Chelmer River meandered towards the North Sea.

Three islands nestled in the estuary's confines. For a couple of hours each low tide these were accessible by naturally formed, raised causeways.

Spindly-legged seabirds searched for food in the black mud surrounding Northey Island. Morning sunshine melted the ice and frost clinging to the green plants on the saltings. The steam rising from the icemelt formed cool droplets that dripped onto the flotsam and jetsam below.

What appeared to be the cadaver of a rotting animal lay almost buried in black mud and herring gulls and crows circled the fleshy object like vultures spotting a likely carcass for dismemberment.

Below the birds, denying them their prey, a non-beating heart lurched into irregular pulsation. Water-sodden lungs ejected liquid and drew in oxygen in a series of violent convulsions. In billowing waves of semi-awareness, its mind drifted between nothingness and despair. Thoughts and feelings were indistinct, as though the creature were a distant onlooker floating above its own body.

Then agony wracked the corporal form as every muscle spasmed, released, and then convulsed again. The tortured soul was dragged towards consciousness as physical agony permeated its whole being. Part of it longed to return to the peace of its previous oblivion.

Eventually, the worst of the creature's cramps abated, with the exception of its calf and thigh muscles. It screamed soundlessly as it struggled to stretch its limbs and relax the contractions. After what seemed like hours the pain eased, only to be replaced by irritating pins and needles. The tingling sensations continued until blood circulation at last returned to near normal.

Gradually, the wretch grasped that it was alive and a human male. The man had been suffering what seemed to him to have been a recurring nightmare. Of profound blackness, hysteria combined with despairing struggle... and of engulfing cold and extreme panic provoked by watery suffocation.

Now, he wasn't drowning. No. In fact, although cold, it was a bright sunny day. The man had a wavering sense of lying on an island shore beneath a bright sun. His body, from feet to chest, was embedded in slimy black mud.

He had a hunch that he had been or perhaps was a Romani boy. Yes, that was it. He was called Edward or Eddie. He thought that was right but it could be just a false perception. In time, a form of personal recognition returned. He felt certain that he was Eddie and had been running from pursuers on a cold winter night.

If that was so and he was Eddie, what happened? Did he have a seizure? His mind floated in and out of focus as he looked around, still dazed and with a splitting headache. He blinked and then did a double take. What appeared to be a number of Viking longships were beached on the mud near the mouth of the creek.

Not far away two men were going through the motions of a mock fight. Both were tall with long blond hair and flowing beards. One swung an axe while the other wielded a heavy double-edged sword with a bone handle.

Alongside the nearest longship another large blond man scanned the horizon out across the sea with a scope. In addition two shorter, dark-haired and swarthy men paddled a wooden board canoe along the creek toward the longships. Was he sleeping, hallucinating, deluded or just dead, Eddie wondered? Maybe this was the afterlife, but was it heaven or hell? Perhaps he'd made it to Valhalla? Could the Norsemen have got it right and all other religions were wrong?

Suddenly Eddie's confusion cleared as he remembered the Norwegian Vikings. They had so recently forced him to be a galley slave. He remembered the Saxons ambushing the Vikings. Were these the Norwegian Vikings' compatriots, Danes or even Swedes?

Whichever race these warriors were, they were likely to be his enemies. It would be prudent to be cautious. Crawling forward, he dragged himself over a weed-covered bank. The plants made good cover while he inched into a position to try to hear what the Vikings were saying.

He couldn't get close enough, and therefore decided it was too risky to get nearer or even stay there.

On the Island's mud flats there were more longships. Eddie also noticed the locations of the few wooden huts on the mainland. He'd seen these when he'd been there recently with the Norwegians. The aroma of woodsmoke and food cooking emanated from the dwellings. Thankfully, the buildings pinpointed the position of the causeway. This escape route was close at hand.

Eddie raised himself and moved off towards the refuge of the land bridge. Unfortunately, he disturbed a blackbird that flew off, noisily crying its warning. The bird attracted the attention of the Viking look-out who shouted his own warning.

Within moments, several Vikings were converging on Eddie's position. The causeway that had seemed so near, in retrospect and with Eddie's panic, seemed much further away. Eddie froze momentarily.

Then, his stomach heaving and sweat running from his brow, he ran. Staring ahead at his goal and not the ground, he stumbled and fell. A giant Viking launched a spear at him. This gave Eddie the impetus to spring up and literally sprint towards his goal. Eventually, enveloped in mud and with his muscles still stiff and painful, he scurried onto the Northey Island causeway. With Vikings in pursuit he had no time to be cautious.

Eddie was almost across the raised mud path. But just before he reached the far side there was a flurry of movement from the mainland. Three short muscular men darted out from the bushes and barred his path. Eddie slowed and looked behind him. Viking archers were now on the causeway, their arrows already dropping around him.

Eddie suspected the men blocking his mainland exit were Saxon warriors. They were dressed in knee-length beige smocks, rough leggings and metal helmets with noseguards. Most worrying were the long scramaseax, the single-edged daggers, spears and clubs they confronted him with.

The nearest warrior shouted, "Surrender, sea pirate, if you want to live!"

Eddie yelled back, "Never!" But when he checked his options, they weren't good. He was unarmed. He couldn't go back because of the Vikings. Yet if he went off the side of the causeway with the tide out, he'd be engulfed in the soft black mud.

Eddie's indecision had calamitous repercussions. He'd momentarily glanced away from the Saxons. As he turned back, he briefly glimpsed a Saxon throwing a club in mid-air before it crashed into his forehead. The weight of the weapon fractured Eddie's skull with a sickening crack, causing excruciating pain before he lapsed yet again into unconsciousness.

Regaining awareness, Eddie realized he was being carried over a Saxon warrior's shoulder. The man took him into a roughly built wooden building. From his upside-down vantage point he could see a central hearth in which a log fire burned fiercely.

What little smoke there was curled upwards and dispersed through the thatch as there was no chimney or hole for it to escape through. Eddie remembered Romani fires and how he'd been taught to use dry, mature wood to avoid creating smoke. Whoever had laid this fire had done the same. The burning timber crackled and gave off an aromatic smell like branches from the deep forest.

Eddie's skull still hurt. His mind drifted. It was difficult to concentrate. He had a fleeting thought… could this all be a hallucination?

In the room were not only the men who had captured him, but also another, dressed in fine clothes. The man wore a scarlet silken cloak over a cream cotton shirt, tan leather breeches and long, brown leather riding boots.

The fine clothes were not matched by the man's stature or appearance. He had short legs in comparison to his long body and was balding, with hunched shoulders and small piggy eyes set close together. Worse still, he had terrible acne or some other skin disease. His face was smothered in fiery red swellings and pustules. The two men holding Eddie threw him down in front of the finely dressed man.

The Saxons held a discussion about Eddie, the gist of which he understood. Over the years he had become quite a linguist. As his tribe moved around from country to country he'd picked up many languages.

Naturally, he was fluent in Romanes, his own Romani tribe's language and he had also become proficient in German and Danish. He had learned some Norwegian after he'd been captured by them and then acquired the basis of Saxon talk from the Norwegians' Saxon rowing captives.

The Saxon race had originated from Scandinavia so learning the Norse languages had been easier than he'd expected. They had words in common but wildly varying accents.

Eddie wasn't encouraged by what he was hearing. The Saxons were discussing whether to kill him now or take him back to be interrogated by someone called Ealdorman Byrhtnoth.

Suddenly, the finely dressed man pointed at Eddie. Two men grabbed his arms and hauled him to his feet again. The finely dressed man forced his face close to Eddie's. Speaking with a high-pitched voice, he said, "I am Eldor Godric. I am in charge of all the Dengie Hundred Peninsula. You accursed Viking, how dare you attack my lands? I have just led my men in a victorious battle against one of your war parties. Now more of you presume to invade my territory?"

Eldor Godric's close proximity was not pleasant for Eddie. Godric's breath, expelled through his black rotting teeth, smelled of a foul mixture of decay and alcohol.

Godric spat green spittle stinking of rotten meat in Eddie's face. "Why do you Vikings dare to intrude onto your betters' lands?"

Eddie protested in broken Saxon, "I'm no Viking!"

The brute's response was to kick Eddie in the stomach. Eddie retched and gasped for breath as waves of queasiness washed over him. He was held so firmly as to be incapable of fighting back. There seemed little point in struggling, so he pretended to pass out.

Godric continued to attack Eddie, but when he got no reaction he gave up and signalled to his men. Two warriors unceremoniously dragged Eddie along the ground by his feet. Eddie felt his head bump against the wooden doorstep and then several stones. They hurt him, but he managed to stay quiet in case he provoked more violence. Eventually he was tied with leather thongs to a primitive trestle. In turn, this was attached to straps on the back of a horse.

The beast dragged Eddie along a dirt track, every bump inflicting more agony to his cracked skull and bruised body. Godric rode at the front on a fine horse while his men followed on their sturdy ponies.

Eddie noticed that as the procession passed serfs, they doffed their hats, bowed their heads and touched their forelocks to Eldor Godric. As the horse dragged him up a steep, cobbled hill, he caught sight of the coast and Osea Island they'd left earlier.

Ahead he could see a log-built church. This was hemmed in by two rows of haphazardly shaped and positioned wooden huts. Most strikingly, overlooking the river was a huge Burh, the Saxon name for an enclosed, fortified town. High earth embankments with intermittent stone towers encompassed the Burh, which Eddie guessed must enclose many acres.

Eventually the horse dragged Eddie through huge wooden gates into the Burh itself. Once inside he was unceremoniously released from the horse-drawn trestle. With the bonds on his wrists remaining tightly tied behind him, he was coerced into a stone building. The Saxon warriors forced Eddie to stagger down steps and along passageways until, finally, they threw him into a prison cell in the semi-basement. There, mercifully, he was untied and left on the earthen floor.

The cell was virtually underground; only the top two feet protruded into the daylight. This was where the tiny window was situated and Eddie struggled to stand on tiptoe to peer out of the barred opening. Being six feet tall, he was able to see out. Anyone of the average height locally wouldn't have that advantage.

He could see the sun was high in the sky. Through the window came an all-pervading stench of raw sewage and rotting carcasses. He noticed the shabby shoes and worn clothing of the many people milling around in the narrow streets.

Eddie turned and looked round the cell. There was a wooden bucket in one corner that he guessed must be the toilet facilities. In another corner was a straw-filled palliasse and a coarse horsehair blanket that was obviously his bedding.

After a couple of hours the door opened and two short, dark men entered the cell. Eddie hadn't seen either of them before. One held a Seax single-bladed sword threateningly and fixed him with a hostile glare. His companion put a tray of food and drink on the ground.

Eddie tried not to glare back, making an effort to look passive. He spoke in a low voice. "Thank you, sir. I'm hungry."

The men looked surprised; perhaps they'd been told he was a Viking and didn't expect him to speak their language.

One man replied, "You don't have to call either of us Sir. We are only slaves doing our job."

"Thank you, my friends. My name is Edward Lavengro. May I ask what yours are?"

The man answered, "My name's Leo and my companion is Dunnere."

Eddie nodded. "I'll remember your kindness."

The two men, still eyeing Eddie suspiciously, withdrew from the cell holding their weapons defensively.

After the men had left, Eddie checked the food they'd brought him. There was some pork that smelled smoky, and heavy unleavened bread. In addition there was a bowl of thick broth with a pungent, herby aroma, plus a flagon of wine.

Salivating, Eddie licked his lips. He tore at the meat with his teeth and hands. Gravy and juice ran down his jowls so he mopped it up with the bread. Then he held the wooden bowl to his lips to drink the broth. By the time he'd consumed all the strong, sweet wine he felt almost normal again. He suspected he'd become dehydrated as his last drink had been twenty-four hours ago.

Despite the pain he was experiencing, he felt exhausted. Stretching out on the straw palliasse, he was sleeping soundly within minutes. It was a couple of hours after midday and he was exhausted.

Eddie half awoke to the sensation of movement on his chest and face, then woke with a start to find himself covered in rats. He jumped up and swiped at the creatures, knocking two from his chest and grabbing the large one on his face. It squirmed round and sank its needle teeth into the little finger of his left hand. Eddie screamed in pain and attempted to shake it off, but the rat bit harder. Using his right hand, he grabbed the animal's neck and crushed its windpipe. The rodent released its bite and Eddie slung it at the wall as hard as he could. He stamped about, trying to crush it underfoot, but couldn't find its body.

Now wide awake, Eddie wrapped the blanket around him for warmth and sat up in a corner until the dawn's light convinced him there were no more vermin. He sucked his punctured finger, trying to reduce the pain but to no avail.

In the half-light, Eddie examined the cell and found the body of a black rat where he'd thrown it. When it was fully light he discovered a rat hole in a corner. As he had nothing else, he stuffed the corner of his blanket into the hole.

Eddie had always hated rats. Was there anything he could do? He wondered if he could perhaps escape. Unfortunately, close inspection of the cell revealed that it was solidly built of stone and the bars at the window would not yield to the strongest of men. The door was solid oak and locked fast.

Later his two jailers, Leo and Dunnere, returned with a tray of food and wine for his breakfast.

As the men didn't speak, Eddie addressed them. "Good morning. May I ask you some more questions?"

Dunnere answered sullenly. "You can, and we'll help if we're able, but it's unlikely we can do much for you."

Eddie said, "There are rats getting into this cell. He held up the black rat by its tail as illustration.

Leo laughed. "You have our permission to eat it raw if you're hungry."

Eddie was not amused. "Very funny. I was going to ask if you could get me something to plug this rat hole with?"

Dunnere spoke. "Yes, I will bring you something next time I come. Did you want to ask anything else?"

"Yes. Like me, you have black hair and brown eyes while most people around here are fairer looking. Is there a reason for this?"

"It's strange you should ask us that," Dunnere replied. "We have been told you're a captive Viking, but you don't look like one. Your skin and hair colouring is more like ours... in fact you're even darker."

Leo butted in. "But we can only just understand your language. You have such a strange accent?"

15

Dunnere agreed. "Leo's right, you're certainly not from around here. And no local would ask such an obvious question." He narrowed his eyes. "Just who are you?"

"Your logic's correct," Eddie confirmed. "I'm not even from this country. I was a rowing slave of the Vikings but escaped when Saxons attacked them."

Leo nodded. "Yes, I can believe you were one of the Vikings slaves, but what nation do you belong to?"

"I'm a Romani; part of a wandering warrior tribe from a place called India, far to the north of this country. I had been working on a farm with my family in Denmark. That was until the Norwegian Vikings captured me and made me their rowing slave."

There was the sound of a violent argument from the road outside. Dunnere peered through the window bars and laughed as two peasants fought over some disagreement.

Leo ignored the scrap outside and addressed Eddie. "I've never heard of Romanies, but I have seen dark-skinned Egyptians on trading boats in Heybridge Harbour that looked like you?"

Eddie smiled. "Sometimes we are called Egyptians, but it's usually shortened to *Gypsies*."

Leo nodded to his friend and said, "There you are, Dunnere. I told you he was an Egyptian."

Dunnere seemed more relaxed now. "We're Britons," he told Eddie. "We dark haired people lived here in peace until the blond Saxons invaded England. Now, under these Saxons, even the name of our race, Briton, is interchangeable with the word slave. We are a slave race."

Eddie screwed up his face, shaking his head as if in disbelief. "So are you saying Britons cannot be free men?"

Leo answered him. "Not quite that. But our only chance of advancement is if we volunteer to fight in battles for the Saxons. Then a Briton can become a free man, an honorary Saxon. But that's a dangerous course, because most who try are given no armour and little weaponry so they lose their lives without reward."

When the two jailers had left the cell, Eddie lay on his palliasse and considered the recent turn of events. He'd been unconscious twice and wasn't too certain of reality. Dreams could seem like realism. With head injuries it was possible to lose awareness of true events in the physical universe. These may have been substituted by warped understandings, perhaps existing in the person's subconscious mind.

Eddie reasoned that if he had the logic to consider these possibilities, his mind must be functioning correctly. He'd suffered enough head injuries in previous battles to know that once his brain's malfunction abated, the confusion would pass. Then he would be as before, if not with heightened psychoanalytical powers.

Leo and Dunnere returned unexpectedly, breaking into Eddie's reverie.

"As promised, we have brought some logs that you can use to block up those rat holes," Dunnere said. "Have a good night."

Eddie was relieved. "Fantastic, guys! Now I should get a good night undisturbed by those rodents. They have fleas, you know. I got bitten by them as well as by the rat."

Both jailers laughed and waved at the door as they left him to position the logs.

Eddie began to think back to his childhood in Germany. His mother told fortunes, either by reading palms or using a crystal ball. Eddie was the oldest of six, having a brother and four sisters. As soon as the children could talk their mother had taught them the Romani ways… to tell fortunes, use mental telepathy and remote viewing.

However, it was only his mother, himself and his sixteen-year-old younger brother, Fero, who had these powers. These three could use extra-sensory-perception as well as remote viewing to explore far away targets.

It wasn't as if Eddie read other people's minds, though he could sometimes interpret others' extreme emotion, which had been invaluable in battle situations.

He could also sometimes accurately predict dramatic forthcoming events. He could feel danger and let his mind travel or remote-view other locations. This had saved him and the family in the past.

His father had been killed in battle fighting for the Visigoths and his mother had died in childbirth. Eddie had therefore become head of the family, so he'd taken them to Denmark. Since he'd been captured by the Vikings, Fero would have had to manage.

Eddie decided to try and contact his brother by mental telepathy. He closed his eyes and covered his ears with his hands. Then he focused his mind on the farm in Denmark.

Eddie also remembered his mother telling him that for generations her Romani family had experienced visitations from strange Druids. One of these had appeared at his birth and nodded benignly before disappearing.

His mental concentration was abruptly interrupted as the cell door was thrown open.

Eldor Godric and two men that bore a family resemblance to him entered the cell. The two men held Eddie against the wall while Eldor Godric kicked him in the stomach before thrusting his boil-ridden face within inches of Eddie's. Eddie turned his head away his face screwed up with disgust. He gagged from the stench of the man's breath.

Godric was enraged by Eddie's obvious distaste and blatant show of disrespect for him. His face turned blood red, and flecks of yellow foamy spittle escaped from his diseased gums and black, broken teeth. His neck muscles expanded into ugly, twisted knots and his facial swellings leaked green pus.

Godric attempted to shout, but in his rage only managed a stammering, strangulated squeak. "Viking... you... you are about to *die*!"

He then drew his ornately hafted, double-edged sword and with shaking hands swung it violently towards Eddie's unprotected throat.

Three

Sunlight streamed through the imprisoning bars of the cell window, Eddie's only link to the outside world, or at least to the inner confines of Maldon Burh, the enclosed fortified town. The cell itse f was cold and damp and he had few comforts.

Discomfort was forgotten for the moment, his very survival taking priority over all else. His captor's sword was being propelled violently towards Eddie's throat.

Instinctively, Eddie wrenched his head sideways. He couldn't avoid the blade completely, and it nicked his neck. His own blood soaked his shirt.

Eldor Godric's hideously repulsive face contorted into a mask of hatred. His slash of a mouth opened, revealing his red bleeding gums and black rotting teeth. His yellow crusted tongue wobbled as a high pitched screech emanated from the freak's grisly cavern.

Godric's skeletal hands swept forward towards Eddie. He signalled to his brothers to join him in enjoying their captive's last moments. His brothers sniggered at their helpless victim's plight. All three began kicking and punching the stricken man mercilessly.

Eddie tried to protect himself by rolling into a ball, his arms and hands shielding his head. But he felt certain they wouldn't stop until he was dead. So, gathering the last of his strength, he kicked out violently with both feet.

One foot hit Godwin in the crotch and the other struck Godwig's bulbous nose. Eddie heard and felt Godwig's nose break. The childlike high-pitched squeals of agony from Godwig, and the retching sounds from Godwin bent double on the floor, gave Eddie some satisfaction.

Eddie was literally fighting for his life. He realized if he were to have any chance at all he needed a weapon. Lurching forward, he grabbed the seax dagger from the floored Godwin's scabbard.

He knew this minor victory would only buy him seconds. The short single-bladed seax dagger wasn't enough protection, certainly no match for the three double-edged swords that the brothers brandished. His attackers' weapons swished from side to side as they relentlessly advanced towards Eddie.

Eddie waved and thrust the small dagger towards each assailant in turn. Each feint getting a reaction when the cowardly targets instinctively pulled back.

Sweat ran down Eddie's face and body despite the cold dampness of the cell. The sneering brothers came closer. Godric's mouth hung open horribly, showing his foul black teeth. His diseased yellow tongue slathered, snake-like, round his thin lips in anticipation of Eddie's imminent murder.

Eddie had reduced Godwig's nose to a pulp that had splattered across his weak features. Nasal mucus mixed with blood streamed down his chin in rivulets, forming thick blobs on his chest as it set. Godwin was bent at the waist, holding his sword in one hand and cupping his crotch with the other.

Despite their injuries, the siblings had managed to force Eddie into a corner of the bleak, stone cell. He had nowhere to go. He was trapped.

Eddie steeled himself to make a last, suicidal, attack on his tormentors. He would not go quietly. He hesitated for a second, feeling other presences nearby. His senses were correct again. The cell door opened and his jailers walked in.

Eldor Godric turned purple and shook with rage. With his sword in his right hand, he shook his left fist at the slave jailers, erupting into a crescendo of profanities and gesturing offensively at them. Finally, in a fit of pique, he flung Eddie unceremoniously against the wall before all three attackers stormed out.

As the brothers left, Eddie heard the unmistakable rumbling of a thunderstorm in the distance. Flashes of lightning illuminated his cell as the storm approached, and the thunder claps became more frequent. Eddie was startled to see, through the window, an abnormally tall, robed figure. He sensed this was a Druid rather than a Monk.

Leo spoke to Eddie, "Hold still."

Eddie glanced at his jailer and then back to the window, but the robed figure had disappeared.

Leo was trying to stem the blood flow from Eddie's neck wound. He'd made a pad and bandages by tearing Eddie's shirt into strips. Eddie thought ruefully that the shirt had had it, anyway.

As well as being cut, Eddie was badly bruised. But because he'd kept himself fit, his muscles had been able to absorb most of the blows. However, he was ready for the painful stiffness that would set in by tomorrow

Dunnere sneezed several times and then blew his nose loudly on a cloth. This coincided with a flash of lightning, followed almost immediately by a very loud clap of thunder. The storm was practically overhead by now.

Meanwhile, Leo had fetched another shirt for Eddie, made of rough cloth, to replace the one they'd torn up. He also brought Eddie a meal of bread, broth and wine. He said, "Eat this, Edward, you'll need your strength."

Dunnere sneezed again, his eyes now red and watering.

"Bless you," declared Eddie. He carefully pulled the clean shirt over his head to avoid getting blood on it. "I've got a question," he said, looking at both jailers. "If that man's an Eldor, why did he stop attacking me when you slaves came in?"

Dunnere sniffled and wiped his nose before replying. "Because we are Ealdorman Byrhtnoth's trusted slaves. He cannot harm us and he knows we report directly to our liege lord."

Eddie said, "So you've Ealdorman Byrhtnoth's protection. But why didn't Eldor Godric have his men kill me anyway?"

Leo answered. "If we'd witnessed you being killed they'd have had trouble from the Ealdorman. You see, Ealdorman Byrhtnoth is the supreme leader around here. He is in fact second only to King Aethelred in England. He'd get to hear you'd been captured and would expect to interrogate you himself when he returns from Ely."

Eddie nodded his understanding.

Just then, during a break in the thunder, they heard raised voices and dogs barking outside. Eddie looked out and saw a dirty, scruffy individual being chased by two men from the communal kitchens, carrying carving knives.

Dunnere and Leo pulled themselves up to the window to see what it was all about.

"Look!" yelled Leo. "That thief's stolen a sucking pig from the kitchen."

A few seconds later, Dunnere continued the commentary. "Its alright. He's been caught. It will be the stocks for him I expect, if he's lucky."

Dunnere climbed down from the window. The storm now sounded less violent, moving away.

"Edward," he said, "as a matter of interest, the two men who were with Eldor Godric were his brothers, Godwig and Godwin. All three are dangerous. Especially as you've humiliated them in front of us slaves, the lowest of the low."

Leo started coughing. "Edward, where did you get the courage to fight three armed nobles?" he asked hoarsely.

"Well, I hadn't planned to do anything like that. But as they clearly intended to kill me, I thought I'd make it as hard for them as possible."

"But you're a slave," said Dunnere. "How do you even know how to fight against three armed men?"

"I haven't always been a slave. I'm a battle-hardened Romani warrior."

Dunnere spoke again. "Your reputation among the slaves and servants will go sky high after this. We Britons were once proud men. But any that fought back against the Saxons were killed on the spot or hung in the town squares. Now, to our shame, we are warriors only in our minds. We have in practice become used to slavery. It's either that or death for us and our extended families if we rebel."

Eddie nodded. "I understand, my friends. But you're not cowards. If you were you'd have cringed outside the cell. Or slunk away and let these so-called nobles kill me. It was true bravery on your part. You came into the cell despite knowing you would receive the wrath of an Eldor."

Both jailers beamed.

Leo patted Eddie's shoulder. "Edward you've lifted our spirits. But it won't be the end of this matter for you, I'm afraid. Eldor Godric will strive to avenge the humiliation you heaped on him. For a Saxon noble to have his dignity and pride challenged by a slave is worse than death. He must now, by the Saxon honour code, take his revenge or lose face amongst the nobles."

Dunnere agreed. "That's true," he said. "And while you're in this cell you cannot escape him. Eldor Godric has a spare set of keys to every cell here. So he can attack you when we aren't around. He'll be back with the rest of his foul brood. We salute your courage, but don't give much for your chances long term."

Leo was shaking his head, his brow furrowed with concern.

Eddie smiled. "Don't worry about me, my friends. I have to die sometime. So if they kill me, I may as well make it as difficult for them as possible. Thank you both again." Eddie grasped each of his jailers' forearms and they patted him on the back and left the cell.

Eddie slept fitfully that night, expecting to be attacked at any moment. But it didn't come.

The next day when the jailers brought his breakfast, Dunnere said. "You're lucky as well as brave, Edward. Ealdorman Byrhtnoth has sent for reinforcements. He's about to confront the Vikings to our north, near Ipswich in Suffolk. Eldor Godric has ridden out with his brothers and two hundred huscarls to join him.

For the next few weeks Eddie continued to work out in his cell. His body recovered with the exercise and good food. He was soon strong again. He made mental contact with Fero occasionally, letting him know he was safe. It comforted him to know his younger sibling was alive and happy.

After a few weeks had passed, Eddie watched through his cell window as some of the huscarls returned to the Burh.

Dunnere told him, "This isn't good news for you. That is the group commanded by Eldor Godric which has come back to the Burh. I've heard that Ealdorman Byrhtnoth and his main force have stopped off at Ely Abbey on their way back here.

Leo said, "But I've also got some good news for you. My friend is a slave in the stables. He overheard two huscarls talking. One told the other that Eldor Godric has been boasting to Ealdorman Byrhtnoth. He said Godric had told him how bravely he'd fought to snatch you from your friends, the Vikings."

Eddie looked puzzled. "Does that help me then?"

"Initially, no," Leo answered. "Eldor Godric and his brothers will almost certainly attack you again…"

Dunnere butted in. "But you see, Edward, now he's boasted about capturing you, he won't be able to kill you. Or at least he can't until Ealdorman Byrhtnoth has questioned you. He's been hoisted by his own petard. He's the victim of his own scheme of trying to gain favour by boasting of your capture."

While Eddie was digesting this news he peered out of the window. At that moment an unkempt young girl walked past, herding a gaggle of geese. She waved her stick in the air as a stray dog tried to bite one of her charges. To Eddie this was a taste of everyday reality. It took his mind away from the nightmare of his imprisonment.

The following day, Dunnere was proved right. Eddie's three tormentors returned.

Eldor Godric shouted at Eddie, "Well you Viking dog, you're not so tough now without your comrades are you? So now you can see before you three men who are of far greater intellect and bravery than you. What can you tell me that will stop me killing you here and now?"

Eddie, emboldened by the news his jailers had given him, replied, "Because you're a very important man, and clever, you'll have noted I'm not a blond Viking. I'm dark skinned with black hair."

Godric looked astounded that Eddie had dared to answer him back. "Just because you're dark and speak our language, you sea pirate, this won't save you from my knife," he spat.

Eddie looked down at the floor, trying to appear servile. He said, "Surely, being a high ranking noble you'd want to show off your prize to the Ealdorman before killing me?"

Eddie's show of servility had been wasted. Godric had turned puce. "You insolent dog!" he shouted. "How dare you tell a highborn noble what he should do? If I don't kill you now, I'll have you as my slave. Then I'll make your life such hell you'll wish you were dead."

With this, the three brothers violently attacked Eddie again, leaving him in no doubt that Godric's words were no idle threat.

Eddie began the next day in great pain, a legacy of the beatings. He reflected that these bastards really knew how to hurt people. They were obviously well practiced bullies.

By now Eddie had been incarcerated for several weeks. Over time, he'd noticed the weather outside was beginning to improve; the passing peasants seldom wore top coats or capes any more.

He had made mental contact with his brother, Fero, several times. Fero now had a girlfriend, a farm labourer's daughter. Eddie hadn't disclosed to his brother that he was in a cell. He didn't want Fero trying to mount a rescue bid, as he'd be killed in the process. It was better for him that he stayed working on the farm, and to be with the girl.

One morning the sun was shining but Eddie's daily routine looked no different than any other day in this place of darkness. However, this time when his jailers, Dunnere and Leo, brought his breakfast he felt it would be different.

Leo had news for Eddie. "Our Lord Ealdorman Byrhtnoth has returned. Maybe he will see you today."

Leo was right. Later in the day Eddie was hobbled and chained and then taken by Leo and Dunnere to the Great Hall. Eldor Godric was there and ordered Eddie to kneel before Ealdorman Byrhtnoth. As Eddie was thrown to the floor, he could hardly decline.

Ealdorman Byrhtnoth was an imposing figure of a man. Eddie estimated him to be several inches taller than he was. Byrhtnoth's torso and arms were strongly muscled. He had long, flowing white hair and beard. Eddie guessed him to be in his early sixties. Byrhtnoth was dressed in expensive-looking purple robes. He had a bejewelled sword at one hip and just as impressive was a silver-handled seax single-bladed dagger, which hung from the other. He also wore several heavy gold and silver rings on each hand.

Ealdorman Byrhtnoth spoke with the deep, assured voice of a man well used to command. "Why are you here, Norseman? We will never pay your Danegeld. You sea thief, we'll not be bought off."

There was a brief pause, a chance to reply, at which Eddie leaped.

"I'm no sea thief or Norseman. My name's Edward Lavengro and I'm of the Romani race."

Ealdorman Byrhtnoth seemed surprised that Eddie could speak to him in his own language and nodded his head to acknowledge this. "You say you are a Romani. I am number two in this country under our glorious King Aethelred, but even I have never heard of such people. I have seen Egyptian traders and a few Moors but never a Romani."

Eddie replied, "You are knowledgeable, my lord. We are often mistaken for the Egyptians you spoke of. Although some shorten that name and call us Gypsies."

Byrhtnoth stared at Eddie for a moment. "You may have learned to speak the heroes' language but your clothes are not East Saxon. You are too dark-skinned and tall to be of our kin. You must be one of the pirates, the sea farers. You, Dane, are now my prisoner."

Eddie protested, "I am no Dane. I'm Romani."

Ealdorman Byrhtnoth's white hair swished as he flung his head back petulantly and his face reddened. He roared, "I don't care whether you are Dane or Romani. You are not East Saxon, not of Offa's kinsmen. You will either die or be my slave unless your kin pay me gold or silver tribute."

Eddie was tempted to speak again but thought better of it.

Byrhtnoth snapped, "King Aethelred has given me dominion over this territory. You were captured on the causeway to the island where the Viking raiders were camped. Thus you are my prisoner by right."

Ealdorman Byrhtnoth turned to Eldor Godric. "I have decided to personally claim this man, either to execute or use as my personal slave."

Eldor Godric's mouth twisted into a strange expression that was more of a grimace than a smile. At the same time he bent his head forward and lowered his hands, open-palmed, in an ingratiating manner. Then he squeaked obsequiously, "Of course, my lord, all battle prizes are yours by right."

Although Godric's words to the Ealdorman were, on the surface, subservient, his body language indicated he was anything but servile. In fact, Eddie saw that Eldor Godric's face had turned purple. He was muttering under his breath and glared at Eddie with unsuppressed hatred.

Eddie concluded that Godric considered him to be some sort of prize and resented losing his worth. Or perhaps he resented being unable to fulfil his promise to make Eddie's life a living hell.

Two hunting dogs started barking in the next room. Ealdorman Byrhtnoth sent a servant to see what was wrong with the animals, at the same time apparently losing interest in Eddie. Especially when a grandly dressed, attractive, middle-aged Noble Lady appeared. She attracted Byrhtnoth's attention. Eddie suspected this was Byrhtnoth's wife and he'd missed her company while away on his campaign.

Ealdorman Byrhtnoth walked towards the lady. With a waft of his hand in Eddie's direction, he said to Leo and Dunnere, "Get this Viking out of my sight." As he did so, he glanced at Eldor Godric with a sardonic grin.

Eddie felt his case was being used as a pawn to bring Godric down a peg or two. Eldor Godric's face was a picture. He pretended he had happily accepted his leader's decision but Eddie could tell that Godric was inwardly fuming. Every barb of Ealdorman Byrhtnoth's irony, mockery and derision had hit home.

Eldor Godric seemed to court and covet praise and Eddie wondered if Godric's physical disadvantages made him feel inadequate, bearing in mind Ealdorman Byrhtnoth's superior intellect, physique and almost regal presence.

He pondered whether he could at some time use this perceived knowledge to his own advantage. True, he'd be even deeper in Eldor Godric's black books. But on the other hand it may just be useful to Ealdorman Byrhtnoth in what could become a minor power struggle between the nobles?

As Dunnere and Leo were escorting Eddie back to his cell, they passed a group of women. Three young girls looked like handmaidens, while the fourth was dressed in fine clothing and was obviously a lady. Eddie was startled as he noticed how beautiful the lady was. She had light, almost white, blonde hair and piercing, light blue eyes. Most Saxon ladies were blonde but this girl was an extreme blonde and exceptionally pretty.

The lady glanced across as the three men passed her. Eddie noticed the grand woman support her chin in her right hand and purse her full lips. Almost haughtily, with a certain indifference, her eyes seemed to be taking in his tall, muscular frame. As Eddie made eye contact with her, she quickly looked away and resumed her conversation with the other women.

Dunnere and Leo hurried him past her. Back in his cell, Eddie asked, "Who was the grand lady we just passed?"

"That was Princess Catherine, the youngest daughter of King Aethelred," Leo told him. "She's here to marry Aefnoth, Ealdorman Byrthnoth's only son."

After Dunnere and Leo had left, Eddie stared out of his barred window. In the distance he could see a wild hawk hovering. It reminded him that Romanies should be free like wild birds, not caged. This situation just wasn't right.

Eddie thought if Ealdorman Byrhtnoth decided to execute him, he had no choice but to use his Romani guile to try to escape. He checked out his cell. It was almost underground and only the top two feet of the walls had any escape potential. He pulled at the window bars and the door fastenings and tapped and wrenched at any protrusions on the walls, floor and ceiling, but didn't find any weaknesses.

With no chance of escape from the cell he tried to plan for a break when he was taken out of it again. He'd grown to respect Dunnere and Leo, his jailers, and didn't want to put them in jeopardy by escaping from them.

Before he could come up with a scheme, his jailers appeared in the doorway.

Dunnere spoke. "We've orders to take you for another audience with the Ealdorman."

Outside the jail several dozen warriors were practising their swordsmanship and archery. The weather was bright and the air felt pleasantly warm.

When they arrived at the hall, Ealdorman Byrhtnoth was talking with Eldor Godric. His jailers held him just outside the doorway. Eddie looked around; if he was to escape this may be his only chance. However, with his wrists shackled, even if he broke away he wouldn't be able to reach the gates because of the practising warriors. His only chance would be to rush up the earth embankments, evade the wall sentries and hope to get away over the other side. Then he remembered the archers. They would almost certainly kill him with their arrows before he could get far.

Eddie could hear Eldor Godric's high, whingeing tone. "You should either kill the Viking prisoner or hand him over to me for punishment," he implored Ealdorman Byrhtnoth.

The Ealdorman was annoyed. "I do not have to take orders from you, Godric," he asserted in his deep baritone. "I shall make my own decisions. Jailers, bring the prisoner here."

Dunnere and Leo propelled Eddie forward and held on to him so that he had no chance of escape or any opportunity to attack their master.

Ealdorman Byrhtnoth looked sideways at Eldor Godric before addressing Eddie.

"So, Edward Lavengro, I am satisfied you are not a Viking. But you are some other foreigner. Not good, but not as bad as being a Norseman."

Eddie was relieved. "Thank you, my liege. You are correct, I am no Viking."

Ealdorman Byrhtnoth ignored Eddie's comments and continued. "I have decided to spare your life, but you will in future be my slave. You will be a servant in my household. If you can contact your kin and obtain tribute to me, you can buy your freedom."

Eddie was stunned. "Sir, I don't understand. I'm a free man. Why should I be your slave?"

Ealdorman Byrhtnoth replied, "In this kingdom, anyone taken prisoner is either killed or enslaved. However, you will find me to be a fair master." Byrhtnoth then directed his Chamberlain, "Find my new slave some new quarters and instruct him on his duties."

Eddie's shackles were removed and the official escorted him from the hall. The Chamberlain was a grey-haired and bearded man whom Eddie surmised was probably in his late fifties. He walked with a limp and his face was thin and drawn. However, the man had sparkling green eyes that made him look intelligent.

Eddie wasn't certain if he should talk to the man before he was spoken to. But he did so, saying, "Excuse me, sir, my name's Edward Lavengro. I'm part of the Romani nation. Can you give me guidance on what I should do to serve the Ealdorman?"

The man replied in a soft voice, "I am Byrhwold, the Ealdorman's Chamberlain. As you are foreign, I'll explain my position. I am the Ealdorman's steward and treasurer. I manage his household. Every free servant and slave works under me so that the Ealdorman can concentrate on the defence of the realm."

Eddie said, "That's a powerful role."

Byrhwold smiled and seemed genuinely flattered. "It is. I've been doing this for seven years. Before that I was a warrior. But since I was badly wounded in battle, almost losing my leg, and am now old, the Ealdorman has honoured me with this 'important' position."

Eddie caught a slight twist of Byrhwold's mouth as he said the word 'important' and realized it was more of an ironic grin. He judged that, to Byrhwold, being Chamberlain was a job and not a status symbol. Eddie resolved to try and cultivate Byrhwold's friendship if the Chamberlain would allow it.

Byrhwold told Eddie, "Saxon slaves are completely owned by their masters. You must do what you are told without question. Your duties will be hauling wood and water, tending to animals, cleaning floors and scrubbing pots and pans. Your first job will be cleaning the kitchen floors."

Byrhwold gave Eddie a leather tunic to wear and showed him where he could sleep. This was to be on a bed of hay in a room with two other slaves.

Each evening, after his allocated work was finished, Eddie concentrated on trying to communicate with his brother, Fero. Some nights he couldn't 'feel' anything, but on others he sensed that Fero was alright and still on the farm.

As he had no choice, Eddie worked hard at all the jobs he was given, but it was a good source of exercise. He needed to keep fit to ensure he'd be strong enough to escape if the occasion arose.

After several days of working in the kitchen, Eddie was sweeping up outside the cookhouse when he had his second sighting of Princess Catherine. It looked as if she was taking a constitutional walk around the Burh. She was carrying a dubious looking tabby cat in her arms and was accompanied by three handmaidens and four guards.

Eddie was mesmerized by Princess Catherine. Not only was she a stunning blonde, but she also looked highly intelligent. He judged that this very petite girl was only a teenager of around sixteen or seventeen. He noticed she had a button nose, tiny hands and a small mole on her cheek.

As Eddie was a new slave he hadn't noticed that all the other slaves and servants had melted into the background. He was also not aware that it was not done for a slave to look at, or even be seen by, royalty.

As he watched the pageant pass by, a fat, black tomcat with a bushy tail ran past at lightning speed, chasing a rat. The creature caught its prey easily. The tabby cat in Princess Catherine's arms instantly jumped from her grasp and fought the other cat for its prize.

The Princess shouted at the cats. "Bodi," she cried, "leave Charley alone! It's his rat."

Eddie watched as the fighting cats took no notice of the princess at all. Without waiting for her entourage to deal with it, Princess Catherine tried to pull the two cats apart. But the felines wriggled so strenuously that the princess slipped and fell towards the muddy puddle in front of her.

Being unaware of royal protocol, Eddie put out his arms and caught her. Princess Catherine smiled at him, but there was a shout and the guard commander held a spear to Eddie's ribs. Eddie realized his mistake immediately, but it was too late by then.

The guard commander shouted an order at Eddie. "Keep your hands off the princess, slave! You will die when the Ealdorman hears of this outrage." He barked another order and two other guards rushed at Eddie, aggressively brandishing drawn seax swords.

Four

A magpie flew past, its black and white plumage glinting in the sunlight. The sun was high but the cool breeze felt uncomfortable on bare skin. In the confines of the Maldon Burh's earthen parapets, the two cats still squabbled over the dead rat.

The princess's guards, outraged by a slave touching their charge, had forced Eddie to the floor. Princess Catherine's handmaidens clustered around her, worried and whispering in dismay at the violent turn of events.

The guard commander apologized to the princess.

"I am sorry about our security lapse, your highness. This will be reported to Ealdorman Byrhtnoth immediately. The slave will be flogged at the very least for his insolence."

Princess Catherine replied sternly, "Leave the slave alone. He is new here and in any case, he was not attacking me. He has just saved me from falling in the mud. This was unexpected chivalry from one of such lowly status." She turned to the guard commander. "Why didn't you do that service for me, Commander?"

The guard commander's face reddened and he stuttered. "I... I would have done but... but I wasn't in the right place."

"Precisely, Commander. If you had been, this slave would not have needed to catch me, would he? Let the slave go."

The guard commander protested, "But your highness, we've orders..."

Princess Catherine smiled coyly at the officer. "Commander Edwig, my father King Aethelred, sent you and your detachment with me from the palace in London to protect me. You have performed your duties admirably; it is far better to over-react than take any risks."

Eddie was still being held by the two guards in the muddy puddle he'd saved Princess Catherine from falling into. He had been startled by the troops' violent reaction, but now realized it had been his misinterpretation of the situation that had caused the problem. He was even more surprised by Princess Catherine's response in defence of him, a mere slave.

Commander Edwig responded to Princess Catherine's order by blushing, then looking confused and, finally, spluttering, "Your highness is, as always, gracious to your humble servant. What do you wish me to do with the slave?"

Eddie noticed Commander Edwig's facial expression. The princess's smile seemed to have had the effect of reducing the older, experienced officer to a whimpering boy. He had the distinct impression that Commander Edwig was infatuated with Princess Catherine. He also noticed that the princess wasn't above using her feminine wiles to manipulate him.

The princess answered the commander, "Let the slave go about his work. I will commend your diligence to the King when we return to the palace."

With a look of pride and satisfaction, Commander Edwig barked out an order to his men. "Release the slave!"

Eddie stood with his head bowed until the princess and her retinue moved away. He had been shocked by the guard's reaction to his social error. He was also beguiled by the princess's beauty and poise. She was the most desirable girl he had ever seen. Unfortunately, she was also as far away from his league and social status as it was possible to be.

He realized he would probably never even see her again. However, this meeting had been the highlight of his life. The fact that she had been gracious enough to save his worthless hide meant he would forever be her slave in the emotional sense as well as in reality.

As soon as the princess was out of sight, the other servants and slaves came out of their hiding places. Alfstan, a slave he'd met a couple of times, spoke to Eddie. "I can't believe you got away with that. Don't you know we must never be seen by royalty?"

"No. I had no idea. I've never been anywhere near royalty before."

Alfstan continued, "Not only did you stay in view. But you got away with touching the princess."

"I wasn't assaulting the princess, but merely saving her from falling into the mud. It was just a reflex action. I would have done the same if it had been a slave, male or female."

"I could see that, Edward. Even so, a slave who touches a royal person is usually summarily executed. You just got lucky. You won't next time. You must learn your place… that's at the bottom of the pile with the rest of us slaves."

Eddie nodded his understanding.

When he was by himself, Eddie thought about Alfstan's words. He realized what a huge risk he'd taken because of his ignorance of Saxon customs. He resolved to find out as much about Saxon history and etiquette as he could. He didn't want to be caught out again.

In the evening, at sunset, he attempted use his powers of remote viewing, concentrating his brain to reach the Danish farm he'd been torn away from by the Norwegian Vikings.

He reached it and felt the calmness and clarity that he'd hoped for. His mind saw Fero and his sisters. They were all safe. Olga, his fifteen-year-old sister, and Tipi at fourteen, were mothering the two youngest. Seven-year-old Mimsy and De is, four, were playing happily in the fields.

Eddie decided not to make direct contact with Fero. That was because Fero may sense his own difficult circumstances.

For the next couple of weeks Eddie kept busy working from dawn till dusk. One evening, instead of going to his shared room, he climbed onto the earthen ramparts. In the approaching gloom he watched as tiny pipistrelle bats twittered their high-pitched calls and swooped around the Burh, catching insects. An owl hooted in the distance. This made him pine for his roving outdoor existence.

He remembered his father, Elward, passing down the Romanies' history to all his offspring in the evenings around blazing log fires. Their father had told them that up until the sixth century, their forebears had been part of warrior tribes in India. They had been forced to leave when cut off from their own lands by the armies of Islam.

Then they had travelled the Silk Road to Byzant um, finding work on farms or fighting as mercenaries on the way for any tribe that would employ them. Romanies were then and still were a freeman nation. It was in their blood. Some had settled permanently on the way along, but at least a third of the tribe had continued moving where and when they could.

Eddie had grown up while they travelled around, developing into a powerful six-footer and an accomplished fighter. He was now an expert at hand-to-hand fighting and proficient with all weapons. In addition, the womenfolk told him he was as handsome as his father before him. He shared his father's dark skin, black hair, brown eyes and muscular torso.

Several more weeks went by and Eddie worked within the confines of the Burh. He was getting restless. The Romani need to keep moving on was playing on his mind.

One day after his daily work he sat despondently on his straw palliasse considering what it meant for him to be a slave. Being enslaved was bad enough for any person, but to a Romani it was doubly so. Slavery wasn't a prison sentence with a release date. Slavery continued for a person's natural life.

He resolved there and then to find a way out. He either had to escape, or in some way earn his freedom. He was confident that he would think of something. He had to be positive or he would become depressed and that wouldn't get him anywhere.

He had already learnt that slaves were often considered invisible. That's why they were expected to hide from nobles. In the days that followed, while he worked with the other slaves, Eddie asked a lot of questions. During these conversations some described what slavery was like for them.

While they chopped and stacked firewood one afternoon, Alfstan told Eddie, "I voluntarily placed my family into slavery."

Eddie was astonished at this revelation. "Why on earth did you do that?"

"It was the only way to save my wife and children from starving," Alfstan replied.

"How come?"

"Well, I once owned a hide of land with a cottage and garden. I grew vegetables and kept sheep and chickens. Then the Vikings raided us. Though my family escaped capture, the Vikings killed all our animals and burned our buildings and crops. We were destitute. I knew that as soon as winter came we'd all starve to death, if we didn't freeze first. At least becoming slaves filled my family's bellies and provided a dry, warm room for them to sleep in."

Remarkably, Eddie found that many other slaves had also voluntarily traded their freedom in return for food and shelter when times were bad. However, there were other, different reasons. Some had been captured in battles. These people had been given the choice of death or slavery. They had chosen slavery. Others had been Britons conquered by the Anglo Saxons. Some were penal slaves, enslaved as a penalty for their crimes, being forced to work hard and contribute to society. Slave prisoners were never returned to society to commit crime again.

Also, he remembered what had happened to him... being in the wrong place at the wrong time. Probably he wasn't the only one. To escape from his situation he needed to learn more details and his chance came while he was sweeping up the floor of the main smithy. He spoke to Ecceard, a blacksmith slave.

The smithy was a baking hot room just outside the Burh's armoury. There were two forges but only one was being used that day. Anvils stood near the forges and smiths' tools hung in racks on the walls. The whole place reeked of oil, sweat and an odd smell he could only describe as metallic steam.

It was a dark room with just one window opening. Apart from the small window, the place was illuminated by the fire from the forge as the logs flared and spat sparks intermittently.

Ecceard was a tall, muscular man. His massive bare biceps bulged and ran with sweat as he worked. He wore no cloth shirt but had a thick leather apron that covered him from neck to ankles.

Eddie asked him, "What's it like working hard as a slave?"

As the big man hammered red hot metal strips into horseshoe shapes on his anvil, he told Eddie, "There are good points to slavery. In practice, slaves work under the same conditions as the Ceorl, the freemen servants."

Eddie had to wipe his brow to clear the sweat running into his eyes. "What conditions are they?"

Ecceard pumped the bellows to his forge and then, using long tongs, put another strip of iron in the furnace to heat.

"Both slaves and freemen servants are treated well, receiving shelter, clothing, food and drink in return for doing exactly what we are told. Neither class is ill-treated as long as we work hard."

Eddie scratched his neck. He found the heat uncomfortable. "So what advantages do the freemen get that the slaves don't?"

Ecceard was silent for a moment as he withdrew the red hot metal from the furnace, hammered it into a horseshoe shape, punched nail holes in it and then doused it in a trough of water. With a deafening hiss, a cloud of steam rose into the air.

"The difference is," Ecceard began, "we slaves do our work unpaid and can be sold on to other masters at our owner's will. We cannot carry arms or leave our master. Freemen receive payment. They carry a single-edged seax dagger as their symbol of freemanship. They can leave if they want. Some earn enough to buy land and become farmers."

Eddie heard a noise from outside and went to the smithy door to see what it was. A donkey was braying and pulling against a rope held by a wizened old man, trying to pull the animal along. He also hit it with a stick on its backside, but the donkey was still obstinate. In the distance, a second donkey brayed. Hearing this, the first animal moved, the rope slackened and the old man crashed to the floor. The ancient man rubbed his backside and started swearing. Eddie laughed at the spectacle, causing the old fellow to swear at him as well.

Returning to the smithy, Eddie asked Ecceard, "Is there no way a slave can be released from slavery?"

Ecceard threw the now cooling horseshoe into a hopper of similar finished shoes. It landed with a clang and the pile of shoes slid across the wooden box like a mini avalanche.

Ecceard looked at Eddie thoughtfully, wondering why this new slave knew so little about real life. With a shrug of his huge shoulders he said, "Well, it is possible. Some slaves, like me, have learned to be skilled craftsmen instead of just subsistence farmers. Sure, we slaves have limited freedom and no legal rights. However, we are actually encouraged by our masters to better ourselves. I've been told the theory is that slaves with some hope work harder and do better quality work. Our masters are probably right there... my dream certainly sustains me."

Eddie was intrigued and heartened by this. "How can a man earn release from slavery, Ecceard?"

Ecceard took a longer, slim piece of metal from a pile and placed one end into the furnace. "Anyone can progress if he gives outstanding service to his master. The quickest way is to volunteer and fight gallantly for his master in battles."

Eddie scratched his forehead, screwed his eyes up and then asked, "Slaves have to volunteer? Don't slaves' masters compel them to fight?"

Ecceard pulled the long piece of glowing metal from the forge and dunked it in the water trough. The hot metal spat and steamed furiously. Some of the steam hit Ecceard's leather apron and Eddie had to jump backwards to avoid being scalded. Ecceard plunged the now cooling metal back into the forge once more.

Eventually, after staring at Eddie and shaking his head, Ecceard answered the question. "Slaves, or any person who'd been forced against their will to fight, would do so half-heartedly. This would be extremely dangerous in a battle situation. Any reluctant warrior would be likely to let his comrades down. Thus no man of any social stratum is compelled to fight."

Eddie bit his lip thoughtfully. "Hm, I see your point. You say anyone can earn this social mobility? How do they do this?"

Ecceard worked on, again removing the hot metal and plunging it into the water before replacing it into the red hot forge. "Slaves can become Ceorls by being awarded two hides of land. Then Ceorls can become Thegns by accumulating five hides of land. I assume you know that one hide is the amount of ground needed to sustain a family?"

"Yes I do," Eddie lied. "Is that what you are aiming to do?"

Ecceard again removed the long red hot strip of metal, hammered it, dunked it in the water and returned it to the heat. He nodded and smiled, more to himself than at Eddie. "Blacksmiths are always needed, particularly when there is a war coming. Since I am now far more skilled and strong, I'll also volunteer to fight alongside my lord at the earliest opportunity. If I fight well I could be granted my freedom and even a hide of land."

Eddie heart was beating faster now, thinking of his situation. He looked quizzically at the long thin piece of metal. "What are you making?"

"It's a scramaseaxe, a seax one-edged sword. It needs a lot of tempering to make it hard and have a degree of elasticity. It's important to make the blade strong enough to both give and receive hostile blows."

Eddie nodded his understanding. "Does the war leader supply all of the slave's weapons if he volunteers to fight?"

Ecceard pursed his lips and made a sucking noise. "No, they don't. That's a big problem. It's because slaves are forbidden to carry any arms, even a seax knife. However, I hope the Ealdorman would make an exception in a battle situation. If not, I'll fight using anything I can find... like a stave? Then hope to find a good weapon discarded by a fallen warrior of either side."

Eddie clicked his tongue and shook his head. "Ecceard, why would you risk your life in such dicey conditions?"

"I'll admit it's a gamble, but if it came off I might get my freedom and my own land and house. If I'm killed in battle, my family will get the best treatment for the rest of their lives."

That evening at sunset Eddie tried to concentrate on his remote viewing. This time he could visualize his brother Fero talking to a young girl. Fero looked like Eddie facially. Being two years younger with a baby face had made him popular with the females. Eddie didn't need to worry about little brother, it seemed.

When the sun had gone down, Eddie closed his cloak around him to combat the cool breeze. A light drizzle, not much more than mist, added to the chill of the evening. Yawning, he slouched back to his straw bed. His two roommates were already there. Wisteric was an unfit, ill-tempered, morose character at the best of times. Tonight he was particularly gloomy.

"Why bother to work hard?" he asked Eddie. "They won't think any more of you for it. You're making us all look lazy. You're letting your fellow slaves down."

Oderald, Eddie's second roommate came back at Wisteric, saying, "Come off it Wisteric, you make old man Wigghelm, the dog catcher, look fast. If you work any slower you'll be going backwards." Then he laughed.

Wisteric snorted something foul-mouthed and made a rude sign. Then he sulked, lay down on the straw and covered his body and head with his blanket.

"Thanks for the back up," Eddie said.

Oderald smiled. "You're quite welcome. Our repetitive work could be depressing if we let it. I try to just take it a day at a time."

Eddie judged Oderald to be in his thirties. Over the short time they'd known each other they'd become firm friends. The man was about average height, quite a bit shorter than Eddie. Though smaller, he had exceptionally strong biceps as Eddie had discovered during their occasional bouts of arm wrestling.

Wisteric was also similar in age and height to Oderald. But he was out of condition and didn't have a good word for anyone.

Oderald said, "I hear you've not only seen our princess but touched her and got away with it. What was she like? Have you seen her since?"

"She was beautiful. I've not seen her again, more's the pity… but I can dream, can't I?"

Oderald grinned. "That's the spirit, Edward. We must dream things will get better, or we will be broken men like Wisteric."

The blanket in the corner quivered as ill-tempered grunts emanated from it.

Oderald and Eddie laughed and patted each other on the back.

The following morning was cold and misty. Eddie went for a walk along the earth embankments.

Seemingly out of the earth itself, a tall figure in a robe appeared. It wasn't a conventional monk; he sensed this was one of the Druids he'd come across before. The figure waved its sleeves across his face. In front of his eyes he saw an image of a huge rock with ants crawling over it. Then he realized they weren't ants, but human masons creating a gigantic statue. He couldn't make out what it was, but understood that it was very important to his life.

Before he could see more it had vanished and, between the screeching of the seagulls, he heard a voice he recognized as Eldor Godric's.

Godric was telling his brothers, "That slave who was disrespectful to me has attacked the princess. I'm going to see Ealdorman Byrhtnoth to demand his execution for assault on her royal person. That's a capital offence in my book."

Eddie froze. If Godric carried out these threats this could be his last day on earth.

Five

Black clouds billowed ominously as a deluge drummed noisily onto roofs. Anyone rash enough to leave shelter was soaked in seconds. The cold wind made the damp conditions feel even more uncomfortable. Smoke curled from the cookhouse, though Eddie noticed that even the appetizing aromas of woodsmoke and pork roasting were diminished by the heavy cloudburst.

Leo and Dunnere, who had been Eddie's jailers, escorted him into the presence of Ealdorman Byrhtnoth. He guessed what it was about and was understandably nervous.

Eddie was right. Eldor Godric was heatedly demanding the death penalty for him, based on Eddie's dastardly crime of touching the princess. The Ealdorman stepped back from Eldor Godric but he was nodding, as if in agreement with Godric. Eddie didn't think it looked good for him.

There was a movement behind the two nobles and Princess Catherine swept into the hall accompanied by a very tall, strongly built man. Despite his worries, Eddie caught his breath. The princess was so beautiful.

Dunnere whispered to Eddie, "That's Eldor Aefnoth, the Ealdorman's son. He's the noble the princess is betrothed to."

Eldor Godric ignored the new arrivals. He was now almost shouting, demanding that the slave Edward should be eliminated.

Eddie noted Princess Catherine talking to her fiancé, Eldor Aefnoth. Then Eldor Aefnoth approached his father, Ealdorman Byrhtnoth. The three male nobles were soon engaged in lively conversation. Eventually, Ealdorman Byrhtnoth turned and addressed everybody in his deep baritone voice.

"I have examined Eldor Godric's valid points."

Eddie froze, expecting calamity.

Ealdorman Byrhtnoth continued, "However, our gracious princess has interceded. She has assured me that the slave Edward had merely reacted automatically to save her from falling into the mud. Therefore in this case I do not intend to take any punitive action. The slave Edward will be allowed to return to his work."

Eddie was escorted back to his work base where Chamberlain Byrhwold instructed him to assist a party of monks that were about to arrive.

Eddie watched as the monks rode their sturdy ponies slowly up Maldon's steep, cobbled hill. Some stopped occasionally as their mounts plucked at the sparse grass protruding from between the cobblestones.

Chamberlain Byrhwold had informed Eddie that the monks had travelled over ninety miles from Ely. Although they would have made overnight stays at churches on the way, they would be tired, thirsty and hungry. He was to take them to the cookhouse to get something to eat and then show them where they could sleep for the night. Byrhwold told him the party was being led by Prior Esmond. He had just been installed as Prior of Beeleigh Priory to the west of the town.

The five monks were soaked to the skin from the earlier rain. As they were so tired and wet, Eddie expected them to be subdued. Not a bit of it, they were laughing in quite a raucous way.

Prior Esmond had a dark complexion, was short in stature and a little portly. Eddie estimated him to be in his late forties. In contrast to the often very outwardly masculine warriors, Esmond came over as slightly effeminate and despite his long ride in difficult conditions, he still looked immaculate. His greying hair was cropped short and the central bald patch was smooth and shiny.

His face was bristle-free, indicating he'd shaved that morning, and his fingernails were clean and neatly trimmed. Even his habit wasn't crumpled. This was in stark contrast to the dusty, mud-splattered garments worn by his four followers.

When the pair clasped hands in greeting, Eddie noticed how soft and limp the Prior's handshake was, though this proved little and didn't matter in the slightest. When Esmond spoke, his voice was light in tone and his hazel eyes pierced into Eddie's in a not unfriendly, rather quizzical way. He had an aquiline nose, black bushy eyebrows and protruding ears. The rest of his facial features were small and even.

Esmond seemed an amiable cleric. Not concerned that Eddie had only the status of a slave, Chamberlain Byrhwold had told him that Esmond's grandfather had been a slave and his father a Ceorl freeman. This was unusual as most senior members of the clergy were the younger offspring of nobles or even royalty.

Eddie guided Esmond and the other monks to their rooms and showed them where to get a meal.

The next morning, the rain clouds had dispersed and it was sunny and warm. Eddie had breakfast with his friend and room-mate, Oderald, before waiting with the other slaves for the day's orders.

Chamberlain Byrhwold came to allocate tasks. He kept Eddie waiting until last and then led him to Ealdorman Byrhtnoth's house. Eddie had misgivings in case the Ealdorman had changed his mind about being lenient with him.

Byrhwold and Eddie entered the Ealdorman's main room and waited. After a few minutes Eldor Aefnoth appeared, followed by Princess Catherine and Esmond. Eddie was confused by this but could only wait and see what would happen.

Eldor Aefnoth spoke to Princess Catherine. Eddie heard the conversation but didn't understand the implications.

Aefnoth said, "Is this the slave you want for your morgen-gyfu?"

The Princess replied, "Yes. He may be useful, but I need to check that he's a hard enough worker first."

"It is good," Aefnoth said. Give him work to do now. Then if he is suitable after our wedding you can have him as your personal slave."

Aefnoth spoke quietly to Prior Esmond who nodded his head. Aefnoth then walked over to Byrhwold and Eddie.

Addressing Eddie, Aefnoth said, "Slave, I have a job for you. The princess wishes to look around the local countryside. She does not wish to go with a full retinue, only a couple of guards and a servant. I have decided to send a male servant instead of another handmaiden. Her highness has chosen you as her preferred travelling male servant, as you saved her from falling."

Eddie caught his breath and his heart fluttered, but he managed to keep his head down and showed no emotion.

Aefnoth continued, "As you are over six feet tall and powerfully built, you may fit the bill. But before I decide, I wish to know more about you. Firstly, can you ride a horse?"

Eddie was surprised at this turn of events and answered boldly, "That I can. I've lived on farms for most of my life, sir."

Aefnoth nodded. "That's good. Of course you would be the most junior person on the expedition and I would insist that you do *exactly* what the armed escort orders you to do. Any deviation and I will personally see to it that you are punished. Do you understand?"

"Yes. I do. It's a great honour, sir and I will obey all orders given to me."

Aefnoth was satisfied. "That is agreed then. As you have told my father you are not Saxon, but Romani, you will be unfamiliar with this area and our customs. Thus I have asked Prior Esmond to acquaint you with some of our great Saxon history and heritage. I shall leave him to instruct you for a few days. Then I will give you your orders later in the week."

Eddie nodded, indicating that he understood.

Byrhwold escorted Eddie back to the slaves' quarters and said, "You must be careful, Edward. Eldor Aefnoth is the second in command in the Maldon area. Mess up and you'll be in big trouble. Do as you're told and you may be given other more responsible roles instead of just cleaning duties."

Prior Esmond had instructed Eddie to meet him early the next day on the earth walls near the gate tower. Eddie was there first. It was a warm morning after a damp night. The condensation rising from the dewy ground shrouded the Burh in sea mist.

Eddie saw the priest arriving. Esmond was leaning forward, his habit dragging on the ground. His cowl covered his face and his hands were lost in voluminous sleeves. Eddie thought the cleric looked more satanic than holy as he emerged from the fog.

Esmond spoke. "God be with you, Edward, on this holy morning. Eldor Aefnoth has asked me to tell you about our Saxon history. I'm also intrigued about your Romani ethnicity. Perhaps afterwards you can enlighten me about your race's history?"

"Thank you, Prior Esmond, I'll gladly do that. I've lived with my Romani tribe in lands across the seas. Now I am determined to integrate into your Saxon society, so anything you can tell me will be welcome."

Esmond smiled. "I'm also the local church historian. I enjoy telling others what I know. Regrettably, few peasants are interested, having enough problems getting sufficient food to survive."

"When did the Saxons come here originally?" Eddie wanted to know.

"After those lovely skirted Romans left." Esmond paused for effect, raising his eyebrows and pursing his lips. "The first Saxons, led by those nice brothers, Hengist and Horsa, arrived in Kent in four hundred and forty-nine. This was at the request of the southern British King Vortgern to help protect his territory."

Eddie's facial muscles contracted as his eyebrows shot up. "Why did the British King need the Saxons' help, Esmond?"

"Because the Romans had been here so long, several generations of Britons hadn't needed to become warriors. The Romans took care of all that. But when the Romans left, every tribe on the mainland raided the almost defenceless Britons."

"So how did you Saxons come to take over?"

Esmond spoke rapidly. "We Saxons were wandering mercenaries who'd been looking for a land of our own for several centuries." His eyes sparkled and his hands swung about as he illustrated each point. "We Saxons soon realized how weak the Britons had become…"

Eddie interrupted. "We Romanies are also wandering mercenaries, but have never found a homeland."

Esmond laughed, "Well, we won't share our land with you."

Eddie screwed up his face, a little hurt by Esmond's last comment. "But you share the land with the Britons, even if they are your slaves?"

"That is because most of us Saxons had real problems changing from the spear and sword to the plough. In fact, we needed to keep the Britons to farm for us initially. That was why they were enslaved rather than killed."

"So how did you become a monk, Esmond?"

"Well, my family were almost starving. The one hide my father owned wasn't sufficient to feed our big family. As his second son, my father told me I must leave home. He suggested I become either a soldier or a monk."

"But why a monk? Had you a Christian calling?"

Esmond looked away and made a strange grimace before answering. "Well, I wasn't strong or butch enough to be a warrior. Just look at me, Edward." He suddenly revealed his almost skeletal arms and hands and held them out wide.

Looking at the Prior's slight frame, Eddie remembered his weak handshake. He had to agree that Esmond wasn't the warrior type at all.

Esmond continued, "So I took the vow of chastity, which was alright as I'm scared of women and didn't want the bother of supporting children."

Eddie smiled and nodded.

"Having no descendents to support, I'm able to help out my parents and many brothers and sisters with supplies from time to time."

"That's very commendable, Esmond. We can't all be warriors or everybody would starve."

Esmond continued with his history lesson. "By the year eight hundred and seventy-eight, the Vikings invaded and took over all the Anglo-Saxon kingdoms, apart from Wessex in the south. However, thanks to King Alfred, most of England was re-conquered by us Saxons."

"Wow." Eddie was impressed. "This King Alfred must have been a brilliant general?"

Esmond nodded. "You're right. He was a strapping, red-blooded man." He sighed deeply, following up with a giggle.

Eddie couldn't work out if this camp display was indicative of Esmond's rather feminine inclinations, or if he was playing it up for effect.

Esmond noticed Eddie eyeing him quizzically, and blushed before continuing. "There was relative peace here until the Vikings started invading East Anglia again recently. They were mainly raiding in small parties on isolated farms for supplies, and on churches and monasteries for gold and silver, or so I've been told."

"I've had a brush with Norwegian Vikings," Eddie declared. "That's how I got here. I was captured by them and made to row in their longship to England. But when the Saxons attacked, I was able to escape."

Esmond beamed and patted Eddie lightly on the shoulder. "Thank you for telling me this."

In the distance Eddie noticed there were dozens of sea birds circling around Maldon harbour. He pointed them out to Esmond. Then, looking closer, Eddie realized one of the small fishing boats had docked.

Esmond also saw this and said, "That fisherman's had a good night. He's gutting his catch and throwing the heads and guts into the water."

"Yes, you're right, Esmond. That's why the gulls are so excited."

They both watched the gulls for a while and then Esmond asked if Eddie would like to hear more about the recent history of the town.

"That would be great. Do you know when the Burh was built?"

In an exaggeratedly high voice and flapping his hand around with a limp wrist, Esmond replied, "I know everything, sweetie. It was in nine hundred and seventeen. That was the year the West Saxon King Edward came to Maldon and repaired and fortified the old Roman town and Burh before he left."

"So it was rebuilt less than a hundred years ago. Has the Burh been needed in earnest?"

"Yes it certainly has. In the year of our Lord nine hundred and twenty, the Vikings attacked Colchester and then besieged Maldon. In both cases the East Saxon army defeated the Vikings. Then it was led by Ealdorman Byrthnoth's grandfather, Ealdorman Ealhelm."

"So Byrhtnoth's family have been in charge here for many years?"

"Yes, indeed. They've held lands here since we Saxons arrived."

"And when did the Saxons reach here?"

"The local King invited Byrthnoth's ancestors, the leaders of the East Saxons, here in the year four hundred and fifty. Eventually the Saxons took over, easily defeating the weak Britons. This kingdom of land was renamed Essex in honour of our tribe, the East Saxons.

"So the Saxons have ruled here for four hundred and fifty years?"

"That is so," replied Esmond, "but if you want to know more, we will have to continue tomorrow. As I'm in charge of the monks, I have to leave now for our dinner and prayers."

Eddie understood. "I'm really grateful for your indulgence and help."

"It's no problem. As I said, I enjoy showing off my knowledge. It's pointless just keeping these facts in my head... and I *love* showing off. If you wish to know more, we will make a date for tomorrow morning. Same place, same time, big boy."

With that, Esmond left, giving Eddie a knowing wink before exaggeratedly mincing away.

Eddie still couldn't decide whether Esmond was just playing to him as the gallery as it were, or was really effeminate. Still, he was certain of his own masculinity and felt that the Prior could be a good ally as well as a fantastic source of information. With a wave, Eddie also left to get his own meal in the Burh cookhouse.

After breakfast the following morning, Eddie returned to the earth wall to meet Prior Esmond. As the monk hadn't arrived, Eddie looked around. Again there was the sea mist and as Eddie gazed into it, he began daydreaming about his family on the farm in Denmark.

Suddenly there was a sharp noise. Eddie jumped and whirled around ready to defend himself, but it was only Esmond who had clapped his hands.

"Got you," he said, in an exaggeratedly deep baritone.

Eddie jumped as his automatic fight or flight reflex clicked in. His heart involuntarily pumped faster, providing emergency fuel for any immediate action.

Recovering his composure, and pleased to see the less than serious Prior, Eddie said, "You took your life into your hands there. I could have turned and killed you."

Esmond wagged a finger playfully. "But you forget something; I know you're a slave and not allowed to carry any weapon... not even a Seax dagger."

Eddie agreed that was true. "Can you bring me more up to date with the local history, please?"

45

"I can. I love a bit of gossip so this is mostly hearsay. Please don't repeat this."

Eddie leaned forward, turning his ear towards the speaker. "You can rely on me to keep it to myself," he promised.

Esmond began. "In nine hundred and seventy-seven, Edward the Martyr became King. But he was assassinated the next year." Esmond glanced round and resumed in little more than a whisper. "It was rumoured that he was murdered on the orders of Queen Elfrid, his stepmother. Whatever the truth was, her son, Edward's half-brother Aethelred, became King."

"Is that the same Aethelred who's the present King?"

Esmond nodded, "Yes it is. Aethelred was only eleven years old at the time. His Mother, Queen Elfrid, acted as regent. Princess Catherine is King Aethelred's youngest daughter.

"So Aethelred has been King for around twenty years now," Eddie said. "He must have learned a lot from all that experience?"

Esmond looked pensive and again glanced round cautiously before speaking. "You'd think so. But coincidentally, almost immediately following his accession the Viking raids intensified." Again he glanced round and quietly continued. "To tell you the truth, I believe King Aethelred relies a bit too much on poor advisers. I think without Ealdorman Byrthnoth's military skills he would have difficulties. Being such a young King, his mother made all the decisions and he hasn't had to rely on his own judgement."

"Thank you for being so frank about this," Eddie said.

Esmond looked solemn. "Remember, I rely on you not to pass this on to anyone. If you do, we both may be executed for treasonous talk."

"I give you my word as a Romani warrior," Eddie replied, and the two men shook hands on it.

Eddie was confused. Esmond didn't seem to be the same person as the day before. All the camp talk had gone and today he seemed far more masculine and serious. He asked, "Are the Vikings causing a lot of problems for the King?"

"Yes. Initially the Vikings raided unopposed. But when the Saxons got their act together the Vikings took heavy losses. Eventually the Vikings realized that small raiding parties were no longer viable. Now most Vikings have changed tactics and are using large fleets of longships. These fleets carry vast armies that are well trained and disciplined. They are powerful forces and they've been making great inroads into our countryside and attacking our main coastal towns."

"But don't the Saxons fight back?"

"Yes, of course. Your master, Ealdorman Byrhtnoth, has been leading the King's armies against them. You should know that Byrhtnoth is regarded as one of the most important men in the kingdom. He's second only to King Aethelred himself."

"Do you know what happened to the Vikings I saw on Northey Island just before I was captured by Eldor Godric?" Eddie enquired.

"That was a small independent raiding party that's now moved north."

There was the sound of rumbling. Eddie looked down at the main gate. He could see several oxen carts labouring slowly up the steep cobbles of Maldon Hill. The carts were loaded so heavily that the spare team of carthorses had to be coupled to each cart. The carter's boy led the huge beasts to the top of the hill, and then returned for the next one.

Eddie asked, "Why are the carts so heavily loaded?"

"Byrhtnoth is stocking up the barns in the Burh in case of Viking attack."

"Esmond, you know… Eldor Godric and his two men attacked me brutally from the moment they captured me."

Esmond, saddened, spread his hands wide. "I do know, yes. Godric has always been a sadistic bully. The other two were probably his younger brothers Godwin and Godwig, who are just as vindictive."

At that moment, one of Esmond's monks, Brother Cedric, appeared. A short, plump man with the monk's regulation shaved bald patch on the top of his head, he walked towards them with short, jerky steps. Politely interrupting their conversation, he whispered something to Esmond and then left.

"Eddie, there's been a message from Eldor Aefnoth," Esmond told him. "You're to report to him immediately at the Ealdorman's house."

Eddie thanked Esmond and hurried off to comply.

Eldor Aefnoth looked at Eddie disdainfully and then gave him his orders.

"Tomorrow you are to report to the stable master at dawn. The stables are by the armoury. I've instructed him to check that your horsemanship is up to standard. If you are good enough you will accompany the princess and two experienced guards on a short trip around the area. You will carry out your orders without question or you will be punished severely." With that Eldor Aefnoth turned around, dismissing Eddie with a wave.

The following day as the first rays of the sun lit the sky over the Blackwater Estuary, Eddie arrived at the stables. He was questioned by the Ealdorman's stable master, Aelfwold.

The weather-beaten, one-armed former warrior asked him, "What equestrian experience have you had?"

"I was brought up on farms, riding and breaking in horses," Eddie replied.

Aelfwold shook his head, unconvinced. "That's easy to say, but few slaves get enough riding experience to become proficient. I want you to prove you're at least a competent horseman."

Eddie noted that the horses were actually squat, powerful ponies. Since most of their riders were also small, the height of the animals was quite adequate.

In the stables, the first thing Eddie noticed was that only blankets were thrown over the ponies' broad backs, while plain hemp ropes served as basic bridles. Eddie wasn't worried; he'd broken in the Romanies' horses so was quite capable of riding bareback.

However, before Eddie could demonstrate his Romani horsemanship, Eldor Godric and his two brothers appeared. Godric whispered something to the stable master, who touched his forelock in deference and backed away.

Eddie sensed something was going on that wasn't good for him. Godric's younger brothers left and returned with a stallion. The pony pranced and pulled against its hemp halter. The animal rolled its wild eyes and showed huge yellow teeth.

The three siblings sniggered as Godric ordered Eddie to mount the volatile beast. Eddie reluctantly approached and quickly mounted the skittish animal. Sure enough, as Eddie had suspected it would, the stallion bucked immediately, trying to throw him off.

He clamped his legs round its belly and gripped its mane and the rope halter tightly. At least this was a short animal, so his long legs were able to hold its belly tightly. Then, bending forward, he was able to keep his centre of gravity low to maintain his balance. Soon the horse was subdued and Eddie brought it to a halt directly in front of Godric.

Eldor Godric spat contemptuously towards Eddie. His facial disfigurements had reddened even more as he stormed off with his brothers in tow.

Aelfwold the stable master smiled at Eddie. "Well done, slave. You've convinced me you're a horseman. But be careful; Eldor Godric is evil and now you've thwarted his will."

"Thanks for the advice, Aelfwold," Eddie said. He dismounted and stroked the horse's sweating flank, handing the rope reins to the stable master's assistant, young Rayhald.

Shortly afterwards, two warriors appeared. The first was a bull of a man, tall and powerfully built. He had massively powerful shoulders and bulging biceps. His face was badly scarred and his left ear was missing.

He introduced himself to Eddie. "I'm Thegn Wulfmaer the Ealdorman's nephew. You will take your orders from me on this journey. This is Eadric, my number two. If I am unavailable, you will obey him."

Eddie bowed his head. "Your word is my command, sir."

Eadric, the second guard, was shorter than Wulfmaer but also well muscled with a deeply indented, purple-coloured battle scar that ran from beneath his left eye to below his ear.

Eddie thought both these guys would make important allies and dangerous enemies. Wulfmaer and Eadric had their own powerful horses brought to them. The stable master brought Eddie a fine and spirited black stallion, giving Eddie a sly wink. Eddie had the feeling he should have been given a small pony, but Aelfwold had upgraded his mount, perhaps to spite Eldor Godric.

Wulfmaer picked out a strawberry roan pony for the princess, who had arrived outside the stables with Edith, one of her handmaidens Edith helped Princess Catherine to mount her pony. This was the first time Eddie had seen the princess without a voluminous gown. For this expedition she wore cloth trousers and a fine blouse with a thick, brown leather jacket. She also wore long, hide riding boots. Eddie tried not to stare but marvelled at how regal the slim princess looked, despite wearing less feminine apparel.

As soon as they moved off it was obvious to Eddie that the princess was an accomplished rider. The morning sun was bright and a few wispy clouds hung lazily in the sky. The four riders headed east led by Wulfmaer, followed by the princess, then Eadric and lastly, Eddie.

On the way out they passed the midden where the town's human dung was thrown. On this warm day the smell was overpowering and Eddie was glad when they reached the water's edge.

When they arrived at a curve in the river, Eddie noted the extensive salt ngs. There were also acres of waterlogged meadow leading down to the estuary. Several small rowing and sailing boats were tied up and fishermen mended their nets nearby. Several seals were sunning themselves on the mud flats.

As it would be impossible to stay near the water's edge, Wulfmaer led the group east along rough tracks that wound around the numerous hides owned by the Ceorls. These hides were plots of sixty to a hundred acres; enough land to erect small wooden buildings and sustain families. Eddie, not being of high enough status to ask questions, contented himself with attempting to memorize the lay of the land.

Eventually the small party reached Mundon. This was a small group of huts where they stopped to water the horses. Eddie was left to do this and while he did so, he was able to subtly observe Princess Catherine. The lady was without doubt the most beautiful woman he had ever seen.

After the short stop they moved on to the hamlet of Latchingdon, the next village being their destination. The few small houses on the local hides were dwarfed by the wooden Saxon church. There the priest stopped them and informed Wulfmaer that Viking longships had been seen in the Blackwater Estuary. He suggested the party turn back.

Wulfmaer seemed inclined to take the priests advice, but the princess would have none of it. She used her position to insist that they carry on; as it had taken them all day to get there, she was not stopping now.

Finally, the four horses carried their riders to Maylandsea, the village Princess Catherine had wanted to visit. This village was merely a few clusters of thatched huts on hides and a wooden church on the hill to the south.

The four rode up the hill to the church and surveyed the magnificent view over the curving estuary at high tide. There were a few hides, the small family farms with thatched houses. The rest was scrubland covered by trees, bushes and seawater.

It was already starting to get dark. Eddie heard Wulfmaer tell the princess they couldn't get back to Maldon before sunset so they would have to stay the night. The burly fighting man approached the church and appealed to the local priest, Pastor John, for accommodation for the night. The tall priest was very obliging and found a bed for the princess in his house. The two warriors and Eddie were billeted in a barn next door. The priest generously supplied them with good food, wine and plenty of hay to sleep on.

Pastor John was quite a character. He was as tall as Eddie and broad shouldered, with a slightly hooked, almost Roman nose. He was pleased to spend the evening in the barn with the three men. He told them he was the youngest son of a nobleman and, being without an inheritance of land, had been glad to accept an ecclesiastical patrimony to enter the employ of the church.

Before long the four men had consumed several bottles of the priest's wine. After this Pastor John challenged all three visitors to an arm wrestling contest. The pastor actually beat the two strong warriors, to their dismay. Only Eddie, using his Romani guile and experience rather than strength, overpowered the black-robed man of God. It was late at night when Pastor John returned to his house to sleep on the floor, having given up his own bed to the princess.

In their state of insobriety, the three men started to speak loosely. Eadric put his arm around Eddie's shoulder in a manly show of friendship. "Do you know," he said, "d'you know, at the Royal Palace the young lady with us is just called Kate? I was told she hates being called Princess Catherine."

Wulfmaer said, "That is true, but you two will only address the princess if she talks to you. Then you must use her full title or you'll have me to deal with."

Full of wine, the two escorts soon fell asleep. Eddie, though, wasn't tired so he went for a walk round the ancient graveyard. The graves were merely long mounds of earth, some supporting rudimentary wooden crosses with the odd word carved on them. One said, 'Dad. Killed by Vikings.' Another read, 'Baby boy and his mum.'

In the shadows something tall and black moved silently. Eddie assumed it was Pastor John, it was his church after all. He called out, "Is that you John?" There was no reply but the darkness around him seemed to have intensified. His eyes, or his mind, became clearer now and he realized it was a Druid. Not the same one as before. This one was even slimmer and taller.

Without any explanation he could see the gigantic statue again with the comparatively tiny masons working on it. He could also see clouds of sand and dunes like those seen at some coastal areas. But these sand dunes weren't a few yards across; they stretched for hundreds of miles.

He sensed he was being taught something of importance but he had no idea what or why. Again, before he could ask, the Druid was gone and Eddie was waking from a deep sleep.

Eddie was the first to wake, and after consuming so much wine the night before, needed to relieve his bladder. He went outside. It was still dark, just before the dawn. He sensed that something was wrong when he noticed the series of fires in the distance. He could see these were not cooking fires; they burnt much too fiercely. The penny dropped when he realized that the flames were coming from some hides in the little village.

Eddie roused the other men. The two guards tumbled outside to see for themselves.

"It has to be a Viking raiding party," Wulfmaer exclaimed. Princess Catherine was woken and expressed concern for the Saxon villagers and their burning houses.

"Your highness," Wulfmaer said, "Norsemen are on their way up to this church, no doubt to steal what treasures they can. I assume they are not aware that the King's daughter is here. If they find you, they will kill all the men and hold you to ransom. It's essential we move you to safety immediately."

Only a slight shiver at the side of her mouth and the involuntary fluttering of an eyelid betrayed Princess Catherine's emotions.

"Your highness," Wulfmaer persisted, "we have been ordered to protect you at all costs. May we have your permission to move you away from the danger?"

The princess agreed and, as Eddie had prepared the horses, the four mounted quickly. In the streaky light of dawn, Eddie noticed that several other groups of Vikings had almost surrounded them. Wulfmaer, seeing the danger, ordered Eddie to escort the Princess across the fields in the only direction where there were no enemies to be seen. He addressed the princess. "Please go with this slave, your highness, while I and Eadric create a diversion."

"We will work our way towards the safety of the Maldon Burh," replied the princess. "Come, slave, let us go."

Princess Catherine and Eddie rode their horses straight across the small field of stunted barley. Meanwhile, the two warriors swivelled their horses around towards the main force of Vikings. Urging their steeds onward, the two Saxon guards screamed out war cries to draw Viking attention away from their princess.

When Eddie glanced over his shoulder he saw Wulfmaer and Eadric dismount. They wasted no time in loosing arrows at the enemy. The Vikings had been taken in and surged towards the two Saxon warriors' new position. Eddie noticed the Vikings were retaliating, loosing their own arrows and hurling javelins back at them. However, the Saxon warriors had gauged the distance well. The Viking's spears were falling short and their arrows were easily avoided or deflected.

As rapidly as they could, Catherine and Eddie headed for the distant woods. When they found adequate cover, they stopped. They could still just see Wulfmaer and Eadric heroically wheeling their steeds, dismounting, loosing arrows and then remounting and riding to another vantage point to repeat the process. Eddie wondered why they always dismounted before loosing arrows. He resolved to ask them this if all went according to plan.

"Shall we move off again, your highness?"

Princess Catherine sighed. "We will in a moment, but I want to speak to you first." Eddie dipped his head. "Your wish is my command, your highness."

"Now this is an order," she said sharply. "Don't keep calling me *your highness*, *princess* or even *Catherine*. Don't you realize if you are overheard you'll be letting our enemies know I'm worth kidnapping for ransom? Instead I wish you to call me Kate, which I much prefer in any case. That's what my family calls me. What is your name, slave?"

"It's Edward Lavengro, your hi…"

She glared at him.

"Edward Lavengro, Kate. Shall we move off now?"

"Yes. We will head south towards the second river, the Crouch. We can follow that westward for a while and then turn north-west towards Maldon."

They moved off but the next few fields were muddy after the recent rain. It was also difficult to navigate as the terrain was becoming more wooded. In fact the woods were effectively blocking the way to the more southerly river Crouch.

At regular intervals Kate stopped to check for signs of Wulfmaer and Eadric catching them up. However, they didn't see anyone until they reached a hamlet called Ashingdon. There, they warned the villagers about Vikings being in the vicinity.

Kate spoke to Eddie in a low voice. "Confidentially, I've sent my detachment of guards back to London. My father needed them for a campaign he's leading. Plus the commander keeps mooning over me and it was getting on my nerves. I thought I could use local troops as guards when I needed them, but I wish my original detachment were here with me now."

Eddie was surprised that a princess would confide this type of information to a slave, but he thought perhaps that was a quirk of royalty.

He felt it would be rude not to answer and merely said, "I expect you're right, Kate."

Kate gave a half smile. "I think we must have moved far enough from the danger now to allow us to turn west towards Maldon."

That was what they did. However, Kate's optimism had been misplaced. As they passed through Althorn hamlet, two Vikings leapt out from a commandeered hut and tried to pull the pair off of their horses.

Because of his slave status, Eddie wasn't armed, but he managed to make his horse rear up. The huge, blond, bearded Viking who had been holding on to him was thrown off. Kate wasn't so lucky. Before Eddie could wheel his horse round to help her, she was pulled from her horse by the other Viking.

"Edward! Save me, Edward!" she screamed, as she was bundled unceremoniously into a nearby hut.

Eddie's first impulse was to rush to her aid, whatever the consequences to his own wellbeing. But he knew if he did that, the gang of marauders would kill him instantly. That would leave Kate at the mercy of these rapists and murderers. He was powerless to help.

Six

It was a dry afternoon on the Dengie Hundred Peninsula. The dark clouds created an atmosphere that mirrored Eddie's depressed mood.

Princess Catherine, Kate, was in great danger. She had been captured by the Vikings and called out for him to save her. He wanted to do just that but he knew that as an unarmed slave it would be impossible.

Eddie's heart thumped as he clasped and unclasped his hands. Not knowing what he could do, he hid behind a clump of elm trees to watch and think. When nobody emerged from the hut, he decided he must go for help.

He gave one more agonized glance towards the hut that sheltered Kate and her captors and then mounted his horse and galloped at full speed to find the Saxon guards, Thegns Wulfmaer and Eadric.

Riding inland, he crossed a stream and breasted a small hill covered with scrubby bushes. Eddie's highly sensitive Romani nostrils detected a subtle hint of something burning. He sniffed the air. It was an acrid smell. This wasn't the strong, clean smoke of a cooking fire. Perhaps it was from a far away building that incorporated some tar-like substance? He felt the chill of the wind against his face.

In the distance, Eddie spotted the Saxon warriors' horses in a depression behind a patch of yew trees. As he rode up to them, Thegn Wulfmaer appeared, sword in hand.

"Where's the princess, slave?" Wulfmaer asked anxiously.

"Vikings have captured her," Eddie said. "Please come. I'll show you where I saw them last." He described the village near to the Crouch river.

Wulfmaer's rugged face turned white. He pursed his lips and shook his head. "I recognize the village you mean. That's quite a way off, so we're in real trouble now."

Eddie expected the two warriors to mount their horses and ride to Princess Catherine's rescue. Then with horror he realized that wasn't possible. Eadric was on the ground, unconscious, his clothes soaked in blood.

Wulfmaer saw Eddie's dismay. "As you can see, Eadric's been badly injured. He killed two Vikings and disabled several more before one of their arrows caught him in the neck. He dropped his shield and was then hit by a javelin in the midriff. I fought the last few Vikings off and then hauled Eadric over his horse's back and led it here.

Eddie shook his head. "Will he survive?"

"He may. I've broken off the arrow shaft, removed the javelin and bound his wounds. He's not losing blood any more. If we can get him to a local farm he has a chance. Eadric's a great guy; he's the father of five and his wife's expecting their sixth very soon."

Eddie knew Wulfmaer was right. Eadric was a fine man who'd gone out of his way to be friendly to him, completely ignoring the fact that Eddie was a slave.

"What should we do, Wulfmaer? We can't leave our princess at the mercy of her kidnappers, and yet this courageous warrior deserves his chance after his bravery, and his family needs him?"

Wulfmaer rested his chin in his hands, shaking his head and tut-tutting to himself. He turned to face Eddie. "How many Vikings were there, Edward?"

"At least ten, perhaps more."

Wulfmaer bit his lower lip and scratched his head. "I'd be unable to defeat so many Vikings alone. Our best plan would be to take Eadric to a farm and then get reinforcements from the Burh."

"I'll do that, Wulfmaer."

"Thank you, Edward, but it would take you too long to find your way back. Plus you would find it very difficult to get anyone to take a slave like you seriously enough to get an immediate rescue party organized. I'm sure it would then be too late."

Eddie was persistent. "I could try. You are needed here."

Wulfmaer nodded. "Whatever we do is risky. But I'm pretty sure I could drop Eadric off somewhere safe and then get back to the Burh and return with a strong force before the Vikings reach their longships."

"What do you want me to do?"

"First help me get Eadric over his horse's back. Then I want you to go and spy on the Vikings. That way you can report their position to me and the rescue force when we return."

"I can do that. Romanies are used to concealment."

"Good. But you mustn't try anything foolhardy or the Vikings may harm the princess," Wulfmaer ordered. "Do you understand, Edward?"

"Yes, Wulfmaer. I'll just watch them."

Between them they carefully lifted the unconscious Eadric onto his horse, securing him with rope.

Before they parted, Wulfmaer reminded Eddie, "Remember we need you as a spy, not as a corpse, Edward. Don't do anything stupid."

Eddie nodded in agreement and they went their separate ways.

Eddie had agreed reluctantly. He felt helpless and desperately concerned for Kate's safety. He went back to hide behind the elm trees near the hut where he'd last seen the princess, hoping against hope they hadn't already moved on.

While he waited, Eddie surveyed the Crouch Estuary. He couldn't see any longships, just a black cormorant in a crucifix stance on a rock, drying its wings.

Through the nape of his neck Eddie sensed that something or someone was behind him. Sweat broke out on his brow and he whirled around, ready for a fist fight or to flee. There was nothing substantial there, just a wispy, indistinct vision of a Druid.

This time his perception told him it was giving him advice. He felt through his skin that when he left this place he was to ride behind a line of deciduous trees and he would find what he needed waiting for him there. Then the ethereal spirit was gone. He shook for a moment, and then shrugged his shoulders.

After more observation, Eddie counted ten Vikings leaving the hut. He was relieved when he saw Kate being chivvied along, her hands tied behind her back with what looked like strips of leather. He noticed that four of the Vikings seemed to be having problems. They were limping and heavily bandaged.

He tried to estimate how long it would take them to get back to their longships but he didn't even know which river they were they going to. Were these the Vikings they had seen coming from Maylandsea? Or were they a completely different party, from Fambridge on the more southerly Crouch Estuary? To be certain, he would have to watch the direction in which they moved.

Eddie followed them, leading his horse, careful to stay hidden in the dense brush. After a while it became clear that Kate's captors were headed north towards Lawling Creek at Maylandsea. He estimated that if they had all been fit, it would take the Vikings about six or seven hours to get to their longships. However, with some of them limping, and hampered by Kate, it might take longer.

Eddie had promised Wulfmaer he wouldn't intervene. But he wondered if he could slow the Vikings down. What did he have going for him, if anything? In a few hours it would be dark. He did at least have his Romani night-stalking skills. He knew it was never completely dark. He'd had plenty of experience fighting with his bare hands and with a staff. He'd also used most weapons when he'd fought alongside his father as a mercenary for the Germanic tribes. However, that was irrelevant as he was unarmed and outnumbered by ten to one.

On the other hand, he did have a horse while they were on foot. At least he could outpace them if necessary.

Eddie kept the Vikings under observation. It seemed the two Saxon warriors had done well against the Vikings, despite their numerical disadvantage. Eddie realized Eadric and Wulfmaer had inflicted enough injuries on the enemy to slow their progress. But could these injuries delay them long enough for the Saxon relief force to arrive? He doubted it.

Still unsure what he could do, but desperate to help Kate, Eddie cautiously rode behind a line of deciduous trees as the Druid had instructed. As it wasn't yet spring, the trees' branches were still skeletal.

In the fading light, he came across a Viking's body on the ground. Dismounting to investigate, he approached the prone figure and immediately saw that the man had a javelin protruding from his stomach. Just in case this was a trap, Eddie nudged the body gingerly with the toe of his shoe. The man didn't move so he touched the back of the Norseman's hand. It was just warm, so it looked as if the Saxon guards had done even better than he'd supposed.

The big, bearded warrior's nose and cheek had a recent cut that crossed older, healed scars. Blood from this wound had matted and congealed in the man's beard. His mouth lay open with his tongue lolling out. The man's expression had been frozen in a twisted grimace of pain, creating a horrible death mask.

The dead warrior was still fully armed. Because of this, Eddie speculated that the man must have been separated from his comrades. Weapons were valuable; the other Vikings wouldn't have left them.

Eddie assessed the dead man's weapons. There was a bow and quiver of arrows, a sword and a short Seax single-edged dagger, plus a Viking thrusting spear. There was also the Saxon javelin impaled in the body. He thought of taking them all and then decided they would weigh too much. In the end he discarded the sword and dagger. With his previous battle experience, he knew if he fought at close range the Vikings would win as he was so outnumbered.

His only chance would be to slow them from a distance by using his javelin or archery skills, while the thrusting spear was his best defensive weapon as it was so versatile. It could be used to thrust or swipe and, importantly for Eddie, an experienced stave fighter, it had a long, strong haft.

Eddie had to retrieve the javelin from the Viking's guts. It was stuck fast but, with difficulty, he eventually pulled it out. Immediately, the dead man's intestines spilled out and lay pooled on the ground. Eddie felt like a grave robber, and bile and vomit welled up in his stomach. But he didn't puke, comforting himself by remembering the man had no need for them any more.

At dusk Eddie noticed the Norsemen making an overnight camp in a clearing within a large wood. He assumed they had been hindered by their wounded and Kate.

He came across a clear stream which he and his horse drank from and he tied up his horse at the edge of the wood where it could graze on the surrounding lush grass. His position was as far away from the Vikings' camp as he could get. However, the animal seemed spooked, and whickered as he left it. Eddie froze. Had the Vikings heard the horse whinny? If so, they would be even more on their guard. In fact, some of them could be heading towards him at this very moment.

He was tense after that. Should he back off and observe, and then just wait for the relief force? Eddie remembered he'd been instructed by Wulfmaer not to get involved. In two minds, he decided to approach the camp stealthily. The moon was low in the sky and intermittently shrouded by clouds, so there weren't many shadows.

Eddie's eyes had acclimatized to the semi-darkness and he knew he must avoid looking directly at the Vikings' fire or it could compromise his night vision.

When he got near enough he lay on the ground, looking around. He noticed a man roasting a deer on a branch over a cooking fire. He was also breaking up loaves of bread to eat with it

By the glow of the Vikings' fires Eddie could see Kate sitting with her back against the base of an ancient oak tree. She was loosely tied to the trunk with leather thongs. She was still bound at the wrists and now also at the ankles. Kate looked grubby and pale with her blonde hair in disarray. Eddie noticed her glaring defiantly at her captors whenever they had the temerity to approach her.

After the deer was cooked, each man was given a share of meat, bread and water. Kate's hands were released so that she could also eat and drink. The aroma of the seared meat tantalized Eddie, reminding him he hadn't eaten since the previous day.

Eddie could see the Vikings weren't expecting any immediate threat. Still, they would be aware that they were in an alien country so would be wary of ambush.

Guards had been set. Eddie could see two of them moving around the perimeter of the makeshift camp. At least, Eddie thought, the Vikings' decision to stop overnight gave the Saxon warriors more time to come to the princess's rescue.

Eventually Kate's hands were re-tied and all but the sentries wrapped themselves in their cloaks and lay down. Keeping still, Eddie gave them time to go to sleep. He hoped he'd somehow be able to cut the princess loose.

A movement to his right betrayed the location of one look-out. A little later he sensed, then saw movements from a second one. It seemed the two sentries had settled on static positions for the night guard. The two sentries were well placed. They could cover each other as well as the camp site so Eddie would have no chance of getting to Kate without being seen.

What could he do? He had been ordered not to intervene, but his Romani senses told him the Saxon warriors wouldn't return in time. Though he'd only met Kate recently, he was infatuated with her. He would rather die than let her be taken to the Vikings' longships. In any case, she'd called out for him to save her. Eddie reasoned that as she was the most senior, her words held more weight than Wulfmaer's.

However, he realized that if he got close and was spotted, any one of the huge men could kill him. He considered a longer range attack. He'd proved he was a competent archer when fighting in Germany as a mercenary. He was strong and accurate at long distance, but he had never used his bow in anger at such close range.

Eddie edged towards the fire. Moving quietly, he lowered each foot carefully so that he could feel the ground for anything like dry twigs that could snap and give him away. He was already tense and when he disturbed a couple of pigeons that flew off noisily, he fell backwards into the bracken.

The nearest sentry jumped up, startled, and drew his sword after hearing the racket. Eddie froze. If the Viking came towards him it would be the end of his rescue attempt and probably his life. He held his breath and his heart rate rose rapidly, preparing for imminent flight.

The Viking sentry stomped around for a while, peering into the gloom, before settling down again. Eddie hoped the man had concluded it had been a fox or other predator that had spooked the pigeons.

He stayed on the ground, allowing his body and mind to return to a state of equilibrium. It seemed a long time but was probably only minutes. While he waited he thought how incredibly dangerous this was. No wonder Wulfmaer had warned him not to get involved.

But Eddie had never been a quitter. In fact he was the opposite. He had a stubborn streak and natural physical and mental prowess. So instead of using common sense and retreating to wait for the Saxon reinforcements, he resolved to carry on.

He crawled carefully for the last few yards until he was lying as close as he dared behind the sentry nearest to Kate. Now what? Having no idea, he sat tight and hoped for inspiration and opportunity.

After a while Eddie became stiff from lying in one position. But he daren't move if he wanted to avoid detection and have a hope of saving Kate. It was an impasse.

After what seemed an age, the far sentry signalled to the one nearer to Eddie that he was going to get them some food and drink. Eddie made a decision to take this chance in case he didn't get another.

Waiting until the second sentry was out of sight, Eddie held his breath with excited anticipation. Then coldly and deliberately, he nocked an arrow, pulled back his bow string and sent the missile into the standing sentry's back. The man was barely three feet from Eddie's bow so he stood no chance and soundlessly crumpled to the ground.

Eddie propped the dead man against the trunk of a tree trying desperately to arrange him to look as if he were still alive. However, he couldn't get the dead man's head to stop lolling against his chest.

There was no time for anything more. The other sentry was returning and Eddie dived for cover as he reappeared. Would the warrior notice something was wrong with his counterpart? Eddie held his breath, sweating profusely.

Initially, the second sentry hesitated, possibly thinking his comrade was asleep, as he didn't raise the alarm right away. The warrior said something in a quiet voice and walked over to his pal. He shook his arm and then jumped back, startled with the realization that his friend wasn't asleep, but dead.

At that moment, Eddie loosed his second arrow. Although it struck the man in the chest, he wasn't as accurate, as the man was moving. This time the Viking screamed a warning before he collapsed. The stricken guard's yell alerted his comrades, who woke and came running in Eddie's direction. Eddie scrambled to his feet and darted into the bushes. He began jinking about, trying to make himself as difficult a target as possible. He could hear the sounds of breaking branches as the Norsemen fanned out to look for their attacker.

Eddie regretted not having had a chance to let Kate know she wasn't alone, that he hadn't abandoned her, but she had probably guessed by now that someone was trying to disrupt her captors. He was startled when out of the darkness a giant Viking came straight at him. Thinking fast, Eddie ducked behind a tree and at arm's length fixed the thrusting spear's butt into the ground. As the pursuing Viking rushed towards him, Eddie aimed the point of the spear at the Viking's gut. The force of the warrior's forward momentum impaled him on the spear's point and wrenched its haft out of Eddie's hands. His foe fell forward, probably badly wounded and he had to jump aside to avoid being crushed by the falling Viking's heavy body.

Eddie was highly stimulated by the adrenaline released automatically in response to the stress of the recent clash. He reached his horse, mounted and spurred the black stallion into a gallop. When he judged he'd gone far enough to be safe, he dismounted.

He had just killed or badly injured three men, but he was used to wounding and killing in battle. He'd been just fifteen when he'd killed his first Hun. It was a chastening experience, but he had eventually subdued any reluctance to destroy human life. In any case, today it was the princess or them, so it had to be them.

Eddie did a quick calculation; there had been ten Vikings to start with and now three were dead or disabled. With the four injured earlier, this left three fully fit Norsemen. That was better odds but it still left three massive experienced fighters with the wounded men as backup.

He wasn't foolish enough to think he'd be so lucky again. This time he wouldn't have the element of surprise. Not only that, there could still be other Vikings nearby, particularly around the longships. If he couldn't stop the original group getting Kate to these reinforcements, she'd be gone from him forever.

Eddie realized he was in love with Kate. This gave him further impetus to try to delay the Vikings until help arrived, despite understanding that there could be no future for him romantically with a princess.

He tried to bring his emotions under control and think laterally. Deliberately, he slowed his breathing and closed his eyes. If he couldn't take them on physically, he'd have to attempt subterfuge.

He must work out a stratagem to outwit this more powerful force and rescue Kate, his princess.

It was still dark and a fair wind had sprung up in the last half hour, coming from the other side of the wood. The Vikings were now awake, having been spooked by Eddie's attack and by the sudden loss of more comrades.

In contrast, Eddie was buoyed up from his recent experiences. He also knew the number of enemies in the camp. Could he make them think they were up against more than one attacker? They might not realize they were only up against one youth.

Searching his pockets, he found the flint and iron that Romanies used to create sparks for lighting fires. This gave him an idea and he remounted and rode round to the windward side of the camp.

He tied up his horse in the wood and then began to gather dried-out elder branches and wild rose stems from the forest floor. He found some dry hay which was plentiful and easily combustible. He arranged his materials into several piles in an area covering a couple of hundred yards.

Eddie struck the flint with the iron and the resulting sparks ignited the first pile. From this, he snatched some of the burning hay and ran along the line, lighting all the heaps. The wind helped fan the flames which spread rapidly across the tinder dry undergrowth. This created a wall of flame that roared swiftly towards the Viking camp.

Mounting his horse, Eddie rode towards the flames. As he approached the heat of the blaze, his horse reared and whinnied loudly. This was just what he'd wanted. He pulled on the bridle rope and swung round the outside of the wood. After moving part way round the wood, he dug his heels sharply into the horse, making it whinny again. He repeated this manoeuvre several times, hoping the Vikings would think there was a big force against them, or at least believe it was bigger than a one-man unit.

As soon as he'd lit the fires, Eddie worried about Kate's safety. A wall of flames was spreading out of control towards the campsite. Would his mad idea kill his princess? What if the Vikings left her tied up to die in the blaze to save their own skins? Eddie was desperately counting on the Vikings realizing she was worth a big ransom. Would the lure of silver be a strong enough incentive for them to take her with them?

Astride the stallion, he watched anxiously as the Vikings rushed out of the clearing, heaving a sigh of relief when he saw in the flickering light that the two leading warriors had Kate with them. Lagging well behind were the four original wounded. They could still escape the conflagration, but were well separated from the others.

What worried him more was the whereabouts of the third fit Viking. He soon found out when the giant Viking appeared immediately in his horse's path and heaved a small throwing axe in his direction.

Eddie flattened himself against his horse's neck and jerked his head to the side. The axe hit him a glancing blow to his shoulder. Blood streamed down his arm. The pain was tremendous. The huge man made blood-curdling war cries and raised his spear to throw at Eddie. Startled, Eddie's instinct was to turn and ride away but he knew that to do so would mean his immediate death with the Viking's spear in his back.

He did the only thing possible and urged his horse on, riding it over the big man who was knocked to the ground. There was a whinny of pain from his horse. The warrior had speared the animal in the chest as it passed over him. The black stallion collapsed and Eddie was violently thrown to the ground.

Both men were winded but the Viking was up soonest. Mouthing obscenities and with eyes blazing, he was swinging his spear in a deadly, scything ark. If it hit Eddie, he'd be slaughtered.

Seven

The once placid dark night on the Dengie Hundred Peninsula was ruptured by the unexpected flames from burning trees. Animals and birds fled the holocaust that had recently provided their habitat. The remnants of the dying moon could just be seen to one side of the conflagration. Even a few stars were visible if anyone had the time to admire them. The smell of burning flora and its smoking residue permeated the area.

Eddie was aware of all this but now had a more pressing problem on his mind. At the edge of the burning wood, a massive Viking was swinging his spear at Eddie with barbarous strength. Automatically, Eddie threw his hands up, grasped his own spear, and managed to parry the crushing blow. However, the Viking warrior's brute force clubbed Eddie's weapon from his hands. Eddie made a grab for his fallen spear before his adversary could strike again.

Eddie was experienced in stave fighting and had used a spear to good effect against the Huns in Germany. The giant changed the angle of attack and this time aimed his spear at the top of Eddie's head. Again, Eddie managed to reduce the effect of the blow with the haft of his own spear, but the power of the blow knocked him backwards and he landed on the soft leafmould.

Before Eddie could recover, the Viking used his weapon as a lance. Its needle-sharp point, guiding a wickedly barbed hook, was aimed at Eddie's chest. Desperately, Eddie rolled to one side, barely avoiding the lethally sharp weapon. The power of the Viking's thrust plunged the spear's point into the ground. While the big man retrieved it, Eddie rolled to his feet. He still had his spear but the Viking was stronger so he felt it safer to retreat for the moment.

Eddie soon out-paced his pursuer who waved his spear and vowed vengeance for his fallen comrades. Within the first few yards Eddie noticed the giant Viking was limping badly. He suspected his horse's hooves had damaged the man's legs.

As Eddie's heartbeat returned to normal after its earlier pounding, he deliberately slowed, encouraging the Viking to go faster to close on him. Eddie hoped his own sure-footedness over the wood and bramble-strewn forest ground would give him the advantage.

Sure enough, the big man was concentrating on Eddie's fleeing form and not watching the ground. He tripped and crashed heavily to the earth. Winded, he dropped his spear.

Immediately, Eddie turned. He ran back and thrust his own spear into the Viking's side. He felt the spear's tip catch in the giant's ribcage and jam. The strong man was wounded but, incredibly, this didn't stop the brute. Even with the spear protruding from his ribs, he still came at Eddie. Emitting a shrill, unearthly war cry, the Viking attacked again.

But as the mighty warrior's blood flowed away, his strength ebbed with it. The Viking sank to his knees onto the forest loam. Eddie snatched the big man's own dagger from its scabbard and cut the huge Viking's throat. Blood spurted from the carotid artery, much of it soaking into Eddie's clothes. The giant's audaciously brave last hurrah faded. The man shook uncontrollably in his death agony as he headed for his personal Valhalla.

Eddie didn't feel triumphant... he'd slaughtered a brave man. Then he gave himself a mental nudge. He had to snap out of these sympathetic feelings for the raiders. He must be ruthless if he was to save Kate.

He was worried that he may not be able to catch up with Kate's captors. After all, he was now on foot and it was beginning to get light. There was a rosy glow over the Lawling Creek. The emerging light illuminated the menacing outlines of several longships.

Smoke from the Viking fires and the scent of breakfast being cooked already permeated the morning air. He had to try and rescue Kate before her abductors reached the Viking warriors who were warming themselves at those fires. He desperately hoped the Saxons would get there before it was too late.

To have any chance of delaying her kidnappers, Eddie knew he must catch them up. So to cut down on weight, he abandoned his heavy weapons, retaining only the bow and quiver of arrows. After that decision he made a faster pace.

In the distance Eddie spotted Kate. She was being dragged by the last two fit Vikings from the original party. He could see that Kate wasn't making it easy for them. She pulled sideways, back and forward, or dropped to the ground. Every step involved a struggle for the two Vikings.

Eddie knew there was no point in going near them. In a straight fight with these two massive warriors, he'd be unlikely to win. Even if he did it would be too risky for Kate's safety. He had to be careful not to be seen, so he dared not take the main track. He would have to circle around. In the distance, he could see the church and its barn. Smoke was billowing from them. So that was where the acrid tar smoke was emanating from.

Keeping track of the two Vikings pulling the reluctant Kate along with them, Eddie edged ahead of the small group and then entered the graveyard. The church where he'd slept two nights previously was now a roofless shell. Still smouldering, the wooden building had been devastated by the raiders. Eddie wondered if the friendly priest, Pastor John, was now lying dead in the smoking ruins.

The Vikings who had Kate weren't far behind. They would pass his position in a few minutes. As Eddie watched their progress he wondered what he could to do to help Kate. He must do something and do it now. But what?

He looked for somewhere to hide in the graveyard, but there were just low earth mounds. Eventually he decided to conceal himself in the bushes that bordered the track the Vikings were coming down. He ensured that his quiver of arrows was fixed securely across his shoulder and used the leather straps to tie it around his waist.

It wasn't as easy to get into the bushes as he'd hoped. They were mostly big holly trees and wild rose bushes. He had to crawl beneath the branches and fronds and was repeatedly scratched and pricked. The dead leaves on the ground crackled as his feet and knees flattened them. The smell of the crushed, long-dead roses still wafted up, ameliorating the pungent smell of smoke from the still smouldering church.

The holly wore its full green armour and even bore a few red berries, but the rose vines were just empty, prickly fronds. At least Eddie could look out through their skeletal branches.

He remembered that the last time he'd been in the graveyard he'd encountered a Druid. What had it told him? From nowhere, the Druid appeared again. He was with him in the bushes. The black cowl covered his face but thin white fingers stuck out from the deep sleeves. Eddie noticed that they were thinner than the rose fronds he was surrounded by.

The Druid made contact with Eddie's mind, instructing him, '*Your historical teachings can wait for now. You must save your princess. She is also a latent Parallaxys. I suggest you make noises like a horse. They will think there is a threat and come to find out where their enemy is.*' Then the Druid had gone.

Eddie thought the Druid's idea was a long shot but he had to try something quickly. He waited until the small group drew level. He tried to neigh as best he could. Then on his knees he crawled behind an old oak tree alongside the bushes.

One of the sea raiders pulled Kate with him and rushed her down the track. The second Viking drew his sword and searched around the area, circling sideways, sword at the ready.

Eddie clucked like a chicken. The Viking, roaring a battle cry, rushed into the bushes, slashing with his sword as he did so. This Viking's chin had only stubble rather than a beard, and lank, blond hair hanging to his shoulders. He had the mightiest upper body that Eddie had ever seen, a barrel chest and bulging biceps.

As the Norseman passed his hiding place, Eddie loosed an arrow at him. It hit the big man in the right shoulder. He screamed in pain and his right arm dropped loosely at his side. His sword fell, clattering, to the ground.

When he saw Eddie, he dragged the arrow from his shoulder and charged towards him, bent on revenge for his agony. As the heavyweight threw himself bodily into Eddie, the impetus sent the Romani crashing to the ground and he rolled into a self-protective ball. The furious warrior kicked Eddie in the side, trying to damage his internal organs. Then he landed a heavy kick on Eddie's back.

Eddie's breath was crushed from his body. In normal circumstances he'd have just lain there and recovered, but this was far from a routine situation. He half rose, using his bow as a crutch. At the same time, the Viking released his long Seax dagger from its sheath on his right hip with his good left hand. The low morning sunlight glittered on the blade. He launched himself towards Eddie's half raised body.

Eddie was only just able to sway away from the knife, but the blade still slashed his cheek. Eddie made it to his feet. Forcing his lungs to suck in a huge breath, he rushed away through the graveyard, making his second retreat in a few hours. Adrenalin gave him speed and he tried to ignore the pain from his bruised side and two bleeding wounds.

He looked back. The Viking had hesitated, perhaps surprised that Eddie hadn't stood his ground and fought him face to face. The big guy was in a fit of violent rage, screaming like a monster and slashing with his seax knife at anything around him, including the grave mounds. Eddie didn't blame him; after all, he'd wounded the big warrior and killed his friends.

As he ran, Eddie almost tripped over two eight-inch chocolate brown weasels he'd disturbed. This stimulated him to a further burst of speed, but the muscular Viking was obviously a fit man as he was catching up.

To try to outwit the giant, Eddie swung sharply round the burnt-out ruin of the barn. But the big Viking wasn't fooled and spun round the corner so easily, belying his greater, muscular bulk, and came even nearer. Close enough to slash at Eddie's back with his long seax knife. The Viking's knife would have cut into Eddie's spine but he was saved by the quiver of arrows he wore there.

Eddie zigzagged through the wreckage of the barn, using his bow to keep his balance. Then he ran towards the church. Reaching a side door in one of the few walls that were still standing, he wrenched it open. However, before he could get through the portal, the Viking was on him.

With a shout of triumph, the giant Norseman again swung the long seax dagger towards his Saxon foe. Eddie managed to deflect the blade with his bow and the Viking's blade thudded into the church door.

The Viking's muscle-bound arm continued its swing and hit Eddie in the face, knocking him to the ground. Eddie was dazed, semi-conscious now.

The massive warrior stamped his large foot and his considerable weight onto Eddie's chest rendering him unable to move or even breathe. Though he still had his bow, he was unable to swing it at the giant.

The Viking nodded and his face twisted into a triumphant gloat, sensing his ultimate victory. The Norse warrior retrieved his seax knife from the door lintel with his good arm and then, with a grunt of exultation, drove the blade towards his conquest's chest. Eddie closed his eyes in anticipation of the pain.

But the cutting torment and Eddie's death didn't come. Instead, the Viking's massively heavy body crashed down onto him. Eddie was trapped beneath the giant.

Unable to move, Eddie realized that the Viking wasn't stirring at all. A few seconds later he felt the big man's body rolling off him. Scrambling to his feet, Eddie noticed the priest, Pastor John, was holding a grave-digging spade still upraised. The spade was covered with blood.

"I'm so grateful to see you, Pastor John," Eddie gasped, "But how did you survive the attack and the fire?"

"I hid in a specially prepared priest hole." He looked down at the massive, but inert body on the ground. "Although my vows won't let me kill anyone, I knocked the heathen out to save your life." Father John looked like he'd been hard pressed to preserve his vows. He seemed ready to hit the Viking again at the least sign of movement.

Eddie needed to move on. "Look, I'm indebted to you Father John, but the other Viking's getting away with the princess." He shook Father John's hand, thanked him again and ran after Kate and her captor.

Eddie knew his chances of catching them up were minimal. He didn't have time to be subtle so he just ran as fast as he could down the same farm track that the Viking had taken Kate earlier. He was relieved when he saw them ahead of him.

Then his blood ran cold. Another band of Norsemen was coming up the Mayland hill towards the Viking and Kate. Neither party was aware of the other yet. At the moment, the relief force was hidden from Viking a line of trees. But in another couple of hundred yards Kate's abductor would have as many reinforcements as he would need.

Eddie felt woozy; he'd lost far too much blood. But there was no time to spare. If he lost consciousness he would also lose Kate forever. He slapped himself about the face several times and then ran towards where his princess was.

When he got nearer, he stopped, nocked an arrow and loosed it. The arrow landed just in front of Kate's captor. Immediately, the Viking stopped. Throwing Kate roughly down, he drew his sword and charged towards Eddie.

Eddie yelled, "Kate, hide yourself in the woods!" She turned her head to look and nod in his direction. He saw her struggle to get up from the rough ground. But with her hands tied behind her back, she overbalanced and crashed to the ground again. She was on her knees dragging herself towards cover. Then Eddie lost sight of her as the big, blond Viking was almost upon him.

This warrior was several inches taller than Eddie and a few stones of muscle heavier. The man had the regulation blond hair and beard. His nose had been broken and when he opened his mouth, Eddie could see that all his front teeth were missing.

Instinctively, Eddie picked up a large flint and threw it at the Viking. There was no time to take aim, but luck was with him. The stone hit the Viking's sword hand and his weapon arched away from him into the undergrowth. But the mighty warrior's momentum carried him right into Eddie, knocking him to the ground.

The adversaries rolled in the dirt of the bridle path. They grabbed at each other's throats. But the Viking was much stronger than Eddie. The giant's hands were the size of hams, and his fingers completely encircled Eddie's throat. Eddie's vision blurred as the life was being choked out of him. His loss of blood had already drained his strength. Now lack of oxygen was weakening him further.

Eddie felt for his fallen bow and whipped it round into the Vikings face. The huge man released his grip on Eddie's neck. Eddie scrambled up and had run a few steps before he was roughly grabbed by several other pairs of hands.

The second group of Vikings had arrived. Eddie struggled to break free but in his weakened state was easily subdued. He hoped that Kate had got away and could stay hidden until help came.

Eddie's original opponent picked up his sword and held its point against Eddie's chest. The big man's face contorted into a triumphant smirk. Eddie closed his eyes and braced himself, resigned to death by skewering by the Norseman's silver blade.

However, the other Vikings shouted, "Glima! Glima!"

Eddie opened his eyes again. It appeared his execution was deferred for now at least. His adversary laughed, stood back, and gave his weapons to one of his comrades.

What was going on, Eddie wondered? But he was still depressed, realizing this reprieve could only be short-lived. There would just be another layer of torture to come.

A Viking with white hair and a scarred, wrinkled face spoke to Eddie. When the man opened his mouth to speak, Eddie noticed the Viking had few teeth left.

The older man, by the name of Omard, said, "You've been fighting our warriors and killing some of our brethren. So we'll have some fun with you before we execute you. In our culture we fight man to man, a great brawl called glima. The normal rules are no kicking or punching. Just wrestling, rushing, tripping or throwing your opponent."

The old Viking continued, "To give us strength, we often struggle unarmed between ourselves until one man is thrown down. But today we have special rules for you, our mortal enemy. You will fight to the death against Halfdan, our glima champion." He indicated the Viking who'd abducted Kate. "Today there are no restrictions. Any blow from any part of the body can be used, but no weapons. Halfdan has already killed four men with his bare hands, so you'll have no chance. But it will amuse the heroes to see you crushed to death."

It sounded to Eddie like a game of cat and mouse and he was to be the mouse. However, he had no choice… die this way or be cut to pieces anyway. He'd fight back as best he could in his weakened state.

Even before the bout started Eddie felt woozy. He had bled profusely from the wounds to his shoulder and cheek. The man Halfdan was a foot taller than Eddie, and very muscular. He must have weighed four stone heavier as well. This, of course, was the whole point of making Eddie fight. To humiliate him and ensure he died in agony.

However, from a young age Eddie had been a korer, a Romani fighter. He was one of the very best at boxing and wrestling and all-round street fighting. Then as a mercenary warrior he'd trained for unarmed combat with various Germanic tribes – the Visigoths, the Avars, and even the Hungarian Magyars. Every tribe had subtle differences so he'd learned and remembered the best moves.

Eddie reasoned he would try and surprise Halfdan with a few street fighting moves. If he did that he may able to postpone his own death but more importantly, this could buy Kate more time to escape.

The Vikings, all fully armed, formed a spear cordon around the two combatants. Eddie would have no chance of escape. There was no ceremony. Halfdan simply grabbed Eddie by his tunic and lifted him off his feet. He swung him round trying to throw him down but Eddie hung on to his opponent's heavy cloth shirt with all his might.

Halfdan's muscular arms now encircled Eddie, the giant Viking's hugely muscled forearms crushing Eddie until he thought his ribs would break again.

Halfdan sneered, "You'll soon die, Saxon. We men of Denmark are stronger than you puny Saxons."

Then he crushed Eddie with renewed force. The pain in Eddie's side and shoulder where he'd been wounded earlier was excruciating. He couldn't breathe and he knew he would pass out unless he could break the titan's grip.

As Halfdan lifted him once more, Eddie kicked out and hit him hard in his crotch. The oldest trick in the world, but it still worked. Halfdan dropped Eddie and rolled on the ground holding his genital area with both hands.

Eddie was surprised to see the surrounding Vikings roaring with laughter. Then they started making ribald comments about Halfdan's future performances with the ladies and the likelihood of him fathering children.

By now Halfdan was on his knees being violently sick. Eddie thought he may as well milk the crowd's good humour. So he kicked Halfdan's behind and the Viking landed on his face in his own vomit. This made the Viking audience laugh again. Perhaps,

Eddie thought, they wouldn't mind if Halfdan were belittled a bit before his ultimate victory.

By now Halfdan had recovered a little, although was still choking. The giant charged unsteadily, head down, at Eddie who stepped aside so that Halfdan crashed into the crowd.

Eddie thought he may be able to slip away in the confusion. He had almost wriggled through a gap when he was tripped and brought back by the other Vikings. He circled round as fast as he could, to keep the even more enraged Halfdan away and give himself a chance to think.

With his face now red and screwed up with fury, Halfdan swung his foot at Eddie. If the blow had landed, it would have broken bones. But this was Eddie's territory. He swung his own foot against Halfdan's approaching knee as hard as he could. The Viking howled and grabbed at his knee. As he jumped on one leg, Eddie knocked the other from under him. The brute went down hard but bounced up immediately and lunged at Eddie.

This was good, Eddie thought. The angrier he was, the less rational would be his thinking. As Halfdan charged, Eddie jerked sideways and punched him in the side of the head. He didn't know how much it hurt Halfdan but his own hand felt as if it was broken.

However, Halfdan was a tough man and didn't want to lose face in front of the other warriors. So, using his superior size, Halfdan stood large, hands and legs spread out restricting Eddie's ability to move around the circle.

Moving forward, Halfdan began pushing Eddie back against the spear circle. Then using one hand and a lightning fast lunge he got hold of Eddie by the throat again. Gripping him with phenomenally strong muscles he lifted him off the ground. Eddie could feel his eyes bulging and he was choking. Desperately, he threw his hand forward and with his fingers sticking out straight, poked Halfdan in both eyes.

Halfdan dropped Eddie, who landed hard on his back, winding him. Eddie tried to draw air back into his lungs. His head cleared. Halfdan was still in pain and rubbing his eyes. But there was no escape for Eddie; the Vikings encircling them made an impenetrable barrier.

Through the surrounding wall of Vikings, a massive left arm emerged and clasped itself round Eddie's chest. Eddie could see it was from the big Viking who'd been felled by the priest. Blood ran from the man's head into his eyes. No doubt the giant wanted revenge for his broken right arm and crushed head.

The warrior's arm tightened around Eddie's chest until he couldn't breathe. It was like an anaconda crushing his life from him. His chest couldn't take any more compression. Simultaneously, Eddie heard his ribs crack and felt the sharp agony as his bones collapsed inside him.

Through his pain, Eddie thought this wasn't fair. This fight was supposed to be a one-to-one bout. But tenth century life had never been fair.

While the second warrior held him in his vice-like grip, Halfdan kicked Eddie in the gut. When he was suddenly released, he folded up on the ground in agony. Before he could get his breath, Halfdan got him by the throat again. Keeping Eddie on the ground he trapped both arms under him then knelt on his legs.

Eddie went white, phlegm choking him. He couldn't move or fight back. There was nothing he could do now. He could feel himself losing consciousness. He was utterly dismayed. This was the end. He screamed out, "Sorry, princess, I have failed you!"

Eight

In the Blackwater Estuary it was an hour after high tide. The sun shone in the blue sky with few clouds to block its rays. There was enough wind in opposition to the current to whip up small wavelets. What started as ripples became swells and then breakers as they reached the mainland shore.

A flock of herring gulls whirled in the air. Most were white feathered, though a few brown chicks already as big as the adults followed the older birds everywhere.

Eddie was regaining a vague awareness. It was as if he were swimming through a thick, soundless bath of cotton wool. He couldn't work out where he was. Strange images swam into his mind. Nothing made sense.

Then he remembered. The Vikings were trying to kill him. Yet he still felt alive Did that mean he was being taken to the longships, to Denmark? He slipped back into dark nothingness.

Sharp stabbing pains in his chest returned Eddie's senses to conscious reality. Strong hands were repeatedly submerging him in seawater. Were the Vikings drowning him?

The smell and taste of swallowed salty brine made him retch violently and repeatedly. Each time his stomach forcibly ejected its contents or he coughed, spluttered and choked, his ribs felt as if a rapier had been thrust between them.

Was this the Vikings taking their revenge for their warriors he'd killed? His mind couldn't take any more pain and torment. He blacked out again.

Later, he realized he was being bounced along a track on another horse-drawn drag stretcher. He could smell the rich, animal scent of the horse and hear the clip-clop of its hooves. The sounds changed with each variation in terrain.

Each time the stretcher bumped over a rock, or skewed to avoid potholes, his shattered ribs sent him terrible reminders of his ordeal. He sought unconsciousness again, but was unable to find oblivion. Instead his mind chose its own coping mechanism. It seemed to him that he was in a strange dream. He fantasized that he could again see the coast. It appeared like a wildly fluctuating, bizarre version of an estuary.

Suddenly, the horse was gone. Where was he now? A blurred figure appeared before him. Was it a ghost? The figure reappeared and he at last identified it as Kate. She was alive… she was talking to him.

"Edward, wake up." Kate took his hand tenderly.

He clasped hers as firmly as he could, not understanding why a princess would hold the hand of a slave.

"Kate?" Eddie whispered. The one word asked all the questions clamouring in his discordant brain.

"Edward," she answered. "You saved my life, thank you. You're back at the Burh. It's okay, you're safe now."

Eddie's forehead puckered and then he gasped. "But how…?"

Kate shook her head slightly. Still talking softly, she explained. "While your fighting was entertaining the crowd, our relief troop of Saxon warriors crept up on the Vikings and attacked them. The skirmish was fierce. But the Vikings eventually retreated to their longships and sailed away."

Eddie coughed up blood and then squirmed from his chest pains. Through tears of agony, he asked hesitantly, "Where… were… you?"

Kate smiled sweetly before answering. "I stayed hidden in the trees until it was safe. Eddie, you were so still and white-faced, I thought you were dead. When you started to spasm, I yelled for help."

Eddie's face contorted in panic as another fragment of memory returned. He blurted out, "But Kate, the Vikings were trying to drown me."

She shook her head. "No, it wasn't the Vikings. It was us Saxons. We were trying to help you. Our salt-water immersion treatment certainly brought you round, didn't it?"

Eddie stared at Kate, still confused, and hurting everywhere, but fascinated by the natural pout of her full red lips as she spoke.

Kate regarded him in silence for a moment. Then she smiled again. "You saved me, Edward, so I've demanded to have you as my official bodyguard in future."

Eddie had never seen such a pretty girl in his life. She was a princess and she was holding his hand. All the fighting and pain of the last few days were suddenly worth it.

"I'll get my girls to bring you some food and drink." Kate laughed when Eddie wouldn't release her hand. She leaned over and gave him a soft kiss on the cheek, then while he was distracted, she gently pulled her hand away.

When Kate left, Eddie looked around him. He was lying on a straw filled palliasse. These were fairly comfortable in normal circumstances, but now he noticed how the sharp bits dug into him and irritated his painful wounds. He couldn't lie on his right side as it was agony.

At least he was near a comforting, blazing fire. The smell of the smoke told him they were silver birch logs crackling and burning in the massive granite fireplace. Silver birch smoke had always been one of his favourite scents. Its aroma was sweet and heady and reminded him of the Romani yogs, or fires, near to the bender blanket tents that made up his travelling home.

But he was not at home. He was in a Saxon log-built and thatch-roofed hall. Eddie could taste his own blood in his mouth. He had a sore throat from retching up blood and salt water. His throbbing head was still bruised and swollen.

Disembodied coughing nearby warned Eddie he wasn't alone. Rolling carefully onto his less bruised left side, he saw Eadric. The Saxon guard lay on a palliasse a few yards away.

Eddie vaguely remembered that Eadric had been badly wounded. That was it, Eadric had also been defending Kate against the Vikings at Maylandsea. Eadric's face was pale. His eyes were closed. His head, chest and both arms were heavily bandaged. Eddie noted the warrior's bandages had fresh red blood stains from his head wound and dark, dried blood marks on his chest.

"Eadric," Eddie whispered. "Are you all right?"

Eadric slowly opened his eyes. Then he replied with his usual bullish confidence, although Eddie noted his voice was now surprisingly weak and light. "Yes, and I'll be ready to fight again as soon as the Viking army comes."

Eadric wasn't tall, but he was a strong man both in body and mind. He was covered in scars from previous encounters. When his bandages were removed there would be more from this latest fight. The massive purple scar on his white face was even more prominent than usual. Eddie marvelled that he'd survived so many substantial wounds.

The two men chatted together with an intimacy that only those who had shared extreme adversity were able to.

"I'm a Huscarl," Eadric told Eddie. "A professional warrior. I've been in Ealdorman Byrthnoth's employ for ten years. I'm forty years old, married to Lilly and we've six children."

Eddie asked, "Do you have boys who want to follow in your footsteps?"

"Yes, I have four boys," Eadric answered proudly, "and they all want to become huscarls. My oldest son, Eane, is now eighteen and has already made it. The others are still too young."

Eddie had taken to Eadric. Although a professional warrior, he wasn't arrogant. He seemed a modest family man. The huscarl was swarthy with curly, jet black hair and a spiky beard. Eddie thought he wouldn't have looked out of place in his own Romani community.

Kate returned and told Eddie, "You'll have met Alfthrith, one of my handmaidens, before. I'm leaving her to look after you on my behalf. That's because the Ealdorman insists I have functions I must attend to immediately."

Then leaving him to recover, Kate smiled and waved. Eddie felt better already. He could dream of his wonderful princess. What a reward! As her bodyguard, he'd be able to be near her legitimately.

Alfthrith was of a similar size to her mistress. Not with Kate's aristocratic profile, but pretty none the less.

Alfthrith gave Eddie water to drink and then fed him spoonfuls of broth. The broth was hot with a sharp, rather bitter flavour. It also had a strong, spicy aroma of mutton combined with a well-seasoned tang of wild horseradish. He swallowed his first mouthful with difficulty, his sore throat contracting as the broth stung on its way down. Though it hurt him, he kept his composure and didn't show his discomfort. "That was lovely, Alfthrith, thank you."

Alfthrith smiled. "I'm glad you like the broth. You deserve it for saving our princess." She continued feeding Eddie until he indicated that he could take no more. Then she held his hands to comfort him. Better still, she produced a long bolster cushion, not soft, but pliable. With the bolster she wedged his body so that he couldn't roll to his right, his broken-ribbed side.

Despite being propped up, Eddie's wounds were still painful. He felt feverish as well, and began shivering and shaking, his mind faltering. He passed out once more.

Eddie dreamt he was a young Romani again, breaking in horses in Germany. A group of giggling Romani girls watched his every move. He loved to show off in front of them. His small grey gelding with plenty of attitude spooked a male blackbird that screamed its shrill warning cry and flew horizontally off into the distance.

He was naked apart from his shorts. Sweat ran down his chest onto the back of the young grey. He was now riding his horse through a copse full of daffodils and heather. His horse's hooves crushed the flowers and forest moss as they passed, wafting delicate floral perfumes into his receptive nostrils. The smells evoked happy memories of sleeping under the stars on hot summer nights.

A dog barked as he rode past, and several deer fled from his path. He heard the snapping of branches as his horse's hooves broke them in their exodus. Suddenly, he noticed a very pretty blonde girl ahead. She was not a black haired Romani, but the girl seemed friendly as she waved and smiled. He dreamt her name was Kate and he knew he wanted to meet her to find out why his emotions were in absolute turmoil. He somehow knew their lives were entwined, but they'd never met. Or had they?

He felt such a strong bond with this girl that he wanted to hold her in his arms and make her want him. Recklessly, he tried to show off to get her full attention. There was a fallen tree near the pretty girl. He tried to get his horse to jump it. But the young colt was too inexperienced and fell forward onto its fetlocks and threw him.

He lay there, hurt. Immediately, Kate was with him. She held him in her arms and kissed him. He felt her breath on his cheek, gazed into those impossibly blue eyes and stroked her long, silky blonde hair.

He somehow knew he wanted to be with her for eternity. But now her pretty smiling face and the German trees were wavering. They were not just fluctuating with the wind. This was different, whole trunks branches and leaves shimmered and then disappeared completely.

He regained consciousness and was even more confused. Was he in Germany with his horse or in the Maldon Burh? Gradually, he recognized he was in the great hall at the Burh.

He was in more pain than before. Neither Kate nor Alfthrith were there, but a kindly looking middle-aged woman stood over him.

"My name is Eadburfi," she told him. While you've been unconscious I've washed your wounds, cauterized them and put on some balsam. Then I re-bandaged them for you."

Eddie's voice was weak. "Thank you, Eadburfi."

Eadburfi's face and hands were deeply creased and her hair was white and thinning. She limped as she walked. She was short with a pronounced stoop and looked to be well beyond her fifties. But she told him she was in fact only forty-two. Life had been hard on her.

"I've had fifteen children," she told Eddie, "though only ten still live. My husband was killed fighting the Vikings." She showed Eddie her red, chapped hands. "They got like this from washing other people's clothes to earn enough to feed my family."

Eddie could smell burnt flesh, then with a start, realized it was his cauterized wounds that stank. There was also a rather offensive urine odour that confused him. "What is that strange smell?" he asked.

"That is just the balsam I've used."

Eddie didn't ask what it was made from.

Eadburfi told him, "Anyone who lives will be helped by the balsam, and anyone who dies will at least be soothed in his last hours. You might have more fever later. You must fight it if you are to live. I'll give you some herbal drink to help you."

To Eddie the drink looked disgusting. It was very green and smelt and tasted salty and acrid. But he drank it. He remembered his mother's words, 'If it tastes horrid it must be doing you good.'

Eadburfi said flatly, "Your cheek will be scarred for the rest of your life. But don't worry, we women find scars like those attractive... a sign of manliness, so it's not all bad news."

Eddie felt he was burning up with fever. He could even smell his own salty perspiration. Yet, despite his sweat-soaked clothing and his pain, he drifted off to sleep.

When he awoke it was dark, but in the candlelight he realized he'd been taken to a smaller room and someone was wiping his brow with a cool, soothing cloth. It took Eddie a moment to recognize that it wasn't Eadburfi, but Alfthrith.

When Alfthrith saw that he was awake, she spoke to him. "Thank God you've come round, Edward. The princess has been worried about you. You've been in a coma for several days, but now it seems as if your fever is reducing at last."

Eddie and Eadric spent most of the next few days trying to find comfortable positions in which to sit or lie so that their wounds could recover. While Eadric slept, Eddie remembered when he was a rowing slave for his Norwegian Viking captors. They'd landed on Mersea Island, the biggest along the east Essex coastline. For exercise, he and his fellow captives had been taken in chains to see a mysterious circle of massive standing stones.

As he was bored and unable to walk, he decided to try his Romani remote viewing powers to explore them more. He closed his eyes, covered his ears and concentrated on the stones. It took a while, but soon his mind used its psychic ability to home in on the target he wanted.

His seventh sense reached out for the stone circle, transcending time and space. He saw in his mind's eye the gigantic monoliths. Then he touched a standing stone. It was black granite, hard and cold. He could taste and smell the ions in the area. The flow of information increased and he detected he wasn't alone there.

From the mists of his mind, figures appeared. A circle of a dozen white-robed druid priests chanted and waved their arms towards the centre of the stone circle. Eddie sensed a stronger force. In the middle of the circle was a small, black figure. The figure was a woman, a powerful Druidess, Magician and Sharman.

The black figure threw potions into a huge smoke-blackened cooking pot over a smouldering fire. As the potions landed, a stream of star-like sparks flew from the vessel. The white-robed Druid priests threw their arms in the air and prostrated their bodies on the floor, surrounding the black-robed Sharman in a star pattern.

The black figure turned towards Eddie's entity and pointed at him with both bony hands.

Immediately, Eddie found himself back on his palliasse in the Burh. He was shaking, not from fear, but from elation. His body felt stronger and his pain had lessened. Soon he was sleeping soundly.

A few days later the big warrior, Wulfstan, came in and spoke to Eadric for a few moments. Then he turned and addressed Eddie.

"Slave, you fought well. We'd expected a bloody fight to rescue our princess or to have to pay a huge ransom for her. But because of you, we were able to surprise the sea pirates and then drive them away without losing any of our men. It could have been very different if they'd been ready for us. You'll be pleased to know the Norsemen have moved out of the Blackwater Estuary. They've now landed at Mersea Island, further north. However, we suspect they will eventually to return to attack us in Maldon because of the Royal Mint that's here."

Eddie asked, "Wulfstan, as Maldon is only a small town, why is the mint here?"

"King Aethered has several rural mints to deflect sustained attacks on London. There are three in Essex alone, the other one near here is at Colchester."

Eadric groaned, then broke in, "I agree with Edward. We'd be safer without the mint."

Wulfstan replied, "Whatever we say, it doesn't matter. The King's decision is all that counts."

Eddie had cramp in his left calf. He rubbed it gently to ease the sharp pain.

"Wulfstan," he began again, "you say the King's treasury is split... so there's not a lot of silver here, then?"

"There's enough. The Norsemen suspect there's thousands of pounds weight of silver here."

Eddie's mouth felt swollen and his lips were dry and chapped. He tried to swallow but his throat was too dry and it was a huge relief when Eadric called out for drinks. Ruth, a short, plump, mature serving woman, brought in a jug of water and three horn cups.

After the three men had drunk, Eddie asked, "Doesn't the Burh afford enough protection for the mint?"

Wulfstan answered, "Although we're aware of our silver's lure, we're always vulnerable. This is because we don't have a permanent standing army at the Burh. At one time there were eight hundred soldiers permanently here. But the cost of manning so many Burhs became prohibitive. They became far too expensive for our King to continue financing."

Eddie winced in pain.

Wulfstan continued, "Some of the time we do have seven hundred huscarls here. But much of the time they are away fighting battles on behalf of the King. If we are threatened while they aren't here, we have to raise a garrison by getting levies of men from around the area. This is called the select Fyrd."

"Is it easy to gather enough men together for this select Fyrd?"

"It's a nightmare, really. Understandably, the older men with battle experience prefer to stay on the farm at harvest times. They send their sons who are very willing, but lack experience so they need to be trained quickly.

Eddie nodded. "That sounds worrying?"

Wulfstan pursed his lips then said, "You're right. When the huscarls are here we are strong. But the Fyrd members, although willing, are part time fighters. In comparison, the Norsemen are all trained warriors.

Eddie had cramp again and forced his foot out in a straight line, trying to stop the pain as his calf muscles spasmed.

Wulfstan waited for Eddie to relax again and then said, "I'm telling you all this because I've asked my uncle, Ealdorman Byrhtnoth, if you can be released from slavery."

Eddie drew in a breath and paid close attention.

Wulfstan continued, "I believe he may do so in gratitude for your brave defence of our princess. Though this will probably be on condition you agree to fight for us in the battle that is surely coming."

Eddie was naturally keen to be free and it was a dream come true to be the princess's bodyguard. But if this also committed him to fight in a battle that the Saxons would lose, what was the point of being a dead freeman?

"So, what's your answer Edward? Slavery? Or glory, protecting our land on behalf of your Lord and King?"

Nine

At Maldon in Essex the Burh, the fortified town, was under siege from a major summer storm. Gale force winds blew the heavy rain against the hall's window openings. Water dripped from the skin coverings onto the earth floor. Rain clattered like hailstones onto the wooden-tiled roof.

Inside, Eddie had been given the choice of staying a bodyguard slave for Princess Catherine, or becoming a freeman and fighting in the coming battle against the ferocious Vikings.

The comparative safety of being the protector of the beautiful princess was extremely appealing, even as a slave. However, his urge to be truly unconstrained, even if his freedom were hollow – and he may well be killed shortly afterwards – won out. After all, he was a Romani. His whole race was naturally restless and footloose, not just from slavery but from any district or country's confines.

Eddie wanted to keep as near to Kate as possible. If he could still do this and gain social advancement by fighting on the side of the Ealdorman, so be it.

"Thegn Wulfstan," he began, "I accept Ealdorman Byrhtnoth's gracious offer of freedom and I will fight loyally for him in future. I also thank you for recommending this to your uncle."

"Good," said Wulfstan. "I'll inform Ealdorman Byrhtnoth that your answer is positive. You've earned your freedom and you've saved me from much shame. As the only Thegn, I was in charge of the princess's guards. Had the Vikings harmed or completed her kidnapping, I would have been blamed."

After the rain stopped, Eddie said, "Eadric, if we're going to rebuild our strength we need to do more exercise. Perhaps we can walk around a bit more."

Eadric nodded. "Great idea, Edward. How about us climbing onto the Burh's walls?"

"Come on then, let's go now while it's dry."

The two men climbed to the high point of the Burh's earth walls. It wasn't far but it was surprisingly steep. Eddie was soon winded, which was indicative of how unfit he had become since he'd been injured.

The sun shone high in the azure sky, although it was still cool after the rainstorm. From the top of the wall they could see Maldon and Heybridge harbours. Also illuminated by the sun's rays were the nearby islands of Northey and Osea.

A flock of rooks cawed and swooped around the tops of nearby trees. The stick nests of their rookeries seemed to hang precariously in the extreme upper branches. Eddie could smell the wild flowers and hay in the surrounding meadows. Also the perpetual hint of raw sewage from the town midden. Puffy grey clouds created patches of shadow that traversed the ground like predatory black ghosts.

More ominously, in the distance, Eadric pointed out vast, black, anvil-shaped clouds heading their way. Bolts of lightning struck the land near Bradwell at the exit to the North Sea. Above the water, a gigantic rainbow splayed across the horizon, displaying the beautiful colours of the spectrum. Thunder could be heard some way off, but was getting nearer by the minute.

Eadric said "We'd better go back, Eddie."

They were aiming to return to the protection of the hall before the storm reached them. The two invalids helped each other down the muddy slope. However, they weren't quick enough. Hailstones hurled themselves from the sky onto the wounded men. Within seconds, both were steaming as the frozen hail and gelid rain soaked their clothes and warm bodies.

A few days later, Eddie stood by the hall door inhaling the cool fresh air after yet another April shower. He spotted a large group of Thegns and huscarls coming towards the hall. Eddie wasn't pleased to see among them, Godwig and Godwin, Eldor Godric's brothers. The brothers were on black ponies, while the others walked.

Eddie wondered what was happening. None of the warriors were in armour but in full dress uniforms. Some were in white tunics and others in brighter shades of silky material.

The warriors filed into the hall, most waiting patiently. But a few, noticeably Godwig and Godwin, showed their impatience by whispering and sniggering together.

Interrupting everybody, two black-haired mongrel dogs ran in and barked at a cat that jumped onto a table to avoid them. They were soon hustled out of the building by Mucil, a one-legged slave. Mucil repeatedly hit the mangy curs with one of his crutches until they ran off, yelping.

Godwig and Godwin were annoying their superior, Thegn Aelfhere. He accused them of being less than soldierly in their conduct. Godwig mumbled under his breath something about telling his older brother, Eldor Godric, to sort out Thegn Aelfhere.

Eddie could feel the tension. Thegn Aelfhere moved as if to grab hold of Godwig. Godwig rapidly hid behind his brother Godwin. This cowardly action elicited taunts and mocking guffaws from several warriors.

Eventually, Thegn Aelfhere marshalled the others into two equal lines about four yards apart on either side of the room.

Through this guard of honour marched Ealdorman Byrhtnoth. Following him, in a procession, were his wife, Lady Aelfflead, on one side and their son, Eldor Aefnoth, on the other. Behind them were Princess Catherine, Eldor Godric and Prior Esmond.

Seemingly spontaneously, the Thegns and huscarls stamped their feet. Then they thumped their spear butts onto the wood and dried earth floor as a salute to their leader. The fine baronial hall echoed with a cacophony of almost thunderclap proportions.

Disturbed by the almost seismic shudders, dust sifted through from the thatch. Grey-brown mice scuttled away in panic and, confused by the racket, swallows abandoned their nests in the rafters.

Princess Catherine looked towards Eddie and, almost imperceptibly, nodded in his direction. A slight upturn of Eddie's mouth served as a smile of pleased recognition. He couldn't believe a princess would even acknowledge a slave in public, despite the Maylandsea incident. Nobody else had noticed this interchange as far as he could see.

Eddie had never seen Lady Aelfflead before. She was a striking woman, probably in her fifties, tall, with a slim, elegant figure, although her angular face and long nose made her look rather haughty.

According to Alfthrith, Lady Aelfflead was the daughter of Ealdorman Aelfgar, a previous Ealdorman of Essex. Her sister, Athelglaed, had become King Edmund's second wife. So Lady Aelfflead was high-born even before she had married.

Ealdorman Byrhtnoth walked towards Eadric and placed his hands on the wounded warrior's shoulders. He said, "You've done well, hero."

Eadric replied, "My lord, I was only doing my duty."

"That's true, but my nephew, Thegn Aelfhere, considered you saved his life despite the fact you'd already been badly injured."

Eadric's scarred face twisted into a lopsided grimace, his bright eyes and a raised eyebrow the only tell-tale clues that the warrior's expression was one of idolization for his leader.

Eadric reached inside his tunic and from the inner pocket, pulled out a small cloth bag which he presented to the Ealdorman. Byrhtnoth loosened the leather drawstring and poured the contents into to his hand. Eddie could see it was a silver pendant and chain.

Ealdorman Byrhtnoth spoke. "I accept your tribute, loyal vassal."

Eadric replied, "My liege lord, it's yours by mandatory right."

Byrhtnoth smiled. "That is so and your reward bounty shall be fifty silver pennies and another hide of land next to your own."

Eadric nodded acknowledgement but didn't reply.

While Byrhtnoth was talking with Eadric, Eddie compared the three senior noblemen. Byrhtnoth and his son, Aefnoth, were fine figures of men. They were exceptionally tall, muscular and handsome, whereas Eldor Godric's appearance, as Eddie had noticed before, was less so. Unarmed and dressed in a knee-length ceremonial robe, Eldor Godric looked scrawny, although he carried a substantial pot belly. He was short, especially when seen beside the other two noblemen, and he was balding. He had hunched shoulders and his small piggy eyes were set close together. As Eddie had observed previously, his face was smothered in red bumps and pustules. The man also had foul, diseased teeth and seemed to have a permanent scowl.

Eddie recalled the stench of rampant decay from his blackened teeth. It wasn't a pleasant memory. He wondered if it was this man's unsightly appearance that had made him take his spite out on him.

Eddie's ruminations were ended when the Ealdorman moved to stand in front of him. Eddie stood as straight as his wounds would allow.

In a voice that carried to the four corners of the room, Ealdorman Byrhtnoth addressed him. "Slave, you have shown bravery and persistence above your station. You left here unarmed, as is fitting for a slave. But you were able to turn the sea pirates' own weapons on them. I don't know where you came from. However you have shown that you are not allied to the Norsemen."

Eddie nodded.

Ealdorman Byrhtnoth continued. "Our King Aethelred needs brave men like you. Besides that, I'm now convinced you weren't born into slavery. Furthermore, that you've had some military training as you're capable of planning and independent thought. Thank God you could do so. If not, our princess would either have been killed or held to ransom. Because of your heroism, I grant you your freedom."

Insolently breaking into Ealdorman Byrhtnoth's speech, Eldor Godric interjected, "Sire, in my opinion we shouldn't free this slave. He's only been here for a short time."

"And what difference does a short time make, Godric?"

Godric curled his upper lip and sneered in Eddie's direction as he replied. "This man attacked us on the Northey Island causeway and his comrades were loosing arrows at us. It was only mine and my brother's bravery that overcame him and his Norse compatriots. My lord, in my opinion he's probably a Viking assassin sent to kill you or the princess." Godric screwed up his nose and his diseased skin lesions reddened even more than normal.

The Eldor sneered again and continued, "I believe this Viking low-life deliberately led our princess into an ambush. He probably signalled to the sea pirates that she was coming so they could take her captive for a ransom. Then, when we brave Saxons outwitted his devilish Danish brood, he pretended to be on our side."

In the background, his brothers Godwig and Godwin brayed agreement with their higher-ranked sibling.

Eldor Godric fumbled for his next words before he blurted them out.

"How do we know he fought those Vikings? He could have made it all up to get near to you and our princess?" Godric lowered his shoulders and waved his hands in front of the Ealdorman in a grovelling manner, saying glibly, "I'm only sounding caution for your safety, my lord."

Eddie gasped, not believing his ears. This Eldor Godric was a clever manipulator and wily as well as vicious. That made him so much more dangerous.

Next, Eldor Godric raised his whining voice to a crescendo, and pointing an accusing finger at Eddie, declared, "I'm sure he's a Viking spy. Why not leave it for a few years? Keep him in irons till we're sure he's no threat to us hero Saxons?"

Byrhtnoth scowled when he replied. "No, Godric. The princess, the priest and my nephew, Thegn Wulfstan, were witnesses to his bravery. I have made up my mind. We have too few heroes these days and we'll need every one of them when the Vikings attack."

Eldor Godric looked down in humiliation. "You are my superior, Ealdorman, so I must accept your decision."

However, when he walked away past Eddie, he spat out a mouthful of rank, green spittle at him. Then he growled, under his breath, "Soon I'll be in charge and your days will be numbered, Viking."

The Ealdorman announced loudly, "This letter of manumission I have caused to be written by Prior Esmond." He handed it ceremoniously to Eddie, "This is my confirmation of your freedom from slavery."

Ealdorman Byrhtnoth then addressed Eddie in a lower voice. "You have, I believe, met Esmond, the new Prior of Beeleigh Priory. He will perform the solemnizing ceremony and witness my signature."

Eddie replied, "Yes, sire. We have met."

Ealdorman Byrhtnoth resumed, "Normally you would have been expected to bend the knee to me to show your subservience. But as you've already proven your bravery you'll be allowed to choose your own crossroads. This is a symbolic gesture that indicates you have been given eternal freedom. It also indicates that you can in future choose your own path in life."

At that moment there was the sound of exaggerated coughing coming from Eldor Godric and his brothers. Eddie noticed them grinning, but looked away unconcernedly.

In contrast, Ealdorman Byrhtnoth's face showed how annoyed he was. He lifted his hand and pointed at the brothers, who stopped their fake coughing immediately. Ealdorman Byrhtnoth turned back to Eddie. "Edward Lavengro, you have proved yourself to be a robust and spirited young man and I would be well pleased if you would stay with us in my service. I would then provide you with arms, shelter and sustenance, plus weapons training. Because you're a stranger in this area, Prior Esmond has offered to help you learn our Saxon and local history… if that's what you want?"

Eddie's face screwed up, his eyes closed. He held both his hands out in front of him palms open. Then he replied, "I'll be honoured to take up your generous offer and give as much assistance as I'm capable of to you and the King."

Ealdorman Byrhtnoth smiled and then announced, "Edward, I have decided that as you are taller in stature than most of my men, from now on you will be called Edward the Tall. Furthermore, for your bravery, I have also resolved to give you two hinds of land from my farms at Maylandsea. There are two good houses and outbuildings available for your use."

Then Ealdorman Byrhtnoth presented Eddie with a Scramaseaxe, a seaxe dagger. This was a knife with an eight inch single-sided blade. This was both a symbol of freemen and of their freedom.

While this ceremony was being carried out, Eddie noticed Godric's youngest brother Godwig leering at the two young girls bringing in flagons of beer for drinking after the ceremony. He was annoyed that these brothers were treating the solemnity of the occasion with such disdain. To Eddie this had been an important milestone.

Following the presentation, Prior Esmond stepped forward. He unrolled a goatskin parchment and handed it to Eddie. Eddie loved the clean, leather smell and silky feel of the thin yellow vellum. The skin was treated to be stiff enough to write on, but soft enough to roll up.

Ealdorman Byrhtnoth dipped his quill in the inkwell. Then he signed his name with his copperplate script near the bottom of the parchment. Prior Esmond countersigned underneath it with an educated but more functional handwriting.

The small, immaculately groomed Prior Esmond straightened up and then pronounced in his light, slightly effeminate tone, "Edward Lavengro, this second parchment is the title to your new lands."

Eddie thanked Prior Esmond and then said to Ealdorman Byrhtnoth, "I'll do my best to live up to your standards, my lord."

Ealdorman Byrhtnoth inclined his head. "I am sure you won't let me down, Edward the Tall."

Eddie spent the next couple of weeks with Eadric, exercising to try to improve their fitness. Getting such grievous wounds to heal had proved to be a slow process. Eddie seemed to have little appetite or energy, but forced himself to eat to rebuild his muscles.

A few weeks later, at the beginning of May on a sunny morning, Alfthrith arrived at the hall. "Edward the Tall," she began, "my mistress, Princess Catherine, wishes to see you."

"What does she want me for?"

"Edward, I'm only her handmaiden. The princess gives me commands. She doesn't tell me what's on her mind. But I'll give you some orders if you like?" She winked sensually at him.

As Alfthrith and Eddie arrived at Princess Catherine's quarters, a young feral dog followed them in as Eddie opened the door. Princess Catherine and her other handmaidens sat at a solid oak table. The princess had a wild-looking tabby cat on her lap.

The scruffy dog started to bark and snap at the cat. Eddie thought, as Kate's bodyguard, he should chase the cur off. But before he got the chance, the cat arched her back, raised her hackles and spat at the dog. Then the cat went on the attack. It jumped on the dog, digging all four sets of talons into the canine's shoulder and biting its neck. The young dog yelped in pain. Having scored a clear victory, the cat jumped off its victim. The dog ran off, still yelping, while the cat pranced round the room, purring triumphantly.

Kate laughed at the cat, picked her up and gave her a stroke. "Well done, Bodi. What great protectors I have. Aren't I the lucky one?"

Bodi jumped down and ran out through the door. Kate said, "Now where's she going? Perhaps she's going to harass that pup further… or boast to the other alley cats of her latest triumph."

The three handmaidens burst into giggles at their mistress's joke. Kate joined in the girls' laughter and they covered their faces with their hands and patted each others shoulders in their mirth.

Eddie stood waiting to be told why he'd been summoned. He tried not to stare, but he couldn't take his eyes off Kate. Not only was she attractive, but she loved her pet. He was pleased she had a softer side to her character.

Kate addressed Eddie. "Edward the Tall, as you are now my bodyguard, I have decided that you should move to a room nearer here. Then I can call for you whenever you're needed. So I've arranged for you to be located in the building next door. Alfthrith will show you where." Kate waved her hand vaguely towards a side door.

Eddie answered, "Thank you, your highness."

Kate said, quite sharply, "Remember, you're to call me Kate in future when no other nobles are present."

Just then Bodi the cat reappeared and rubbed her back against Eddie's legs. He stroked the animal and then answered the princess. "I'll remember, Kate."

Bodi the cat seemed jealous that Eddie was talking to her mistress and kept pawing at his legs. Kate said, "She's a pest. If you don't pick her up she'll bite you, Edward."

Eddie picked up the tabby as Kate had told him. The cat purred and then nuzzled up to him, her tail curling and twitching.

Kate looked pleased. "You see, my brave Bodi likes you now. She accepts my choice of bodyguard."

Alfthrith took Eddie to his new room, It was certainly better than his previous shared bedroom. At least it was just for him, if rather basic. Instead of a straw palliasse he now had a wooden bed and two blankets.

Two weeks later Kate called Eddie to her quarters. She told him, "I've arranged for Prior Esmond to give you lessons on Saxon and local history as Ealdorman Byrhtnoth mentioned. I've organized it because it's important for you, as my bodyguard, to understand us Saxons so that you can do your job efficiently."

"Thank you Cath... Kate. I want to learn as much as possible."

Kate said, "I also like to understand about other cultures and sometime I will get you to tell me about your Romani race. In the meantime, I wish you to meet the Prior after breakfast tomorrow outside the Armoury."

"Thank you Kate, I'll do that." Then he went to leave her presence, walking backwards.

Kate's eyes opened wide and her cheeks flushed. "There is no need to back out, Edward. That only applies to my father, the King. I hate formalities."

Eddie loved to see the fire in Kate's big blue eyes when she was annoyed. He was fascinated by everything about this remarkable girl.

The next morning was warm and dry with the sun shining. Four jackdaws strutted about near the cookhouse, scavenging for scraps. Woodsmoke spiralled vertically, indicating a windless day.

Eddie saw Prior Esmond arrive and greeted him with a pat on his back.

Esmond spoke first, "Princess Catherine has asked me to inquire into your background."

With his heart racing Eddie asked, "What do you need to know, priest?"

Esmond cupped his chin in his hand looked at Eddie quizzically then asked, "How do you come to understand the Viking language?"

Sweat broke out on his brow, then Eddie answered, "I've learned several languages on my travels. I already spoke Romanes, our Romani language. I learned German while I was fighting for Germanic warlords. I've worked on Danish farms. I was also a galley slave for the Norwegian Vikings – that is how I arrived in this country. During my captivity I learned Norwegian and also Saxon from my fellow Saxon captives."

Esmond said, "Only a privileged few get the education to learn to speak several foreign languages. These are usually restricted to the nobility, clergy or scriveners. How did you do so without formal education?"

Eddie answered, "Languages come easily to my Romani tribe. The reason being, as we rove the world we've had to integrate as quickly as possible with each new tribe or nation we meet. If we don't speak their language we can't find employment and we'd be liable to attack. That's understandable as most foreigners are traders or invaders."

Esmond asked, "But how can you speak and think in so many languages? I myself can only speak Saxon, Latin and some Danish."

Eddie replied, "Well I'm sure you know that most languages in this general area of Europe have many words the same, or with similar variants. They are all derived from a Germanic or Scandinavian base that includes Saxon. The exception to that rule being Latin that comes from a Roman source. I cannot speak or read a word of it. So my manumission document is unintelligible to me. I have to take it on trust that it says what you say it does."

Esmond advised Eddie, "I suggest that you don't confide your prowess with this language gift to others. Some Saxons like Eldor Godric may see this as proof you're a Viking spy. However Edward, perhaps in the future this unusual talent could be of service to Ealdorman Byrhtnoth or King Aethelred. If it's God's will, that's what will happen."

Esmond suggested, "Edward, as your superiors wish you to know more about Saxon and local history, it seems more sensible for you to come to stay with us at Beeleigh Priory."

Eddie said, "Won't I upset the Priory's routines?"

Esmond replied, "Actually, I do have a lot of work there. But we can go for some walks when I'm free. That way you can recuperate by resting most of the time but getting some exercise while we walk and talk."

Eddie smiled. "The idea sounds very appealing, a rest in the country."

"The Priory is just a couple of miles west of Maldon, near the village of Langford. Come at the end of next week, then I will have dealt with most of my immediate tasks."

Esmond left for the Priory and Eddie agreed he would follow later.

The next day Eddie was summoned by the princess to her house in the Burh.

Kate waved Eddie into her presence. "Prior Esmond tells me he wishes you to go to the Priory with him. He says it will be easier to teach you the Saxon ways there."

"Yes, Kate. He tells me I can convalesce better there as it's quieter."

Princess Catherine nodded. "I agree it would be the best option. After all, until you're fit you won't be strong enough to act as my bodyguard."

Eddie left the princess reluctantly. Just to be able to see her beautiful face was heavenly.

The next week Eddie left the Burh to walk to the Priory. He paused in the meadow near the river to watch Byrhtnoth's head falconer, Modda. He and his two assistants were training hawks by swinging meat on ropes around their heads and whistling.

Modda told Eddie, "Falconry is Byrhtnoth's favourite relaxation." Then he showed Eddie a magnificent peregrine falcon that was sitting on his shielded arm. The bird was attached by a leather jess on its leg to a leash. "This is Byrhtnoth's favourite falcon, Talon."

Eddie was suitably impressed and thanked Modda for the information. With the hawks around, Eddie assumed the small birds would keep well clear but that wasn't so. A field lark flew above their heads, singing its trill, repetitive song and sparrows and starlings foraged in the long, dead grass only feet away from the birds of prey. Did they understand that these magnificent killers were restricted by jesses and so unable to catch them? Were they mocking the great creatures?

A group of small boys and girls sat on a bank, fascinated by the whole scene before them.

Eddie limped painfully on towards the Priory, along the banks of the Blackwater Estuary. Seagulls swooped and screeched above his head and one defecated onto his shoulder. The bird's white mess stunk of fish and he knew it would be difficult to clean from his tunic if he left it. So, dipping a piece of cloth into the seawater, he washed it off as well as he could.

Eventually Eddie reached the end of the tidal Blackwater. There it met the Chelmer River that flowed from the other side of Chelmsford. As the Chelmer was at a higher level, it cascaded over a wooden slatted weir into the tidal reach. The spray smelt clean and fresh, not salty like the estuary.

Sitting motionless on a branch above the river was a kingfisher. Suddenly, in a flash of cobalt blue and cinnamon, it dived and returned with a stickleback.

From the middle of a family of seals fishing in the centre of the estuary, a figure rose and floated across the water towards the Romani. The Druid reached Eddie's mind once more. He felt the Druidic entity again showing him the massive statue in the desert. This time Eddie could tell it was a cat or a lion. The Druid explained this was called the Sphinx.

Now Eddie felt his spirit entering the Sphinx. He was in a vast hall with sweeping aisles so long that the far ends merged into one as far as his eyes could see. Shelving filled all the aisles from the floor to the distant ceiling that he estimated to be ten times his own height. The shelves, the Druid instructed, held manuscripts and books of all kinds and a vast array of maps. In the distance he could see a long corridor leading downwards at a gentle angle. He somehow knew this long hallway held the key to a mystery he needed to unravel.

Then the Druid had gone and Eddie was left sitting on the river bank contemplating the situation. Everything seemed peaceful, but the calm was short-lived.

All at once Eddie heard horses galloping towards him from the direction of the Burh. The riders charged along the riverbank, their horses' hooves pounding a malevolent tattoo. They travelled fast in a two beat stride, all four hooves leaving the ground at once.

Eddie turned and saw three black horses kicking up a vast cloud of dust. Moorhens and ducks scattered out of the path of the imposing equine charge. As they came nearer, Eddie realized with a shudder it was Eldor Godric and his brothers. Eddie was wary as he was unarmed except for his seax dagger, and vulnerable to attack.

The horses pulled up short, almost crushing Eddie under their hooves. Godric's stallion rose onto its hind legs, its forelegs kicking the air.

"I have you alone at last, you charlatan!" Eldor Godric roared. "By rights, you should be my slave. You've just been lucky. The Ealdorman's blinded by your sort. I don't trust you myself as you refuse to show me the homage that is my right."

Eddie shouted back, "Godric, you know I am no threat to you. Give me a break for once?"

Godric spat at Eddie. "Why should I? I would do my King a service if I disposed of a wastrel like you."

Eddie spoke softly, trying not to antagonize the noble. "Eldor Godric, think of your good reputation. If you harm me, the Ealdorman will know who it was. You will have been seen riding this way."

"You think so, do you?" Godric bellowed with elation. "But not if your disposal is seen as an accident."

Godric signalled to his brothers, Godwin and Godwig, who edged their horses closer and closer to Eddie. He could smell the horses' sweat, they were so near. He could see they were going to force him off the muddy bank into the deep water of the estuary.

Godwig shouted, "Now you'll pay for breaking my nose!"

Godwin squeaked, "And for my balls, Viking."

Godwig urged his horse to walk sideways. As the mare's bulky belly pressed against Eddie, its horsey smell was overpowering. Eddie tried to slip away along the bank but Godwin's horse blocked this escape route. He daren't go through the animal's legs as both horses were prancing around and he knew just one kick could be fatal. Eddie had nowhere to go to escape Godwig's mount.

The powerful flanks of Godwig's horse jostled Eddie off the bank. He desperately grabbed at a clump of grass. But agonizingly, its roots gave way, propelling him backwards into the salt water.

Eddie heard a horse whinny before he plunged below the surface, into the cold depths.

Ten

Around the Blackwater Estuary, two miles west of the Essex town of Maldon, the weather was sunny with little wind. The natural elements were tranquil. That was more than could be said for the scene at the beginning of the tidal inlet.

Seconds before, Godwig had used his horse to nudge Eddie into the brackish water. Eddie was weak, and his broken ribs excruciatingly painful. He sank, dragged down by his clothing and the powerful undertow from the weir race. He had been caught in undercurrents before and he knew they could trap you underwater until you drowned.

Eddie was desperate. He needed oxygen immediately. Allowing himself to float upwards, he gasped for air as soon as he broke the surface.

There was a shout from Eldor Godric. "Don't let him escape! Kill him."

All three brothers launched javelins that splashed into the stream. One landed in the water, inches from Eddie's head. There were few choices for him. If he stayed on the surface, a missile would skewer him for sure. Gulping air convulsively, he managed to get his bearings. Locating the position of the weir, where the fresh water from the Chelmer River tumbled into the estuary, he took a last breath and dived.

Eddie plunged as deeply as he was able and then swam underwater, barbs of agony shooting from his broken ribs at each stroke. He tried desperately to avoid the powerful drag and rolling undercurrents. His only chance was to get right underneath its surface power. He felt the strain in his whole body; if his weakened muscles gave way now, he'd be done for.

A large, evil-looking pike swam towards him out of the gloom, its visible, needle sharp teeth threatening more pain. Eddie recoiled, but it swam past in pursuit of a shoal of green striped perch.

With his lungs at bursting point, he barely made it the thirty yards to the point below the crashing cascade. Had he submerged enough to locate the smooth water behind the weir pool?

Abruptly, he came up under the current and in the placid trough next to the waterfall's mud and wooden wall. He rose to the surface. The falling water created an effective aquatic curtain in front of him.

Gasping for oxygen, he struggled to brace himself against the muddy bank. He somehow had to avoid the engulfing force trying to tear him back into the maelstrom of the whirlpools created by the descending waters.

He felt the wooden planking of the weir, his fingers gripping it like a limpet. Then he felt several fingernails slide off the slippery green wood and break. But he knew he mustn't lose his grip.

Eventually, Eddie brought his breathing under control. Clenching his teeth to avoid giving voice to his anguish, he worked his way, hand over hand, along the weir's planking. The thunder of water crashing onto the wooden boards near his head was deafening, but despite his distress he reached the relative safety of the far bank. He stayed there until his chest pain eased and his swirling consciousness became stable. Then he peered cautiously from his spray-curtained refuge.

The three brothers were still scrutinizing the point where Eddie had submerged. It had only been minutes since he'd entered the water but it seemed like hours to him. Eventually, the brothers seemed to be satisfied that he would never surface again. They turned their ponies and rode back towards the Burh.

Eddie crawled from the brine and collapsed, exhausted onto the muddy bank. He lay there for some time. Then bedraggled, mud splattered and fatigued, he began to make his way towards the Priory. Now that his sodden clothes were exposed to the air, even the slight but cold breeze made him shiver and shake.

There was a towpath of sorts to walk along, but it was overgrown with brambles criss-crossing the path and he tripped more than once, almost staggering backwards into the sluggish water of the Chelmer River. A black moorhen paddled past, ignoring Eddie, its red and yellow tipped beak in the air.

At last he reached Beeleigh Priory. This was a large multi-roomed wooden structure topped with thatch. In front of it, a rotating water wheel creaked and groaned. The monks had waterpower to mill corn, and the river provided plentiful drinking water and fresh fish. It seemed a tranquil place for convalescence.

Eddie approached the massive oak door. He rapped the impressive iron knocker against the wood and a diminutive novice monk answered his summons. The young man quizzically took in Eddie's six-foot muscular frame, rugged good looks and dark appearance before going to call the Prior.

When Prior Esmond appeared he greeted Eddie in his high, sing-song voice. "I am pleased to see you Edward, and looking forward to our future conversations." He addressed the novice monk. "Brother Gregory, please show Edward to a cell where he can rest."

Brother Gregory was a slight, handsome young man of about sixteen years old. The shaved bare patch on the crown of his head was surrounded by fine, blond hair. He had a deep voice for such a small youth. His eyes flitted around nervously and his whole demeanour was one of insecurity.

Eddie noticed that the boy had particularly small feet and hands. When Gregory placed his hand on Eddie's arm to guide his direction, Eddie noted how soft Gregory's skin felt. It was smooth; completely without callouses. He imagined that being a monk must be the ideal vocation for the lad. He didn't seem big or strong enough to farm, and certainly not bold enough to be a warrior.

The priory was fairly dark as there were few window openings. It was sparsely furnished, though spacious and airy. Large wooden beams supported the thatched roofs and the mud-daub walls were decorated with carved Christian artefacts.

Brother Gregory showed Eddie to his cell. This was just a bare room with a palliasse covered by two rough sheepswool blankets. Fixed on the wall was a large wooden cross, embellished with horn.

"This is a small community, not big enough to warrant an Abbot," Gregory explained. "Esmond was appointed 'Prior in charge,' after our previous leader, Prior David, was taken seriously ill."

Later, when Eddie had rested, Gregory returned and took him to visit Prior David, the former senior cleric. Prior David was also a tiny man. His wrinkled face bore an unhealthy pallor and his blotched, skeletal hands were indicative of his advanced years.

The old priest's left arm seemed immovable, locked across his chest. He walked with a shuffling gait, his left leg apparently frozen. A dribble of saliva crept from a corner of his mouth. His hair, what little he had left, was tidy, and his habit was clean. Eddie detected a faint smell of urine, but not the stale odour associated with unclean garments.

The old man had just returned from the chapel where he'd taken the service. This indicated that Prior David was by no means senile. His old eyes, though sunken, had shone with pride when he heard Gregory tell Eddie that Prior David was blessed with a prodigious intellect.

Prior David spoke to Eddie in a halting, laboured way. He was difficult to understand and was fully aware of this. "Please… forgive my diffi…culty with comm…uni…cation and God bless you, my son."

Eddie replied, "I am honoured to meet such a revered Christian leader as you, Prior David."

Prior David waved his good right arm in a dismissive gesture. "We've been ex...pecting you for many a year. I felt your... presence today even before you arrived. You've been... sent to us from a long way off. My pre...decessor's predecessor proph...esied your coming."

From thinking the opposite, Eddie now wondered if the old man's mind was rambling. He said, "Thank you for your blessing, Father, but I think you've mistaken me for someone else."

Prior David looked tired after his walk from the chapel. He smiled as if he was amused by Eddie's denial of what he knew was the truth. He suddenly spoke strongly as if he'd gained composure from somewhere, no hesitancy now.

"There is no mistake. Oh no, no. I am honoured to be the one to be here at your arrival. I can rest now."

Prior David tried to lower himself onto his bed but he began to shake as though he were suffering some form of seizure. Both Gregory and Eddie supported him and helped him to lie down. Eddie attempted to turn the thin old man onto his side in case he was sick. But Gregory became almost hysterical and insisted on his mentor being laid on his back.

Prior David coughed, choked, and held his throat. He sat up, looking right through the two watching men. Then he smiled and held out both arms as if to reach something or someone in the distance.

Gregory looked horrified and raised his normally deep voice by two octaves in alarm. "Prior David! What's wrong? Can I help? Let me assist you?"

Eddie put his arm around the young brother to comfort him.

Prior David's eyes were wide open. With his arms still outstretched, his hands started to quiver and slowly, he subsided onto his bed. Then, holding his crucifix in one hand and his rosary in the other, Prior David mumbled the Lord's Prayer in Latin. Slowly he closed his eyes, becoming calm, almost serene.

Brother Gregory crossed himself, said a mumbled prayer and ran from the room. He came back with Prior Esmond, who went to check on his predecessor. "Our Saintly brother has gone to his maker, his God," Esmond declared matter-of-factly. "He is now in glory and whole again."

Eddie thought about what David had said. His seeming recognition of Eddie was curious. Then his dying like that, straight after his utterance, was bizarre. Perhaps David had been having a vision of his own demise and Eddie's arrival at that moment was merely a coincidence?

A couple of days after Prior David's death, his funeral was led by Prior Esmond. The old cleric was buried in the grounds of the chapel. Next to the graveyard was the priory's extensive kitchen garden which had been Prior David's pride and joy. He had also been proud of the many domestic animals. These included several ponies for transport between this priory and their mother community in Ely, over ninety miles to the north, in Cambridgeshire.

In the following days, Eddie accompanied Esmond for walks by the River Chelmer. They mostly headed westward towards the village of Ulting. Bordering the paths were willow, ash, and majestic oaks, providing shade from the worst of the sun.

Esmond reclined on the riverbank, surrounded by soft green grass. Picking out a succulent stem he put it into his mouth and sucked it for a moment. "You know, Edward," he began, "I've always found chewing on grass relaxes me. What do you wish to ask me about?" Eddie sat down beside Esmond and scratched his head. "Can you tell me about Ealdorman Byrhtnoth, please?"

"By all means. I studied his family history when I was at this priory as a young monk."

Eddie grinned and leaned forward to listen.

"Ealdorman Byrhtnoth is descended from the Mercian royal house. His father, Byrhthelm, is a Duke as well as an Ealdorman. He is the youngest son of the Mercian King, Harrold the second.

"From the age of seventeen he travelled in the armies of the King and fought in the northern campaigns. He served the best possible apprenticeship for a warrior leader. At twenty-six, by then already a seasoned fighter and general, he was made Ealdorman of Essex."

"So the title of Ealdorman isn't hereditary?" Eddie queried.

"No. It literally means 'King's deputy.' That title has to be earned by exceptional martial service."

Eddie nodded. "So Ealdorman Byrhtnoth is essentially a military man?"

"He is much more than that," Esmond replied. "He has also reformed the monetary, legal, artistic and architectural systems in England. Consequently we are now the most advanced in the world. In doing so, he has become immensely wealthy and powerful, having estates in nine counties. He's also the highest judge in England and is the leader of the English armies. So he's second in overall power to the King."

Eddie raised his eyebrows. "That's pretty impressive. Does he command a large army?"

Esmond choked and forcibly ejected the piece of grass he was chewing. He shook his head and laughed ironically at Eddie's naivety. "No. He only has a few hundred personal huscarls who are the professional warriors. He has to raise a militia from the farmers and other citizens as needed."

"But doesn't that take a long time? What if the Vikings spring a surprise attack?"

"Ealdorman Byrhtnoth has spies around the coast, so he has some warning. With the Vikings marauding locally, Byrhtnoth has already called for the select fyrd to be mobilized.

Eddie pursed his lips. He was confused now. "Select fyrd?"

Esmond broke off a thin twig and used it as a toothpick to remove a shred of meat lodged in his teeth. Then he patiently explained to Eddie, "This is a part-time army, dependant on each freeman's land tenure. For every five hides of land, one well-armed man must be sent with provisions for two months."

Eddie coughed, still wincing slightly from the pain of his healing ribs. "What if that's still not enough?"

Esmond was warming to the subject. "If the invasion's bigger, Byrhtnoth could ask for the great fyrd to be mobilized. This is simply every able-bodied freeman, armed with whatever weapons they can lay their hands on."

Eddie had been listening intently. "So, if Ealdorman Byrhtnoth is experienced in warfare, this area should be safe?"

To Eddie's surprise, Prior Esmond didn't look too confident about this. As he gnawed at a fingernail, he replied, "Ealdorman Byrhtnoth has been an outstanding leader. However, I'm rather worried now for his personal safety. You see, he's exceptionally brave and has such great pride that he always insists on personally leading his army from the front."

Eddie was impressed by this, "That's brilliant; if he's at risk himself, he'll only fight if he thinks he can win. That's a real leader in all senses of the word. The warriors would surely follow a man like that…"

Esmond interposed. "You're right, Edward. He is a true leader and it's his personal charisma that inspires his men to fight harder. But he's now over sixty years old. He's also much taller than most of his men, with long grey hair and beard. That makes him too obvious a target for his enemies."

Eddie stood up and spread his hands as if in disbelief. "But surely his best men can protect him? Surround him and kill the enemy's toughest warriors while they're concentrating on attacking Byrhtnoth?"

Esmond shook his head. "You're right," he replied. "Ealdorman Byrhtnoth galvanizes and inspires his warriors, and so far that's what has always happened..."

"But?" queried Eddie.

"Sadly, that well proved battle plan could now be a two-edged sword. You see, should Byrhtnoth fall in battle, it could have a devastating effect on his army's morale."

Eddie nodded. "Surely, though, if he's the wise general you describe, he will realize that?"

Esmond wore a resigned look. "Apparently not, although I've tried to persuade him to stay back and marshal his men from the rear. But he'll have none of it."

Esmond and Eddie walked down to the estuary's source and watched the water cascade from the Chelmer into the sea mouth.

They sat down on a grass-covered hillock and watched a family of wild boar amble by. The dark brown sow showed some concern at their presence. She snorted at her little striped piglets as if telling them to keep away from these strange animals, which could be dangerous. The piglets trotted in energetic circles around their mother; to them, mum meant safety. Eddie smiled at the porcine family, but his mind was on other matters.

"Do you know why Eadric gave that pendant to Ealdorman Byrhtnoth?" he asked.

Esmond was still watching the piglets. He snapped out of his reverie. "I can make an educated guess. I think it was a silver Thor's Hammer pendant that Eadric may have taken from the Vikings at the raid on Maylandsea. You see, Thor is their false heathen god of thunder. He is always depicted wielding a hammer that is emblematic of the thunderbolt."

"Are you saying all the Vikings have one of them?"

"Probably not all, but many do. You see the Vikings carry them as good luck charms. I believe they use them in marriage ceremonies and the acceptance of newborn infants. So no Viking who had one would give up his Thor's Hammer pendant while he still lived."

"But why did Eadric give such a valuable piece away if he had to kill for it?"

"It's accepted here that all booty from battles is the property of the leader. This makes practical sense. The pendant has only ornamental value to Eadric. By presenting it to Byrhtnoth, it provided him with land and silver coins that he can spend easily."

Eddie kicked the heads off some seeding dandelion clocks and watched as they floated away on the breeze.

Esmond continued, "This arrangement is also a clever move for Byrhtnoth. By rewarding Eadric handsomely, others will realize that serving him can bring them great advantages."

Eddie didn't answer this, but spread one hand and nodded his understanding.

Eddie was shown round the home farm by Brother Augustus, who looked after the livestock. He was a short, skinny, sour-faced man with a ruddy, weathered complexion.

Augustus was bald apart from small patches of wispy hair above his ears. Not for him the need to shave the round circular portion at the top of his head to denote celibacy, chastity and purity.

At about five feet tall and not weighing more than seven stones, Augustus had initially seemed to Eddie to be a weakling. However, he soon realized that this was far from the truth. He'd noticed Augustus invariably won the arm-wrestling contests held by the monks most evenings after dinner.

Talking to Esmond one evening, Eddie asked him, "Esmond, I've noticed Viking sentries looking through parchment tubes. I've also heard these tubes referred to as scopes and that they let them see objects from further away. Do you know what they are?"

"No." Esmond's reply was emphatic. "I've never seen or heard of such a hellish instrument. God gave us eyes to see, so there can't be anything more."

The monks often drank wine to excess and sang quite raucous and vulgar songs. There had been relaxing evenings in front of blazing log fires that gave off the enticing aromas of smoke as the monks alternated the types of woods burnt.

Eddie met a rotund monk called Brother Paul in the priory's kitchen. He was foraging for his customary between-meals snack. Paul's job was to maintain and harvest fish from the fish traps and to gather and market sea salt.

Paul was a short, portly man weighing eighteen stones. Eddie thought Brother Paul looked the perfect stereotype of the jovial fat monk. Observing the grey hair surrounding the shaved scalp, he put his age at somewhere in the late forties. Paul had a red bulbous nose and smelled a bit from his regular breaking of wind.

Each evening, Brother Paul imbibed prodigious quantities of alcohol and double helpings of food before relating bawdy jokes to the others. The problem was that he invariably burst into uncontrollable fits of laughter before he got to the punch lines. Seldom did the others laugh at his ribald comments. However, his overall good humour, red face and flopping belly never failed to put everyone in a good mood.

"Edward," Paul ventured, "would you like me to show you where we harvest our fish and collect our salt?"

"Why, yes Paul, that would be very interesting. Thank you."

As the two men walked east towards the Blackwater Estuary Eddie asked how Paul caught so many fish. "There are some for dinner every night," he pointed out.

"We use tidal traps," Paul replied. "I'll show you. Look, the seawater flows from the North Sea. It reaches us via the Blackwater Estuary into the tributaries of the Chelmer River."

Eddie examined the traps studiously.

Paul was gratified by Eddie's obvious interest and continued with enthusiasm. "The salt water streams have been lined with long timbers enclosing wickerwork cones. These are fixed so that the fish can swim in with the seawater tides, but they can't get out again. All we monks have to do is take the catch out at every low tide, you see?"

"That's fascinating, Paul. Ingenious, in fact."

Eddie and Paul watched as the novice monk Gregory waded into the water and removed the dabs, dog fish and sea bass from the fish traps then placed them into a wicker basket.

Gregory brought his baskets ashore and showed Eddie the catch. "I've got a great job here, Edward. Look at these healthy fish." He held up a large dab, a flat fish, and then a fine silver sea bass.

Eddie nodded, greatly interested. "What are those big fish that look like sharks?"

Gregory laughed, pleased by the attention he was getting. He picked the fish up by its tail, a three-foot long, brown, spotted, wriggling fish. "You're right Edward, this is a spotted dog fish. It is, indeed, a small shark. He handed the writhing fish to Eddie, who held it at arm's length, away from his body. He noticed its tail was surprisingly rough, so he quickly handed it back. "I've caught many fish myself," he said, "but never with such rough skin. Is that normal with sharks?"

"I don't know about all sharks, but these dogfish skins are so rough we use them for smoothing down wood and metal. Come and see the other shark I removed from the trap earlier."

Eddie's eyes widened with surprise and he stepped back a pace when Gregory hauled a five-foot long, dark grey shark from one of his baskets.

"Good grief! What's that?"

Gregory smiled at Eddie's reaction. "This is a Tope…"

"A Tope?"

"Yes. We only catch a few each year, but they taste fine. We'll roast it tonight so you can judge for yourself."

At that moment, the Tope jerked sideways. Its huge mouth, full of serrated teeth, snapped at Eddie. He jumped out of its way, his face anxious and his heart beating wildly.

Gregory and Paul burst into laughter. "I like their taste," Paul said, "but not handling them."

With difficulty, Gregory manoeuvred the big tope back into the reed basket which he secured with a leather strap. The basket jerked about as the angry fish thrashed around.

Afterwards, Paul took Eddie further along the estuary banks. "See those shallow oblong seawater reservoirs? Those are our sea salt beds."

Eddie followed Paul's pointing finger. "How does that get you salt?"

"We allow a few inches of salt water to flow in. Right? Then we close the inlet and the warmth of the sun creates evaporation. When all the water is gone the salt lies on the top and is removed with shovels."

"I see. Do you just use it for flavouring?"

"Not only for that. We preserve meat and fish for the priory's own use. Some of it is taken by pack ponies to Ely monastery. We also sell bags of salt and preserved food. In fact, it produces as much income as our farm rents."

A few days later, it was the twenty-third of April, St George's day. At the priory, the monks took every saint's day seriously, especially the feasting part. They had prepared roasted suckling pig, barbecued sea fish, masses of hot vegetables on the side, plus steaming fragrant soups and stews. The evening feast was held in the Priory's biggest hall with its ancient wooden beams. The long, oak refectory tables and benches were set out around the walls. Two flaming torches secured in low positioned ornate metal holders lit the area, the flickering flames creating variable light and shade.

The roasting pig aroma made Eddie's mouth water. As soon as Grace was said, everyone was ripping mouthfuls of meat from bones and dribbles of fat-laden saliva cascaded down their chins and into the folds of their habits.

Belches and breaking wind were frequent. After they'd quaffed a great deal of alcohol they began some very raucous singing, hardly befitting the ecclesiastical setting. An owl hooted censoriously from the rafters and outside, a fox cried its plaintive howl, possibly attracted by the scents of cooked meat.

Eight days later it was the first of May. Winter had turned to spring and the deciduous trees vigorously shook their boughs, now clothed in new season's greenery. The sun shone down on Esmond and Eddie as they sat on a fallen tree trunk. Above them a white willow rustled its slender branches, reaching for the nearby stream.

Eddie asked another question. "Esmond? You told me that there are Scandinavian settlements here. Can you tell me more about them?"

Esmond cracked his knuckles and settled himself comfortably. His manner suggested that he relished telling this story. "Yes," he said. "There's quite a large Norse colony on Mersea Island, especially around the ancient pagan standing stone circle."

Eddie wasn't surprised to hear about the stone circle. He'd been there with the Norwegian Vikings and revisited it via his Romani remote viewing. However, he was curious to learn more.

"That's interesting," he said. "Tell me about the stones?"

Esmond nodded and smiled. "Yes. In fact I was there last year, on the twenty second of September at the autumnal equinox. That was when I witnessed a pagan ceremony that no true Christian should be exposed to."

Eddie heard the excitement in Esmond's voice. "What happened?" he asked.

Esmond leaned forward towards Eddie, cupped a hand to one side of his mouth and then whispered in a low, conspiratorial tone, "Near sunrise, a dozen white-robed druids appeared. Their faces and flowing hair were as white as their regalia and they were all identical... the same height and everything. At the exact second of sunrise they threw their arms in the air in salutation. And at precisely that moment, the sun's rays entered through a hole in the biggest stone and struck a mark on the smallest stone. From nowhere, a small, black-robed Druid appeared."

Eddie leaned nearer to the Prior, scarcely able to contain his curiosity or his excitement. "Yes? What happened then?"

Esmond looked up into the sky and put his hands together in a praying position, as if he wanted forgiveness for committing some heresy.

"The druids croned strange incantations in some language I'd never heard before. I didn't feel the presence of evil, but an aura of pure peace. These were not devil worshippers, but they were not Christians either. They seemed to be followers of some ancient religion. I was frozen to the spot."

Eddie was on tenterhooks. "Yes? And then?"

Esmond looked rather frightened and his speech became mumbled, "What was spooky was that without any noticeable signal, the druids walked down to the sea, then... well, then they were gone. I didn't actually see where they went to, they just... vanished."

"Vanished?"

"Just so. Disappeared in an instant. Later, I asked the Norsemen about the druids. I was told they came from a far away civilization and it would be death to interfere with them."

Eddie spoke in a low, whispered tone. "Oh, now that is odd. And did you see the druids again?"

Esmond didn't answer immediately. He appeared to be studying a pair of white swans as they floated past with their three brown signets.

Eddie waited for the prior to reply.

"No," he said at length. "Even though I visited the Norsemen several times to try to convert them to Christianity. I didn't get anywhere trying to save their souls, but I did become interested in their lifestyle."

Just then an orange fox dashed past them, attempting to catch a mallard, but the green-headed drake flew off, quacking indignantly.

Esmond said, "Those foxes are cunning, but ducks have sharp eyesight, so foxes will seldom catch them in daylight."

"Hm, cunning or not, that fox needed patience this time. Talking of cunning, can I ask what may seem to be an impertinent question, Esmond?"

"Certainly. What is it?"

Being in close proximity to the clear, trickling water of the stream, the fallen tree was slightly damp. At odd intervals, a water vole swam across to the bank and a fish momentarily breached the water's surface creating ripples. Eddie stared at the water for a moment before he spoke.

"It's about Eldor Godric and his two brothers, Godwin and Godwig, who captured me near Northey Island."

"Yes, what about them?"

"They've always been very aggressive and have attacked me several times since then. What I really can't understand is that Godric is downright disrespectful to the Ealdorman. Are there reasons for their churlish behaviour? And why doesn't Ealdorman Byrhtnoth censure them for their disgraceful conduct?"

"They have no excuses, but there is a reason. You see, their father, Odda, was for many years chamberlain to Ealdorman

Byrhthelm, Byrthnoth's father. During the war campaigns, Odda saved both Ealdormen's lives by his exceptional bravery."

Eddie listened intently, his hand supporting his chin.

Esmond continued. "In recognition of this, Odda persuaded the King to promote Odda to the hereditary title of an Eldor. In a later battle, Odda died while defending his two lords and that was how his eldest son, Godric, inherited his father's title of Eldor. He also succeeded to the Lordship of the Dengie Hundred, that is, to the Lordship over all the hides of land on this Peninsula that went with it. That doesn't mean he owns it, but he can collect taxes on each piece of land."

"I see now," said Eddie, "how he comes to hold his high position at a young age. But that still doesn't explain why he is so aggressive to me, and insolent to the Ealdorman."

Esmond shrugged, spreading both palms in front of him. "Well, you see, when their father was mortally wounded saving the Ealdormen's lives, as Godrichelm lay dying, Byrhtnoth promised him on oath that, because of his selfless bravery, he would always protect his three sons."

Eddie expelled his breath sharply.

Esmond explained, "To us Saxons, a sworn oath's obligation must be carried until the last breath of the Swearer. Unfortunately, the brothers know this, and the fact that they can never be punished, whatever they do. So they take full advantage of that fact."

"I'm beginning to understand," Eddie said. "Have they got many friends and allies?"

"None. And local hostility towards the brothers has worsened lately. This is because, a year ago, all three of them attempted to rape a young girl called Athelflaed. She is the daughter of Thegn Maccus and the girlfriend of Eldor Aefnoth, Byrthnoth's son. Luckily for the girl, Aefnoth was coming to meet her, heard her screams for help and beat all three attackers to within an inch of their lives."

Eddie was shocked. "But in that poor girl's case, why didn't Byrhtnoth deal with them? He's the top law keeper and Judge in this area, isn't he?"

Esmond nodded. "In any other case, they'd have been executed or banished. But Byrhtnoth's oath protected them, even from this heinous outrage."

Eddie was feeling physically better. He missed seeing Kate, his princess. So he decided it was time to return to the Maldon Burh. He said a somewhat reluctant goodbye to Prior Esmond, and also to the many monks whom he now counted as his friends.

Briskly, Eddie walked away, past the weir and along the banks of the Blackwater Estuary where a small gathering of seals lolled about on the mud banks. As he waded across the ford on the far bank, he was met by a white-robed Druid. Shorter than the ones he'd met previously, he sensed this one was female. Eddie felt his skin tingle as he was contacted. Now he had images of mountains of ice. Snow was falling so thickly it was hard to see through it, and strong winds drifted it up into wild, contorted cathedrals of whiteness.

The Druidess swept her robed arms in an arc and the image changed. Now he could see that under the ice there was a strange city. Not like the town of Maldon... this was a hundred thousand times bigger. Not wooden buildings, either; they were like smooth stone, as if carved from a single block. Then the image and the Druidess vanished and Eddie continued his journey.

He knew that on his return, he was to go for weapons training. This reminded him he was almost certain to have to fight in a fully-fledged battle against the Norsemen.

This was quite an exciting prospect in one sense. But it was marred by the thought that the psychopathic Eldor Godric and his brothers could be behind him in battle. Even now, they were a more imminent and dangerous threat to him than the Vikings.

Eleven

Maldon was a hive of activity. Farmers loudly advertised their wares, and barbers, bakers, butchers and shoemakers also vied noisily for trade in the narrow streets. Cutpurses stealthily pursued the unwary.

Carters urged sweating carthorses or oxen to drag their loaded, creaking wagons up the steep one-in-ten cobbled Maldon Hill towards the Burh, the fortified town. Many wagons were so heavy that the carters needed spare horses from the inn to supplement their own beasts' strength to drag them up the hill.

Gulls whirled above the town and nearby river. The rays of the morning sun glinted on spearheads as the sentries nervously patrolled the earthen walls.

Reaching the town and entering the Burh's main gates, Eddie tried to ignore the rumpus and made his way through the throng. He was longing to see the beautiful Princess Catherine… Kate.

However, before he reached her quarters he was waylaid by Thegn Wulfstan. "I'm glad I spotted you returning," Wulfstan said. "My uncle Ealdorman Byrhtnoth asked me to watch out for you."

Eddie's mouth turned down at the corners and his brow furrowed.

Thegn Wulfstan continued, "Our leader informs me that Viking longships are nearing this area. So it's vitally important that you join the other fyrd members for weapons training. It just so happens it's starting in the armoury almost immediately."

"Of course I'll do that, Wulfstan. May I get some food and report back to the princess first?"

Wulfstan shook his head. "No, I'm sorry. There's not time for either. I will personally inform the princess that her bodyguard has returned and has reported for training."

Eddie reluctantly nodded his agreement and walked towards the armoury. Once he was out of Wulfstan's sight, he kicked a loose rock in frustration, immediately regretting it as he stubbed his toe painfully.

The armoury was situated inside the Burh's walls. It was connected to the fortified keep for use as a last line of defence. The building was sixty feet long by twenty wide, constructed of stone with closable arrow slits.

Inside was a metal grid over an emergency well by the side wall. Prior Esmond had explained to him previously that there was also a second water source in the main keep building itself. Both wells tapped into the underground spring before they emerged into the Burh courtyard itself, the earliest of the fount's connections to the stream being the one in the main keep. The point being that even if enemies poisoned the water in the courtyard, it wouldn't affect the two wells inside. Nor could the armoury pool be used to contaminate the well in the keep. Thus the garrison couldn't be forced to surrender by lack of water.

Inside, Eddie met the other new trainees – about forty teenage guys plus one mature man. The older guy was Ecceard, the big blacksmith slave, who'd told Eddie he wanted to earn his freedom by fighting on behalf of Ealdorman Byrhtnoth.

Thegn Maccus, who was in charge of the armoury, Eddie knew by reputation to be an experienced warrior. Although fairly short, he was strongly built. He wore a tan-coloured leather jerkin over his linen clothing, and his feet were clad in strong tan hide. Maccus had several facial scars and the first two fingers of his right hand were missing.

Thegn Maccus addressed the trainees in a soft but compelling voice.

"Usually, when people first meet me, they speculate as to how my hand got injured in this way." He held up his mutilated right hand.

One of the trainees made a high-pitched sucking noise. Others shuffled their feet or subconsciously put their hands to their mouths.

Thegn Maccus ignored their reactions and continued. "To clear this up now, I'll explain the circumstances that led to my injury so that we can get on with your training. I'd been sent on a spying mission by Ealdorman Byrhtnoth. Unfortunately I was captured by the Vikings. I expected to be slaughtered on the spot, but the sea pirates had other ideas. They cut off my bow string fingers, thereby ensuring I could never be an efficient archer again. Then I was allowed back to the Burh. Presumably, the Vikings hoped this life-changing deformity would deter other Saxons from standing up to them. I was lucky to survive as I'd lost so much blood."

Eddie noticed some of the lads had turned white and others looked sick. From the back a voice shouted, "Did it hurt?"

Thegn Maccus snapped, "Of course it bloody hurt, Gadd. It was so bad I thought I was dying from the wounds. However, I survived and have been able to take my revenge on many of those Vikings' comrades. The point of explaining this is to emphasize to you that war is not a boys' game. It's deadly serious. Many of you will receive painful injuries and others will be killed. Obviously, if you die immediately, you're beyond help. However, although injuries are painful, most like mine are survivable."

There was a lot of mumbling from the class, which Maccus stopped by holding up both arms. "Later you'll be shown how to treat your own minor injuries so that you can keep yourself alive until you can get help. Many who have died from blood loss would have survived if they'd been taught what to do. You'll be given ligaments to use as tourniquets and a bandage pack to keep with you. What's also very important is not to let pain from your wounds stop you defending yourself. If you do, you're more likely to take another blow that will kill you."

There were a few whispers and shaking of heads among the youngsters.

Thegn Maccus had the trainees' full attention now. "Few weapons will be issued to you because they're expensive and therefore in short supply. However, you'll be taught how to use all categories efficiently. This is so that you will know how to use any weapons you can scavenge that are discarded during a battle."

There were more whispers in the crowd.

Maccus paused until there was silence and then resumed. "Shields are essential to our strategy. They are not just defensive; they can also be effective offensive weapons." Maccus held up some shields made of wood with central metal bosses to protect the user's hand. "As you can see, most are round and all are big enough to cover the head and torso."

A wag at the back shouted, "You'd need a much bigger one than that to cover Atfelwulf's head!"

Most of the trainees laughed, including Eddie. Then a scuffle broke out between two trainees. Eddie recognized the bigger guy as Atfielwulf and guessed the smaller one was the comic.

The big guy, Atfielwulf, sneered. "We all know a daisy-sized shield will cover your little parts, Elfgifu." By then the whole class was in uncontrollable fits of laughter.

Maccus turned red in the face and tried to regain his authority. Speaking loudly and firmly he said, "Elfgifu, Atfielwulf, behave now! I've already told you this is not entertainment. It's in deadly earnest."

The two combatants did as they were told and looked suitably shame-faced.

Maccus continued. "Light woods are used to make shields as they don't split like hard woods. Instead, the light fibres bind around blades, arrows and spear points, in most cases preventing them from cutting or piercing deeper and hitting the shield's user."

There were many whispers as the young boys made comments to each other.

Maccus persisted. "You'll be taught to construct and get the best from shield walls. These are vital to our battle defences in open country."

Next, Maccus showed them two types of arrowhead. "Barbed arrowheads are for general use as they are difficult for your enemies to remove from their flesh," he said. "Now these bodkins that have a long iron point are utilized against opposing fighters wearing chain mail, as they are more likely to penetrate this type of armour."

At that moment an imposing, older warrior appeared and Maccus introduced him. "This is Thegn Aelfhere, who will take you for practical training."

Aelfhere was taller than Maccus, and wiry, though still muscular. He had what were likely to be battle scars across his cheek and neck, and most of his right ear was missing. He had a deep, booming voice which he used with great effect.

Aelfhere said, "Each of you pick up a bow and a quiver of arrows from Edwold and Dunnere, our quartermasters over there. They all contain the two styles of arrows."

Edwold and Dunnere, were two elderly slaves. Eddie had met them when he himself had been a slave. They were brothers, short in stature, wizened and balding. Eddie remembered Edwold had always seemed cheerful, while Dunnere was a morose character. True to type, as Edwold handed Eddie a bow, he smiled in recognition. In contrast, Dunnere thrust a quiver at him with a sullen scowl.

Aelfhere led his group of trainees to the archery range. This was in a meadow with a high log wall at the far end. Protruding vertically from the ground in front of this were several poles. Feathers adorned the tops of some, and old chain mail vests were fixed to others.

Eddie noticed the masses of paigles and bluebells in the meadow. They were being brutally crushed beneath the trainees' boots. The bruised petals released flowery scents that mingled with the sharp smell of sweat. The weather was fine but dew still lingered in the longer grass. The few clouds roaming the sky provided some relief from the heat of the sun.

Aelfhere stopped, gathering his group in closely. "In massed battle situations," he began, "showers of arrows are the most effective. However, individually aimed arrows are a good sniping option. A skilful archer can get four of his arrows in the air at the same time."

Aelfhere personally demonstrated that this was possible. He nocked an arrow and released it; another three were nocked and sent into the air almost too quickly for the eye to follow. As he'd promised, all four were airborne before the first landed. Eddie was amazed that all four arrows hit the same post target.

Aelfhere explained, "Loosing the arrows can be speeded up by sticking them in the ground in front of you as I've just done. Taking them individually from your quiver slows the process down. Break the action into the basics… notch, draw, loose."

Under Aelfhere's instructions, they practised loosing arrows from various distances. Eddie noticed that his fellow archery students faced towards their targets, pulling the bowstrings to their chests as was their custom. He'd always used the Germanic and Romani method. This was by holding his bow standing sideways on, which allowed him to pull his bowstring further back and so get more power.

Aelfhere noted that Eddie was using this side-on method and suggested he change to the Saxon way. Eddie did so, but without much success. There was a consistent resonant twang of the bow strings and thump of arrows striking the log targets. Or in Eddie's case, a twang and swoosh as he missed and his arrows buried themselves in the long grass, or a thud as they hit the log barrier.

Using the Saxon front-on method, Eddie was without doubt the most inaccurate bowman in the group. Several of the younger trainees laughed at his clumsiness. In particular, Gadd and Oswold, two short but strong lads of about fifteen years old.

Gadd was scrawny and short with a round face. He had very strong forearm muscles that were able to bend the heavy wooden longbows fully. Eddie assumed that Gadd must have already been a practised archer as he hit the targets every time. His sidekick, Oswold, was a few inches taller than Gadd. He seemed to Eddie to be a little simple, concurring with anything Gadd said.

Gadd sneered at Eddie. "You're no good as an archer, you're even worse than Oswold."

Oswold echoed, "You're even worse than Oswold."

Eddie just smiled. He couldn't argue. After all, Gadd was right as he couldn't get the hang of the Saxons' unfamiliar archery stance. His worst problem was being struck on the left forearm by the bow string when he released an arrow. He was soon very sore from elbow to wrist, and striped with thin, red wheals. When he'd fought for the German warlords he'd always strapped on a leather bracer. The small arm guard would have saved him all this pain.

Someone shouted, "There are refreshments on the way, you guys!"

Eddie turned and saw two middle-aged ladies he knew, Sibyrht and Ruth, who were auxiliaries. The slight, grey-haired women were approaching with pails full of drinks and food suspended from wooden yokes across their shoulders. There were cheers and claps from the lads, who were looking forward to a rest.

Aelfhere said, "We'll only take a short break. I'll call you when I want you to recommence."

The women gave Aelfhere his supplies first and there were a few mutterings from Gadd.

"Favouritism, I call that, he grumbled," but as Aelfhere turned to see who said it, Gadd hid behind the others.

There was goat kid meat that had its own pungent aroma, dark and chewy bread and bitter acorn ale. The trainees sat in a circle to eat, drink and rest. Eddie really needed the liquid as he was becoming dehydrated in the heat.

All too soon, Thegn Aelfhere called, "Time!" and the trainees reluctantly reassembled. Aelfhere instructed them to aim at targets from a greater distance than any attempted that day. Eddie, like most of the class, had been unable to reach the target. Because of that, he decided to revert to his Germanic side-on stance. As soon as he did this he was able to extend his range and make the furthest mark easily and accurately. Something none of the other trainees could manage. He suspected that using his side-on stance brought his strong back muscles into play as well as his arms. That was allowing him to impart more power with his longbow.

After watching Eddie do well at the long distance archery, Gadd pointedly ignored him. Oswold, however, was impressed and said approvingly, "Gadd, this new boy Eddie, he better than you. Maybe he stronger?"

Gadd gave Eddie a strange look, and then slapped Oswold round the ear.

Oswold flinched. "But he did beat you, Gadd. I see it."

Several others were curious enough to try to emulate Eddie's side-on position. But none got the hang of it and soon went back to their accustomed front-on stance.

Maccus' explanation on using different arrowheads was proved accurate. When they shot at the chain mail targets, the standard arrows bounced off, whereas the thinner bodkins penetrated.

Maccus told them, "You'll never be able to carry enough arrows in your quiver. So the answer is to retrieve the arrows your enemy has aimed at your side and use them again."

The training had been physically hard, leaving Eddie exhausted with sore bowstring fingers, his left forearm stinging and both arms aching. Judging from the overpowering smell of sweaty bodies, the others would also be tired.

As the training was finished for the day, Eddie returned to the Burh and had a wash down and a change of clothes. Then he reported to Princess Catherine's court.

Edith, the smallest of the princess's handmaidens, ushered him in to Kate's royal presence. Kate, looking resplendent in a purple robe, sat on cushions on a wooden chair, with the wild she-cat, Bodi, curled up on her lap. When Kate smiled in his direction, Eddie was speechless with admiration for her beauty.

"So, Edward the Tall, I hear from Thegn Aelfhere that you're a very skilful, if unconventional, long distance archer. For a Romani gypsy boy who's not been brought up as a Saxon, you have many talents."

"I learnt archery from a young age and have used it successfully in German battles." Eddie informed her.

"You're different, I grant you that, Kate remarked. "Convention says commoners must only speak to a royal personage when they've been asked a direct question by that royal."

Eddie's face reddened. He wanted to speak but, unsure whether he was being rebuked, he just looked down.

Kate spoke to him again. "However, you're not Saxon… and in any case, formality bores me. So I give you permission to override that convention when no other nobles are present. But I'm only allowing you this dispensation as I owe you my freedom, and even my life."

Eddie fidgeted. "I was just doing what any man would have done, Kate."

"I'm glad you're calling me Kate now; I doubt I could persuade any Saxon freeman to do so."

Eddie smiled self-consciously.

"Thegn Aelfhere tells me you're already a warrior. However, you need to understand our Saxon way of fighting and Aelfhere has to assess your capabilities. For now, I suggest you get a meal and rest."

"Thank you Kate. I'll do whatever you want."

"Anything?" Kate asked. Then she winked in a conspiratorial fashion.

As Eddie left the room, Kate's three girls, Edith, Alfthrith and Bretwalda giggled. Then they squabbled as each girl tried to take him by an arm. He loved all this female attention.

Edith spoke. "Come back later, Gypsy boy. This is my night off."

He left confused. Did Kate's wink mean what he thought it did? He'd love a liaison with the beautiful princess. But he knew if he did he'd be in real trouble as that could even be viewed as treasonable. After all, as well as being a princess, Kate was engaged to Eldor Aefnoth, the only son of Ealdorman Byrhtnoth, England's top general.

Edith, on the other hand, was in his league. She was pretty rather than beautiful, but willing, it seemed. However, he was crazy about Kate and wary of making any other emotional alliances.

On Eddie's second day of training, Thegn Maccus showed the group two types of spear. Light, throwing javelins and heavier thrusting spears for hand-to-hand combat.

"It's usual to go into battle as the Ealdorman does, with three javelins in the shield hand and a thrusting spear in the other. I know three javelins don't seem enough. However, as with arrows, your enemies will be throwing theirs at you. So you retrieve these to throw back at them."

As the trainees were examining the heavy thrusting spears, there was a noisy interruption. Eldor Godric and his brothers swaggered in. All three delinquent siblings were unsteady on their feet. They smelled of alcohol combined with their normal bad breath and accumulated body odour.

Eldor Godric shouted belligerently, "What the hell are you doing Maccus? You couldn't teach your grandmother to suck eggs! This load of wasters will never be any good to anyone. They all look like halfmen… mummy's boys, to me. Let us demonstrate how real men fight, you load of pig's dung." Godric drew his sword. His brothers Godwin and Godwig sniggered as they followed his lead.

The next moment, Godric visibly shook with anger. His pot belly wobbled and his face turned even redder when he spotted Eddie in the crowd. Then he spat green phlegm and waved his sword in Eddie's direction.

Eldor Godric snarled at Eddie, "You must be using supernatural Wicca practices to live underwater like the fish. No Christian could do that. For your sorcery and occult practices you should be burned at the stake. Ealdorman Byrhtnoth was wrong to free you against my advice. Kneel and beg for my mercy, warlock."

Eddie didn't move. He looked Godric in his piggy eyes and said, "You're not a warrior, Godric. You're only brave if you have your brothers to back you up. Even then you only attack women and unarmed subordinates."

Eldor Godric's eyes bulged and his pox-ridden face turned purple, the left side twitching uncontrollably. His hands shook so much his sword almost dropped to the ground. "You'll soon be dead, you worshipper of demonology. I'll have you executed for treason. Your failure to obey a superior's orders gives me the right to summarily execute you if I see fit."

Maccus intervened. "Eldor Godric, Edward told me how you tried to drown him. You're lucky you didn't succeed. You know quite well if you had killed a wounded hero of the Maylandsea battle, all three of you would have been declared lily-livered nioings by the huscarls council. You'd have been cast out of that noble order and you personally would have lost your title, position, money and lands."

Godric's bloodshot eyes bulged. Veins stood out on his spotty face and his mouth hung open exposing his black, rotting teeth and bleeding gums. Then, perhaps attempting to prove he didn't care about what Maccus thought, he led his brothers towards Eddie. All three siblings were swinging their swords with obvious homicidal intentions.

To Eddie's surprise and delight, the massive Ecceard moved alongside him, arms akimbo. He didn't say a word, but his towering presence caused the brothers to hesitate.

Godric began to harangue the trainees again. "Don't you peasants realize my noble position? I'm an Eldor and no one here would dare to protect this foreign follower of necromancy. Or bear witness against me, as I am everybody's superior."

However Godric's prediction was proved wrong. When the three brothers again advanced towards Eddie and Ecceard, both of the Thegns, Maccus and Aelfhere, interposed themselves between the two groups.

Pushing his thrusting spear to within inches of the siblings, Maccus stated, "The youth's right. Just because your father was a brave man doesn't mean his sons are."

Godric bawled at Maccus, his high pitched voice rising another octave. "How dare you men mutiny? I'll have you all executed for this!"

Maccus replied with loathing in his voice, "Why don't you try your luck physically? You three 'brave' nobles, against two mere Thegns and a few trainees you describe as mummy's boys. That's if you have the nerve, which I doubt."

Eldor Godric squeezed a pimple on his face and yellow pus shot out. His features screwed up into a leer and he licked his lips suggestively. Then he sneered, "Maccus, how's Athelflaed, your little daughter?"

Godwin's upper lip curled licentiously and Godwig made explicit hand gestures.

Maccus was under no illusion about what the bullies meant. He easily translated the aura of chilling amoral menace in Godric's eyes, demeanour and words. With his upper lip quivering, Maccus spat out, "You keep away from my daughter, you repulsive perverts." He lunged towards Godric who cringed away. The blood drained from his face so that the inflamed pustules stood out like holly berries against the snow.

Aelfhere held his fellow Thegn back, knowing that Godric would indeed report Maccus for attacking a superior if he did so.

However, Aelfhere's intervention had emboldened Godric. "Don't forget, Maccus," he snarled, "I'm the Eldor in charge of all the Dengie Hundred hides. You know that includes your farm. I can get you thrown out whenever I want."

At that point Thegn Aelfhere thought it had gone far enough, so he took charge. "Class, carry on with your spear use training. Lower your spears and move forward, and don't stop for anything or anyone."

The class, including Eddie, did as ordered and advanced with their spear points at waist height in the direction of the brothers. Godric held both arms in front of him, his palms facing the trainees as if to push them back or make them stop. The trainees, as ordered, ignored him and when their spears points came dangerously close Godric turned on his heels and stormed off.

With his brothers trailing behind him Godric shouted back, "You've not heard the last of this. All four of you had better watch out, I'll have my day."

When they had gone, Maccus spoke to Eddie. "You did well there, young man, but don't be too brave. They're amoral idiots, but no less dangerous for that."

After the disturbance, Thegn Aelfhere led the trainees back to the practice field. Aelfhere showed them the light, throwing spears called javelins.

"A javelin weighs only about two pounds. However, when thrown with sufficient force a warrior can impart enough speed to the shaft that it can go through a wooden shield. Sometimes javelins will penetrate chain mail, but even if they don't they can cause quite a bruise. I know... I've been hit by several and it's very painful."

Oswold groaned and shook his head.

"Where possible, several of you launch javelins together," Aelfhere instructed. They travel relatively slowly through the air. Thrown singly, the enemy often has time to dodge, deflect or even catch them and throw them back at you. However, if javelins arrive in volume they'll have great difficulty avoiding them all, so you're more likely to be successful. Aim at your enemy's head or body."

Oswold shouted out, "What if they got in shield wall and we can't see their head and body?"

Gadd rebuked him, "Don't be so stupid Oswold."

Thegn Aelfhere interrupted the boy. "No, leave him alone, Gadd. That's a good question."

Oswold beamed.

"If you can't see their upper body, try to hit their legs. I assure you, a foe with one of these through his calf, ankle or foot won't fight on for very long. Especially if the javelins' points have been pre-dipped in poison." At that juncture, Thegn Aelfhere finished the training for the day.

By the time Eddie had returned to his room, cleaned himself up, changed and had a meal, it was getting late. When he did report to Kate's quarters, Alfthrith told him Kate wasn't feeling well and had retired to her bedchamber.

"Why don't you hang out with me for the evening, Edward?"

Although he was tempted to dally with the attractive girl he replied, "I'd love to, Alfthrith but I'm exhausted from training at the moment. Another time perhaps?"

Alfthrith pursed her lips. "What a pity," was all she said.

As he walked away, Eddie wondered why he was turning down dates, when he knew he was never going to have any chance with Kate. But the lovely princess had such a hold on his affections that he was pining for her, despite realizing his longing to be with her was only a pipe dream.

The following day was sunny but fresher as there was more of a breeze. Eddie had no training sessions that day so he went for a walk around the Burh. Inside the Burh's outer walls several scruffy, feral dogs had encroached from the outer town's streets. Wigghelm, the town's elderly hunch-back dog catcher arrived.

"I've got orders to capture or kill these mutts," he told Eddie.

Eddie saw Wigghelm loose an arrow and heard one cur's howl of pain. The rest of the pack bolted past him, heading for the Burh's main gates with their tails between their legs.

Later, Eddie was summoned to Kate's presence. She ordered him to accompany her on her daily walk. Kate led the way. He and

Alfthrith followed her. By Saxon custom, a princess's servants had to walk two paces behind her.

The three kept to the centre of the cobblestones. This was essential to avoid the human sewage and rubbish strewn in the gutters. Among this debris wild cats, dogs, rats and mice fought for scraps or chased any animal smaller than themselves.

After successfully negotiating their way down the steep Maldon Hill the trio reached Heybridge Harbour. They sat down on the edge of the old mud baked quay watching the water flow past them, the salty ozone and other sea tangs wafting around them.

On the shingle in front of them, cabbage-like plants were growing. Some had enormous domes of white flowers, hundreds of the blooms making up areas of up to a yard across. Their sweet, honeyed scent drifted towards them on the breeze.

"These are Sea Kale," Eddie told Kate. He plucked a flower and a leaf for her to see. Kate fingered the purple leaf; it was hard to her touch and felt waxy.

"This feeling is caused by the substance the Sea Kale uses to protect itself from the wind and sun," Eddie explained.

Kate pointed out that the white flower had several insects feeding on the pollen.

"Those insects are important to the plant. While they eat the pollen, the Sea Kale's male gametes stick to the insects' legs. Then they transport it to other Sea Kale plants and this fertilizes them. It's a fair exchange for supplying the pollen isn't it?"

"Yes," Kate Replied. "The plants are crafty. I learn something new every day."

On this sunny morning the rays reflected from the seawater created shafts of light which highlighted Kate's pretty face every few seconds. Eddie thought how truly beautiful she was… there was not a blemish on her classic features.

Kate yawned and stretched out in the sun, allowing the warmth and slight breeze to caress her face. Her body was covered by an ankle-length ivory gown with red flowers embroidered on the bodice and long, hand-made, lace sleeves. Eventually Kate did remove her long white cotton gloves and blue hat, giving them to Alfthrith to look after.

"It's nice here, Edward. Better than in that stuffy Burh."

Eddie agreed. "You're right, as usual Kate. It's so peaceful."

Kate closed her eyes and began to doze. Alfthrith fussed around her mistress, making sure her clothes didn't ride up in the breeze. Eventually, Alfthrith also fell asleep wrapped in her cloak.

Kate, in her sleep, flung an arm sideways very near to a patch of thistles. With Alfthrith also sleeping, Eddie took it on himself to move Kate's arm out of the danger area.

He carefully lifted her hand and arm and replaced it at her side. Her white skin felt so soft. Not the red and calloused hands of most girls he'd known, who worked manually. As he bent forward her breath touched his face and a shiver of excitement ran through him. She smelt so clean and feminine, he was reluctant to move away, having to force himself to do so. But he stayed close, watching with wonder as her bosom rose delicately with each breath.

When Kate awoke she asked Eddie to tell her more about his culture.

"I know you Romani gypsies can read people's fortunes. A gypsy woman was brought to the palace once when I was a child. She told our fortunes. It was fun."

Eddie sat up, leaned forward and turned his ear in her direction as the breeze carried her words away from him.

Kate continued, "My mother, the Queen, let the Romani gypsy woman stay in an outhouse near the palace for a while. This was so that she could show off the Romani's psychic talents to her friends. The Romani lady had a small crystal ball by which she used to tell people's fortunes and she also read their palms." She looked at Eddie with interest. "Can you do this Edward? Are you psychic?"

"Yes, Kate, to some extent. My mother was very good at it. You say the Romani lady told your fortune. Was she right, Kate?"

"Yes she was. She told me I would meet another Romani gypsy one day. He would be a handsome young man who would have a permanent effect on my life. At the time my sisters and I giggled about it. We considered it unlikely, considering our privileged positions. But she was right; I have met a handsome young gypsy boy. That's you... and as you saved my life, the gypsy's second prediction has already come true."

Eddie coloured, not knowing how to react at being described as handsome by such a beautiful and exalted young lady.

Kate noticed Eddie blushing; she thought he was so different to the brash royal and noble males she was used to. She decided to amuse herself for a little longer, by inquiring about his Romani powers.

"Can you sense anything about this harbour's past, Edward?"

Eddie concentrated and then, when he felt the vibes, told her, "Yes. I feel this place has been the site of Stone Age, Iron Age and later, Roman, settlements. My intuition also tells me that even before that, families from the pre-homo sapiens, Clactonian ethnic tribe lived here around four hundred thousand years ago."

Kate looked hard at Eddie, not knowing whether he was making it all up. "Really? One day I'll ask you to tell my fortune, but not now. I think I'd rather not know at the moment, with the Vikings so near. That's why I asked about the past."

Eddie's reply was cheeky. "In that case you'll have to keep me with you for a long time, Kate."

She gave him a beaming smile. "You're quite correct. I will need you as my court jester as well as my bodyguard."

"Anything to be near to you, Kate."

Kate laughed, assuming he was joking.

When they'd returned to the Burh, Kate's cat, Bodi, rubbed herself around Eddie's legs, purring. Eddie wondered what Kate's reaction would have been if the scruffy feline hadn't taken to him. Later, Kate's second adopted cat, Charley, arrived carrying a dead starling. Bodi immediately lost interest in the humans and vied with the black tomcat for the bird's carcass.

Later that evening, when Eddie was alone, he climbed up onto the Burh's earthen walls. It was a clear night with few clouds masking the full moon and the millions of stars.

Floating from the ramparts, a white-robed Druidess entered his view. His mind was taken over once more. He was back beneath thick ice, peering at the strange single element buildings. Now he was inside and standing on a floor that moved, taking him with it. He was in a room with odd artefacts. What he initially thought was a portrait changed every few seconds into other scenes.

Then suddenly he was back on the Burh wall and the Druidess had gone. This Druid factor was getting to him now. What on earth was going on?

Twelve

The emerging sun was slowly dispersing the morning mist over the Maldon Burh. Despite this it was hot for late May; an early heatwave. There was little breeze to alleviate the sun's already powerful rays.

A blackbird screeched a warning cry as a wildcat hunted close to its nest. However, this was the only natural sound that penetrated the relentless creaking and rumbling of cartwheels. More farmers were delivering their produce to the Burh in case there was a Viking attack.

Eddie had woken far too late to get any breakfast and his stomach grumbled in protest as he hurried towards the armoury for his next weapons training session.

He could already feel his shirt sticking to his back as he perspired freely. Stopping briefly at the Burh's spring, he mopped his brow and drank a scoop of cold, clear spring water drawn for him by a kindly old lady.

At the armoury, Edwold and Dunnere, the two elderly quartermaster slaves, issued a shield to each trainee. Edwold grinned at Eddie while his brother, Dunnere, scowled in his usual irascible fashion. Eddie was surprised how light his shield was, despite the metal boss over the hand hold.

Aelfhere led them to the same meadow they'd used for archery practice. By now much of the grass had turned yellow after being trodden down and baked in the early summer sun. Eddie sniffed the air, pleased that he could still smell the scent of the crushed paigles and bluebells. In the distance he could see the Blackwater Estuary and even a few seals fishing. He envied them in the cool seawater.

Aelfhere stood to address the trainees from the crest of a hillock. The Thegn was all but engulfed by the heat haze from the evaporating morning dew, making him appear like a fantasy character in some dreamlike hallucination.

"Shields can be offensive as well as defensive weapons," Aelfhere began. He demonstrated this on Oswold by telling the boy to attack him with a thrusting spear. The willing but rather dim lad charged straight at Aelfhere with his spear, screaming the Saxon war cry, "Ute, Ute, Ute!"

With a deft movement, Aelfhere used his shield to knock the boy's spear from his hand and cracked Oswold over the head, all in one flowing manoeuvre.

Oswold sat on the floor rubbing his cranium and swearing profanely. Several of the class laughed nervously, not wanting to be made examples of themselves.

Aelfhere told them, "A strong shield wall is essential in any open ground battle." To prove his point, he formed the trainees up into four lines. The front line interlocked shields and held them in front. The second line's shields were held over the heads of both the front row and themselves. Those at the edge covered the sides. This was repeated until only the rear was unprotected. The effect was like a tortoise's shell.

Back on the Burh's earthen walls, Eldor Aefnoth stood on the highest point of the tower. He had climbed up there having been notified that a signal fire had been lit at Bradwell at the entry to the North Sea.

Aefnoth strained his eyes to try and spot any interlopers. As he couldn't see any longships he came to the conclusion that the Vikings were just probing the entrance to the Blackwater Estuary. Therefore no defensive action was needed at the moment, although it was a warning that Vikings were in the area.

Meanwhile, inside the shield wall the smell of closely packed, sweaty bodies was overpowering. Making matters worse, somebody loudly broke wind. This instigated complaints, swearing, accusations and denials from beneath the cover of the shield wall.

Without warning, a large reddish-brown hunting dog appeared from the hedgerow. The animal, upset by the simulated fighting, barked aggressively and snapped at the heels of the exposed rear trainees.

Oswold broke off from the shield wall. "Bad dog," he shouted, and swiped his shield at the hound, hitting it on the back. The dog yelped and slunk away with its ears flat and tail between its legs.

Gadd told him, "That's Bruce, the Ealdorman's favourite hunting dog you've just hit."

"I don't care. He's a bad dog," replied Oswold.

Thegn Aelfhere's face contorted, his eyes blazed and he clasped and unclasped his fists. He shouted at Oswold, his deep booming voice dropping yet another octave. "You young fool!"

The shield wall disintegrated as the trainees peered out to see what was happening.

Oswold cowered away from Aelfhere, stung by his censure.

Thegn Aelfhere shouted at everyone now. "Don't you all realize what this dolt's done? He has just broken one of the most important battle rules. When you've made a shield wall it must be held in position at all costs. He pointed an accusing finger at the dim boy, causing Oswold to cringe even more. "If anyone does this in battle, your whole army could be slaughtered.

"Even if someone's killed or injured, the others must close ranks immediately. Injured warriors should crawl away if they can, or just lie still. In no circumstances should anyone attempt to help them. You may only split up when your leader gives you the order to do so. It's all your lives that are at stake. Do you get that Oswold? Everybody?"

Oswold was crying and shaking. He nodded and sobbed, "Yes, Thegn Aelfhere. I'm sorry."

There was a welcome relief for everyone with the arrival of Sibyrht and Ruth. They brought buckets of water hung from the wooden yokes, some round loaves of unleavened bread and pats of white goat's cheese. The food was welcome and the water essential in the heat.

As the ladies were leaving, Gadd made a ribald remark to them about joining the boys under the shield wall. For his pains, Ruth hit him over the head with her wooden tray. Oswold laughed, relieved that he was not the object of derision any more.

After the day's training, Eddie leisurely strolled back towards Kate's quarters. Since he'd been appointed her official bodyguard he'd had unrivalled access to the beautiful princess. This was something that few of his station in life could dare to dream about.

However, as he neared the great hall that incorporated Kate's rooms he sensed that something was very wrong. The heavy door that was always open during daylight hours was shut. His heart rate doubled and he snapped out of his languor, becoming instantly alert.

Eddie ran to the hall's big oak door. He tried to lift the cast-iron latch and push the door open. Though it budged a fraction, it wouldn't move enough for him to enter. He realized with horror that it was being held shut by someone's muscle power.

Now concerned for Kate's safety, Eddie crashed his shoulder into the door. It was solid initially. Then at his second attempt the door gave way far too easily, allowing him to pitch headlong through the doorway, landing in a heap on the earthen floor.

Before Eddie could rise he was struck on the head with a wooden club. Everything went red, his mind swam and he lost the ability to focus. He was aware of an almost overwhelming sharp pain in his skull.

He was dazed, barely aware that Eldor Godric's brothers had tied his wrists behind his back and secured them to the hasp and staple of the door and post. This had not only restricted Eddie's movements, it had also effectively secured the door from outside interference. He had also been gagged with a foul-smelling, filthy cloth and had to fight to stop himself retching.

Through the blood trickling into his eyes from his head wound, Eddie could just make out Kate and her girls. They were all at the far end of the main hall, being threatened by Godric and his brothers. In desperation he tried to wrench his wrists free from his bonds. But for once the brothers had done a good job; the knots held.

Godric shouted at Eddie, his slurred diction and unsteady movements indicative of his inebriation. "So, you waster, you've decided to join us? Unfortunately for you, your only participation will be to watch. You can admire how your superiors enjoy their women. Then I'll personally slice your throat and laugh while you bleed to death."

Eddie could see Kate's girls huddled together, shaking. They were sobbing and wiping away tears on their cuffs. However, Kate herself stood in front of her handmaidens protectively, looking both regal and defiant.

Godric leered at Kate. "C'mon girls… uh, and boys, let's party," he slurred.

Eddie saw Godwig make a grab for Kate and wrenched his whole weight repeatedly against his bonds, desperate to prevent this assault on his princess.

To Eddie's surprise he wasn't needed. Kate kicked Godwig in the throat, sending him sprawling, and his weapon fell to the floor. As Godwig got up, choking, he grabbed for the sword he'd dropped. But before he could wield it, Kate clutched his wrist and twisted his arm upwards behind his back. Once more, the sharp blade clattered to the floor.

At the same time, Eddie was amazed to see the cats, Bodi and Charley, attack. Bodi the wild she-cat was growling. Her back was arched and her neck hair stood on end. With one leap she was on Godwin, digging her unsheathed talons into his groin. When he tried to push her off, she bit deeply into his hand.

Meanwhile, Charley, the big black tomcat, mewing dementedly, had leapt onto Godric's shoulders and was frenziedly scratching at the man's acne-ridden face. Godric let his sword fall to the ground so that he could use both black-finger-nailed hands to drag Charley from his badly lacerated face.

Godric screamed in pain. "Kill the accursed animals," he commanded his brothers, but neither could do anything about it. They had all dropped their weapons in the fray. Overcoming her terror, Bretwalda retrieved one of the brothers' swords. Then she sprinted down the hall and cut Eddie free.

By then the two cats had relinquished their hold on their victims and were standing in front of Kate. Backs still arched and hackles raised, they spat viciously at the three brothers. The felines were unmistakably standing guard over their mistress and lunged at the brothers each time they attempted to retrieve their weapons.

Kate had also taken up a defensive unarmed combat stance. Understandably, the brothers were looking in some consternation at Kate and the cats at this quite unexpected turn of events.

Now freed, Eddie took the weapon from Bretwalda and joined the melee, sword in hand. He shouted at the brothers, "Stop that! Go now or by God, I'll kill you all."

The disarmed brothers shambled away, rubbing their wounded bits of anatomy. As a parting threat Godric screamed at Eddie, "That's it! You and those damned cats will die for this. You're a mutineer and a traitor, Edward the Viking."

When the brothers had gone, Kate held her arms out and Bodi jumped up into them purring loudly. Charley came to Eddie, who lifted the tomcat onto one arm and stroked him.

"Weren't my kitties magnificent, Edward?" asked Kate. "They are real little heroes. Who needs a guard dog with them around? I think they deserve a reward. There should be some fresh fish in the kitchen. If there is they shall have one each." She sent Alfthrith to try and track down the fish for the cats. Eddie was delighted that the cats had fought to protect their mistress, though he somehow sensed there was more to this incident than just feline instinct.

At the Bradwell end of the Blackwater Estuary, white smoke spiralled into the windless sky. In the tower on top of the Burh wall, Eldor Aefnoth's shoulders relaxed. He turned and walked towards the tower's exit steps. The white smoke indicated that the Viking raiders were sailing away. The immediate emergency was over, but…

Back in the hall Eddie asked his princess, "Where did you learn to fight like that, Kate?"

"I pestered my father to let me go with my brothers to learn hand-to- hand fighting. He wasn't keen but because I was a tomboy and nagged him continually, he gave in. Were you impressed, bodyguard?"

"Very," Edward replied, with feeling.

Kate smiled proudly. "Mind you, doing high kicks wearing this long robe wasn't as easy as in the boys' trousers I borrowed from my brothers. But those idiots never expected me to fight back so I caught them off guard."

"You were magnificent, Kate."

She smiled demurely pleased that he'd praised her.

Eddie nodded. "So why didn't you use your fighting skills on the Vikings when you were captured in the raid at Maylandsea?"

"That's because they had a blade at my neck and I was tied up. Not to mention being outnumbered by real warriors, not poltroons like Godric and his brothers."

Eddie smiled self-consciously. "Quite. It was rude of me to ask, Princess."

"Changing the subject," Kate said, "my father, King Aethelred, is coming to the Burh this weekend and will stay here all next week. I suggest you take a few days off to visit your new farms. My father's troops will be here so I won't need a bodyguard until the week after."

"That would be good Kate, if you're sure you won't need me?"

"It will be nice for you. Tell you what, Edward, Prior Esmond's here in town at the moment. Why don't you take him with you? You could learn more about our local history from him."

Eddie agreed to her suggestion as did Prior Esmond as soon as he was asked. Consequently, later that week the two men set out on horseback to visit Eddie's recently granted farm on his two hides of land.

As they rode away from Maldon, Eddie was already missing Kate. However, he still had a thrill of anticipation at going to see his new land acquisition as he had never owned any before. He looked up at the sky. The sun's heat was projected through a layer of grey stratus cloud and the muggy air was still making him sweat profusely. Droplets ran down his forehead into his eyes.

It was now low tide and the exposed black mud was thronged with long-billed sea birds searching for shrimps, lug and rag worms in the silt. As they passed the midden it was impossible to avoid the stench of the decaying human sewage.

On the journey Esmond asked Eddie, "Did you know that Byrhtnoth is the patron of many religious houses? Well he is. In particular the Ely, Ramsey, Abingdon and Mersea Island abbeys. Then there's the Beeleigh Priory, where I have the honour under God to be the senior cleric."

Eddie pretended to be interested despite it not really being his thing. So as not be rude he replied, "Fascinating."

As they rode through a small stream, a family of otters swam past. One emerged from the water with a brown trout in its mouth. After another few miles they passed a hamlet called Steeple. It had been so named because the church there was one of the few that had a pointed wooden tower. Later, a lone buck deer with half grown antlers watched their progress from a coppice of elder bushes.

"I've found out more about the Druids' stone circle on Mersea Island if you're interested," Esmond said.

Eddie pricked up his ears at this. "Oh, do please go on; I'd like to hear about that."

"I met an old hermit called Odda who lives in a small cave on a remote part of Mersea Island's coast. He told me he survives on nuts, berries, sea fish he catches himself, and food left for him by the locals. Odda has the looks one might expect of a hermit... skinny, with long grey hair and a beard reaching almost to his bare feet. He's of indeterminate age and has strange piercing green eyes that seem to penetrate into your very soul."

Eddie scratched his head. "Did he speak to you? Did you learn anything interesting from him?"

"Oh yes, he spoke to me alright, although he had a very strange accent and intonation. He told me a local legend."

Esmond's horse suddenly stumbled and almost threw the prior, but the man of God clung on to the beast's mane and kept his balance.

Eddie was intrigued. "So what was this legend?"

Esmond was pleased by Eddie's show of avid interest and warmed to his tale. "Well, according to Odda, Mersea Island's history is tied in with an extreme Druid sect from pre-history. He said that's because of an alternative magnetic North Pole."

Eddie's mother had shown him what she called a compass. This was a small, flat metal needle she balanced on a pin and it always pointed north. His father had traded it with a sailor for furs. He'd considered it a curiosity. But Eddie's psychic mother said a Druid had told her it pointed to a massive iron deposit in the extreme north. She told him this created a strange pull and was called the North Pole.

But Eddie wondered how there could be an alternative pole. More than one iron deposit? He looked quizzically at Esmond. "How do you mean, alternative?"

"Well, Odda insisted that in the old pagan days the North Pole was in a different position to now. It was centred at a place called the Yukon... wherever that was, or is."

Eddie shook his head. "Really?" he exclaimed.

Esmond coughed a little. "Yes. Odda told me that long, long ago there were several sacred sites in England linked to this ancient Yukon magnetic Pole. In fact he showed me a piece of wood that had a reference carved on it. He swore this had come from a Chief Druid of pre-history. I memorized it and then recorded it onto parchment. It said sixty-three degrees north and one hundred and thirty-five degrees west."

At that point Esmond dismounted to check which of several bridle paths they needed to take. Eventually he decided on a rough track passing a small hut. As they rode past, Eddie smelt smoke and what he took to be the aroma of herbal pottage. Stopping briefly to reconnoitre, they couldn't see any humans around, so they continued on their journey with Eddie salivating.

Eddie was curious about what Esmond had been saying before their stop and wanted him to continue with the story. "I wish I'd been there with you when you met the hermit," he said. "What else did he say?"

Esmond smiled, pleased by Eddie's enthusiasm and more than happy to tell him more. "Odda said the Yukon Pole is linked by that strange written reference to all the major sacred druid sites around the world, including England."

"What did he mean by sacred sites?"

Esmond cleared his throat. "He wasn't referring to sacred Christian sites. No, he must have meant ancient pagans, druids... or something more sinister even.

Eddie's horse reared up as an adder slid past the powerful animal's eye line. The horse's hooves clattered down again but it was still spooked and difficult to subdue as it threw its head around inside the rope bridle.

When Eddie had brought his mount under control he asked, "Well, did Odda tell you where these sites were?"

Esmond nodded his head, his brow deeply furrowed. "Places called Avebury, Glastonbury, Stonehenge and Mersea Island. I don't know where these other places are so I concentrated on the Island..."

Eddie interjected, "You did say Mersea Island?"

"Yes, Edward. In fact Odda told me that's why he was living there. He insisted that the Pagan legend says the most important of all was, and still is Mersea Island. This was because the stone circle there was linked to a fabled land or world called Atlantis."

Eddie was confused. "Atlantis? Have you heard of this place?"

Esmond nodded. "Yes. Our founder, Cedd, knew of the legend and instigated the Christian Abbey to be built on Mersea Island right by this pagan site. He wanted to smother the heathen influence of the stone circle with our Christian God's power…"

Again Eddie broke in. "But Cedd left the stone circle in place? I'd have thought he would have used the stones to build the Abbey?"

Esmond nodded his agreement. "That had occurred to me, but it appeared the locals were scared of disturbing the stones, saying they were evil magic. Coincidentally, one of the Christian brothers attempted to split one of the smaller stones with a wedge and a hammer and then with an axe."

"Did he succeed?"

Esmond gave Eddie a strange look. He blinked slowly several times and gazed into the distance. His reply was hesitant. "That… that's the strange thing. The instant the axe head hit the rock…" Esmond stopped, shaking his head.

Eddie had picked up the tension in Esmond's voice. "What?" he asked eagerly. "What happened?"

Esmond's voice quivered. "The axe head broke in two. One half rebounded and hit the poor brother between his eyes and killed him instantly."

"How terrible! I expect it was pure coincidence?"

Esmond looked away. "Probably, but Abbot Cedd ordered that none of the Christian brothers was to go near the stones from then on. Brother Berthold was buried in hallowed ground, just outside the stones. There is a small rock memorial there to this day." He paused and then turned back to face Eddie. "Later, the Pope in Rome canonized Abbot Cedd so he's now referred to as Saint Cedd."

"Wow, well that's quite a story."

Esmond tried to finish his tale off as he was now feeling uncomfortable, thinking he'd told Eddie far too much already.

He said, "As the original basis of this legend is pre-Christian I don't expect it means anything. The first part of the story is obviously just a myth." He shrugged then, as if to make light of it. "But I collect and record all these silly tales as a hobby."

Eddie was more than interested in the tale; he was fascinated. That was because it tied in with his own visits with the Norwegians and by remote viewing. However, he sensed it would best not to probe Esmond any more.

But he resolved to try to find out more of the mystery of the stones on Mersea Island by his own methods. Perhaps it was the key to this Druids enigma?

Thirteen

It was still warm after the main heat of the day had dissipated. A light breeze wafted the combined smells of ozone and seaweed over Eddie and Prior Esmond as they rode their sweat-lathered horses near to the Blackwater Estuary in Essex.

After a short stop to rest and water the horses from a stream, they turned right, following the course of the two adjoining creeks. They knew these led to Eddie's newly acquired farming properties.

As the tide was right out, Mayland Creek contained little water apart from a few pools where seabirds searched for shrimps and black lugworms. Further on, Lawling Creek was just mud, with one tiny channel of flowing water meandering around with seemingly no logic to its course.

Prior Esmond muttered a short prayer of thanks that they were nearing their journey's end.

Eventually they arrived at the tiny farming hamlet of Maylandsea. Apart from the muddy river, the rest of the scene was arable land growing various crops, and woodland. This was divided into hide farms with a few houses and farm buildings spread out in no apparent order.

A Ceorl freeman greeted them and introduced himself as Wistan.

"I was informed you were coming," he said. "I'm your neighbour; I own the farm next door to your property."

Wistan was small in stature but rugged. Eddie judged he was probably in his late forties. He had a craggy, weather-beaten face and when they shook hands in greeting, Eddie felt the calloused palms and fingers of a long time manual worker.

Wistan added, "I've been farming Ealdorman Byrhtnoth's two hides of land as well as my own for many years. These two hides to our left are now your land. They comprise of around two hundred acres in total and the soil is good."

Eddie came to the point. "I'd be grateful if you would continue farming my new hides. You can keep all the produce from my land in exchange for supplying me and my friends with food when we visit."

"That's a bargain," Wistan replied. "Let me take you round your farm now."

The three men walked down to Lawling Creek. Eddie was pleased to realize that his property started from the water's edge. He'd always loved the waterside, finding it relaxing.

He owned a small log-built dwelling near the water. He looked forward to sitting in front of it on balmy evenings, watching the sun go down. He daydreamed of sharing these experiences with Kate. Although that was too much to hope for, he could at least dream, but should he feel inclined, for two hours before and after high tide, he'd be able to swim or fish to his heart's content. Inside the building were two rooms – one with two bed platforms and the other with a small fireplace and cooking implements.

Wistan took Eddie and Esmond round the rest of the holding. As Wistan had said, the land seemed excellent. Many healthy crops were growing, including corn, turnips, carrots and cabbage. There were extensive woodlands and grassed areas where sheep and goats roamed in natural herds. At the centre of his land stood a large house with a barn, workshops and animal pens.

The house had several rooms, including a long hall with two bedrooms leading from it. He sensed he would enjoy his time in this beautiful place.

"There's one problem," Wistan told Eddie. "I've had trouble from the Dengie Hundred's Eldor Godric. He's doubled the rental his father, Eldor Godrichelm, expected from us. Now we have to give him a full tithe, one tenth of our crops. If we don't pay it on time his brothers become violent. I'm only mentioning this in case he tries to do the same to you."

Eddie nodded. "Thanks for the warning; I do know of Godric's treacherous character."

Wistan continued. "I work these farms with the help of my wife, daughter and a family of slaves."

"After so recently being a slave myself I'd much rather they were freemen," Eddie replied.

"Oh, these weren't forced into slavery. They were my neighbours till recently. Let me introduce them to you."

With that, Wistan took Eddie and Esmond to a neighbouring hut and introduced them to Wigelm. He was a big, jovial man and the father of the slave family.

Wigelm said, "I'm pleased to meet you both, may I explain my position?"

"By all means," said Eddie.

Wigelm explained, "I begged my kind neighbour, Wistan, to accept my family as slaves. This was because the Vikings raided us a few weeks ago. They killed my eldest son who tried to fight them off. Then they destroyed our property and pillaged all our animals and food.

"Without this temporary slavery arrangement we would starve. This way, Wistan has agreed to free us when we've rebuilt our house and gathered enough goods together to be self-sufficient again."

Eddie pursed his lips thoughtfully. "As you're working on my land, feel free to use my house and buildings when we're not here."

"Thank you sir. At least I've still got my wife Naomi, two teenage daughters and three younger sons. We're all grateful to the kindness everybody's shown us."

Prior Esmond then spoke to Wigelm. "God bless you and your family, my son. I'm sorry to hear of your elder son's death. But as he saved his whole family, he would have died happy."

When they returned to Wistan's house Wistan asked the two men to take supper with him.

"I'd be honoured if you will both join my family for an evening meal. You'll find my wife is an excellent cook."

Prior Esmond answered for them both. "We'd be honoured, Wistan. I, for one, am very hungry."

Outside Wistan's dwelling Eddie had noticed the family could gather clean water from a small stream with a widened sump pool. The cottage was made of logs with a thatched roof through which the smoke percolated. Inside was a large family dining room that incorporated a fireplace in the kitchen area. Leading from this room were two smaller rooms that Eddie guessed were probably bedrooms.

There was a pleasant redolence of mixed herbs. These heady scents even overpowered the smoky aroma from the cooking fire.

The family room had an earth floor and only one small window opening, so it was quite dark and the flames from the crackling log fire projected a strange flickering effect onto people's faces.

That evening, Eddie and Prior Esmond shared a fine meal with the family. It smelled and tasted wonderful, comprising as it did of slow roasted lamb that melted in the mouth, and piping hot vegetables – wild cabbage, yellow carrots and green beans. These vegetables had obviously been freshly picked and lightly cooked immediately. Consequently they crunched pleasingly as they were bitten into. This was all washed down with turnip wine that Wistan had made himself. It had a fruity rather than the vegetable flavour that Eddie expected.

This wonderful feast was reminiscent of the open-air Romani meals he'd eaten round the campfires when he was young. The tasty fare was served to them by Wistan's wife Edigh and daughter Emma. Eddie judged Edigh to be in her late thirties and their daughter Emma looked like a teenager. Both were small, slim, attractive blondes.

After dinner Wistan walked with Eddie to his house on his new property.

"Edward, I understand you're not married?" Wistan asked.

"You are correct; that is so."

Wistan, rather boldly, continued, "In that case, my daughter Emma, my youngest and only surviving child isn't promised to any man. She'd been about to marry Wigelm's son, Aetheric, when he was killed. He died a hero in the same battle as Emma's brothers. My own two sons," he added softly.

"When you move next door, you'll be welcome to call and see us for a meal at any time. Then perhaps you will get to know Emma."

"I'll certainly take you up on sharing your meals; your wife is a wonderful cook." Eddie didn't comment on Emma, feeling it unwise.

Esmond, sensitive to Wistan's emotions, spoke quietly. "It's always hard to lose your children, but God has blessed you with a fine wife and daughter to comfort you."

Eddie commented, "It's a dangerous time; none of us can be sure of our safety."

"Without you, Edward the Tall, my family would all be dead by now," Wistan said.

Eddie did not understand. "How do you mean?"

"It was when you came to Maylandsea as a lowly slave and fought so hard to save Princess Catherine from the Vikings."

Eddie scratched his forehead before answering. "But I didn't come near these farms then."

"No, that's true, but the sea raiders had their longships in this very creek. My two sons Eanwold and Eddgar, with Wigelm's oldest boy Aetheric, held them off heroically. Our wonderful boys fought well, killing many Vikings. Then they were overwhelmed by a vastly bigger force and slaughtered."

Prior Esmond crossed himself then shook his head slowly.

Wistan continued. "Our boys sacrificed their lives for us and delayed the Vikings long enough for the rest of us to hide in the woods. However, the Vikings had spotted us fleeing and started to search the woods to kill or enslave us all. But that was when you intervened."

Eddie was puzzled and asked, "How come?"

"We didn't know it at the time, but the sea raiders got word that their scouting party were under attack and needed help. They temporarily left us alone to go to their comrades' aid. When the Vikings had rescued their comrades they would have returned. Then they would have destroyed our little farm, including the animals and crops. Eventually they'd have caught us for sure, and then killed or enslaved us."

Eddie held out his open hands nonchalantly. "I still don't see how I helped you with that?"

"Don't you see? While you were fighting to save our princess from the Vikings' scouting party, it deflected their main force away from us here." With his head raised and shoulders back, Wistan's next words were spoken with feeling. "Edward, while you were putting up such stiff resistance you gave our Saxon relief force time to arrive. Also, it distracted the Vikings' attention enough for our forces to surprise them. By doing so, the sea pirates were driven back to their longships without being able to harass us any more." He paused, not sure that he had convinced Eddie. "So without you realizing it, Edward, you saved all the families living on this Dengie Hundred from those murdering invaders."

Eddie's face had reddened. His hands fluttered in front of him and his only reply was, "Really?"

"Yes, Edward, it's true," said Wistan, nodding. "Of course we had no idea it was you who had saved us. Until, that was, I met the warriors from Maldon Burh. They told me the whole story. It was then I learnt your name, and that for your bravery you'd been freed from your slavery. I was also told that you'd been awarded two hides of land by Ealdorman Byrhtnoth for your valour. Also that, coincidently, your new land was adjoining ours."

Eddie self-consciously brushed his fringe away from his eyes. "I'm pleased you were helped as a by-product of my actions. I was just trying to rescue Princess Catherine."

Wistan nodded his head sagely, his mouth turned up at one side and he leaned on his fists. Then he said, "I'm told that Princess Catherine is absolutely beautiful."

Eddie blushed, put his hand to his mouth, tapped two fingers against his teeth and nodded.

Back at the Maldon Burh, King Aethelred, Ealdorman Byrhtnoth and his son Eldor Aefnorth were discussing the country's security situation. With Viking longships marauding along the east coast, defensive plans had to be drawn up.

King Aethelred spoke. "I have been informed of a simmering rebellion near York."

Byrhtnoth stood to attention and immediately said; "I will lead all my professional warriors to York to back you, Your Highness."

King Aethelred held up his right hand, the third finger of which bore his seal of office ring. "I knew that would be your reaction, Ealdorman Byrhtnoth, and I thank you for your loyalty as always. However, in this case I am only making a show of force to dissuade any local lords who may be considering alliances with the Vikings."

Eldor Aefnorth bowed to the King. "I would be honoured to ride with you Sire, if you so wish."

King Aethelred leaned forward, placing a hand on each of the two nobles' shoulders. Smiling benevolently, he addressed them both.

"In this case I do not anticipate any martial action at York. However, I have another important task for you. I wish you, Byrhtnoth my premier general, to keep a watch on the coast from East Anglia to London as it's impossible to tell where or when a Viking attack will come."

Byrhtnoth bowed and said, "Your wish is my command, Sire. It shall be done.

At that point Princess Catherine swept into the room in full make-up and wearing a voluminous gown. She smiled at her father.

"You've been neglecting your youngest daughter, Sire, talking about soldiering with the boys. Will you come and walk with me for a while?"

King Aethelred's stern facial expression softened into a paternal smile. "You are right, daughter. I should relax a while before my long journey." Turning to his two nobles he said, "If you will excuse us gentleman, even I, your King, must deal with family matters.

As the King walked off holding the arm of his daughter, Princess Catherine, he reflected that she had not looked once at Eldor Aefnorth. As she was betrothed to him he would have preferred her to show some interest in him. He was aware she was to marry Aefnorth at his, the King's, instigation to join the two premier English dynasties into one strong unit. He knew she would carry out his wishes but she was his youngest child, the apple of his eye, and he wanted her to be happy.

Back in the hall, Ealdorman Byrhtnoth spoke to his son, Eldor Aefnorth.

"Let us hope we don't get a major insurgency. If the Vikings realize the Royal Host, England's main full time army won't be here along this Eastern territory, they could try to take advantage."

Aefnorth answered, "Our numbers will be inadequate if they do. We'll need to call on the select fyrd or even the grand fyrd if it gets too bad."

The following morning in Maylandsea Esmond asked Eddie, "If

it's all right with you, I'd like to use this time away from the priory to read my religious texts and pray?"

Eddie answered, "Yes, that is perfectly in order. I need to explore the farm and rest my sore ribs."

"Good. Thank you. In that case I intend to go for long walks along the sea wall and in the countryside to try and get closer to my God."

A couple of days later Eddie walked up Mayland Hill to visit Pastor John at the burnt out church. Pastor John was the brave priest from Maylandsea who had saved his life by knocking out the Viking who was about to kill him.

Pastor John greeted Eddie and showed him where the farmers had already started restoring the church and outbuildings. He told Eddie, "I've been living in the subterranean priest hole where I hid when the Vikings torched the buildings."

"It must get cramped in there. How do you get supplies to survive?" Eddie wondered.

"Yes it is a little tight in my bolt hole," Pastor John agreed. "But dryer and warmer than sleeping outside. As for rations, my parishioners bring me what food they can spare and I gather water from the nearby brook over there. I'm continuing to hold services in the open air. Subsequent to the Viking raid I held the funeral service for Wistan's and Wigelm's sons. I also saw to it that the Viking dead were buried in a mass resting place outside the confines of the consecrated graveyard."

Pastor John, a strong man, had been labouring with his parishioners to restore the church. Eddie joined them for two days, moving logs and carving wood. After all, he owed his life to the Pastor.

Later in the week Prior Esmond went to see his old friend Pastor John and he also helped John with his rebuilding. He then arranged to send a team of monks from the Priory as a work party. He also promised to donate furniture and religious items for use when it had been fully restored.

Most evenings, Esmond and Eddie enjoyed a meal with Wistan's family. During the day Eddie traipsed round every part of his farm. As a Romani he'd soon realized how easy it would be to live there off the land. Apart from the fish in the sea, the woodland also had great potential. There was soft wood to burn on the fires, hard wood trees from which to build houses and boats, and although it was only June, he recognized fruiting trees and bushes that would supply abundant food later in the year. He found trees that would provide sweet chestnuts, acorns, crab apples and hazelnuts. There would be strawberries, blackberries, elderflowers and wild cherries. Also deer, hares and wild pigs abounded.

Eddie followed the smaller of the two streams on his property into a wood. The water was quite shallow but he noticed several trout in the strong current. Following the stream became difficult when a tangled bramble thicket blocked his path. Eventually, despite getting badly scratched, he reached a deep, clear pool.

Surrounding the pool were several large, gnarled oaks and half-rotting beech trees. In the under wood beneath them were nine hazel trees covered in long yellow catkins – the male flowers known as 'lamb's tails.' The female flowers were small, red and bud-like in appearance. What was extremely unusual for the time of year was that on the female flowers were several fully formed hazel nuts. He knew it was far too early for them to fruit.

Eddie became very confused when, within a few seconds, every one of the dozen or so nuts fell from the tree and landed in the pool. To his astonishment, a large salmon broke the surface of the water and swallowed all the nuts. Eddie felt lightheaded and had the urge to swim in the pool. He stripped off his garments and entered the cool water.

From nowhere, it seemed, a Celtic Druid appeared at the side of the pool. He was wearing a white robe and had pure shining white hair although he only looked to be in his twenties.

The Druid spoke, '*Edward Lavengro, I am Fionn MacCumhail. I am here to explain that these hazel nuts contain all our Gaelic concentrated wisdom and poetic inspiration. Our revered salmon has, by eating the hazel nuts, absorbed our wisdom. You must eat all of this fish yourself. In no circumstances must you give any to another.*'

Eddie was bemused by this and wanted to ask how he could catch such a large fish, but he was unable to speak. He didn't have to. Fionn MacCumhail put his arms in the water and lifted the big salmon out. The Druid passed a hand over the fish's eyes and it was instantly dead. He passed the fish to Eddie who carefully waded out of the pool with it in his arms. He turned to ask Fionn MacCumhail a question but he had vanished.

Eddie was confused but strangely at ease, as if this were natural. He dressed and took the salmon back to his smaller house by the bay. After lighting a fire he roasted and then ate the fish. The fish smelt of salmon, but it tasted rather too sweet.

Eddie felt that his mind was swirling around. Then his brain suddenly became exceptionally clear and positive.

The following day, he decided to go back to look at the spot, but he couldn't find the sacred pool, just a shallow river. He intended to try again. However, that day Esmond told Eddie he needed to get back to the Burh because he had important religious duties to perform – two marriages and a baby's christening, to be exact. Consequently Eddie agreed to return with him and shelved his plans to find the pool until a later visit.

Rather reluctant to leave, the pair thanked Wistan's family and then rode back towards Maldon. Eventually, Eddie and Esmond rode their horses up to the main gates of the Maldon Burh, the earth-walled, fortified inner town. Esmond didn't enter, but continued on to the Priory with a wave to Eddie.

The smells of the town's life were as Eddie remembered them. Woodsmoke from fires and food of all types cooking, and on such a muggy day, the stink of raw sewage dominated all others.

As Eddie entered the Burh, dogs barked and gulls screeched. Axles squeaked and the continuous clatter of metal-rimmed cartwheels on the cobbles grated on his nerves. The multitude of carts was the biggest difference from the last time he'd been there.

"Why is there so much extra traffic today?" he asked one of the carters.

The old grey-haired driver replied, "That's because we're delivering extra supplies to fill the Burh's stores in case of a siege."

Eddie looked up at the clouds that were now covering the whole sky. He decided the atmosphere was so heavy there must be a storm due. He wiped the sweat from his brow. His shirt was sticking to his chest. It was generally too uncomfortable to do anything energetic, so he lay on his bed and contemplated his future.

He hoped he could resume his duties as Kate's bodyguard. He just wanted to be near his beautiful princess.

But it wasn't to be. Next morning he was summoned to see Ealdorman Byrhtnoth.

This sounded ominous.

Fourteen

The thunderstorm overnight had re-oxygenated the air within the Maldon Burh. Eddie shivered as the cool breeze penetrated his light tunic. He was careful to avoid the puddles as he approached Ealdorman Byrhtnoth's headquarters.

A slight movement to his right revealed an old bedraggled ginger cat staring at a rat hole, poised to spring if a rodent emerged. The feline turned its moth-eaten and greying head towards Eddie as if admonishing the interloper for interrupting its hunting concentration.

Eddie was nervous, having been summoned to see Ealdorman Byrhtnoth. He wondered if he'd done anything to offend the country's most senior general.

Byrhtnoth's headquarters was in an impressive detached building with a slatted, wooden-tiled roof. An armed guard allowed Eddie into the Ealdorman's house. Inside he was shown into the long baronial hall by Oderald, one of the slaves he'd shared a room with when he himself had been enslaved.

Oderald smiled at him. "You've done well for yourself, Edward. You've given us slaves a glimmer of hope that we, too, could be freed some day."

"I was just in the right place at the right time, Oderald, my friend. Do you know why I've been instructed to come to see the Ealdorman?"

"No, I've not overheard anything. But the boss seems a bit edgy lately."

Oderald went off to tell the Ealdorman Eddie had arrived and Eddie took stock of his surroundings. The hall had three high, wooden-shuttered window openings. All were ajar to allow light in. At one end was a great hearth that held a massive log fire ready to be lit.

To one side there were woven wall drapes of heroic scenes. Byrhtnoth's personal battle standard stood in a corner attached to a long ornate gilded staff, topped with a metal spike. The pennant itself was grey with triple red-handled silver Scramaseaxe single-bladed swords embroidered on it.

Eddie's mouth hung open, his eyes widened and he shook his head. On the end wall hung two huge portraits. They were fully five feet high by three feet wide, set in gold-encrusted carved wooden frames.

He had heard of such images but never thought he would ever see one. These paintings indicated extreme opulence. Eddie suspected few would be able to paint portraits of this complexity and even less would be able to afford to commission them.

These were not images he would like on his wall. They were of stern looking men in full battle armour with black backgrounds. The subjects' faces, clothing and armour were also painted in depressingly sombre hues.

One portrait had a resemblance to Byrhtnoth so he guessed it might be of the general's father, Ealdorman Byrhthelm. The other was of a younger man wearing a crown so that was probably of King Aethelred.

Eddie was ushered into Byrhtnoth's study by Oderald, who shrugged his shoulders and opened his hands in a gesture that indicated he still had no idea why his friend had been summoned.

Byrhtnoth was pacing up and down with his right hand cupping his chin. With him, but seated on ornate carved wooden chairs, were his son Eldor Aefnoth, and Prior Esmond.

Byrhtnoth turned on his heel and faced Eddie. "Edward the Tall, I hear your wounds have healed and you've completed your weapon training. Also, Prior Esmond tells me you're now conversant with our local Saxon history?"

Eddie stood to attention. "That's correct, my lord. Prior Esmond has been exceptionally helpful. I've recovered well, apart from some pain from my ribs."

The Ealdorman nodded. "It's good that you're on the mend, we need fit men. Oh, er please relax... there isn't any reason to be formal."

"Yes, my lord."

"Prior Esmond has also informed me that you can speak the Viking languages. This would normally make me consider you a potential spy. However, because of your bravery in defending our princess, I realize this is not the case."

"Thank you, my Lord. You are right, I'm no Viking."

"Esmond also tells me you've seen the Norsemen use an instrument that enables them to see details of our forces from long distances?"

"Yes. I've observed them using a device that I believe is called a scope..."

Esmond interjected. "I understand they use crystal lens to make these scopes work."

"That's also what I've heard," Eddie replied, "although I can't confirm it."

Byrhtnoth put his hand on his chin and tapped his cheek for a moment. "Hm, that's highly interesting. You see, at this moment there's a Danish Viking raiding party in the Blackwater Estuary. They've beached their longships on Osea Island."

Eldor Aefnoth addressed his father. "Let me lead a force against the Vikings and teach them to avoid our territory in future."

"No, my son. I have other plans. I'll explain in a moment."

Eddie listened intently, not knowing where this was leading.

The Ealdorman spoke to Eddie. "I want you to accompany my son on an expedition to spy on the Vikings. As you can speak their language, you may be able to hear what their plans are and report back. I'd also like the two of you to try to capture one of these scopes. I'm curious to examine one and establish whether it may be of some military use to us."

Eldor Aefnoth spoke petulantly. "I can do it by myself, Father. I'm a noble and an experienced warrior. I don't need any help from underlings."

Byrhtnoth's response was low and paternal. "I understand your feelings, my son. But in this case I need you to have an interpreter."

Eldor Aefnoth sighed.

Ealdorman Byrhtnoth attempted to humour his son. "King Aethelred has ordered me to defend the whole coast from East Anglia to London while he's away on an expedition. Thus it would be extremely useful to glean as much intelligence about the Vikings' plans as possible."

At that moment on Osea Island an old grey-haired and bearded Viking sat with his most experienced men round a cooking fire. The burning logs were still full of sap so they spat and crackled as the flames curled around them.

A young giant of a man was giving vent to his feelings. "I say we raid the Maldon Burh tomorrow at dawn. The Saxon King's mint is there full to the brim with silver. Why are we wasting time raiding isolated farms and churches? If we capture their silver hoard, there will be plenty for all of us to return home rich men!"

Eric Greybeard nodded his head. Eric was a muscular man, very tall with long grey hair and beard, and a drooping moustache, both ends of which he was rolling in his fingers. He had old battle scars on his nose and cheek. Eric was fifty three, much older than most of his men. He was exceptionally fit for his age.

"Agnar," he said, "I understand your feelings and your haste to return to Denmark. Your young wife is with child and will deliver your firstborn to you in a few weeks."

Agnar reddened. He stood up and kicked a pile of logs. "That's not the only reason I want to raid Maldon Burh. I need the silver to buy us our own farm. Also I'm a warrior and crave to fight in a real battle. Intimidating a few farmers or priests isn't what I've trained all my life for."

A few of the younger Vikings nodded, murmuring agreement with Agnar.

The Viking Chieftain Eric Greybeard also stood. He looked Agnar directly in the eyes. "Agnar, we are a small party… ten longships with three hundred warriors. Do you realize how many men they will have? We'd be outnumbered by ten to one at least."

Agnar snapped, "We Viking warriors are ten times braver than those soft Saxons."

Eric Greybeard sighed. "Yes, we may well be braver, but think! They hold the silver you crave in a walled town, a Burh. To take a fortified town we'd need to vastly outnumber them, not the other way round. In addition, they're on their home territory and could muster reinforcements, while we are limited to the men already here. They could also defend until our supplies run out, which wouldn't be long."

Agnar's shoulders hunched, his mouth sagged at the corners and he slowly shook his head.

Eric Greybeard put his arm round Agnar's shoulder. "Agnar, you're a brave warrior like your father before you. But you must understand that in attacking such a numerically superior force, we would be unlikely to succeed. If you are killed for no gain, not only would you never get to meet your first child, but you would also leave it and your pretty young wife destitute."

Agnar put his arm round Eric's shoulder and the two came together briefly in a man-hug. "You're called Greybeard for your wisdom. You're our leader, so I'll defer to your judgement."

In the Maldon Burh the Saxon General, Ealdorman Byrhtnoth turned to his son and Eddie. "You are both tall, so with the right clothes the Vikings will hopefully mistake you for some of their absorbed ex-captives. We have genuine captured Norse clothing in stock to supply you both with an authentic Viking look."

He addressed Eddie. "So will you do this for me?"

As it had been more a command than a request, Eddie realized it was impossible to refuse without looking less than loyal.

"Yes, my lord, I will do it."

"Aefnoth," said the Ealdorman, "your best chance of getting onto Osea Island unseen would be to try to cross the causeway tomorrow night. There will be a neap tide. That means an extremely low water level, allowing more time to traverse the raised path."

Eddie said, "May I pose a question my lord?"

"Go ahead."

"Why don't we sail over on our warship, or go across in a rowing boat in the dark? We could pick an area to land far away from the Vikings camp?"

Byrhtnoth immediately shook his head. "That's a smart question, but my boat spies tell me the Vikings are aware of their vulnerability to this option. They have sentries at crucial points so they can ensure no sea craft get near them. I authorized a dummy run with a muffled-oared rowing boat. It was a dark night, but they were still spotted and attacked by the Viking's archers."

Eddie nodded his understanding.

Ealdorman Byrhtnoth gave them each two silver coins worth sixpence to use in emergencies. Eddie examined the coins. King Aethelred's name was on them so he assumed the image that was similar to one of the paintings was also the King. He also noted they'd been hammer stamped with a die rather than being moulded.

Ealdorman Byrhtnoth then said formally, "This is my son, heir and battle deputy, Eldor Aefnoth, who will be in charge of the expedition."

Eldor Aefnoth was a fine figure of a man, very tall like his father. He had a rough-hewn handsome face with long dark hair and shaved chin. Eddie thought if he himself was considered tall, Aefnoth and his father were giants in comparison to the average Saxon male.

After the audience with Ealdorman Byrhtnoth, Eddie accompanied Aefnoth to the armoury a hundred yards further inside the Burhs earth walls. The two men were fitted out with Viking clothing by the battle-training instructor, Thegn Aelfhere, and the quartermaster slaves, Edwold and Dunnere.

These were long woollen smocks with separate front and back panels and set-in sleeves. Roughly rectangular brick-red cloaks were held together with very large cloak pins. They were also given a pair each of itchy, woven-wool trousers. These were yellow and red, baggy garments held up with drawstrings.

Thegn Maccus, the weapons expert, supplied them each with a Viking style double-edged sword and a short single-edged seaxe dagger. Ealdorman Byrhtnoth had decided any more arms would be out of keeping in a non-battle situation, as well as too cumbersome for covert operations.

Eldor Aefnoth ordered Eddie to meet him at the stables two hours before sunrise. Then Aefnoth turned his back and marched briskly off towards his own quarters. Eddie had the distinct impression the Eldor was not keen to have him as company on this mission.

That evening, Eddie returned to Kate's quarters in the great hall and told her what Ealdorman Byrhtnoth had asked him to do.

Kate commented, "As my bodyguard you're never here to guard my body. Perhaps I shall have to find someone more reliable."

Eddie's face fell. He looked down at the floor and started to shuffle his feet. Then he glanced up and realized the beautiful princess was stifling a grin with her dainty hand over her pretty mouth. She was just teasing him.

Eddie pretended to look hurt and Edith, one of Kate's handmaidens said, "It's alright, you can be *my* bodyguard, Edward."

With that, Kate and her three maids burst into girly laughter.

Kate said, "Don't worry. My fiancé, Eldor Aefnoth, had already informed me that his father wished to borrow you for a few days. I am a princess, remember. I could have refused had I wanted to. I've agreed to release you for this mission only. But I have insisted you're restored to my service as soon as you return."

Eddie breathed a sigh of relief. "Thank you, Kate. I'll be your servant and bodyguard for as long as you'll have me."

Kate wrinkled her nose. "Er, there is one problem, Edward."

Eddie shook his head, scratched the side of his nose and gave her a pensive glance.

Kate pushed her tongue against her bottom lip. "Those balloon trousers," she said sternly. "Viking funny pants; I don't like them at all."

"I know what you mean, Kate. They do look odd, but they're surprisingly comfortable, apart from being a bit itchy."

"That's okay, then. Although you're dark, and as you've not shaved and your hair is long and lank, you really look the part of a Viking. Mind you, I don't like you in that horrible scruffy beard. It makes you look old. When you get back, I'm going to have it shaved off whether you like it or not."

All three of Kate's handmaidens offered to shave off his beard on his return and Bretwalda said, "Then I shall bath him, as he'll be in no state to serve our princess after several days in those horrible Viking clothes."

"Behave, girls," Kate said, giggling with them. "Just keep safe," she said to Eddie and then beamed at him.

Eddie was overcome by Kate's smile. Her wide blue eyes sparkled and her naturally red lips pursed into a heart shape. He tried to answer his beautiful royal patron. "I w...will be back as soon as... as I can, Kate." Eddie didn't usually stutter, but he was quite overcome by Kate's allure.

The expedition was leaving early the next morning and Eddie needed to get some rest. As he left, he glanced back, noticing with surprise that Kate's cheeks had coloured to a fetching blush. She even wore a shy expression. Surely that couldn't have been caused by his presence?

As he walked away from the girl he idolized, Eddie daydreamed that one day they would become an item. But he knew in his heart this was only wishful thinking on his part. A princess and a freeman just couldn't match up socially. Even worse, he was about to go on a two-person mission with Kate's fiancé. If Aefnoth had any suspicions about his relationship with Kate it could be extremely dangerous for him.

In the early hours of the following morning, Eddie rose and dressed in his Viking apparel. It was still dark and stars filled the clear sky, suggesting a lack of cloud and a hot day to follow. But at that moment a cool sea mist hung around the Burh, making him shiver.

As Eddie headed towards the stables, an orange-coloured, mangy fox crossed his path. It had a struggling wild duck in its jaws. The canny fox ignored him and disappeared into its lair under a pile of horse manure.

When Eddie arrived at the stables meeting place, Eldor Aefnoth introduced him to their escorts for the trip. Thegn Leofsunu, a short but powerful man, was in charge of four other tough-looking, scarred veteran warriors, all dressed in their normal Saxon attire. This, Aefnoth explained, was to trick any Vikings into thinking they were an escort party guarding two Norse prisoners.

They left at dawn astride short but strong dumpy ponies, except for Aefnoth's and Eddie's, whose heights necessitated bigger mounts.

After riding down the very steep, cobbled Maldon Hill, the party progressed to Heybridge Basin. When they reached Mill Beach, they moved on to cross two shallow rivers. By now, despite the early morning chill, their mounts were sweaty from their efforts and a distinctive horsy smell blended with the ozone and salty air that wafted in on the sea breeze.

Nearing Decoy Point at the mainland end of the causeway to Osea Island, they dismounted. Thurston, one of the escorts, a short, balding man, tied the horses behind the elm and beech tree line. This was to shield them from the island.

Aefnoth sent two other escorts, Byrhwold and Aethelgr, out as scouts, one in each direction. This was an attempt to locate the positions of the Vikings on the Island. The rest of the party moved as near to the water's edge as they dared. This was to check if there was any hostile movement on the causeway. The men lay down in the rough shore grasses. Unfortunately, the scent from the sea holly's grey-blue flowers was so sweet and overpowering it made Eddie sneeze. Aefnoth shot him a stern glance, concerned that his sneezing could attract the enemy's attention.

From their position on the high point of the promontory, Eddie gazed at the panorama to the seaward side of Decoy Point. Their position was adjacent to the causeway. A quarter of a mile away across the sea into the estuary, he could see Osea. It was a large island obscuring the whole horizon to the east from their ground level viewpoint. In the moonlight he could see that the island appeared to be mainly covered with trees and bushes.

Eddie pointed out to Aefnoth a cart track leading from the end of the causeway directly into the island's interior.

"We daren't use that," Aefnoth replied. "It's probably guarded nearer the Viking camp. We may have to cut our way though the undergrowth to avoid detection."

Eddie's eyes followed the island's shoreline. "There's another alternative," he suggested. "A ring of sandy beach surrounds the island. That will give us the option of skirting around it to try to find a subsidiary path that would lead us inland."

Aefnoth looked irritated. His reply was terse. "It's possible. I'll decide on the strategy later."

The three guards lying in watch for any Viking movement with Aefnoth and Eddie were Thegn Leofsunu and the two brothers, Wulfmaer and Thurston. They were all huscarls, professional warriors. Tough looking guys, they had fought many skirmishes. This was indicated by the amount of obvious battle scars each one had on his face and arms. After the two scouts returned, they'd make a potent fighting force. The pair's backs would be well defended while they tried to cross to the island.

As the tide ebbed, Eddie was surprised that the causeway meandered rather than going straight to the island. Because of this he surmised it was a natural bank rather than a man-made roadway.

While they waited, Aefnoth spoke in a very authoritarian tone to Eddie. "You must always remember that I am in charge and you must obey my orders immediately."

"I agree with that while we are here, or alone on Osea Island. But this will have to be suspended should we contact the Vikings, because if they hear you speaking Saxon, we'll both be killed."

Eldor Aefnoth instantly flew into a rage. He stood up and drew his sword with its horn pommel handle, pointing it at Eddie threateningly. "You must remember your place. I am Eldor of the Langford Hundred, Lord of a hundred hides. That's over ten thousand acres of land that reach all the way to Ulting in the west."

Eddie automatically raised his hands protectively in front of him. "You're the boss, but you may be giving our cover away by standing?"

Aefnoth lay down again but was definitely not amused at having his potentially disastrous mistake pointed out by a Ceorl. He spoke again, even more aggressively. "You must not attempt to tell me what to do. You have to accept my supremacy without question. I am a noble by birth and a seasoned warrior, while you were only a slave until a short while ago. Just because my father in his generosity made you a Ceorl, a common freeman, that only makes you that. You're not even a Thegn."

Eddie was taken aback by this rant. Then he replied in a low conciliatory tone, "I agree you've a far higher status than me. But your father ordered me to accompany you as I'm the only one who can speak the Viking languages. Without that skill, your father's mission will probably fail."

Arrogantly Eldor Aefnoth spat out, "Haven't I just told you not to question your better's authority?" Aefnoth's countenance contorted into a snarling grimace. His eyes widened and he lunged towards Eddie.

It was only Thegn Leofsunu's intercedence that calmed the volatile situation. "My lord, wouldn't it be best to carry out your father's instructions first, and then you can discipline him at your leisure?"

Aefnoth hesitated then sheathed his sword, uttering a threat. "Edward the Tall, you have not heard the last of this."

Eddie could not remain silent. "I do understand... and agree that you are by far my superior. However, if we don't resolve this disagreement now it will be too late when we cross the causeway. Please consider this: it is true I was initially enslaved by your father. But this was because the unreliable Eldor Godric made an error as usual, and mistakenly identified me as a Viking."

Aefnoth was red-faced and indignant. "So? What difference does that make?" he roared.

Eddie persisted. "Well, my lord, what slave do you know who can read, write and speak several languages? Aren't these talents normally restricted to priests, nobles and scriveners?"

Aefnoth thought for a while. His reply was spoken with some reluctance. "Yes, that is true, but you are still of a far inferior status compared to me."

"Of course that is so. I am completely your subordinate. Though remember I killed several Vikings at the Maylandsea raid despite initially being unarmed. Could I have done that if I were not a warrior? Also, would I have dared contradict the son of England's premier general if I were naturally a slave or even a peasant?"

Aefnoth's face turned red with rage and Eddie expected another tirade. However, Aefnoth hesitated, considering this for a while before calming down. His shoulders relaxed and his tight fists opened.

"I had not considered this. You are right; you must be a noble warrior or you would not possess the knowledge to have done those things."

Eddie also felt calmer now. "Then may I make some suggestions?"

Aefnoth's mouth opened, baring his teeth as he curled his bottom lip. Eddie was wary, expecting another haranguing from the Eldor. But Aefnoth's face took on a more benevolent expression. He nodded at Eddie. "Go ahead."

"As your father commanded, if the Vikings see us, we must pretend to be local absorbed ex-slaves. It's important as they will know we didn't come in the longships with them."

"I suppose so," Aefnoth mumbled sulkily.

"I'll have to do the talking, because you can't. You are tall, so you will not seem suspicious unless you speak. For just this phase of the mission, could you pretend to be a mute Ceorl? This will obviously be hard for you, having always had your will obeyed immediately."

"Yes, I see your point. I'll do it," Aefnoth agreed half-heartedly.

Some time later the Saxon spies returned. Byrhwold, a sturdy bearded warrior, had circled to the left. He reported that he'd seen campfires and ten longships on the opposite side of the island to the causeway. This confirmed the intelligence the Ealdorman had supplied.

Aethelgr, a taller, swarthy warrior with long, lank, black hair had investigated the island to the right. He had not spotted any longships. But he described how he'd seen two sentries in the bushes. These were to the right of the causeway on the island side.

He also noted that two fresh guards had been substituted for the original sentries about half an hour earlier.

Aefnoth instructed Aethelgr to continue watching the sentries to see if a pattern could be established as to how often they were relieved.

He announced to Eddie, "We'll cross after dark and kill the sentries."

Eddie was worried about this impulsive reaction. "With respect, my lord, if we try that, they will resist and raise the alarm. Even if we could kill them quietly, the next relief sentries will find their predecessor's bodies, or at least that they're missing. The Danes will then know they've got enemies on the Island and our cover will be blown."

Aefnoth sneered, threw his head back to shake the long hair out of his eyes and said sarcastically, "So have you got a better plan, then?"

"Well, I have a suggestion for your consideration. May I propose that under the cloak of darkness we creep across the causeway and lie low? Then, when the sentries change, we may get the opportunity to slip past unnoticed."

Aefnoth was unhappy at not making all the decisions. But he reluctantly agreed to this plan, adding petulantly, "Don't try to push me too far."

Eddie could feel the presence of a Druid. He couldn't see anything but he knew it was there. It was telling him to be careful… that if they were seen at this stage there wouldn't be a second chance. Then the Druid's influence faded completely. He couldn't fathom out what the Druids wanted from him, but they seemed to be always there in the background. However, at least they seemed to be friendly and certainly not malevolent.

He thought about the mission, wondering what chance it had. He was going onto an island occupied by homicidal Vikings. His only companion was an arrogant man more used to challenging opponents by direct force than subterfuge.

He had real forebodings about the entire assignment. This whole escapade could become an extremely dangerous blunder.

Fifteen

The earlier warmth was fading as the evening sea breeze drained its strength. This made lying motionless by the seashore far less comfortable for the Saxon spying party. To the east, Osea Island had taken on a reddish glow as the sun descended below the line of trees. Wavelets on the Blackwater Estuary shimmered red and silver.

A pair of narrow-winged arctic terns hovered above the concealed Saxons. The two birds repeatedly swooped towards the men, calling with their distinctive 'Kee! Kee!' Aefnoth's inclination was to swat the birds away, but he resisted in case it compromised their own camouflage. The irritation of course did nothing to improve his mood.

Aethelgr, who had been watching the Viking sentries' movements, crawled towards the Saxon group through the blue-green spiky sedge grass. This further infuriated the aggressive birds who turned their full fury onto the unfortunate man. Aethelgr shielded his scalp with his hands, only to have his fingers viciously pecked. The guard cursed the birds loudly. Aefnoth ordered him to keep his voice down.

Eventually the terns seemed satisfied they'd made their point about the unwelcome human invasion of their territory. As the tidal water receded, they flew off, landing on the re-emerging mud banks, most probably to feed on crustaceans and worms.

Aethelgr sucked on his fingers where the tern's sharp beak had drawn blood. Then he made his report to Eldor Aefnoth. "Sir, the Viking sentries were changed after about four hours."

Aefnoth nodded. "Well done, Aethelgr. If they keep roughly to that timing, the next change-over will coincide with the night's low tide. That will fit in with my plans admirably. We need to be in place on the far side of the causeway at the earliest time the tide allows."

Aethelgr found a piece of cloth and wound it around his bleeding fingers and then lay back, contracting his brows and staring sullenly at the first emerging stars.

While waiting for the tide to recede, Eddie made a mental assessment of the two islands nearest to Maldon in the Blackwater Estuary, considering their suitability as Viking bases.

The nearby Osea Island was the bigger island. Its causeway looked to be about a quarter of a mile long. Ealdorman Byrhtnoth had said it was only crossable for two hours per tide. Because of

Osea's situation on the north shore of the Blackwater Estuary, it was a considerable distance from the Maldon Burh. Logistically it would be a nightmare to use as an attack platform. In contrast, it would be easy to defend, as any large scale troop movements coming from Maldon were likely to be detected, even in the dark.

Northey Island, on the other hand, though smaller, was situated on the south side of the Blackwater Estuary. It was less than half a mile away from the Burh. Its causeway was only a hundred yards long, giving ample time for an attacking army to cross at low water and reach Maldon. From Northey any Viking assault could be mounted quickly with reinforcements and supplies easily accessed at low tides. Thus he reasoned it had more invasion base potential against the Maldon Burh.

Eddie's final evaluation was that, logically, any attacking force would use Northey and a defensive one, Osea. Therefore, he considered these Vikings on Osea Island at the moment were likely to be resting and, hopefully, their sentries would be fairly relaxed.

Eddie told Aefnoth of his conclusions and the Eldor grudgingly agreed with his assessment.

After covering all their visible skin with the black, evil-smelling mud, the duo moved cautiously from their hiding place at Decoy Point. It was now 1.00am; half an hour before low tide. Seawater was still washing over the causeway, making it difficult for them to keep their footing. This worried Aefnoth as he'd admitted he couldn't swim.

Salty spray flew over them on the increasing wind, leaving their clothing soaking wet and the two men themselves cold and uncomfortable. In addition they were engulfed with the overpowering odours of salt water, ozone and rotting seaweed.

Startled by strange whooshing noises above their heads, the pair dropped to the waterlogged ground. Eddie's heart raced and adrenalin pumped in anticipation as his fight or flight response kicked in. With relief he realized it was only the wing beats and white ghostly shapes of two swans flying low overhead. In the darkness, reflections from the flowing waves and the sound from the magnificent birds had given a touch of surrealism to this already tense situation.

When the two men approached the island they stopped and lay down on the wet and slimy causeway. Although it was early summer, the freshening breeze and dampness created a potent wind-chill factor that made them both shiver.

After a few minutes Aefnoth spotted the glint of what was probably a weapon, pinpointing the sentry's positions in the bushes just to their right.

Eddie whispered to Aefnoth, "If we get slightly off the causeway on the left where it slopes down, we can crawl forward. Then wait for an opportunity to creep into those elderwood clumps just ahead on the island."

On the east side of the Island, Eric Greybeard and most of his Danish Vikings were sleeping, wrapped in their cloaks and blankets. 'Strong-arms' Rasmussen, a trusted older warrior, had woken up and allocated the last replacement sentries for the night.

Rasmussen was the same age as Eric Greybeard. They had *gone Viking* together since their first raid at fifteen. It was Eric who'd nicknamed him Strong-arms as his massive biceps were disproportionate to his otherwise wiry frame. Rasmussen's body was scarred from many battles. Now he was balding, the long red weal on his scalp from a Saxon sword blow was always visible.

Now Rasmussen's job was finished for the night he could rest. He poked his fire and then threw more fir branches and cones onto it. The veteran Viking smiled with satisfaction as newly kindled flames warmed his chilled body and the smoke's fragrance relaxed him. Wrapping his cloak around him and pulling his knees up to ensure his feet wouldn't get cold, Strong-arms settled down for what was left of the night.

However, Rasmussen was unaware that two interlopers were attempting to break through his carefully prepared defensive cordon.

On the causeway on the west side of the island Aefnoth whispered to Eddie, "My tactics are to try to get into the cover of the island before the new sentries take over, as I assume fresh minds are likely to be more alert initially."

Eddie nodded. But they hadn't been able to move off before the replacement sentries arrived. Confusingly, the new Viking sentries kept low and crept up on their comrades. Suddenly, these ran into the bushes screaming loudly. Obviously this was a game the youths enjoyed playing.

While the Vikings distracted each other, Aefnoth and Eddie took their chance. Bent double, they sneaked onto the island and were soon concealed in the elder shrubs.

Large clusters of white elderflower swayed in the breeze. Unfortunately, as Eddie well knew, they smelled like sugared cat pee. Although smelling awful, Eddie remembered the Romanies ate the flower umbrellas raw, fried them as fritters or made them into elderflower champagne. He picked and ate some of the flowers, but Aefnoth couldn't get past their vile scent.

Aefnoth again whispered to Eddie, "I've decided the moon's too bright for us to attempt to walk along the sand to locate another path to the interior. Our only logical route will be to go directly through the undergrowth."

Eddie wasn't certain that Aefnoth was right, but he didn't want to antagonize the Eldor. "You're the boss," was all he said.

Unfortunately, as Eddie had suspected, when they crawled away the terrain was less than hospitable. In the semi-darkness an abundance of stinging nettles made their presence felt. Both men were badly stung. The stiff hairs of the plants' leaves had effectively injected formic acid and histamine into their bare skin.

Luckily, being Romani, Eddie knew the best way to soothe the nettle rash. By the light of the moon he located some clumps of dock leaves. Using the soothing sap found at the base of the leafstalks, they coated the hives, reducing the pain immediately.

When Aefnoth considered they were far enough away from the sentries, they stood up. Although they could now walk upright this didn't save them from being prickled and scratched by the masses of brambles and thorn bushes in their path.

Blackbirds flew away, sounding their warning cries. Unseen animals scuttled out of their way. Flowers, crushed under their feet, gave off their varying scents. In stark contrast was the stench of the methane fumes, or marsh gas, from the decaying material in the rotting bogs. These organic stink bombs were inescapable as the pair couldn't tell what was underfoot.

Eddie, who had been there briefly when he was a Norwegian galley slave, was aware that Osea Island was fairly narrow and shouldn't take them long to cross, even through this inhospitable terrain, especially now that their eyes were fully attuned to the moonlight.

However, they were thankful when they reached a small stream. This allowed them to drink by cupping the sweet tasting spring water in their hands. They used it to clean off their mud camouflage and further soothe the irritation from the nettle rash.

As they moved over the top of a ridge they saw flames and smelt the smoke from cooking fires, indicating the direction of the Viking camp.

Aefnoth told Eddie, "It's essential that we press on to find a place to hide before it gets light."

"I agree, boss."

Soon they could see in the moonlight a line of ten Viking longships pulled up on the far beach with sentries guarding them. They could also see several campfires near some wooden farm buildings.

"I can only pick out a few blanketed figures lying by the fires so it's likely most men are in the buildings," Eddie mentioned.

"You are probably right, Edward. We will take cover on that ridge overlooking the Viking camp."

Aefnoth had made a good choice. The mound was covered with elm and crab apple trees. They had soon eaten a few of the small, sharp apples. Hidden in the bramble bushes, they settled down to rest for the few remaining hours of darkness. Wrapped in his cloak, Aefnoth was soon asleep. However, Eddie sensed they were not alone, and sure enough, a black-robed Druid appeared. He could feel its communication rather than hear it. It was saying, '*These Vikings are led by a wise man. Be bold and he will teach you important truths. Now sleep.*'

When they awoke there was a lot activity round the camp fires with the mouth-watering smells of breakfast food cooking. The smell of porridge and roasting pork wafted in the wind, making them feel hungry. Apart from the few crab apples and elderflowers, they hadn't eaten for twelve hours.

From their hiding place on the ridge they could see a multi-coloured vegetable patch, no doubt originally owned by the previous Saxon inhabitant. Now the Saxon peasant's lovingly tendered kitchen garden was being plundered by the Vikings.

Further away, between two narrow avenues of trees, could be seen the blue-green of the shimmering sea under an azure sky. Only a few wispy, white cumulus clouds broke the perfect, natural vista.

Unfortunately, this peaceful panorama was completely spoilt by a foreground that was filled by armed men and instruments of warfare. Ten Viking longships were pulled up on what, at any other time, would probably be an ideal fishing beach.

The Vikings had affixed their shields along the ships' gunwales. This gave an attractive, though chilling, scalloped effect to the tops of the warships. At each end of the line of ships stood sentries holding spears, their burnished blades flashing menacingly in the morning sunlight.

"Look," Eddie said. "Can you see what that look-out's holding to his eyes?"

"I can see something. Is that the instrument you were talking about?"

"Yes. It looks like a scope of some sort."

Aefnoth asked, "How can we get hold of one?"

"We've got two choices. Try and obtain one either by force or by guile. What do you think, boss?"

Aefnoth paused to consider this. "We're well out numbered. There are at least three hundred of them, I'd judge, against two of us. I'm a warrior, a natural fighter, but I can see the odds aren't good here. Although I am not afraid to die, that would not fulfil this expedition's objective. So if you know a way we can do it, let's try cunning."

"Right."

A few moments later, in the distance, Eddie saw a couple of Viking canoes being paddled across the water towards the longships. He pointed them out to Aefnoth. "They're probably some of the settled Danes. If they are, it may be our chance. Let them land and then we'll attempt to join in with them and hopefully neither group will realize where we really came from."

Boldly, Aefnoth and Eddie broke cover and, swinging their arms, laughing and gesticulating, they strolled down to the beach. The canoes were about fifteen feet long with open decks. They were 'clinch built', using overlapping boarding in the same way as the longships. Knowing he was a competent canoeist, Eddie was certain he could handle one of these if they needed to use one to escape.

However, he was surprised when he realized these were combination vessels. As well as single-bladed paddles, they were also fitted with rowlocks to accommodate the two oars that were on board. Additionally, there was a small, folded down mast and flattened sail, making them extremely versatile craft.

As the canoes beached, Eddie spoke to the paddlers in Danish. "You're welcome, friends."

The first canoeist smiled. "It's our pleasure to visit you," he replied.

Aefnoth and Eddie walked with the newcomers towards the campfires. Aefnoth remained at the back, so nobody spoke to him. As they neared the Vikings' camp the pair dropped back, so neither Norse faction would realize they weren't from the other party.

The newly arrived Norsemen moved into the Viking camp. When the canoeists were out of sight, Aefnoth and Eddie followed them into their enemy's temporary headquarters. Both hoped they didn't look too out of place in their disguises.

Eddie's palms were sweating and he could sense that Aefnoth was as tense as he was. The big warrior's eyes had developed a twitch. Both men's hands had the tendency to automatically wander towards their sword grips. Eddie had to mentally stop this habit or it would have looked suspicious.

As they reached a small clearing they were stopped by a Viking who told them his name was Ericsson. He was a muscular warrior, at least as tall as Aefnoth and powerfully built.

The mighty Viking asked, "Who are you, ex-slaves who've joined our great Danish Viking community? Do you live here at peace with the enemy? Are you cowards?"

"No," Eddie answered in Danish. "We're not cowards or great warriors like you. We were born in Germany and have rowed in your comrades' longships. Now we're just ex-slave farmers in England. However, we'd like to learn more of your Norse ways so we can fight by your side."

Ericsson leaned towards them. He was so near that Eddie could smell wild garlic on the Viking's breath. The big warrior's eyes narrowed as he examined the pair's faces suspiciously.

Although still dubious, Ericsson nodded. "You speak well but you'd not be ready to do battle like we Norse heroes do. Come to meet our leader, Eric Greybeard. I'll see if he'll explain about our legends and Gods that make us great."

With apprehension, the pair followed Ericsson into the largest clearing. This had several Saxon buildings and was surrounded by ash, elm, and fir trees. Viking weapons were stacked in neat personal piles ready for use immediately if needed. Some Vikings sharpened their blades with elongated steels. Others tended fires and cooked food. A youth was slowly rotating a pig on a spit. That was where the delectable pork aroma was coming from.

Ericsson led them to the biggest campfire. There, an older, grey-haired man was using a wooden spoon to taste the sweet-smelling broth cooking in a large cauldron. His young cook companion was roasting a hare on a spit.

"This is Eric Greybeard, my father. He is our great leader and wise man."

Eddie was impressed with the tall and muscular physique of the Viking leader, estimating that Eric was well over fifty. However, if the big man's hair, beard and moustache hadn't been grey he could have passed for a much younger man.

Ericsson spoke softly to the older man who nodded his head as if in agreement. "Eric has agreed to tell you absorbed Germans how you can become brave Vikings like us," Ericsson said.

Eric Greybeard spoke, "I see you are surprised at my age for a Viking leader. The reason for that is because the grand Danish council exiled me for two years, as I'd killed a man with my bare hands in a fight. Although I'll be glad to explain our sagas and phenomenal history, be warned, Germans, any sign of betrayal will result in your immediate death."

Eddie replied, "We would be greatly honoured. When I was very young I lived with my family and worked on a farm near Thyboran in the north of your great country of Denmark. Unfortunately, as a teenager when I was fishing in the fiord, I was captured by marauding Norwegians and made to row in their longships."

Eric face relaxed. "I know Thyboran well, and that's only a little to the north of my own home village."

Eddie continued, "When they came to this country, I escaped. However, as you may imagine, I regretted that my capture took away from me the opportunity to learn your Danish ways so that I could fight alongside your heroes."

Eric pointed to several large logs. "Sit there by the fire and take some broth and hare, and I'll tell you a little of what motivates us."

Gratefully, the two newcomers accepted the food. The sweet-smelling broth tasted of mixed herbs. The roast hare smelt delicious and was soft and tender with a strong game influence.

Eric told them, "You see, we Vikings have to raid because the sparse amount of farmland in our mother country has become over-populated. Another of the reasons we need new land is because we follow the system of primogeniture. This means all of a Norse family's fortune is left to the eldest son. This is done to ensure that the farms are not reduced in size until they're incapable of supporting a big family.

"Consequently, the younger sons of Norsemen need to gain wealth, fame and land to get homes of their own. So they're forced to go to other countries to seek their fortunes. Thus our drive to *go Viking* and expand is fuelled by this need."

Eddie stretched his legs out. "Yes, I understand."

"Our great pagan religion guides all our people's lives. We believe death is the end for all but a few, such as the chosen warriors who die in battle. These fortunate ones enjoy the pleasures of Valhalla. Other good men who die naturally go with the Goddess Hel to the underground. This is a kind of boring waiting room where dead people's souls float around as shadows without a body. And then the really bad people, like oath-breakers, thieves and the like, are taken to Niflheim for eternal torment."

Eddie nodded and leaned nearer to the Viking leader.

"So you see, since there's no acceptable afterlife for most people, the only thing that survives after death is reputation.

Therefore it is worth risking everything to gain and protect your good name."

Eddie gestured his understanding. "Yes," he said, "I can see how important reputation and honour must be."

Eric expectorated noisily, depositing a gob of phlegm on the ground, and then continued. "Our second key belief is that the time of your death is determined by fate. There's nothing one can do to change the moment of one's demise. But what you do up to that moment is in your own hands. Therefore you should make the best use of every second of life. This is because the worst that can happen is a dishonourable death and the best is fame. Since your death is predestined you cannot affect its timing. So there's nothing to lose and everything to gain by being bold and adventurous. You must bear in mind that the power of fate is limited in one respect. It cannot touch the core of any man's being."

Eddie scratched his head. "Eric, I'm having difficulty understanding what you mean by that. Can you clarify it for me?"

"I'll try." He looked pensive for a moment. "I know... I'll tell you a saga to illustrate my meaning."

"Oh, thank you. What an excellent idea."

Aefnoth was fidgeting, his lips silently moving. His boredom was obvious and he made as if to speak. But Eddie shook his head and held a palm up to stop him. Aefnoth regained his composure and sat down, putting his elbow on his knee and leaning his chin on his hand.

Eric looked suspiciously at Aefnoth, and then relaxed again. He entwined his fingers together and clicked all his knuckles. Then, with his eyes gleaming, he stood in a heroic pose and with obvious relish began telling the saga.

"A farmer accompanied his young son to the warship for his first raiding party and gave him the following advice. 'Be valiant and hardy in all perils.' Then he asked his son, 'How would you act if you were engaged in battle and knew beforehand you were destined to be killed?' His son answered, 'I'd fight hard for my reputation.' The farmer smiled with satisfaction, then asked his son, 'Now suppose someone could tell you for certain you wouldn't be killed?' His son replied, 'Then there would be no reason not to be brave.' So the farmer stated, 'In every battle where you're present, one of two things will happen: you'll either fall or come away alive. Be bold, therefore, for everything's preordained. Nothing can bring a man to his death if his time hasn't come. Also, nothing can save one who is doomed to die. Remember, to die in flight is the worst death of all.'
"

Eric smiled. "So you see, it's expected that every Danish man should take whatever befalls him with unshakable courage and equanimity, fighting to the bitter end, even in the face of certain defeat and death."

Eddie said, "Thank you, Eric, for that story. You have great wisdom. Now that we understand, we would like to become as bold as you Danes."

In the Maldon Burh, Princess Catherine was by herself. She had sent her handmaidens away as their constant chattering and giggling was getting on her nerves. She was pondering what was happening to her fiancé, Eldor Aefnoth, and her bodyguard, Edward the Tall. She was fully aware that both could have been killed by now. Many of her relatives and girlhood companions had died violently. Her uncle, King Edward, the previous King, had been stabbed to death on his horse.

Kate sighed, reflecting that she was not in love with Aefnoth. She had been ordered by her father, King Aethelred, to marry him. Saxon princesses had to marry whom their most senior male relative ordered them to.

Princess Catherine, Kate, as she preferred to be called, looked in the mirror. She adjusted the pins holding her blonde hair in a bun and let her flowing tresses fall to waist level. She felt more comfortable that way.

She was well aware Aefnoth didn't love her either. He had a girlfriend called Athelflaed, a strikingly pretty girl. Despite this, he'd been ordered by his father, Ealdorman Byrhtnoth, to marry Catherine. Their marriage was purely a business arrangement to link the two premier families of England. Not the romantic love match she'd longed for.

She walked up and down restlessly and, unintentionally, her mind began to wander. Kate remembered being told many stories by her nursemaid when she was a child. They were often about handsome princes who saved princesses like herself, by their gallantry. Then the heroic prince and the princess fell instantly in love, married and lived happily ever after.

Unfortunately, the princes and higher nobles she had met were generally oafs interested in casual sex, but had no romance in their souls. Edward, then just a slave, had been the first gallant male she'd encountered. He'd saved her from falling in that muddy puddle. That act had been spontaneous and even courageous on his part. After all, he could have forfeited his life for merely touching her.

Edward was brave; that was certain. He'd saved her life at the Maylandsea raid. She shook her head, reflecting that he should have been killed. Unarmed and outnumbered, he must be an exceptional warrior to prevail against overwhelming odds. Such valour was befitting a noble, not a lowly slave. She was secretly pleased Ealdorman Byrhtnoth had now freed Edward from his slavery.

He wasn't a prince or even a noble. He was only her servant, her bodyguard. He was even of a different race, a low cast Romani. Forbidden fruit to a princess like her. But he was also tall and handsome… the prince of her dreams.

Kate was aware that Edward fancied her. She'd seen it in his eyes and expressions. In fact, she'd been playing up to him, flirting subtly just to see his reactions. Now, despite her closeted, trained upbringing and royal breeding, she realized with a shock that she was missing Edward and not her fiancé, Aefnoth. She had feelings for Edward, or Eddie as she'd started to think of him. She realized that now. But she knew it could never be. The social gulf was completely impossible.

Why couldn't she have the boy she wanted? Why was it always the men who told the women what they should do?

On the Island, Aefnoth drew in several breaths and brought his hands together lightly and silently. He was a man of action, not used to pretending he couldn't hear. He was used to being a leader, not a follower. He was bored stiff. His inclination was to draw his sword and fight all the Vikings, but he knew that would be stupid.

Aefnoth looked at Eddie contemptuously. This ex-slave was deep in conversation with a hated Viking. He had been taught from a small boy to loathe Vikings. He detested them and their pagan ways. He didn't know how much more humiliation he could take before he exploded into violence.

Eddie asked Eric "Are there any other important points we should know?"

"Yes. Another thing that's vital to understand is that theft is abhorrent."

Eddie looked puzzled by this, contrasting that statement with the fact that the Vikings were constantly stealing from farms and churches.

Eric said, "I see from your expression you don't understand the difference between theft and raiding."

Eddie nodded. "You are right, Eric. Isn't plundering other people's goods theft?"

"Not to us. You see raiding is different as it involves a battle, with the victors taking the booty. That's not only acceptable but is also highly desirable since it enhances men's fame and wealth. Shall I tell you another saga to clarify this?"

"If you would, it may help my understanding."

Eric put some dry branches on the fire, and sat on a log. "The Viking Egill's band, were raiding a coastal farm but were captured by the farmer's family. In the night, Egill slipped his bonds and grabbed the farmer's treasure and went back to his ship. But then Egill realized he was acting like a thief and that was shameful. So he returned and set fire to his former captor's house and killed all the occupants. Then he returned to his ship as a hero. That was because he'd fought and won the battle, so he could justly claim the booty."

"Ah. I think I see the difference now. Thank you, Eric."

Eric smiled then poked the fire with a stick, sending a shower of sparks flying up. One large spark landed on the back of Aefnoth's hand. He shook his arm and then licked his wound.

Eric regarded Aefnoth, who was looking none too happy. "Are you all right?"

When Aefnoth didn't answer, Eric pushed the tip of his tongue between his lips, narrowed his eyes and furrowed his brow. Then with his hand on the hilt of his Seax dagger he stood up and moved towards Aefnoth.

Aefnoth, noticing Eric's hand on his dagger and the Viking coming his way, started to rise. Then the Saxon went red in the face in preparation for a fight. Eddie, seeing this as a confrontation that would end their mission and possibly their lives, intervened. Circumspectly holding Aefnoth down on the log, he addressed Eric. "I'm sorry Eric. This is my fault. I forgot to tell you, my comrade Aefnoth doesn't speak Danish, only German. He means no harm. I'll explain your sagas to him later."

Eddie thought it prudent to ask another question quickly to take Eric's mind away from Aefnoth's suspicious behaviour. "Eric," he said, "Do you Danes raid all the time?"

Eric sat down again, though he was still watching Aefnoth closely. "No," he answered. "What you should remember is that for much of the year most Norsemen are farmers. However, in the summer we farmers have little option than to lead raids if we want to extend our territory sufficiently to feed our multiplying families. Of course only a few members of each family can go on raids, as we have to tend our own crops and gather them in. That's why most Vikings are the young men who can be spared from their fathers' farms."

"I did wonder why most of your Vikings were so youthful."

This relaxed Eric, who went back into his story telling mode. "Most young Norsemen see going on a raid more as a rite of passage to manhood. So at the age of around fifteen, the prospect of forever continuing the daily toil of working on his father's farm has lost its charm. Remember that from an early age they would have heard sagas of heroism and adventure told around the fires by the heroes. Added to this, most lads would also have seen their older brothers and friends come back with booty, including captured women. So you see, to them the prospect of a raid is like an adventure or a holiday. In fact, it's their only chance of gaining honour, treasure and affording their own personal territory."

Eddie nodded. "There's a lot of common sense in what you've just told me, Eric. I appreciate you taking the time to share such wisdom."

After listening to Eric's tales, Eddie and Aefnoth moved away from the clearing towards the sea and the longships. Eddie tried to tell Aefnoth quietly what Eric had been saying. He also complimented him on seeming interested without being able to understand the language.

But Aefnoth did not accept Eddie's attempt to pacify him. He said loudly, in Saxon "I'm unhappy about not understanding what's been said. You might be betraying me, for all I know. I want to leave here now. I'm a warrior. I should be fighting the Vikings, not talking to the heathens. I've seen the carnage they create amongst my people and I will not cosy up to them."

Eddie looked around and realized this had already created a difficult situation. He saw that Aefnoth's demeanour and noisy aggressive talk had been noticed by a group of Vikings. All these Vikings had now drawn their swords and were approaching Aefnoth and Eddie. They looked decidedly menacing.

Sixteen

The sun was shining over the Dengie Hundred in Essex. High in the sky a flock of noisy geese passed over in a chevron, heading north.

On Osea Island, east of Maylandsea in the Blackwater Estuary, Eddie and Aefnoth were walking towards the seashore. Injudiciously, Aefnoth had been loudly ranting at Eddie in his natural Saxon language. In his fury he had not noticed the group of Danes standing within earshot. As they were in the middle of the Viking camp this oversight was at best imprudent, and at worst suicidal.

Some of these Danes had indeed overheard Aefnoth's outburst in what to them was a foreign language. Quite naturally they were suspicious, being on alien soil and close to potential danger from the Saxon fortification at the Maldon Burh. Understandably, it was a group of distinctly hostile Vikings that was now approaching Eddie and Aefnoth.

Eddie whispered to his superior, "I understand your feelings but please don't talk any more now."

Aefnoth looked annoyed with Eddie but then saw the Danes closing in menacingly and just nodded his acquiescence.

The first Viking to reach them, whom Eddie had heard addressed as Agnar, spoke with obvious suspicion in his voice. "What language were you speaking? It certainly wasn't Danish."

Eddie replied in Danish, "You are right. We were speaking German. We are absorbed ex-slaves being taught to become Vikings by your great leader, Eric Greybeard."

Agnar was sceptical. "If that is so, why was this man raising his voice?"

"He's just overwhelmed by the complexity and meanings of your sagas that Eric Greybeard has just told us."

Agnar looked at them dubiously. "Hm, that may be so, but remember I'll be watching you two."

Eddie's palms were sweating again and his arm muscles twitched, but he'd covered up well by using Eric Greybeard's name and they'd got away with it... for now.

When they were well out of the Vikings' earshot, Aefnoth apologized to Eddie. "I'm sorry about that outburst. It is so difficult, pretending to be subservient when I've always been in charge."

Eddie nodded. "I do understand your difficulties. But we must both play this cool or we'll blow your father's mission and lose our lives into the bargain."

When Aefnoth had calmed down, Eddie related Eric's sagas to him. Aefnoth was genuinely impressed. "Now I understand how their mind games allow the Vikings to fight so valiantly, even to the death."

A pair of oystercatchers with black backs, white bellies and long, bright orange bills, screeched noisily at the two men. The feisty and pugnacious birds dived and complained repeatedly at them until they moved further down the beach. Eddie surmised they had a nest nearby. A few seals were fishing in the main channel.

In the far distance, a small rowing boat disappeared into Lawling Creek.

"That's one of my father's spies keeping tabs on the Vikings," Aefnoth exclaimed.

The wind swung round to the west, bringing with it traces of woodsmoke and the aroma of food cooking. Both men were hungry and, following the scents, made their way up the sloping sandy beach. Then they threaded their way through the sea grass and elm trees towards the clearing and the Viking camp.

Crossing the wooded area, Aefnoth spotted a patch of wild strawberries and they picked a handful each. As the fruits were only tiny, this took a few minutes. However, it was well worth it for the unique flavour of the firm, succulent fruits.

When they reached the camp, Ericsson ensured the pair was given some food. It was a meal of roast chicken and vegetable stew washed down with acorn ale. Afterwards they casually walked along to the beach to check out the longships.

The wooden craft were impressive. Most were about eighty feet long by thirteen feet wide, and the largest about a hundred and fifteen by eighteen feet.

On the biggest ship, Eddie noticed there were thirty rowing benches on each side. Most had only room for one rower per side although the rear ones had wider double seats and spaces for sixty-four oarsmen altogether.

He also checked the canoes. These had single bladed oar-like paddles. He'd used similar before, though these were longer and thinner. That didn't matter. He could use any style in an emergency. He was curious about the crafts' other modes of propulsion; the rowlocks and oars, plus the folded down mast and sail. This was a combination he'd never seen before. He concluded that these alternatives indicated they were communal craft, used by various people with different preferences.

At sunset, Eddie was about to settle down by the fire to sleep when, without warning, he felt the strange mental swirling as his Romani higher senses automatically activated. He was having psychic cerebral sensory feelings that only happened spontaneously at times of extreme danger.

Moving from the crowded camp fires area, Eddie walked down onto the deserted sandy beach. He lay down, wrapped himself in his cloak, closed his eyes, relaxed completely and let his mind dictate its own progression.

The automatic remote viewing capacity took over his mind. Immediately he was picking up impressions of waves on an endless sea, not hemmed in by banks. Piece by piece, his brain revealed its targets… wavering mental images of many longships in full sail.

His mind focused on a white and black pennant flapping from a mast in the wind. He sensed this was somehow important and concentrated on the flag. He sensed an image of an evil bird… it was black… a crow.

His mind then flipped away from the pennant and was within the clouds, looking down on the longships. How many longships? He counted ten… sixteen. No, twenty. Yes, it was definitely twenty. Eddie felt as if time and space were spinning together, moving fast in front of this new longship fleet. He was mentally moving at great speed down a coastline he didn't recognize.

Then he noticed something – an ancient Roman signal beacon. Why? Soon he detected images of ten longships on a beach. It was Osea Island again and in his mind, he was lying on the sand.

He realized this new fleet of longships was heading towards Osea Island. He sensed the crews from this new fleet were not friendly. But who were they unfriendly to? Were they a danger to the Saxons in the Maldon Burh? To the Danes? Or to both?

Now his consciousness had rejoined his physical body again. He felt certain he hadn't been dreaming; the images had seemed so authentic. When he'd experienced these spontaneous remote viewing episodes before, they had always been portents of danger and, inevitably, accurate.

He suspected that these episodes were something to do with the Druids. In fact he sensed from the deepest reaches of his brain there was a higher reason controlling him, tied in inextricably with these Druid high priests. Frustratingly, he couldn't work out what.

Intuitively, Eddie also sensed he was meant to pass on what he'd learned. That he was just a conduit between a higher reality, 'them' and the 'normal' world, whatever that was. His difficulty was how to pass on this psychically obtained information to either the Saxons or the Danes? It would be pointless trying to explain the danger to Aefnoth. He wouldn't understand and there would not be time to contact the Burh, even if he did.

Then Eddie's subconscious indicated that he was to warn the Danes. He was happy about that as Eric had been friendly and helpful to him. But how could he do this without revealing what to them would be an improbable source of information? He would have to think about this, but there was very little time, so he knew he had to do it soon.

Eddie went with Aefnoth for breakfast with the Danes. The thick, salty porridge and acorn beer filled his stomach. But he still felt an emptiness inside his mind, knowing he'd been given a mission from somewhere in the psychic realm and had to find a way to fulfil it.

After breakfast Aefnoth and Eddie walked briskly along the sandy beach. They came across Eric and a group of his Danes in a circle. Eric was throwing rune stones to predict the future.

Aefnoth told Eddie, "I've heard of the mystical rune characters that are inscribed on these stones. I remember my monk teachers at the monastery I attended telling me that the runes language was developed from an ancient Germanic alphabet."

Eddie smiled. "I'm impressed, Aefnoth. You really are well educated."

Aefnoth looked pleased. Eddie himself understood the runes' meanings well enough. His mother who had been born into a German Romani family could divine answers to complex problems with them. From an early age he'd been taught the runic meanings and how to interpret them. He'd even ascertained the Danish variants after they had moved to Denmark. This gave Eddie inspiration on how to pass on his psychically received warning. He felt that the solution to his dilemma hinged on Eric and his runes.

When Eric had finished his runic predictions, Eddie asked if he could also try to foretell the future with the runes. Eric sounded dubious but told him, "You can attempt to, but I doubt you'll predict anything as you haven't the lifetime of rune experience I've had." However, he half-heartedly handed Eddie the rune bag, shaking his head as he did so.

Eddie shook the soft leather bag and then cast the runes onto the hard yellow sand. The ones that had landed face upwards he lined up, trying to look deliberately precise about it, and then made his pseudo divination.

Eddie pronounced to Eric and the surrounding Danes, "The runes tell me twenty more longships are approaching this island."

After hearing Eddie's predictions, the big young Viking called Agnar, who had questioned them earlier, laughed contemptuously.

"I don't believe you can predict anything as you're not a Dane, or even a Norseman, just an ignorant German," he sneered. Agnar was very tall with a massive, barrel chest and biceps bigger than any Eddie had ever seen. Agnar had a handsome, unscarred if rough featured face. with the classic Viking's long blond hair, beard and moustache.

Aefnoth didn't understand what Agnar had said, but realized the derisive laughter was aimed at his mission subordinate. Eddie could see that Aefnoth was about to make a protest as his leader, but was able to prevent him with a hand gesture.

Eddie faced Agnar. "You're laughing, but what if I'm right? If there are twenty alien longships sailing towards us along this creek, would they be friends or foes?"

Eric replied for him. "If they existed, they would be rivals as we've no friends near here at the moment."

Not believing a word of Eddie's prediction, Agnar snorted. Then he challenged Eddie by arrogantly announcing, "If there really are twenty more longships in this creek, on my oath I'll give you my gold amulet. However, if you're wrong you must fight me in a glimmer bout for inconveniencing me." He laughed again, waving his hands in an upward gesture from his waist. This was to orchestrate general derision among the crowd and it worked as his friends whistled, cat-called and gesticulated in Eddie's direction.

However, they were silenced when Eddie held up his right arm and replied, "I accept your challenge, Agnar. Your amulet against a glimmer bout t is. So shall we see who's won the wager by checking the estuary for another fleet of longships?"

Agnar bit his lower lip. With a furrowed brow, he opened his hands in front of him and turned to Eric.

Eric sighed. "Agnar, this is just youthful verbal jousting. You young warriors are prone to make oaths and challenges you know you'll win. You're merely trying to establish a higher place in the male pecking order outside of battle conditions."

Agnar blushed and shifted from foot to foot.

Eric then shrugged his shoulders. With some reluctance, he said, "Okay, let's clear this up. We will check the German's prediction."

To do so, Eric led the crowd to the east, towards the seaward facing end of the elongated island. The Danes were buoyant, enjoying the excitement that oaths brought.

A warrior called Oman Claw-hands was attempting to take wagers that Agnar was wrong, but there were few takers. In the end he reversed the odds and took many bets that Agnar was right.

Oman Claw-hands was a ginger-haired man with freckles and a rather bulbous nose. He was aptly named. As he held up his arms to confirm a bet, Eddie could see that the last two fingers on both hands were bent permanently into his palms.

Eddie hoped in one way that he was correct about the longships. He didn't want to glimmer wrestle with Agnar, who was obviously far too powerful for him. But on the other hand, if these other ships did arrive they would probably herald danger. That wouldn't be good at all.

It was almost dark now. The moon was full but clouds covered most of the sky. Small waves splashed onto the beach. Otherwise, all seemed peaceful.

Shattering the calm, a fox's eerie shrieks rent the air. This was answered by chilling, blood-curling replies. Several animals howled repeatedly and what sounded like threatening calls echoed all around the island.

"Wolves," Aefnoth whispered to Eddie.

The Osea Naze, the easterly facing marshy headland of the island, was the perfect place to check the Estuary. From that position, had it been light, they could have seen as far as its entrance to the North Sea.

Agnar proclaimed triumphantly, "There, you see guys, there's nothing visible but water. I win my oath challenge. Pay out on those wagers, Oman. Tomorrow the rest of you can win even more silver coins, betting I'll win the glimmer bout. I'll ensure this German won't make any more fake predictions."

Oman Claw-hands pushed his palms towards the crowd to prevent them demanding their winnings. "Hold on, my friends. The German said twenty more longships were *approaching* this Island. He didn't say how far away they were. They may not get here for days."

The crowd of men, who had made what seemed like winning wagers, grumbled, but had to admit that Oman Claw-hands had a point.

Eric said, "Oman's right. We must give the German the benefit of the doubt. I will decide when or if he's proved wrong."

Eric couldn't see any craft, but had reluctantly taken from his sack a tube of hardened goatskin and put it to his eye.

Eddie realized it was obviously a scope. So now he knew somebody who had one.

The men all lay down on the Island's Naze Bank behind rough marsh grass and gorse bushes. Eddie could smell the distinctive strong coconut scent of the yellow gorse flowers. Trying unsuccessfully to avoid the thorns, he picked some of the dark yellow flowers. He licked the spots of blood from his fingers where the sharp thorns had torn them. Then he ate the flowers that tasted like strong lettuce. That was why the Romanies used them in salads in the summer.

Eddie remembered that gorse flowered most of the year, which no doubt accounted for his mother's old Romani saying, 'When gorse is out of blossom, kissing's out of fashion.'

Ducks could be heard calling from saltings in the estuary. Small white caps were creating a shimmering luminescence as the moonlight struck their flowing course.

Eddie had begun to wonder if his psychic information and thus his predictions were wrong for the first time ever. He watched Eric, who was patiently, but without much conviction, scanning the choppy seawater and the horizon with his scope. The old Viking was struggling to recognize anything in the poor light.

Suddenly, Eddie noticed that Eric was holding the scope steady and staring intently at a point directly east, far out into the North Sea.

"I can see something!" Eric suddenly exclaimed with surprise. "It could be longships. Yes, there they are. Five... no, nine. Now I can see more, it's... there are twenty. You are right, German."

In a shaft of moonlight, Eddie glimpsed some of the Danes looking at him with astonishment and a few even with admiration. However, these didn't include Agnar, whose face showed only despair.

Oman Claw-hands patted Eddie on the back and then shook his hand. Eddie felt the clusters of lumpy growths on Oman's first two fingers and palm that were obviously causing his clawing problem. Oman knew he was a lot richer and was a very happy man, for a while at least.

Eddie asked Eric "Can I look at the ships?"

Eric nodded agreement and handed the scope to him. Eddie put the tube to his eye and at that moment the clouds parted to allow a pool of moonlight to shine in the distance. It illuminated the advancing fleet.

Eddie was excited as he'd never looked through a scope before. The longships looked at least five times bigger than they were to the naked eye. He thought for a moment that they were almost upon them. But of course it was an illusion. When he checked without the scope, they were still far away.

Impressed with the scope, he looked inside the goatskin tube and noticed a crystal lens at both ends. He resolved to ask Eric how the lenses were produced or obtained after this situation had been sorted out.

As he watched, the fleet was again plainly lit up by the moonlight. As the biggest longship tacked towards him, he could clearly see a white banner streaming from the mast. Emblazoned on it was what appeared to be a large black crow in flight as he'd seen in his remote viewing.

Eddie asked about the pennant. Eric took the scope and checked again.

"I believe that may be a Norwegian Royal Raven banner. If so, we're in real danger."

Eric handed the scope to Aefnoth. He looked at the longships and was noticeably startled. Not breaking his silence, but nodding his thanks and with a bewildered expression on his face, he returned the scope to Eric.

Eric gave an order to his men. "Rouse anybody sleeping and fetch all the warriors and your arms in case of attack."

While Eric and most of his group returned to the camp, two Danes stayed behind, watching the suspect longship fleet with the scope.

Aefnoth and Eddie moved away from the pair of observer Danes. As soon as they were out of earshot Aefnoth said, "I don't understand how that scope works. But it's a wonderment I never knew existed, or even dreamed about. These scopes could revolutionize our spying and early warning systems. We must obtain one to take to my father."

"I agree, but we will have to wait our chance."

Quietly, Eric and his men returned and lay in the long grass covering the Naze. Eric told Eddie, "The crew of the approaching fleet will almost certainly see our craft as they navigate past."

"You're right, Eric, but there's nothing you can do about that."

The group all watched with growing tension as the twenty suspect longships approached them along the Blackwater Estuary. It was by now fully dark apart from the cloud-shrouded moon. The wind had dropped so the dubiously crewed longships had furled their sails and were rowing with muffled oars.

The longships moved closer and a challenge rang out from them, "Who are you and what's your business with us Norwegian heroes?"

Eric replied, "We're proud Danish Vikings."

There was an immediate aggressive shout from the Norwegians. "This is the first flotilla of the great fleet of Olaf Tryggvasson, Prince of Norway. We intend to raid the Maldon Burh for their silver. You are in our way. Flee now or we will kill you all."

Eric shouted back at the Norwegians, "Danes will never yield to pirates from Norway. Sail back from whence you came."

After a short delay, a dozen fire arrows flew through the air from the Norwegian flotilla. Some hit the beached Danish longships targets. Then volley after volley of flaming arrows from the Norwegians lit the darkness.

In reply the Danish archers sent showers of arrows back at the Norwegian longships.

Eric shouted to his men, "Try to stop their longships from landing so they can't use their extra manpower to full advantage. We have the stable platform at the moment. Tell me if any of their longships manage to beach."

Eddie and Aefnoth moved back inland, away from the Danes and the immediate danger from the Norwegian arrows.

Eddie asked Aefnoth, "What should we do in this dangerous situation? Should we flee the island or stay and observe the battle in the hope we can obtain a scope?"

Aefnoth thought for a moment before answering. "I've always fought any Vikings as the pagan interlopers they all are. However, I've heard that Olaf Tryggvasson's a fearsome warrior who's been plundering the whole of the east of England. King Aethelred's spies report Tryggvasson has a fleet of over one hundred longships altogether around these coasts. As you tell me they said this is the first flotilla of Olaf Tryggvasson fleet, I presume that he is not here in person. However, anything that reduces his overall forces can't be bad."

The smoke from the flaming arrows made Eddie choke.

Aefnoth continued. "In contrast, these Danes are just a small party controlled by an old Chieftain. They're only strong enough to plunder a few hamlets and farms, just sufficient to keep them alive. That tells me Maldon Burh would be in much greater peril from the larger Norwegian force than these few Danes."

"You are right, Eldor," Eddie replied, with a cough."

Aefnoth was also coughing. "Because of that and the fact that I've always liked fighting in battles, I consider we shouldn't just observe but actively help the Danes. After all, they've fed us and informed us of their sagas."

Another volley of fire arrows emanating from the Norwegian longships arched through the air and landed on the beached Danish longships.

Aefnoth resumed. "It's possible this inter-Viking fight could, in the long run, give us Saxons some advantage. If the Danes win the battle, Eric may help us obtain a scope. While if the Norwegians carry the day, we can make our way to the mainland when the causeway's dry and unguarded. Either way there would be less Vikings to attack Maldon."

"I agree with your analytical assessment, Aefnoth. You must have been taught your war tactics by your father, our great General." He noticed a beaming smile on Aefnoth's face in the flickering light from the flames.

"Edward the Tall, I'm glad you've now acknowledged my superior expertise. I was ill at ease deferring to you because of your language skills. However, I feel we now have a mutual bond of respect."

Eddie replied, "I concur, Eldor. May I ask your opinion on an idea of mine? As neither of us are experts in the Viking ways of fighting, wouldn't we be better restricting ourselves to putting out the fires on the Danes' Longships?"

Aefnoth now looking his self assured best again, replied, "I agree that seems the safest way for us. We can assist the Danes and still leave ourselves free to withdraw should we need to. Let's do it."

Aefnoth led Eddie in a flat-out run to the beached longships. With flaming arrows landing around them they scrambled on board a Danish longship that was already well alight. The smell of burning wood and the salty mist combined, and on any other night it would have been pleasant. But today, in the circumstances, it only added to the prescience of menace and imminent death.

Grabbing sacking from the longship's prow, they beat at the flames. The wooden sides of the longship were shielding them from the Norwegian invaders' missiles, although each time any part of them showed above the gunwales they became silhouetted by the flames and targeted by the Norwegian archers. This was especially dangerous when they moved from ship to ship, as they had no shields with them. It was more by luck than judgement that they managed to evade the arrows.

The cacophony of battle, including the screams of the injured and dying, and noises of clashing blades and crashing battleaxes, was terrifying in its intensity. Eddie wanted it all to stop, and to return to Kate at the Burh. But the terrible pandemonium wouldn't go away. In fact it intensified further.

When they'd put out most of the fires, Eddie paused. Sheltering behind a mast, he looked to see how the overall battle was going. He could see that most of the Norwegian longships were being kept at sea by the ferocious Danish resistance. Unfortunately for the Danes, a couple of the Norwegian longships had now beached. On landing they'd immediately disgorged the ships' full complement of homicidal warriors onto the island.

Furious fighting was taking place around the landing areas. The Norwegian Vikings were attempting to clear the beach to allow more of their longships to land and reinforce them.

Meanwhile, the Danes had formed two shield walls. These were being used to press the attackers back, attempting to force the Norwegian warriors into the sea and deny them the space to bolster their numbers. From behind the shield walls the Danes were loosing arrows and throwing javelins at the Norwegians who had already landed. For their part, the Norwegian invaders were also loosing volleys of arrows from the shelter of their ships.

Chillingly, out of the darkness, a lone man's terrifying screams and shrieks of wretched physical torment made Eddie feel physically sick. The screeching and high pitched squealing continued unabated for what seemed like an eternity until it ceased mid-wail. Eddie had no idea if the poor wretch was Dane or Norwegian. However, he assumed the unfortunate's anguish had been ended by his enemy's coup de grace.

Suddenly, Eddie realized that they themselves were far from safe. A Norwegian longship was coming straight at the grounded Danish ship they were occupying. There were just the two of them against what could be up to fifty Vikings aboard the incoming longship.

Eddie pointed and yelled to Aefnoth, "Pull back, Aefnoth! Norwegian longship…"

But before either could escape, a Norwegian javelin flew towards Eddie. Fortunately, because of the remaining glow, he'd seen it early. He was able to duck and catch it in mid-air.

With sickening force, the Norwegian longship crashed into the Danish ship the pair was sheltering in. The collision knocked them off their feet. Immediately, a Viking leapt aboard the Saxon vessel. The huge man was swinging a long-bladed, double-handed sword at Aefnoth who was still on his back. Automatically, Eddie threw the javelin he'd caught at the big Viking. The shaft stuck firmly into the attacker's chest, his sword falling to the deck harmlessly.

"Thanks Edward. Now run for your life!" Aefnoth shouted to Eddie, as several other Norwegians swarmed onto the Danish longship. They both vaulted over the inland side of the grounded Danish vessel with the invaders' missiles thudding into the gunwale behind them.

Scrambling around the line of vessels, they took shelter in the darkness. Eddie yelled out to the nearest Danes to warn them of the Norwegians' latest breakthrough. Within moments, thirty or so Danes rushed towards the newly-beached Norwegian ship.

Hurriedly the Danes formed a new defensive shield wall. Aefnoth and Eddie retrieved discarded bows, arrows and shields from fallen Danes. Now they were able to release arrows from the comparative safety of this shelter.

Screams of pain, despair and the overwhelming clamour of battle were horrific and overwhelming. The smell of blood and the ear-piercing shrieks of the mortally wounded were spine-chilling.

A blackbird flew out of the gorse bushes, emitting its high-pitched warning cry and was immediately pierced and killed in mid-air by an arrow from within a vast shower. Eddie felt sorry for the innocent creature that found itself in the wrong place at the wrong time.

Looking around at the overall battlefield, it was impossible to see who was winning because of the darkness. The only light came from the flames of the burning ships as black clouds obscured the moonlight.

However, when the clouds cleared for a while, Eddie could see that not all the Norwegian longships had moved shoreward. Their biggest longship was surrounded and tied up to four smaller craft, forming a stable platform from which to attack. This had been anchored some way out in the estuary. The Norwegian archers on board this longship raft were releasing a withering shower of arrows from there, aiming well inland to avoid their own men.

Eddie reasoned that eventually the overwhelming two-to-one Norwegian manpower superiority must prevail. Then the Danes would be slaughtered. Either way, many more men would die there on Osea Island. As he watched, like some insane nightmare two gargantuan men, wearing what looked like bear or wolf skins, appeared. They charged at the Danes' shield wall nearest to him. These monsters screamed like animals and swung massive battleaxes.

Aefnoth pointed at the ogres and shouted to Eddie one word, "Berserkers!"

The fearsome warriors were being pushed like battering rams. Other Vikings were forcing them bodily right through the Danish shield wall. The fur-clad giants were ferociously swinging their oversized battleaxes. They were creating a breach for the other Norwegian Vikings to penetrate the Danish lines.

Several Danes went down, cut almost in two by the berserkers' mighty battleaxe blades. The mortally wounded men's horrific screams of agony lasted only seconds before they died. This was hideous, gruesome slaughter in the extreme. Blood and gore sprayed over all the warriors, Dane and Norwegian alike.

This was not the gentlemanly clashing of swords as in training. This was, literally, bloody reality. The berserkers' ferocity and utter brutality made Eddie's flesh creep. He'd been in several battles before, but never anything as ferocious as this.

Eddie tried to help the beleaguered Danish warriors. He loosed a thin, metal-tipped bodkin arrow at point blank range at the nearest Titan berserker. Exactly as his weapon instructors had promised, the narrow iron point deeply penetrated the berserker's chain mail armour. But even this had little effect. The mammoth-man still charged towards Eddie, bellowing obscenities. Eddie was perplexed. What type of unholy being was this massive creature?

The berserker wrenched out the bodkin arrow from his body. His blood spurted from the wound. This had the effect of infuriating the creature even more. Howling a chilling war cry, the berserker swung his colossal battleaxe at Eddie. The monster was obviously bent on revenge for the outrageous pinprick.

With lightning reactions, Eddie dropped to the ground and the axe blade missed him by a whisker. Unfortunately, the axe's wooden haft continued its motion and struck Eddie such a hard blow on the head that he felt groggy.

The berserker howled like a wolf and stank of something that had gone rancid. Eddie expected to be killed at any moment. However, the berserker seemed to be rather dazed as if he was in a trance. The savage's dirt-encrusted hair hung in clumps, and green snot tangled with the knots in his scraggy beard.

The colossal warrior semi-recovered. Then, screaming manically, he swung his axe in a wild arc around his head towards Eddie again. Initially Eddie was frozen to the spot, but quickly snapped out of the berserker's hypnotic hold on his senses.

Eddie's heart started pumping nineteen to the dozen. The increased supply of blood and adrenalin gave him the speed to move away fast. It was senseless to fight this 'thing' head on. He dived behind a sturdy oak tree and attempted to climb into its branches.

Unfortunately the berserker spotted him again. Hollering elatedly, the giant again swung his battleaxe. Eddie flung his legs into the air and wrapped them around the branch he was hanging from.

The big man's axe head narrowly missed Eddie's body and thudded into the tree trunk. The Herculean force of the blow made the whole tree shudder. Eddie knew he had to move quickly as he was a hanging target for the next attack. As the maniacal bearskin-clad giant freed his axe blade, Eddie grabbed for a higher branch. But it broke and he crashed to the ground winded, near the heinous berserker's swollen feet.

The savage opened his mouth to bellow. From the ripped lips, bleeding gums, black teeth and green tongue emitted the worst stink Eddie had ever smelt. Something between cat's mess, marsh gas and rotten meat. Eddie choked and had to resist vomiting. The berserker's face, encrusted with dirt and dried blood, showed a malevolent look of triumph. His mighty double-bladed axe swung back to strike the blow that would end Eddie's existence on this earth. Eddie tried to scramble away but slipped on a pool of blood and spilled guts. He was sweating and cold at the same time. As the axe swung towards him, Eddie steeled himself for extreme pain and death.

Seventeen

The half moon illuminated the night. A countless array of celestial stars appeared to fill every inch of the cloudless firmament. Below, at ground level on Osea Island, it was a very different world. Hell on earth rather than heaven above.

Palls of choking black smoke drifted like shrouds at eye level just above the Essex island. Deliberately generated combustion caused by Norwegian Vikings' flaming arrows had heralded the intense conflagration.

The extreme heat generated from a still glowing, recently burnt Danish Viking longship, spewed out black clouds of noxious fumes. Pitch used to fill and waterproof between the boards, combined with the wood preserving oils, produced a toxic mixture when smouldering.

The black clouds afflicted both nations' fighting men without favour, impairing their ability to see, or even think. Tears affected vision and the foul tasting fumes made many nauseous.

It was a peaceful night elsewhere on England's east coastal region. But not on this cursed island in the Blackwater Estuary. The clamour of the battle between rival Danish and Norwegian Vikings was deafening. Steel striking steel and the screams of wounded and dying warriors were incessant.

Among this fracas were Aefnoth, a Saxon noble, and Eddie, a Romani. They were the only outsiders caught up in this inter-Viking dispute. Eddie was in mortal peril, having fallen from a tree in front of a homicidal Norwegian berserker. Closing his eyes, he anticipated his own immediate death from the scything blade of the berserker's raised battleaxe.

Mercifully, the blow never came. Instead he felt and heard the thud of something heavy landing beside him. Eddie tentatively opened his eyes. In the moonlight, only inches from his own face, he saw the gruesome visage of the berserker. The monster's red eyes were frozen wide open, staring lifelessly, his swollen slash of a mouth open in a hideous grimace of death rictus. Broken and blackened stumps of teeth surrounded a swollen, blood-soaked bitten-through tongue.

The huge man's corpse stank of an accumulation of months of sweat, urine, faeces and gore. The berserker's long, unkempt hair was matted with mud. Nasal mucus glued together clumps of tangled, voluminous beard and moustache.

Eddie twisted his face away in disgust and vomited. As he slowly recovered, he saw Aefnoth standing over the giant's cadaver, sword in his hand, its blade still dripping blood.

Aefnoth helped Eddie to sit up. "That's in repayment for saving my life on the longship, Edward. It was a close thing though. The berserker was so intent on slaughtering you, he wasn't aware of me coming up behind him. That proves anyone can be vulnerable if they get over-confident."

"Uh, than… thanks," Eddie stuttered. "I thought I was going to die." Such an inadequate response was merely stating the obvious but, still numb with shock, that was all he was capable of.

Eddie could see shimmering waves breaking on to the yellow sand of Osea Island's beach. In that direction the world went on as usual, seemingly peaceful. This was a momentary illusion; the clamour of the fighting to his right impinged on his reflections. The screams of the injured and expiring all around them put his own personal survival into context.

The pair weren't out of danger, far from it. Eddie asked Aefnoth, "How's the rest of the battle going?"

Aefnoth helped Eddie to his feet. "It looks as if the Danes we've been helping are losing badly. But I'll never criticise Vikings' courage. Both nations really do fight to the death."

It was still night, but the moonlight illuminated the scene of carnage. Eddie could see that by then most of the Norwegian longships had made it to the shore. He noticed the Danes had changed their tactics. Instead of using shield walls they were now skirmishing. Attacking then withdrawing, spreading the scope of the fighting to a wider area of the Island.

Osea was a fantastic place in peacetime. However, the island was physically far too small for any side losing a battle on its shores, as there was nowhere to retreat to. The victors only needed to seal off the causeway and destroy their enemies' ships. Then they could hunt down and annihilate or enslave the enemy at their leisure.

In the estuary the tide had turned and was running strongly east towards Bradwell. Also, the wind had veered in the same direction. Thus it would be easy to go with the tide towards the North Sea but almost impossible to sail west towards Maldon.

The larger mammals on the island had panicked and hidden away from the humans in the woods and scrublands. As Eddie and Aefnoth were temporarily doing the same, they unintentionally flushed some of them out. A small herd of deer crashed away even deeper into the woods. A wild boar nearly had Aefnoth over as it broke cover, squealing in terror.

"So do we fight and die with the Danes or withdraw while we still can?" Eddie asked.

They moved into a hazelwood copse before Aefnoth replied. "It's not our battle after all, Edward. In fact, as they're killing each other, it's already served our purpose by reducing the threat to the Maldon Burh. It wouldn't be cowardice for us to leave. We've not sworn allegiance nor have we any kin loyalty to these Danes."

"You're right," Eddie said, "but without some outside intervention the Danes will be wiped out. It won't matter how bravely they fight as they're massively outnumbered."

Aefnoth shrugged. "That's war for you, Edward."

Eddie nodded. "True enough, but I like Eric Greybeard and his men. They've been friendly, fed us and supplied us with useful information. Even more important for our mission, Aefnoth, your father wants us to obtain a scope. We know there is one in Eric Greybeard's possession. If Eric survives, he may trade or sell one to us."

Aefnoth scratched his head. "Hm, true, but this is a life or death struggle so it's almost certain Eric will be killed. What will happen to the scope then?"

Eddie leaned against a tree, considering the question. "If the Norwegians kill Eric, they'll capture his scope. I'm assuming Olaf Tryggvasson doesn't have one already. Just imagine, if he now gains one he'll have even more of an advantage. With his huge force, that would be the Saxons' worst nightmare, wouldn't it?"

"I agree. We need a scope ourselves… or at least to keep it out of Tryggvasson's clutches. But to do either we'd have to prevent the complete rout of the Danes. That seems improbable."

At the Maldon Burh, Ealdorman Byrhtnoth was listening to a report from one of his most trusted lookouts. Thegn Augustus, a venerable warrior, had just appeared. He was out of breath even though he'd ridden to the Burh.

Augustus was old, short and balding with a curved spine and wasted left arm. His wizened, scarred appearance made him look dependent on others. This was far from reality. The old soldier had been a fearsome fighter in his youth. Though his physical body had been damaged by many battle wounds and the ravages of old age, his indomitable spirit drove him on as hard as ever. He was in fact one of Ealdorman Byrhtnoth's most dependable aides.

The Ealdorman asked him, "What news, old man?"

Thegn Augustus, still puffing, gasped out, "I can confirm that my men at Bradwell reported twenty more longships entering the Blackwater Estuary yesterday evening, coming this way."

Ealdorman Byrhtnoth's brow furrowed. "Have you any more news of their whereabouts since then?"

"My son, Augustine, rowed me out to the end of Lawling creek." He paused to take a few deep breaths. "We saw the twenty extra longships arrive in the moonlight and assumed they were joining up with their comrades on the island." Augustus paused again, coughed and wheezed, mentally cursing the Viking spear point that had destroyed his left lung.

Byrhtnoth understood the wounded old man's problem. Patting him on the back, he said, "When you have the breath, my brave, tell me what happened?"

Augustus was purple of face by then but carried on his report as best he could. "I was wrong, sire. The second group of Vikings must have been rivals of the ones already on Osea Island."

"How do you know that, Augustus?"

Augustus coughed again, his breathing punctuated by whistling breaths. "Because there were aggressive shouts, followed by fire arrows loosed from the new longships and aimed at the already grounded longships on the island."

"Hm," Byrhtnoth said thoughtfully. "That's pretty conclusive evidence. What could you see in the darkness?"

Augustus wheezed and gasped again before he could answer. "When I last saw them, the two groups were fighting an all-out battle on the foreshore of the island. I could see burning ships and heard the sounds of fighting and the screams of the wounded.

"And what's your estimate of the danger to us at Maldon Burh, loyal Thegn?"

Augustus was now holding a hand to his throat to avoid choking. "In my opinion," he croaked, "none of these two tribes of Vikings will cause any immediate trouble at the Burh. As they're fighting among themselves they're unlikely to be fit enough to tackle us Saxons any time soon."

Byrhtnoth held his chin in his hand. "As usual, your analysis is logical, Augustus."

"It's good that our Saxon brothers from Osea Island reached the Burh a while ago, sire. No Saxon is in danger from this battle as far as I can see. My son is still watching the battle from my rowing boat."

Then the old man slipped to the floor, exhausted and gasping for breath.

Byrhtnoth said, "Well done, Thegn Augustus." Then he addressed two slaves, Wisteric and Deshler. "Take our brave comrade to the sick bay and see he's looked after."

As the slaves gently helped the old man away, Byrhtnoth sighed, remembering when he himself once had four fine sons. The oldest three had died bravely in battle. Now he just had his youngest son and heir, Aefnoth. In some ways he regretted sending his remaining son into such danger but his personal rule had always been to lead his men by example. That entailed taking the most dangerous position for himself in battle and not sparing his own children while risking others. Having such high principles had inspired his men to idolize him, but it still brought him mental pain as one by one his beloved boys died for their neighbours' safety. He was still his boys' dad, after all.

Thegn Leofsunu had confirmed his son and Edward the Tall had reached Osea. That meant they could be in grave danger on the island. Byrhtnoth hoped they would be in hiding, just observing the battle. He prayed that Aefnoth and his companion were safe and hadn't been caught between the two lots of Vikings.

On Osea Island, a barn owl swooped down near to the pair and rose again with a mouse in its talons. Eddie watched the magnificent bird and envied its ability to fly away from danger. He wondered if there was some way to help the Danes. Then he had an idea.

"What if we paddle a canoe out to the Norwegian longship raft to try to cut it free?" he asked Aefnoth. "That's if we can find a serviceable canoe, of course."

Aefnoth looked worried. "There is a problem. I don't know how to paddle a canoe. I can't swim, either, and I'm terrified of water."

Eddie tried to reassure Aefnoth. "I can paddle the canoe by myself. The Viking canoes are broad and flat bottomed, so virtually unsinkable. You'd be quite safe. Although you can stay here on dry land if you wish, two of us would have more chance of success. If we can't free the raft, I could paddle us to the mainland so we could escape these killing fields."

Aefnoth's shoulders had slumped forward. He was gripping his hands together and breathing heavily. Eddie could see Aefnoth still wasn't overjoyed about the idea.

"But there's no point in talking about it till we see if there's still a canoe there to use," he said.

Aefnoth nodded and then pulled himself up to his full height. Without speaking, he strode down towards where they'd last seen the canoes. Eddie followed closely behind, glad to be doing something, at least.

While they walked to the beach, Eddie noticed with amazement that many wild creatures seemed to be ignoring the noisy battle nearby. Turnstones ran about rapidly as they searched for titbits on the beach, and out in the estuary a family of seals were fishing quite calmly as if nothing was amiss. Their lives went on as normal. The equation was simple: without food they would die. Humans made life too complicated.

Eventually the two men found the canoes in the dark. One was burnt out but, miraculously, the other was only slightly charred. The oars were missing but the strange slim paddles were still there, as were the mast and sail.

Eddie said, "From this island at dawn, I've noticed what looks like a range of mountains on the horizon. Of course it's only clouds, but it could disorientate anyone for a few minutes. I was thinking… if this happens we may be able to achieve this sabotage.

At the same time, just two hundred yards away on the same beach, the furious fighting was continuing. The Danes were being forced back by the Norwegians' greater numbers. The clash of metal blades against chain mail provided percussion, but against flesh, the agonized screams from the unfortunate recipients would have put the most robust soprano to shame.

There was a heavy mist now and coupled with the wind chill factor, it was rather cold just before the dawn. The Danish longships shielded the pair from the melee so they were able to launch the canoe into the sea without being seen.

Aefnoth sat on board looking anxious as Eddie, standing up to his knees in the cool water, pushed the heavy wooden canoe the last few feet until it floated. Then he scrambled on board, keeping his centre of gravity low to avoid capsizing the small craft.

As the canoe slid onto the water, waves broke over the side. On this rough, gusty morning, it soaked the two men to the bone. The scent of charred wood didn't completely mask the smells of salt water, ozone and seaweed. Aefnoth looked terrified and was seasick already.

Eddie noticed four black-robed Druids floating over the sea just in front of the canoe. They were only with them for a few moments but it made Eddie feel more secure. It was as if they were saying, 'We're with you.'

Heavy mist blanketed the area from sea level to several feet above it and Eddie could not see the longship raft. High above the mist the stars shone, so he was able to get his bearings. He also knew the tide would take him in the direction of the longship raft and the North Sea.

As well as the thin-bladed paddle, Eddie had to contend with the strong tidal swell, the crashing waves, and the handling of a very unfamiliar Viking canoe. He found the curious paddle was more use as a rudder than to propel the canoe along. By the time he'd worked it out, the canoe had spun round in a full circle a few times.

This made Eddie disorientated in the sea mist. It also left them too far out into the main current. He knew they mustn't be swept past the raft as he would not be able to paddle it back against the strengthening wind and tide. It would be just as bad if they were directly in front of the longship platform. At the speed the tide was running, they would crash right into the raft. This would betray their presence to the Norwegian defenders. That would be suicidal.

By now the smells from the sea and the canoe lurching rhythmically on the rough seawater was having a detrimental effect on Aefnoth. He'd turned deathly white, and looked sickly and terrified. Eddie knew Aefnoth was unquestionably a brave warrior, but he'd now met a terror he was unable to handle. Aefnoth was unable to hold back any longer. He threw up, violently, over the side.

As the first shafts of dawn broke through, the clouds produced strange Castilian effects on the horizon. Eddie hoped it might distract those on the raft long enough for the canoe to approach unnoticed.

Even before the sun rose it had started to warm the air and was producing even more sea mist. This was good to hide in, but it also made precise navigation difficult. There was now a ghostly appearance to the scene.

Were they still on course or had they passed the moored ships in the dark and mist? It was difficult for Eddie to judge. But it seemed to him that what should have been a short journey was taking a surprisingly long time.

Then he saw at last that they were approaching the dark, menacing bulk of the longship raft. But the canoe was not in the right position and going too fast. If they passed it on the left between the raft and the shore they'd be seen and attacked with spears and arrows. If they hit the raft, the same thing would happen.

Eddie used all his strength to swing the canoe round to the right. Then he hauled the long paddle through the water to slow it down. After that he leaned out to the right, applying hanging draw strokes to try to drag it to the far side of the platform where there was less current.

His paddling skill was sufficient and luck was with him. The canoe nudged sweetly and softly into the mainland side of the longship. By good fortune, no Vikings were in this craft, having moved to the ones adjacent the island. Eddie tied the canoe to the longship and hauled Aefnoth on board the bigger vessel.

Aefnoth looked terrible. He was white-faced and repeatedly vomiting over the side.

"Haven't you been on the water before?" Eddie asked him in a low voice.

Aefnoth whispered his reply between projectile vomiting. "Only to ford rivers. Never on tidal waters. Edward, I feel I'm dying. I want to get to dry land as soon as possible. I'm terrified of drowning. As I told you, I can't swim at all. Don't let me drown."

"Hold on, it won't be for long," Eddie assured him. "You've only got what is known as seasickness. As soon as you get ashore you'll be alright again."

Aefnoth didn't look at all convinced that he'd ever recover from this terrible malaise. However, with Eddie's help he managed to walk to the stern of the longship. Once there they could see that just two heavy hemp hawsers were anchoring the whole raft. One rope was attached to the longship they were in, so it could be reached easily. But the other was right at the back of the biggest longship that was full of Norwegian archers.

Eddie whispered, "I'll have to try and swim to the far rope and saw through it with my knife. Can you cut the other as soon as you feel the ship lurch when the first hawser parts?"

Aefnoth swallowed hard. "I should be able to manage that, despite being sick. It'll give me something else to think about."

"In that case, cut all the ropes by the sails on this longship as well. Then when they try to raise them, they'll collapse."

Aefnoth mumbled, "Okay," then tried to be sick, but as his stomach was already empty his internal muscles contracted painfully.

Eddie told him, "I've calculated that as long as you push off hard you'll be far enough out of the stream to be left behind as the raft's swept away in the main current."

Aefnoth's mouth turned downwards at the edges and he shook and hung onto the gunwale till his knuckles turned white.

Eddie said, "If I'm able, I'll swim back to you. But if I don't make it you'll eventually be washed ashore somewhere. Of course I may not be unable to sever the other mooring rope. So in around fifteen minutes, if you don't feel the raft lurch it means I've failed. If that does happen just get in the canoe, cut it loose and drift away in it."

Aefnoth looked utterly miserable and even had tears in his eyes, more from frustration than anything.

Eddie stripped naked and left all his clothes in the canoe, knowing it would be impossible to try to swim in the Viking baggy trousers and voluminous shirt. As he took off his clothes he was distressed to see they were soaked with his own blood from his head wound.

Eddie slipped unclothed into the sea, griping his short Seax dagger in his teeth. He managed to swim round the back of the main raft. This wasn't easy as there were now massive waves smashing against the longships. All this time the tide was running strongly and trying to drag him under the ships' keels.

The water was cold before the dawn and Eddie couldn't create enough muscle heat to warm himself. Eventually he got to where the rope was streaming out behind the ship platform. Unfortunately the rope was too high for him to reach from the shelter of the ships' water line. The only way to make any contact would be to swim towards the hawser as hard as he could against the current.

Using all his fading strength, Eddie swam past the rope. Then he grabbed the wrist-thick, rough, hemp hawser as he was swept back towards the longship. The rope was too thick and difficult to hang onto, even with both hands. So he wound his legs round the rope cable and gripped it with those as well.

Then, hanging on perilously, with his right hand he took the knife from his mouth. He slashed furiously at the hawser with the Seax knife. The blade was sharp and the rope parted with a jolt. This threw him violently into the seawater and he lost his knife to the depths.

When Eddie surfaced, he watched fascinated as the longship platform swivelled round sharply. This threw the Vikings on board off their feet. Immediately after that the raft swung wildly again the other way. So he knew Aefnoth had cut the second rope.

The whole raft floated off at a great pace downstream towards the North Sea. He could see its occupants attempting to regain control. The canoe broke away towards the mainland. Aefnoth had done well in his sick state and with his terror of seawater.

Eddie was being swept along by the tide behind the longship raft. He started to swim furiously, desperately trying to escape the current and reach the canoe.

The canoe was floating on the tide out of his reach, but with a last frantic effort he'd nearly made it. Then a volley of arrows from the longship raft struck the water around him and the canoe.

Panicking, Eddie swam around the mainland side of the canoe trying to find some shelter. Somehow he felt so much more vulnerable without his clothes. This was illogical as an arrow would go through cloth just as easily as skin. But it was a psychological thing, he supposed.

Eddie grabbed the canoe's gunwale and was pulled aboard by Aefnoth. Eddie noticed that the main tide was running so strongly that the platform had now floated well away. Luckily, that put the canoe out of the range of the Viking archers which was a good thing as several arrows were stuck into its wooden side. The arrows had to stay there in case water came in through the holes they'd made.

Picking up a paddle, Eddie was able with difficulty to get the canoe under control. But even out of the main stream they were still floating towards the North Sea. A dozen black-headed gulls flew over them making plaintive cries before the birds were lost in the mist.

Out of the water the morning breeze and mist was making Eddie very cold so he stopped paddling to put his clothes on and felt better immediately. Aefnoth was still retching, so Eddie thought keeping him occupied might take his mind off his malaise.

"Come on Aefnoth I'll show you how to drag the second paddle through the water. Hopefully if we both paddle we'll get to one shore or another quicker."

Aefnoth still looked terrible but said, "I'll give it a go as long as I don't fall in."

Eddie tried to instruct Aefnoth to paddle but the big Saxon's efforts did little to propel the canoe forward. However it did help Eddie control its direction. This allowed him to pull harder on his own paddle strokes without needing so many time wasting steering strokes.

Blood was still running from Eddie's head wound and getting in his eyes, making them smart. But he couldn't take his hands of the paddle to wipe it away.

The full dawn lit up the sky, but there was still an impenetrable sea mist hanging from the surface up to four feet above the water.

Because of this they had no warning as the dragonhead prow of a single longship emerged from the mist. The duo could hear the oars creaking as its crew propelled it into the current in pursuit of the longship raft. As the two men watched, the longship's sail was set. The strong wind filled the mainsail, sheets were pulled to ensure direction and the longship sped away.

Aefnoth and Eddie lay in the bottom of the canoe, fearful but fascinated at the same time. The canoe was wide bottomed but had little draft. Therefore they had no option but to lie on their backs. From their supine position they watched an awe-inspiring sight. More and more dragonhead prow longships appeared, fourteen in all passing them, in formation.

As Eddie and Aefnoth stared, linen sails were unfurled on the longships and billowed in the wind. Just as soon as the ghostly longships appeared, it seemed they'd disappeared from the men's sight into the thick mist heading towards the North Sea.

What did this mean, Eddie wondered? Was the battle over? Had the Danes been annihilated? At least the longships weren't heading towards Maldon.

He said, "We've drifted away from the mainland shore. I don't think we're strong enough to paddle through the main current. I think we'll have to try and make landfall on Osea Island again."

"I don't care where we land as long as we get out of this rocking boat as quickly as possible," Aefnoth grumbled.

Despite both paddling as hard they could they were making little progress. Eddie realized they needed more power, so he raised the mast and secured it with the wooden peg that was attached to it by a leather thong. Then he fixed the sail to the mast using toggles and loops, finally securing it with ropes. The sail flapped around, but by getting Aefnoth to haul on the sheets while he used his paddle as a rudder, he was able to tack the craft towards the island.

Eventually, to Aefnoth's great relief, the canoe grounded on the island. They'd made landfall on the far eastern tip of the sand split, the Naze. Aefnoth immediately leapt over the side and laid face down on the sand shaking.

"My whole body feels as if it's rocking... as if I'm still on the water. Will it ever stop Edward?"

Eddie reassured Aefnoth, "You'll be the same as normal soon. As you've found out, Aefnoth, the sea demands its own type of courage."

Aefnoth shook his head and spat in the sand. "I'll never go in a boat again."

The sky was completely blue and without any clouds, it looked a perfect summer day. A robin was singing its heart out on the branch of a fir tree and a family of sea otters fished from the beach. There was little sign of the travail and suffering of the previous night.

Eddie wondered if perhaps it had all been a dream, but knew it hadn't.

When Aefnoth had begun to recover they walked wearily along the beach and up the slope onto the main part of the island. Reaching the clearing where the Danes had made their encampment, the change was startling. All the Saxons' houses were now just piles of ashes. Chillingly, in front of where they had stood were lines of Danish warriors' corpses.

However, Eddie was surprised that there was no air of gloom about the place. In fact the atmosphere was one of high excitement. Eric Greybeard was noting the name of each slain Dane. Other wounded men were lying away from the corpses. Some were more dead than alive. Many were unconscious and barely breathing. Blood still ran red from their bound wounds over dark, dried blood they'd shed earlier.

Other young men, little more than boys themselves attended to their fitter comrades. Around the clearing were about half of the original crew of the Danish longships. Most seemed to be wounded somewhere, as they were bandaged about the body or limbs.

A vast firewood pile was being constructed in the centre of the clearing. In addition, aromas of burning wood and food cooking were surprisingly seductive, if one considered the so recent trauma of the bloody battle, followed by the death of so many brave men.

The big warrior, Ericsson, who had first introduced them to Eric, greeted them.

"My father's busy now, listing the glorious ones who'll soon be in Valhalla. He'll talk to you both when he's finished. In the meantime come and take food to help you recover from the battle and we'll sort out your wounds."

They did eat, not realizing how hungry they'd become. Surprisingly, a certain amount of adrenalin still seemed to have them on a high. Aefnorth had emptied his stomach repeatedly while on the water. Although he was still feeling tender, he didn't take long to eat the roast meat, barley porridge and acorn beer that they were offered.

Subsequently Oman Claw-hands the bookie approached them and said that he would attend to their wounds. Eddie hadn't even realized Aefnoth had been wounded.

Aefnoth had an arrow head stuck into the side of his leg. He said, "Those bastard Viking archers from the longship raft hit me through the gunwale of the canoe. I broke off the haft so I could move away from the side to try and avoid any more hits."

Aefnoth hadn't complained once; Eddie was impressed with his bravery.

Oman washed Eddie's head where the berserkers battle-axe handle had struck him and it stung intensely. When Eddie put his hand to it he could feel a large swollen area which was also badly lacerated. Blood was running down his face again.

Oman Claw-hands dabbed his damaged skull with honey and then bandaged Eddie's head. Afterwards, he did feel a bit more comfortable.

Oman removed the arrowhead from Aefnoth's leg by pushing it right through the other side of his flesh. He told Eddie that this was less damaging than cutting the barb out through the entrance wound. Then Oman stitched Aefnoth's wound and cauterised it with a red-hot knife.

Throughout this painful operation Aefnoth hardly flinched. Eddie remembered when in the past he'd had the same treatment, he'd passed out with the agony.

Eddie realized he was lying on the wild strawberry patch. Although the fighting had flattened it, he still managed to pick a few to eat. Then he crushed some in his hands and held them to his nose. The strawberry fragrance masked the stench of burnt human flesh and spilt blood for a while.

Eric came to see them and said, "Almost half of my men have either died or are about to die. This has been a great day for them. They'll go straight to Valhalla. What's more, although we were out numbered two to one, we've still not lost the battle."

Eddie said, "I was impressed how bravely your young warriors fought. They are indeed heroes."

"My men have exceptional courage. They fight to the death for each other. You have both done well today also. My men saw you two putting out the flames on our longships. Then fighting on our side behind the shield wall. They believed you'd been killed by the berserkers."

"One of the berserkers nearly did kill me. It was only Aefnoth's bravery that saved my life."

Eric said, "It's good that you lived. You wouldn't go to Valhalla with my men, as you aren't of our pagan religion. I say that, but I'm not sure if I'm correct. When I saw you leave the island in the canoe you had several druids with you. Am I right?"

Eddie looked curiously at Eric. "You're the wise man the Druids told me you were." I've been watched over by Druids since my birth but I'm neither Pagan nor Christian, just Romani."

Eric nodded. "You're guided by the universal Gods. The Druids are everywhere. They come from an ancient society that ruled the universe before our cultures existed. I believe they originally came from a land of ice and snow. We have sagas about them from the ancients. We don't know them but they know us all. You were sent to us and guided by these Druids."

Eddie blinked, pursing his lips thoughtfully. "They tell me things, these Druids, but I don't understand why?"

Eric said," We may only know the truth about the Druids when we reach Valhalla, but they mean good, not evil, to us and you. Be grateful you have these guardian angels."

"The Druids encouraged me to go on with my idea to cut the Norwegians' longship raft free."

Eric smiled. "It was a good thing they did. By then my brave warriors had been forced back and we'd all expected soon to be in the glory of Valhalla. But just as all seemed lost the Norwegian pirates shouted that their great raft was being swept away. When I checked through my scope I saw the canoe pull away from the raft and realized it was you two who had cut it free."

"Even I wasn't sure our plan would work. But I'm glad it had the effect it did."

Eric mentioned, "I suspect their longship raft had very few men on board. There was certainly not enough crew to sail or row the five longships it was comprised of under full control. Furthermore, all the Norwegians' plunder, including their silver and gold, would have been on board their leader's big longship."

Eddie understood. "I see, so they'd no alternative – either continue the battle or lose their most valuable assets?"

"That's so. Plus they'll need all their fighting ships when the main flotilla comes to attack Maldon."

"We were just glad we were able to help you."

Eric's face seemed to be wavering. Eddie was weakening from loss of blood. He sank to the ground.

Eighteen

On Osea Island a slim black rat foraged in the grass near a cooking fire. It grabbed a scrap of discarded bread and dragged it down its hole to feed its brood.

In the middle of June the sun shone on the calm Blackwater Estuary. No craft moved on its smooth surface. This was in absolute contrast to the previous night's nautical and land based battle.

Aefnoth, a Saxon from the nearby town of Maldon and Eddie, a Romani, had fought on the side of the Danes. Both had been wounded. Eddie had lost a lot of blood. Weakened he'd sunk to the earth.

To Eddie's incoherent brain, the face of the Danish leader, Eric Greybeard, seemed to be fluttering around. Aefnoth had strange noises escaping from his mouth. Eddie thought he heard his name, but wasn't certain. His world disappeared and came back bigger and then smaller. Scents of bluebells, sweat and ozone combined into a strange hotchpotch of smells. Gradually his life came back into focus.

Aefnoth asked, "Are you alright, Edward?"

"Yes I think… I'm okay."

Eric spoke. "Rest now, warrior, you're not due to go to Valhalla yet."

After Eddie recovered his senses, Eric asked him, "May I ask you some personal questions, Edward?"

"Sure. Whatever you like."

"Well then, are you two really absorbed Vikings from Germany, Edward? I ask because you've been heard speaking the local language, so I think you're Saxons."

Eddie's heart raced and he looked askance at the big Viking leader, wondering if he and Aefnoth were in trouble again and knowing, if they were, that he wasn't fit enough to fight or escape."

Eric noticed Eddie's worried demeanour and tried to reassure him with an open handed gesture. "It's okay, Edward. Even if you are Saxons, this doesn't matter to us as you warned of the Norwegians' approach and then fought alongside us. You saved our longships from burning, then cut the Norwegians' longship raft free, changing the battle's outcome in our favour."

Eddie nodded. "You are correct, Eric. We are from the Maldon Burh. We were just checking you weren't any immediate danger to the town."

"I thought so. That's all right. Your bravery has made us blood brothers. I give you my oath we won't attack Maldon or anywhere else in the Blackwater Estuary."

Eddie visibly relaxed and smiled with relief. "That's good of you, Eric."

Eric Greybeard continued. "Also, should you ever need help against the Norwegians, just get word to us and we'll return and fight by your side."

Eddie patted Eric's shoulder and said, "A military alliance. That's fantastic. However, I'm not a member of the Saxon nobility, I'm merely a translator, picked because I speak your language. As such, I cannot make any pledges on the local Saxons' behalf. However, my comrade here is Eldor Aefnoth, who can speak for them. Have I permission to translate your generous offer to him, as he doesn't understand Danish?"

"Certainly. He's also a hero. You both helped saved my men. However, please emphasize that my oath and offer only applies to this single party. Others from Denmark will not take notice of me. I'm just an old chief, not Danish royalty."

"I understand you and I'll ensure I make that plain."

Eddie interpreted Eric's offer and oath to Aefnoth.

Aefnoth said, "That's great, Edward. It was well worth helping the Danes.

Please tell Eric from me that we concur with his magnanimous offer and we will reciprocate with the accord. Edward, there's no need to translate everything that Eric says. Just let me know later. I now trust you to negotiate for me, my father... and therefore, the Burh."

Eddie passed Aefnoth's acceptance of an alliance on to Eric Greybeard and then Aefnoth and Eddie in turn shook Eric's strong hand.

Eric asked, "We'd like you both to join us as our guests at the cremation and interment of the deceased."

"We will both be honoured to be present at the funerals of such brave warriors."

Simultaneously, in the Maldon Burh, Ealdorman Byrhtnoth had just given Princess Catherine some disturbing news. It was that his son and her fiancé, Eldor Aefnoth, could have become embroiled in a battle between rival Viking armies.

Kate was worried. Byrhtnoth had told her neither Aefnoth nor his interpreter, her bodyguard Edward, had been seen since the Osea

Island conflict. She prayed they were both still alive and perhaps in hiding on the island.

Later, the princess walked with her three handmaidens up to the top of the tallest lookout tower on the Maldon Burh's walls. She stared towards Osea Island, but could see little detail, only trees and the smoke from several fires curling into the sky.

Alfthrith whispered to Bretwalda and Edith, "I think our mistress is pining for her fiancé, Aefnoth. The other girls giggled when Alfthrith said, "Well I'm pining for my fiancé, Edward."

Bretwalda sniggered. "You'll be lucky. Your fiancé... huh, he hardly looks at you. It's me he fancies."

Edith interjected, "No way, you two. He kissed me the other day, so I'm going to seduce him when he gets back."

Their princess was pining alright, but her handmaidens would have been surprised had they known it was Eddie she was longing for, not Aefnoth.

On Osea Island, swallows swooped around the clearing. Diving down to the estuary, they scavenged mud portions in their sharp beaks. Then the birds transported the tiny mud balls to the sheltered branches of mighty oaks to construct their nests.

Under the flight paths of the streamlined blue-black birds, in the centre of the clearing, was a hive of human activity. The fittest Vikings were digging a trench in the sandy soil. It was eventually dug to four feet deep by seven feet wide, extending to a hundred feet long.

When the trench was finished, the remnants of a partly burnt-out longship was carried from the beach and carefully placed in the ditch. One by one, each of the dead Danes, shrouded in their sleeping cloaks or blankets, were lowered reverently into the trench. They were placed deferentially on top of the remains of the longship.

Each corpse was dressed in full battle armour, including some personal weapons. With each body was placed their personal feeding bowl full of food, a bottle of mead and a silver coin. Subsequently, piles of dry wood were laid in and over the trench, several feet thick over its whole length.

Aefnoth coughed loudly, which sounded like a thunderclap in the context of the funereal silence. A few Danish warriors looked round, but nothing was said.

The only other sounds that impinged on this solemn occasion were the leaves rustling in the wind and a solitary blackbird's requiem.

Eric Greybeard, the chieftain, lifted his hands and all the men who were capable stood to attention, holding spears and shields. Those who were badly injured and unable to stand, had been laid where they could see the burial trench.

Eric swung his arm in a wide arc encompassing the whole trench and proclaimed in a deep loud voice so that all could hear, "My brave warriors, you will today sail to Valhalla where you will fight all day, every day, alongside Tyre, the god of war. In the evening all your injuries will be healed and you will feast on the best food and have young girls to look after your every need."

Eddie noticed several Danes looking to the heavens before bowing their heads to observe the funeral trench once more.

Greybeard continued, "My braves, your threads of life have been cut by the Norns and you will be met by Odin and Freya and be as gods yourself. You will be taken straight to Father and Ragnarok; you are the fortunate ones, our ultimate heroes.

"This great longship will transport your souls across the waters of darkness to the afterlife, to the Other World. The flames and smoke will carry you straight to our great Pagan Gods."

With a deft stroke of his seax dagger on a flint, Eric created a myriad of sparks that lit the dry hay of a torch. As it flared, ten other men lit torches from Eric's and cast them into different parts of the trench. The flames shot up and burned fiercely for quite a while.

Eddie was startled to see that, in front of the flames, figures of dozens of Druids lined the edge of the trench. They weren't solid, as he could see the flames through them. Eric looked into Eddie's eyes and swept his hands in the Druids' direction before falling to his knees and then prostrating himself before the Druids and his dead. The rest of the fit Danes did likewise. Eddie, overcome by the solemnity of the situation, also dropped to his knees before lying face down in submission to the deities.

Aefnoth remained standing, unable to understand the latest phenomenon. But he was so overawed by the ceremony's gravitas, his mouth hung open and he clasped his hands tightly together.

Eric stood up and then spoke to Eddie. "You could see our masters were there, friend?"

"Yes, Eric. Lines of Druids. Your warriors will certainly go to Valhalla today."

Eric nodded and walked back to the funeral pyre.

Aefnoth didn't understand a word Eric had said. But he empathized with the solemnity of the ritual. He also felt solidarity with the deceased warriors as they had been fighting on the same side only the day before.

Overpowering the woodsmoke and ozone smells was an overwhelming sweet stench from the burning bodies. This was quite natural, but Eddie was relieved when it was all finished. He thought how composed the Danish warriors had been, mostly solemn or smiling, although he did notice that one young boy had tears running down his cheeks. He recognized the lad as one half of identical twins whose brother had been killed.

When the flames had died down, the trench was filled in with earth until a mound was formed. After this, stones were piled on the trench, creating a tumulus or barrow. Then finally a large flat stone inscribed with Runes was placed on top, hopefully establishing a permanent memorial to the slain.

Eddie read the runes. They said: 'Fly quickly to Valhalla, Heroes'. He interpreted the chiselled runes' meaning for Aefnoth.

He nodded his head. "That's how I'd like to go, as a hero. But not yet, until I have many sons to carry on my mission."

Later, everybody involved moved to the beach. Another trench had been dug. The remains of the burnt-out canoe was put into it. It was followed by the Norwegian dead and then dry branches were laid on top of them.

Eric said a few appropriate words, similar to those for his own men, if somewhat truncated in this case. But considering these men had been killing his warriors only a few hours earlier, it was still surprising to Eddie that he would do it at all.

These dry branches were also lit and eventually the same sweet stench of burning bodies assailed Eddie's nostrils. When the flames had died down, the ashes of the Norwegian dead were covered with a mound of sand.

Aefnoth scratched his head, looking confused though fascinated with the whole procedure. He whispered to Eddie "What's going on here?"

"I'll have to ask Ericsson to explain it to me."

After the Norwegians' cremations, Eddie asked, "Ericsson, why, if these men were trying to wipe out your warriors, are you showing them such reverence?"

"Although they were our enemies in battle, they were also men who have fallen in war. As such, they will also be allowed their place beside our brave warriors in Valhalla."

Eddie was puzzled. "I still don't get it. They killed your friends?"

Ericsson tried to explain. "You see, Edward, it's our belief that the dead can return to haunt the living. They can become revenants, or malevolent ghosts, if they're not treated with sufficient respect. If that happened it would be an omen that others would also die soon."

Eddie face turned white at the very idea of malicious spectres returning to haunt them.

Ericsson continued, "When Ragnarok, which is the end of the world, comes, these warriors will also rise with our own battle slain. Together they will fight by Odin's side against the people of the fire realm."

Eddie thanked Ericsson and then explained what he'd been told to Aefnoth who, as a Saxon warrior, seemed to accept the idea of solidarity between dead combatants more readily. Although Eddie was also a warrior, his Romani culture was more into revenge than unanimity with their enemies.

Aefnoth looked up as a fat pigeon flew out from the poplar tree they were standing beneath. The bird's wings knocked down several red catkins onto the trio's heads.

Eddie had a question for Ericsson. "I'd heard rumours that some Viking funerals are held by laying the corpse on a ship and then setting the ship aflame and letting it sail out to sea, leaving it to burn and sink with the cremated body on board. Is that just a myth?"

"Not entirely, Edward. That does happen very occasionally. However, it's only evoked for some of our greatest kings and high chiefs.

"Why only a few of the top men? Surely every warrior's important?"

Ericsson nodded. "You're right, but longships are very valuable and take so long to build. It would be such a waste to destroy one for mere warriors. In any case, if a longship was burnt for each warrior, how would the fallen men's comrades sail home after a battle?"

Eddie smiled. "A good point... I hadn't thought of that."

Ericsson said as an afterthought, "Mind you, I have heard of raids where so many warriors were killed there weren't enough survivors to crew all of the longships. In those cases the dead were loaded aboard the spare ships and then they were floated and burnt. That was killing two birds with one stone. Not only were they Viking funerals, but those longships were denied to their enemies."

Eddie thanked Ericsson for this information. Then he remembered an equivalent dilemma in his own ethnicity where it was a Romani tradition to burn the goods of the deceased when the owner 'mullered' or died.

First the Danes had the solemnity of the funerals. Then they moved on to the ceremonial feasting. Apart from the sentries, everybody ate and drank all through the night. They fed on spit-roasted sheep and stews made with lamb bones, white thin-rooted carrots, wild parsnips and cabbages. They drank mead, a sweet alcoholic drink made from honey, as well as barley and acorn beers, plus an apple wine not unlike the cider enjoyed by the Saxons.

Aefnoth was particularly taken with the barley beer and had soon drunk too much of it. So much so, he was having trouble standing. Eddie tried all four types of alcohol but didn't like any of them much, so stayed sober.

The following day, as Eddie had expected, most of the men had hangovers. That was with the exception of the previous night's sentries who were now making up for lost time with the food and alcohol. Eddie reckoned the best day to attack the Vikings would be the day after a previous battle.

Eric approached Eddie and said, "Agnar wishes to speak to you."

Agnar, the tall young Viking, spoke to Eddie solemnly and directly. "I didn't believe you could interpret the Runes. As I was wrong, I am bound by my oath to give you my father's amulet." He held out the amulet out for Eddie to take.

Eddie raised his right palm. "There's no need. You can keep your amulet as it's a family heirloom."

However, Agnar went white in the face, shook his head and cast his eyes down.

Eric took Eddie to one side. "You should take the amulet," he whispered. "If you don't, he believes that according to our great pagan religion, he will go to Niflheim when he dies. Failure to complete an oath's terms brings the oathmaker great dishonour, even if they have tried to keep the oath. If the other party refuses, it's seen as the ultimate insult. Many men become depressed and kill themselves, rather than live with an unfulfilled oath on their conscience."

"I understand," Eddie replied in a hushed tone. "I had forgotten how strong your pagan beliefs are."

Eddie addressed Agnar again; "I will be honoured to accept the amulet and will treasure it as you have. I commend you on your integrity and rectitude."

The big fellow nodded and then passed Eddie the wide gold armband talisman with an amber Thor's Hammer mounted on it. Agnar looked relieved. Death was obviously no problem to him. But not being able to keep his actions in line with his beliefs would be catastrophic.

Aefnoth was trying to amuse himself while the others spoke in Danish. Looking around, he noticed the oak trees had bunches of parasitic mistletoe growing from them. He'd heard of the Druids' belief that mistletoe growing on oak trees was the most sacred form of the plant. He knew they picked the white berries to use in many of their pagan potions and in particular to create aphrodisiacs and improve fertility.

Eddie examined the beautiful carved metal and amber amulet. "How was such a piece of art available to you Danes?" he asked Eric. "I'd not realized that amber was naturally attainable in Denmark?"

Eric replied, "You are right, it's very rare. But you should understand we Norsemen are great travellers and traders. We're not afraid to explore anywhere in Odin's world."

"I've travelled far on land. Is that how most of your trading is done?

"Sometimes we go by land routes. But we travel vast distances by sea."

"But how do you navigate in the vast ocean? Surely you'd get lost?"

"No. You see, we Vikings know the entire ocean is completely surrounded by landmasses. It's like a colossal pond inside a gigantic village green. If we keep going in one direction, we know we'll come to land eventually."

Eddie persisted. "So was this beautiful object part of a trading deal?"

"Yes. The amulet was traded by Agnar's father, with an artisan in a village called Wolin in Poland. We barter for articles in amber and gold, for textiles, food and, in particular, weapons. For example, without doubt the sharpest double-edged swords come from the Frankish Rhineland. The very best are made by the smiths Ingelrii and Ulfberht."

Eddie clasped his hands. "What goods do you have to trade for such exotic merchandise?"

"Because we're excellent hunters and there are plenty of fur bearing animals for us in Denmark, we have a large surplus of furs that are prized elsewhere, so they are ideal for trading."

After this, Eric went off to check that his wounded warriors were being looked after. By this time Aefnoth had become so bored by a conversation he could not understand, he had laid down in the sun and fallen asleep.

Eddie sat on the sandy beach watching with interest a flock of the small, round, dunlin wading birds running about by the waterline, emitting their staccato cries of 'Shrit! Shrit!'

Later, Aefnoth woke and Eric returned, so Eddie joined them in a walk along the now peaceful sandy beach. Eddie used the time to ask further questions of Eric. "Is there any significance in the big black bird image that's on the Norwegians' banner?

"Yes. Many Vikings use similar banners. You may have noticed the actual banner was made in the shape of a battleaxe blade. This indicates it's the axe raven banner, the personal standard of Prince Olaf Tryggvasson of Norway.

"The raven emblem is indicative of the live wild ravens all Vikings carry on long voyages. You see, we know when we release one that it will always fly in the direction of the nearest land. So we follow its direction of flight to safety. Also, the raven is a sacred bird. In the sagas, our great God, Odin, invariably had two ravens as companions It's believed by the Norwegians that if a flying wild raven appears when they're in battle, their side will win. If it's at rest they'll lose."

"So, in that case Eric, why is your banner just plain white?"

"Well you see, Tryggvasson and all the Norwegians have it wrong. We Danes know that in battle a raven's image has been known to appear on our plain banner and bring us Odin's blessing."

Aefnoth, still uninterested, threw a stone at a black headed gull, but missed.

Eric resumed. "Mind you, it takes a brave warrior to carry either banner into a fight, as that man becomes a prime target and is very often killed while holding it."

The three walked in silence for a while and then Aefnoth spotted a rowing boat over by the mainland.

Eric followed his gaze. "That's your Saxon friends in their rowing boat, spying on us again. I don't blame them. It's sensible to be forewarned of any danger."

"You're probably right about that rowing boat, Eric," Eddie agreed. "Can you tell me who these berserkers are? I saw two of them crash through your warriors' shield wall on the beach. My arrow hit one at close range and he didn't even go down."

Eric grimaced. "Oh yes, the berserkers. They are all big, strong, professional warriors who dress in bear or wolf fur. They use these outer garments to create a larger physical profile. This is also to create a look of terrifying invincibility that is implied by their ferocious animalistic appearance."

Eddie nodded. "The monster that attacked me looked to be out of his head. You know, not fully aware of reality. Is that normal berserker behaviour?"

"Yes, that's usual. You see, berserkers always swallow fungal agaric drugs before battles to become fearless. After taking the drugs, these men fight in an ecstasy which makes them extremely aggressive. Those drugs' effects also ape localized anaesthesia, so they can also disregard pain."

"But in reality they can die, the same as anybody else," Eddie pointed out. "I've just witnessed one berserker's death on this island."

"Of course, you're absolutely right. We all die in the end. But remember that our pagan religion says the time of your death is predetermined by fate. So it doesn't matter when it happens, that's your time by predestination."

"I'd forgotten you told me that."

Eric continued, "Before combat, berserkers achieve a particular drug-induced state of mind that encourages them to fight fiercely and tirelessly for hours or even days. Unfortunately when the battle's over, even if they've not been wounded, they sometimes die from exhaustion."

Eddie released a surprised sigh. "That's amazing, Eric. Please tell me more."

Eric coughed up some phlegm and spat it out before continuing. "Often, before combat, berserkers stand grinding their teeth and even biting the edges of their shields. They're so drugged up that some of them even remove their armour and clothes.

"Most of them belong to a berserkers' sect, which is a cult dedicated to Odin. berserkers in the sect generally have psychological 'attributes' such as being psychopaths, and intentionally provoke drugged seizures."

Eddie scratched at his cheek and shook his head, unable to fully understand this concept.

Eric explained. "The berserkers become so completely fearless, battle commanders consider they give the other warriors more courage by their example. They will always use them to lead the charge, if available. Berserkers therefore are usually the first men to go into hand-to-hand combat with the enemy.

A berserker is inevitably picked for the lead man in a Boar Snout charge. This is the wedge formation you saw them using on Osea beach. This is when one berserker, equipped with almost complete body armour, is pushed at speed like a battering ram by the other Vikings at the opposing shield wall."

Eddie loudly drew in his breath, remembering the Boars Snout charge he had witnessed in the recent battle.

"The sheer weight and momentum of the charge usually breaks through any defensive wall. Then the following warriors can get behind the enemies' shield wall and attack the unprotected opposing warriors. This generally spreads panic amongst our opponents. As often as not, it turns the battle in our favour."

A hornet danced round Aefnoth's face and he became agitated by the insect, swiping it away several times before it left him alone.

Eddie continued to quiz Eric. "But this constant excessive drug taking must have long term detrimental effects on the berserkers?"

"Yes, indeed. It has many secondary effects, even well after a battle has finished. As an example, we were in the middle of a victory party when one of our berserkers' ecstasy returned. He jumped up, took his sword and began swinging it in the air... his comrades had to duck. And then he began to hack uncontrollably at a rock until his aggression disappeared. Additionally, there have been many times when berserkers have killed their own men in battle, or afterwards."

"But surely this must make them a liability when there's no battle?"

"True. When there is peace, many berserkers travel around the country. They fight, for payment, as mercenaries or soldiers of fortune, sometimes in battles but at other times in single combat to settle feuds.

Unfortunately the berserkers stay extremely violent and quarrelsome and will sometimes enter a trance state involuntarily. This makes it impossible to control them. Therefore, during peaceful times they have to live in the woods, separated from 'normal' people."

"So don't these men have a family life at all?"

"As a rule, they live alone," Eric replied. But some berserkers challenge farm owners to combat. Their only goal is winning the duel and taking everything, including the farmer's family. The challenged farmer cannot refuse because it would compromise his honour, although sometimes he can see that he has no chance in a duel. So then, without any fight, the man gives all his belongings to the challenger, including his own wife."

Eddie's mouth was hanging open and he scratched his head.

"Berserkers seldom marry or even have steady girlfriends. However, in their mentally degenerate state they often become violent rapists. We Vikings have a bad name as rapists and pillagers. But the raping is usually down to the berserkers so it's an unfair slur on the rest of us. That's why I haven't brought any berserkers with me on this expedition. Except in a major battle, they're more of a liability than a help."

Aefnoth was shifting from foot to foot. Then he picked a long grass stem which he sucked on noisily.

"I'll tell you all about this later," Eddie told Aefnoth. "It's fascinating." He then asked Eric, "Can you tell me about this fungal agaric the berserkers use to drug themselves?"

"Agaric's just a woodland fungus. I'll show you some growing if you like?"

"Thanks Eric, that would be most useful."

As the three men left the beach and walked off into the woods, Eddie passed on what he'd just learned to Aefnoth.

Eric pointed out various fungi, under evergreens, on dead wood and organic waste. They had yellow or scarlet caps. He also indicated other fungi that the berserkers used, including the death cap and destroying angel.

Eddie picked a few death caps from under an oak tree. They were egg shaped, greenish in colour and felt a little slimy. They looked a bit like straw mushrooms. Some young ones had a faint honey-sweet smell, but the mature ones had an overpowering, sickly-sweet objectionable stink. Aefnoth also picked one and had to be restrained by Eric from tasting it.

Eric said, "Both of you must wash your hands now you've handled them, as there's no antidote to that plant's toxin. You could both die from liver and kidney poisoning. I've been told the Roman Emperor Claudius was reputed to have died from eating death caps."

Eddie explained to Aefnoth about the poisonous mushrooms and they walked to a stream to wash their hands.

Aefnoth told Eddie, "We also use mushrooms to poison our spears and arrows, but these are a different variety."

"What are the symptoms of being drugged by agaric fungi?" Eddie asked Eric.

"Well, Edward, the berserkers take agaric well before battle, because they have a delayed effect. After about twenty minutes they go into a deep sleep and then wake up with hallucinations and feelings of euphoria. Sometimes the agaric also gives them severe digestive upsets. Also they can get dizziness, psychological distress and convulsions, so the quantity eaten is crucial. Because of this, they test various amounts in training to produce the greatest aggression with the least after affects."

"But surely they can't rely on finding supplies when they need them?"

"You are right, Edward. That's why they keep a bag of dried agaric and other drugs with them, in case it's needed "

"I see. That explains a lot."

Aefnoth was again bored as he didn't understand a word the others were saying. He was watching with interest as a green woodpecker, with its distinctive red head, flew over. The bird dipped with closed wings and then rose again in a series of enormous swoops. Its mocking cry was like a human laugh.

Eddie was fascinated by Eric's description of the drugs' effects and decided to find out as much about them as possible.

"How do these drugs work, and what effects do they have?"

Eric explained. "The last two types of fungus I told you about, death cap and destroying angel are deadly poisonous. We use them to coat spears and arrowheads. Even a scratch from these tainted missiles causes real problems. After an hour, the person injured by these contaminated weapons feels intoxicated, confused, anxious and delirious."

Aefnoth sighed and kicked at an ant hill, displaying his mounting boredom.

Eric continued, "Any weapon-poisoned enemy can get paranoia and tremors and altered perceptions of speed, light and colour. None of which is any good for the affected warrior in a long battle situation."

Eddie nodded.

"Effectively, then, being hit by any poisoned missile puts that person out of action in the long term, even if the actual wound doesn't. Of course, if they get a large dose they die in agony with stomach cramps as their internal organs are destroyed."

Without warning a loud commotion broke out from the direction of the campfire area. There were the unmistakable sounds of screaming, shouting and weapons clashing, it sounded like another Norwegian attack.

If it were an assault by Olaf Tryggvasson's full fleet, the few fit and sober Danes would quickly be overcome and they would all be annihilated.

With fear and trepidation, Eric, Eddie and Aefnoth rushed back towards the camp and the increasing uproar.

Nineteen

On a hot June day, a rowing boat dropped anchor in the Blackwater Estuary. The Saxon, Augustine, occasionally cast his fishing net from the boat. However, this was just a distraction to conceal the fact that he was spying on the activities of the Vikings on Osea Island.

On Osea, beads of perspiration trickled into Eddie's eyes. Despite being in the shadows of the woods he found it difficult to breathe, as if there were a storm brewing.

The Danish Viking leader, Eric Greybeard, had been showing Eddie and Aefnoth the poisonous and hallucinogenic fungi that grew there. Only rooks cawing in their roost disturbed the peaceful scene. That was until sounds of shouting and weapons clashing were heard coming from the direction of the Danes' camp.

Eric shouted to Eddie and Aefnoth, "Come on! That sounds like another Norwegian attack."

The three men ran back towards the camp as fast as they could, swords at the ready. To their relief, when they entered the camp clearing there were no foreign attackers to be seen. Instead, two young Danes were bellowing threateningly at each other. Their faces were almost touching; each was trying to stare the other out, determined not to be the first to look away.

Eric shouted an order. "Stop this madness, you two! Come here and explain what this is about."

Sihtric said, "When we get back home to Denmark, I intend to marry my girlfriend, Aelfald."

Leifur retorted, "That's nonsense. She's marrying me."

Ericsson intervened. "You're both wrong. I know she told you both she'd make her decision if and when you both return."

"So what's the problem then?" Eric asked the two warriors.

Leifur said, "Its Sihtric's fault. He's just challenged me to a Holmganga duel…"

Sihtric butted in. "That's right, I have, if he's not afraid to accept it."

Eric stood between the two men and asked Sihtric, "What brought this on? Can't you wait till we get home?"

"No. I've lost so many comrades in the last few days, I've decided I want to be certain of my future now, not in a few months time."

"So be it then," Eric pronounced, "but you'll fight to the lesser traditional formalized rules."

The two adversaries agreed to this and that the reward to the winner would be the hand of the girl, Aelfald, in marriage. That was if she accepted the winner.

Eric told them to make their preparations, "Come back here in an hour and then I will go through the procedures with you."

Sihtric was very tall and muscular. He had the Vikings' classic long, blond hair, beard and moustache. His rough masculine face sported blue eyes and a rather hooked nose. His opponent, Leifur, was marginally shorter, brawny with ginger hair. He was clean shaven with a similarly rugged countenance to his opponent, but with a snub nose, freckles and piercing green eyes.

Eric explained to Eddie, "Historically, our quarrels are settled by a Holmganga duel. The two warriors fight on a tiny deserted island, in hand-to-hand combat to the death.

"Isn't that rather drastic, Eric?"

"It certainly is, particularly as our force has already been depleted by the Norwegians' attack. So in this case, I've imposed a lesser option. To fight until one of them is badly injured."

"But if they fight, won't it split your warriors into two camps?"

"No. Everybody, including the fighters, will accept the result. Honour having been satisfied, both fighters will become comrades again. It's expected in our culture. However, if I banned the fight, resentment would grow between them... not good for overall morale."

Later, Eric announced to the two rivals and the whole community, "The rules are that you must fight within the area you're given. There will be a two-metre light coloured square cloak in the centre, with further areas around it marked by hazel sticks. This is representing the Holmganga.

If either steps outside of this area, they'll be declared a coward and will lose the fight. If anyone's hurt badly enough for their blood to hit the cloak, the fight will be stopped and the one whose blood was shed will have lost."

Aefnoth was moving from foot to foot, and then held out both hands to Eddie, palms upwards.

Eddie got the message and told Aefnoth what was going on.

Eric led all his men towards the east end of the island where he knew there were many open, sandy areas.

As they walked, Eddie asked Ericsson what Holmganga meant.

"It literally means to go to a small island," Ericsson replied.

"What weapons are they allowed?"

"Each man is allocated three shields, plus the offensive weapons they agree between them. I believe in this case it's a double-edged sword and a seax single-edged dagger."

"And are these fights usually over women?"

"Quite often they are. This is because we Danes practise polygamy. Many Scandinavian men have several wives. A legitimate one and others who are concubines belonging to the slave classes, captured in raids. I myself have four wives including three concubines. Unfortunately this results in fewer females being available for the younger men to marry. Consequently, these two young men have none. You see, it's considered a point of honour to at least have one wife by the time their second raid's completed and this is theirs."

Quietly, Eddie told Aefnoth what Ericsson had said.

Aefnoth whispered to Eddie, "I'm intrigued, as a warrior myself, to witness a Holmganga duel. I want to compare the Viking close combat techniques with the way we fight."

Eric told Eddie, "I've appointed Ericsson as the fight referee as he's taller and of superior rank to the two antagonists. His task will be to control or stop the fight and disqualify anyone who cheats."

"Thanks for telling me. Aefnoth and I are interested in all your customs since you told us some of your sagas."

Eric smiled and then went to find a suitable sandspit. When he did, he positioned the cloak in the centre, weighed it down with four large stones and gestured to Ericsson to carry on.

Ericsson marked out the borders in the sand around the cloak. Hazel staves were placed in the corners and finally, stones to mark the edges of the formulaic pattern arena called the Tjosnublot.

When this was all set up, Ericsson declared to all, "This area is now hazelled."

The whole space of the Tjosnublot, Eddie judged to be approximately twenty square feet. Not large for two long-armed men wielding swords, he thought.

The rest of the Vikings made a circle around the Tjosnublot, about two swords length away from the outside edge. The crowd of Danes were slapping hands vertically or mutually punching fists, then shaking hands. While they did so, Eddie could hear sharp verbal exchanges between them.

He was intrigued and then realized they were taking or making bets on the result of the fight. Eddie couldn't understand this. It was barely twenty-four hours after the funerals of many of their comrades. Now they were gambling on a possible extra death. Then

Eddie remembered the Vikings' belief that dying in battle was a good thing as the dead went straight to Valhalla.

As before, Onan Claw-hands was at the hub of it all, collecting stakes. He seemed to delight in any form of wager. When Eddie explained about the games of chance to Aefnoth, he understood the situation well enough.

"I love to bet," he replied, "And would have had a flutter on the fight if I spoke Danish."

Eric appointed two of the more senior Danes, Guthlac and his trusted lieutenant, Strong-arms Rasmussen, to act as sentries in case the Norwegians attacked again. Eddie heard Guthlac complain to Rasmussen, "I'd rather watch the fight." Rasmussen merely shrugged his shoulders. He had seen many before.

Eddie noticed both antagonists were pacing around. Leifur's mouth had developed a twitch. Sihtric had sweat running down his forehead, which he wiped away with the back of his hand. He was also bending his knees and flexing his arms.

Both stood on the edges of the sandspit Tjosnublot area. They were dressed in long chain mail tunics and wore metal conical helmets with nose protecting strips. They each held a sword in one hand and a shield in the other, with a seax dagger tucked into their waistbands.

As was the custom, before the duel, Sihtric, who had issued the challenge, reiterated it. This was followed by the man being challenged, Leifur, reciting the rules of the Holmgongulog, including the reward to the winner.

Waves lapped onto the sand only feet from the Tjosnublot. About fifty yards out, a seal watched the humans with interest, its big, dark eyes unblinking. Halfway across the estuary, the Saxon Augustine up-anchored and rowed his boat nearer, to better observe the action.

The crowd fell silent and Ericsson lowered his spear for the contest to begin. As he did so, a flash of lightning in the distance followed by a rumble of thunder, gave a surreal feeling to the situation.

Ignoring the changing weather signs from the heavens, the combatants rushed resolutely at each other. No doubt it was their pent-up nervous energy and adrenaline kicking in. The two men forced their shields against one another, each hoping their opponent would show some weakness.

Neither gave an inch so they both backed off. Leifur swung his sword over his head in a tight arc. If it had found its mark, it would have split his opponent's skull in two despite his helmet. But Sihtric sprang back and side-stepped. At the same time he swiped horizontally with his own sword.

Leifur swiftly deflected his opponent's sword with his shield, clashing the metal boss into the weapon. As his opponent's sword crashed away on to the ground, he lunged with his own sword, then swung it in a circular motion, trying to knock his adversary's shield out of his hand.

This had no effect and Sihtric dived sideways and retrieved his dropped weapon. Soon both swords were engaged, parrying their opponent's blade. Sihtric forced his weight vigorously against his adversary, but as he tried to lean on him, Leifur smashed his shield's edge into his face.

Sihtric crashed sideways onto the ground, a long purple bruise already swelling on his cheek. While Sihtric was down, Leifur swung his sword and then his foot at Sihtric. Hurriedly, Sihtric rolled away from the sword, but was kicked on the forearm. Desperately, he made a grab at Leifur's leg and pulled upwards sharply, bringing his opponent down on the ground with him.

By now, Eddie could smell the fighters' sweat after their strenuous efforts on this muggy afternoon. Aefnoth and many of the Danes had been twitching, ghost- riding blows and feinting… fending off the attacks as if they were themselves fighting in the Holmganga.

Now both warriors were on the ground, wrestling and punching each other violently. Sihtric broke free and was up first, swinging his sword vertically and hard at his foe. This Leifur took on his shield. It split; the sword going straight through the soft wood. But this was not as good for Sihtric as Eddie had assumed. The sword had snared in the shield's fibres. Leifur dragged his shield vertically, forcing Sihtric's sword out of his hand.

Just then the storm arrived with a vengeance, turning the sky black. Lightning and thunder filled the air, adding to the tension. A summer hailstone deluged the brawlers and battered the assembled crowd. The storm hurled the pellets of ice vertically, smashing into bare flesh and causing discomfort to everyone.

The instant change to cold, atrocious weather caused Sihtric to pause momentarily and Leifur took advantage. He swung his sword offensively back and forth at speed. In the crowd, arms were raised to cover faces, and hands sheltered eyes so that they didn't miss any action by the combatants.

Pugnaciously, Sihtric parried repeatedly with his shield that was splintering, but just holding together. As he fended the sword off for the fifth time he swung his shield upwards so that the central metal boss hit Leifur hard in the face, at the same time grabbing his own seax knife.

Leifur's mouth was split and swollen but he slashed again and again at Sihtric. The two fighters attacked and fended most blows off with their shields. But inevitably some blows got through and both were looking worse for wear, bruised and bloodied.

During a comparative lull, the combatants called to Ericsson, asking to change shields. Ericsson gave his permission and they threw down the old ones and picked up replacements. Ericsson checked that they were ready and then lowered his sword once more for the duel to restart.

Despite the continuous hail storm, none of the watching Vikings had moved away as the spectacle was too engrossing. Gone was the stifling heat. The re-oxygenated cool air altered the whole atmosphere on the sandspit. Everybody's clothing was soaked through and their extremities were freezing cold. Scents of wet grass and soaking leaves mingled with the ozone to intensify everybody's senses.

A warrior in the crowd, Thorsson, called out, "Hey you two, why don't you kill each other? I'll look after pretty little Aelfald for you. She fancies me more than you two, anyway."

Both fighters gave Thorsson black looks and Leifur shouted back at him, "I'll fight you next for that insult, you sick bastard."

This caused bawdy laughter from the rest of the crowd and some ribald comments about Thorsson's carnal prowess. Thorsson's mouth turned down and he hunched his shoulders noticeably.

The thunderstorm was relentless. Lightning, thunder and hail caused consternation and confusion to the adversaries. Sihtric forced his shield into Leifur's face, at the same time placing his leg behind his opponent and pushing him backwards onto the soaking ground. Sihtric stabbed at Leifur with his sword but he rolled out of the way and kicked upwards into Sihtric's groin. He went down as well, clutching his bruised crotch. Red in the face, Sihtric gasped for breath, his pained expression betraying his agony.

Thorsson shouted, "You'll be no use to Aelfald now, Sihtric! Leave her to me."

Leifur had risen to his feet and raised his sword to strike the winning blow when, without warning, a lightning bolt stuck the earth near the Tjosnublot. A discharge of celestial electricity flashed across the ground, stunning both combatants on the rain-soaked sand. An almighty crack of thunder followed within seconds with deafening intensity.

Everyone in the watching crowd felt the shock through their feet, making them jump about. Some also covered their ears that were still ringing from the thunderclap's explosive boom.

Eric and Ericsson had been shocked with all the others. Ericsson recovered quickly and stepped into the Tjosnublot area. Holding up both hands, he ordered the men to cease fighting for a few moments. Eric climbed onto a high sand dune and addressed the assembled men.

"My friends, our great Thor, God of thunder, who is emblematic of the thunderbolt, has intervened to show his pleasure at this Holmganga duel, indicating he's put his seal of approval on the event."

The crowd cheered at this and began chanting, "Thor's hammer, Thor's hammer," over and over again.

Aefnoth asked what was going on and Eddie told him what Eric had said.

"Oh," Aefnoth said, "Perhaps the Viking Gods are the authentic ones after all. I'll be careful not to deride them in future."

While the bout had stopped, the two fighters asked Ericsson for permission to change shields and get a drink of water. Ericsson agreed and they did just that, not needing to wash their wounds as the rain had cleaned them naturally.

In the Maldon Burh, Kate and her handmaidens had sheltered inside her quarters to avoid the thunderstorm. Water dripped from the window openings as the skin coverings were blown in by the force of the wind.

Edith was terrified of the thunder and lightning and cowered on the floor, covering her head with a blanket. The other girls, Alfthrith and Bretwalda, giggled nervously while Kate comforted them.

Princess Catherine considered storms to be magnificent expressions of a god's power. When she was a child she had met a Druid who appeared during a storm. With arms aloft, pointing to the sky, he told her not to be afraid as she was more than a princess. She was above mere mortals and would never be harmed by the earth's minor turbulences. The Druid said when she was a young woman she would meet a young man who was also from the same ancient race. Their destiny would be shared and by the direction of a heavenly storm's power, she would sense who he was.

Although she was only seven years old at the time, Kate had never forgotten the Druid. Or that, despite the druidic priest standing in the pouring rain, his habit did not get wet. She had blinked and the Druid had vanished.

A massive flash of lightning filled the room with brilliant white light, followed by a deafening clap of thunder, making Edith shake violently and start crying. But it had a far more profound affect on Kate.

In that instant she realized her own bodyguard, Edward the Tall, was the young man from the ancient race the Druid had foretold would come to her. Had the Druid meant a Romani? But the Druid had said they were from the same ancient race, so it had to be a different one?

On Osea Island, Ericsson judged the weather had improved enough to restart the fight. He lowered his spear again to let the dual recommence.

Leifur struck the second session's first blow, swinging his sword at Sihtric who took its full force on his shield. Sihtric retaliated with a horizontal swing with his own sword which Leifur parried. They both fought bravely for another half an hour, neither gaining any advantage.

The combatants' ability to concentrate was made more difficult as regular lightning flashes were filling the cloud-blackened sky with ultra brightness every few seconds. The sounds of clashing of weapons were punctuated by peals of thunder and the drumming of the massive hailstones on the sea, the sand and their hot bodies.

One thunderbolt hit a majestic but dying old oak on the island just behind the sandspit. The rotting tree instantly burst into flames and one massive branch that comprised nearly half the tree, came crashing down. It landed so near the Tjosnublot area that several warriors had to dive out of the way to avoid being crushed. The huge hollow branch burned brightly despite the deluge of hail.

The Danes obviously considered this was another sign from the hammer of the thunder God, Thor, as they chanted his name again and again.

Eddie was distracted by a vision on the surface of the sea. He thought he saw a Druid rising from the depths in a white robe. He sensed it telling him 'they' were with him and his role was important to 'them'. Then, just as quickly, the opaque figure submerged again.

The duel continued. Both fighters had been buoyed up by the obvious signs of approval from their thunder God, Thor. However, both warriors were now tiring, using up their last reserves of energy. Incredibly, the duel had already been going on for over two hours. By now, after both giving as good as each other, they were mutually black and blue and covered in blood from sword wounds and shield swipes, particularly on the face, arms and legs. Eddie realized that in this type of fight, the shields had indeed become the main offensive as well as defensive weapons.

The end came when Sihtric slipped on a patch of hailstones. Leifur took his chance and swiped his seax knife yet again at Sihtric. This time the blade connected with the momentarily undefended Sihtric, catching him across the neck. Blood spurted out like a fountain and landed on the cloak. Once his blood hit the cloth, Sihtric had lost.

Ericsson stepped between the adversaries and announced, "Enough. The victor is Leifur. He wins the prize of the young lady Aelfald as his wife. If she'll have him"

As if on cue, the storm abated and the sun heated the men's wet clothing making them steam. The crowd saw this as yet another sign from Thor, the God of thunder. They assumed Thor had lost interest now the Holmganga duel was over. The pumped up warriors chanted 'Thor's hammer' over and over again.

There was chaos around the Tjosnublot, partly from the ecstasy of Thor's perceived approval but mostly as the crowd were settling up for their wagers with Oman Claw-hands. Still more were toasting the winner in mead.

In the confusion, Sihtric was being ignored and blood was pulsing out of his neck. Eddie doubted he could live long in that condition and felt he must to do something to help. He forced the heel of one hand hard against Sihtric's neck but the arterial blood pressure was pushing his hand away. Placing his other hand on top of the first, he then pressed down as hard as he could. Eddie's clothing was soon saturated with Sihtric's blood. Sihtric was losing consciousness.

Eddie yelled to Eric, "If you want to keep this man alive, he needs help now."

Eric and Ericsson had been sidetracked by the excited warriors, so they hadn't realized the severity of the loser's plight.

Eric rushed over and told Eddie, "We must get him stitched up straight away." He barked out his orders and Guthlac ran over with a horseshoe-shaped needle and some thread to stitch the wound. A rolled cloth pad was then brought and forced down over the wound and bandaged.

Sihtric was wrapped in blankets and carried back to the camp, and then laid near the fire to recover. Eddie seriously doubted whether Sihtric could survive the night, but there was nothing else he could do for him.

Eddie was still covered in Sihtric's blood and as he had no spare clothing he dived into the sea fully clothed to wash it off. However, when he emerged, the salt seawater, sand and mud particles swirling in it had made his skin itchy. He found a clear freshwater brook and rewashed his clothes and body. He then lay naked in the hot sun until he and his clothes were fully dry.

When Eddie eventually returned to the camp, Aefnoth said, "The duel was fantastic. I'd have liked to fight that way myself. But though I'm strong, I doubt if I could have lasted for such a long time. The lady must be very pretty; they both wanted her so much."

Eddie acknowledged Aefnoth's sentiment with a laugh. "You're right, and if I've learned anything here, it's that Vikings like to party as much as fight."

Aefnoth smiled. "I don't mind that at all. It's a good way to build camaraderie again after a setback."

Despite the post-battle shindig barely finishing, food and mead were soon available again. This time, stew was being consumed from bowls with the use of wooden spoons.

That night Eddie found sleep difficult with all the carousing and good-natured mock fighting going on, but he eventually dozed off.

In the morning, Eddie checked on Sihtric to see if he'd survived the night. He had, but was very white and drawn. To Eddie's surprise, Sihtric's erstwhile opponent, Leifur, was feeding him with thin gruel from a small wooden spoon.

Eddie noted that although Leifur was the winner, his face was badly swollen and his lips split. His head and limbs were bandaged and his face had a definite pallor. In fact he looked almost as bad as the loser, Sihtric.

Leifur explained to Eddie why he was feeding Sihtric. "Before our rivalry over the girl, Aelfald, we'd been good friends. In fact we are cousins who played together as children."

"If you didn't want to hurt your cousin, why not hold back?" asked Eddie.

"Unfortunately, in the heat of any battle or fight, it's not possible to be that clever. If you hesitate, you are more likely to be killed yourself. Literally, it was survival of the fittest."

"Why did it take you so long to reach a conclusion?"

"The problem is that in a normal battle situation your opponents will have many different styles. But in this case we had both learned the same fighting moves together, so we anticipated each other's attacks and defences, making it really difficult."

"As you were fighting over a girl, what status do your women have in Norse society? Do woman have to do their men folks bidding?"

"Not at all. In our land, free women, as opposed to slaves, are considered equal to men. You see, their husbands are away much of the time hunting, trading or raiding, so they often have to take on the entire management of the farm as well as the home. This is vitally important when you remember their men often don't survive raids."

Aefnoth scratched at his face and wiggled his shoulders.

Leifur continued, "Because of the importance of their work, it's of more significance to find a capable wife. Looks are of secondary value to us Norse men. However, the girl, Aelfald, we fought over had all the best skills learnt in her farming childhood and is beautiful as well. She's a real prize."

After Eddie had translated all this to Aefnoth, the big Saxon understood the sentiments entirely.

Eddie had been fascinated by the Holmganga duel. However, he was confused. When the white lightning bolt had smitten the oak tree in half, he'd had such a strange vision and feeling... that as well as being a Romani, he was from a more ancient culture still. Who were '*they*' the Druid from the sea had psychically told him about?

This whole situation was an enigma. He now knew, or rather felt, there was a great deal more he didn't know about himself. He sensed it was somehow tied in with Kate, but he had no idea how.

Adding to his confusion, he now felt strongly that something even more dangerous was waiting around the corner for him.

Twenty

On Osea Island in the Blackwater Estuary, the grass seemed to be greener after the rain storms. It was sunny with a mild sea breeze distributing the scent of smoke from the aromatic birchwood cooking fires. At the Danish Vikings' camp the morning seemed peaceful. A solitary robin sang his territorial song on a nearby elm branch.

Eddie and Aefnoth went to check on Sihtric's condition. The wounded Viking lay by the main fire. He was white and shivering despite the heat from both the fire and sunshine, as well as being wrapped in his cloak and sleeping blanket.

Sihtric was still being looked after by his cousin and erstwhile Holmganga duel opponent, Leifur.

Eddie whispered to the still bruised and battered Leifur, "Sihtric looks pretty down today."

"Yes, he's depressed after losing the fight and with it the chance to marry Aelfald. I wish now that we hadn't fought over her. We should have just thrown lots. But we're both proud men and we can't go back now. It's happened."

Eddie then tried to reassure Sihtric. "You're looking better today."

Sihtric gave a weak smile. He shuddered, pulled his blanket around him and then spoke in a barely audible whisper. "Thank you for trying to cheer me up. I'll not survive this, I'm soon for Valhalla. Without Aelfald to meet me, it's not worth going back to Denmark."

Worryingly, Eddie noticed that Sihtric had deteriorated so much he looked double his age.

Later Eddie and Aefnoth breakfasted with the other Danes. They ate thick barley porridge, sweet tasting acorn bread that needed a lot of chewing and a nutty, acorn beer that tasted and smelt bitter. Eddie had noticed the Vikings used acorns extensively, particularly as grain substitutes in breads, soups and stews as well as for beer. His Romani race did much the same, as acorns were free and plentiful in the well forested countries they travelled through.

When breakfast was over, Eric approached and spoke to Eddie. "Thanks for your help in treating Sihtric, and I've enjoyed sharing my knowledge of our Norse culture with you. Are there any other aspects of our lifestyle you don't understand?"

Eddie seized his opportunity. "Yes. I'm curious about where you got your scope from."

Eric smiled. "I'm glad you asked me that, as there's a unique story there and you know how we Danes like sagas."

Eddie nodded. "I noticed, and I have learned a lot of your wisdom from them."

Aefnoth, sensing yet another long conversation that he couldn't understand, wandered off to explore the island by himself.

Eric stood up, entwined his fingers and cracked the knuckles. Then with a flourish of his arms, he divulged the big 'secret' he'd been telling around the camp fires for years.

"We've had these scopes for a generation. A trading party led by my father, Garbold, with Agnar's father, Alfgar, as his number two, arrived in a city called Constantinople in Byzantium. There they discovered these crystal lenses. They were shown them by a master craftsman called Ali Espigatt."

Eddie pricked up his ears at the master craftsman's name, as it sounded Romani.

Eric continued. "The master craftsman showed them polished green and blue translucent rock crystal samples. My father thought they would make good ornamentation, so he offered what he considered to be a fair price for them. However, the craftsman said this was nowhere near enough as the crystals were unique to him."

"So what did they do?"

Eric waved his arms about. "The master craftsman demonstrated how remarkable they were by holding a crystal a few inches above a tiny, finely carved statue. My father was amazed to find that by looking through the crystal he could see minute details that were not visible before."

"That must have seemed like a miracle to them."

"I'm certain you're right. Next, Ali produced a tray of dry tinder. He held the crystal up against the sun's rays and concentrated the light through it until it was a red-white pinpoint of light on the dry wood chips. To their astonishment the tinder smouldered and burst into flames. The craftsman told them it was the refraction of the sun's light that produced that startling effect. He said the lenses could also be used to cauterise wounds in a more sterile way than using heated metal."

"Amazing as well as useful," Eddie interjected.

At that point there was a sudden rain shower so Eric and Eddie quickly moved under the cover of a large oak tree. A bushy tailed red squirrel, disturbed by the men's approach bolted up its trunk.

When they were out of the rain they sat on a fallen branch and Eric resumed. "Next, the craftsman showed them a scope. This comprised two crystals affixed into a goatskin tube, like the one I've got. He let them look through it, pointing it at a hillside several miles away. Without the scope the hillside looked bare. But through the scope, the panorama was absolutely transformed. It was suddenly alive with people and animals moving around."

"What on earth did your father make of that?"

"He and Alfgar thought it must be magic sent down from their Norse god, Loki, the wizard of lies. But Ali Espigatt told them that it wasn't supernatural. He explained it was his skill that made the crystals worth so much more than the two men had offered. He mentioned that he'd spent months mining to locate absolutely pure transparent rock crystals. Then he polished them, using sand impregnated cloth and a foot-powered turning lathe."

Eddie nodded, spreading out his hands, palms upwards, enthralled by what he was hearing.

"Originally, Ali said he'd intended to make the crystals into jewellery. But as he worked on them, he'd noticed that they magnified things. By trial and error he'd developed a precise elliptical optic shape that gave the optimum magnification."

As he listened, Eddie bent down and picked a handful of the tiny wild strawberries, giving half to Eric and eating the others himself. The small strawberries' sweet flavour and fragrance reminded Eddie of Kate's scent.

Eric paused to eat his strawberries before resuming. "Ali Espigatt told my father and Alfgar that even when the configuration was perfect, the crystals all had to be buffed. He did this until he found some that were unblemished and smooth. Then he reworked these until they were a very accurate shape and flawless. Ali Espigatt said only one in fifty fitted his exacting standards to be used for a crystal lens."

Eddie scratched his temple and nodded.

"Additionally, Ali Espigatt told them he'd discovered that using two lenses at opposite ends of a tube quadrupled those two lenses' individual magnifications. Plus it improved clarity and allowed him to see things far away. Ali had also said it took him on average four months to make each unique lens."

"The master craftsman sounds as if he was a very skilled man," Eddie commented. "So I understand why he deserved a good price for his ingenuity and hard work."

Eric nodded. "Garbold and Alfgar asked Ali Espigatt how many perfect crystals he'd made that were still in stock, and also how much he wanted for them all. Ali told them he had only ten and they were priceless. The two Danes were overawed by the potential of these crystals, so they resolved to give the craftsman everything they had for the treasures.

"After a lot of haggling, the craftsman agreed to accept all the Danes' silver and gold as payment. That, plus their entire stock of furs and double-edged Frankish Rhineland swords."

Eddie's elbows rested on his knees and he cupped his chin in both hands, completely engrossed in Eric's tale.

"My father, Garbold, and Alfgar figured correctly they'd then be the only people in Scandinavia with these wonders. They also calculated that this would bring them immense prestige and be useful militarily."

Just then Ericsson and Agnar arrived in the clearing, carrying the carcass of a large tusked wild boar they'd caught. Lashed by its hooves to a carrying pole, the beast was so big the two strong warriors had difficulty supporting it. The thick carrying pole sagged in the middle. The big men whooped and shouted, obviously delighted at their successful hunting abilities.

Ericsson noticed Eric under the tree and shouted, "We'll feast tonight, Father!"

Eric smiled, waving his approval.

When the excitement had died down, Eddie asked Eric, "What has become of those crystals?"

"My father Garbold died in battle and left his four to me. Agnar's father Alfgar, who was his deputy, went with him to Valhalla in the same fight. So Agnar also has four. The other two went to others on the expedition. I'm not sure where those are now."

"Can I look at some of these crystals?"

Eric seemed pleased by Eddie's request. "Certainly," he agreed.

While Eric had gone to fetch the crystals, Aefnoth reappeared after his exploration of Osea Island and Eddie was able to explain to him what Eric had said about the crystal lenses. When Eric returned he let Eddie and Aefnoth examine a crystal each. They were both about two inches in diameter and one inch thick at the centre and were perfect ellipsoid shapes.

Aefnoth was spellbound when he looked through the crystal. Then he held it up to the sun to focus the rays as he'd been told the craftsman had done. Unfortunately, he focused it on to his own hand and the intensely concentrated shaft of light burnt his skin. He shook his hand about to cool it and looked quizzically at the red mark it had made.

"That hurts. These crystals are magical, whatever they say," he remarked to Eddie.

Eddie also examined one, and an already assembled scope. "These are fantastic and exceptionally beautifully coloured," he said, handing them back to Eric.

Later, as Eddie and Aefnoth walked through the elm and beech tree thicket towards the sea, a wildcat crossed their path. This feline was far bigger than the domestic cats, but still had the classic tabby markings.

The wildcat arched its back, spat at them and, screaming a terrible prolonged mewing sound, darted towards the two men. They didn't wait to be attacked and ran back the way they'd come. The wild cat stopped when it had driven them off, but was still spitting and mewing belligerently.

Aefnoth warned Eddie, "Never get too near to a wildcat, Edward. They bite and could rip an arm or leg apart with those vicious talons. I've seen one kill a feral dog.

"Don't worry," Eddie replied. "After that, I'll give them a wide berth. I'm only used to domesticated moggies."

"You should also watch out for so-called domestic cats, Edward, as most are partly bred from wildcats. Look at the one Princess Catherine has adopted and calls Boadicea, or Bodi. That was a kitten we found after its wildcat mother had been killed."

Eddie nodded. "I'd suspected as much. It looks and acts like a wildcat."

A few miles west in his quarters in the Maldon Burh, Ealdorman Byrhtnoth was waiting to hear a report from Thegn Augustus and his son, Augustine.

Byrhtnoth commanded, "Tell me what you actually saw, young man?

Augustine said, "I was in my father's rowing boat watching Osea Island as ordered. It had been quiet until I saw a lot of Vikings on foot heading for the Naze sandspit to the east end of the island."

"Then?" Byrhtnoth inquired.

"I upped anchor and rowed nearer so that I could see well…"

"Get on with it, son," Thegn Augustus interrupted. "The Ealdorman doesn't want to hear your every move. Just skip to the chase."

"Okay. Well, two Vikings started to fight with swords and shields, while others stood in a circle, egging them on. Well… I thought one of the Vikings watching the action looked like your son, Aefnoth, in Viking clothes. But I must have been mistaken, sire."

Byrhtnoth's expression changed. He leaned towards the boy and asked, "What made you think that, Augustine?"

Thegn Augustus coughed and wheezed. "Tell our lord, boy."

Augustine looked down. "I know it's silly. Why would a Saxon noble be dressed in Norse clothes and standing with Vikings watching two of their number fight a duel? But the way the man moved reminded me of him, sire."

Thegn Augustus interrupted again. "Son, I expect Eldor Aefnoth is somewhere around the Burh. Come, we will leave the Ealdorman in peace now." He coughed and spluttered for a moment and then apologised. "I'm sorry, sire. We'll go now."

Ealdorman Byrhtnoth spoke loudly in his deep commanding voice. "Leave Augustine alone, Augustus. I wish to hear more of this. Carry on, Augustine. Now, why did you think it could be my son?"

"This man was as tall as you and when the duel was going on he was aping every blow, just like I've seen Eldor Aefnoth move when there've been fights at the Burh. I'd know those movements anywhere."

"Well done, Augustine," Byrhtnoth exclaimed. "You are right to report what you think you saw. It doesn't matter if you're mistaken. I'll be the judge of that."

Augustine smiled and bowed.

"Tell me, was there a second man, tall, black-haired, with this guy you thought could be my son?"

"I didn't see one, as a violent thunderstorm broke out and I had to row for the shore. I only just made Lawling Creek. The rowing boat was almost swamped."

"You've both done well. Please return to your lookout station and report anything you see, however trivial. Especially let me know if it's about the Viking who looks like my son."

On Osea Island, Eddie again sensed the vibes he'd felt earlier. Now these were getting stronger by the minute. While Aefnoth went to get a bite to eat, Eddie walked into the wood where Eric had shown him the magic mushrooms. He moved into the undergrowth well away from any paths and then lay down, relaxed and concentrated on clearing his mind of everyday thoughts.

Soon he felt his mind drawing him involuntarily into an automatic remote viewing experience. This invariably heralded extreme danger. Eddie felt his mind moving on the psychic plain again, transcending time and space. Gradually his brain was opening a window to a remote target that was towing his psyche to it.

When he instigated the viewing sessions he remained in charge of the flow of information. His mind moved fast, concentrating his consciousness into clarity of some other power, probably Druid.

Instantly he was somewhere where it was misty. His mental senses boiled, surged, and then settled down. He was once again over a wide stretch of water. It had to be the sea as it was too big for a river or even an estuary. The water was fairly calm. No white caps, just a gentle swell.

Eddie concentrated. He could only detect a vast stretch of water and sea birds. What was he supposed to see? Then he knew. A gigantic longship was at his peripheral psychic horizon.

His mind moved in closer until he could see a lone man, a Viking. This was a giant over seven feet tall and extremely muscular. He sensed this man was very important… royal even, and ruthless. Now a name came to him: Prince Olaf Tryggvasson.

Once he'd taken this in, his target widened and he was high in the sky. He could see other longships. Many more. In fact, the sea was filled with the craft to the horizon. There must have been ninety to a hundred in this mighty fleet. He sensed the huge armada was sailing north from the Kent coast, heading towards Essex. Within seconds he was back in the wood on Osea Island.

If the huge fleet's next destination was Essex, Colchester and Maldon would be the most likely to be attacked because they both held King Aethelred's silver in the Royal Mints.

Probably the flotilla that had attacked the Danes would by now have joined up with Tryggvasson. If so, and the huge fleet went straight for Maldon, they would pass Osea Island. Then it would be inconceivable that they wouldn't try to destroy the Danes on their way past.

As Eric Greybeard had made him and Aefnoth his blood brothers, Eddie felt obliged to warn him of the new threat before it was too late. However, he realized he still daren't tell Eric how he 'knew' more danger was coming.

He went to find Eric. Walking out of the wood, he crossed the camp clearing where the colossal wild boar was already cooking on an oversized spit. Two cooks' strength was needed to rotate the huge beast above the hot ashes, while another cook prepared vegetables and was cooking unleavened bread on a flat griddle suspended from a tripod. This would be another feast indeed.

Eddie found the roast pork aroma intoxicating as it mingled with the birchwood smoke. Even the wounded Sihtric was licking his lips.

Before Eddie found Eric he had to pass several Vikings arm wrestling by a fallen tree. As he approached, Agnar challenged him to join in. Eddie was reluctant, as his mission to warn Eric was urgent, but he decided he'd better be sociable, not wanting to antagonize Agnar further.

Agnar picked out Oman Claw-hands who acted as a bookmaker, taking bets on almost anything to arm wrestle with Eddie. What the Danes weren't aware of was that Eddie had been arm wrestling with other Romanies from an early age. The ginger-haired Oman Claw-hands was taller and weighed several stone heavier than Eddie, in muscle, not fat.

Oman and Eddie took up the required positions with elbows on the log and clasped each others' right hand. Oman Claw-hands, as his nickname suggested, had his ring and little fingers of both hands permanently bent into his hand. Eddie could feel large growths on those two fingers and his palm. He assumed this was causing Oman's tendons to contract, permanently displacing the fingers.

Agnar said go, and Oman tried to force Eddie's arm sideways. Eddie just braced his arm, so using far less energy. With Eddie not giving an inch, Oman turned red in the face with the strain.

Oman started to sweat. As well as running off his brow, Eddie felt the Viking's palms dampen. When Eddie sensed Oman was weakening, he jerked his own arm sideways and forced Oman's arm down, winning the bout.

Agnar cursed Oman, and then demanded Eddie have a bout with him. But Eddie told him he had to see Eric urgently, and would take him on at a later date.

Agnar's lips curled and he dismissed Eddie with a rather disdainful smirk.

At that same moment, in the Maldon Burh Princess Catherine – Kate – had been summoned to Ealdorman Byrhtnoth's house.

Byrhtnoth addressed the princess. "I have possible news of my son, Aefnoth, your fiancé. One of my spies thinks he saw him yesterday on Osea Island."

Kate clenched her tiny hands and smiled. "That is wonderful news. I'd been worried about him."

"Naturally I'm also pleased. But this might be an inaccurate report. So we shall have to wait for confirmation, or his return."

Princess Catherine, with a quiver in her voice, asked, "Was there any news of Aefnoth's companion, my bodyguard, Edward the Tall?"

"None at all, I'm afraid. It doesn't look hopeful for him," Byrhtnoth replied. "I will let you know if there is any more news."

Kate left Byrhtnoth's house with her head bowed and as she walked to her own rooms she was shaking, and tears rolled down her cheeks.

Back on Osea Island, Eddie had located Eric. He was at the beach examining the fire damage his longships had sustained in the recent battle.

"Can I try making another prediction with your rune stones?" Eddie asked him.

"Yes, but only if you can prove to me you really understand the runes' meanings," Eric said. "I'm asking you to do that as the ones you cast last time wouldn't have indicated what you predicted."

"That's true according to your Danish interpretation," Eddie told him. "However, my Romani tribe uses a quite different system."

"Possibly there's more than one system of rune interpretation. After all, you were right last time. However, will you explain what you know about the runes?"

"Certainly, Eric. I understand the runic alphabet or Futhark, as it is correctly called. It gets that name from the runes' first six sounds. F, U, TH, A, R and K. I'm also aware that each rune not only represents a phonetic sound, but also has its own distinct meaning connected with Norse mythology."

"For me to believe you're even a novice rune master, Edward, you must also show me that you understand the runes' full meanings. Not just a few items you could have learnt by rote."

"In that case Eric, set me a test."

Eric ordered a Viking to bring him his shield and then challenged Eddie. "What do the three runes carved on this man's shield symbolize?"

Eddie looked at the carving and pronounced, "This three rune sequence is the runic name for Tyre, the god of war. It gives the shield's owner the belief that nothing can overcome him."

"That's correct," Eric said. "But now can you tell me the significance of each of those runes separately?"

Eddie's brow furrowed for a moment. "Yes," he said. "The upward facing arrow is called teiwas or spiritual warrior. For meditation it means to gain strength over an adversarial situation and keep serious physical harm away. The two vertical vees are called jera or the cycle of one year. Its meditation meaning is persistence and foresight. The R rune stands for raido or journeys, meaning journeys are a call for learning and most are favourable in retrospect."

Eric was impressed. "Hm. You undoubtedly have some knowledge of the runes. So you may again try to see what you can divine."

Eddie took the rune bag and threw the individual stones to the ground. Then he lined up all those that landed face up. After considering them for a while, he made his purported divination and made his announcement with a flourish.

"I see many longships coming from the south. It's a very big fleet, probably allied to the Norwegians you've just fought. You should sail north soon, or you'll be trapped in this estuary."

"How many do you see coming?"

"Ninety to a hundred longships. A huge fleet, I think."

"I don't know how you made that divination from the runes you threw, Edward. However, you were correct before, so I must trust your prediction again this time. We shall move north, just in case you're right again. We can't take any chances as we're not strong enough with our depleted force to fight a sustained battle against what would be overwhelming odds."

"You'll not regret it. After all, if I'm wrong you can sail back again should you wish."

Eric's brow furrowed. He looked at his feet. Then he started tapping a forefinger on his teeth.

"Is there another problem?" Eddie asked.

"Well... there could be, if this is Prince Olaf Tryggvasson's battle fleet.

"In what way do you mean?

Eric shook his head. "Because Tryggvasson is reputed to be the son of our chief god, Odin."

"I don't understand that, Eric?"

"Well you see, Odin is in the habit of roaming the earth in human disguise, seducing and impregnating women. That's why many mortals are able to trace their ancestry back to him. This applies to Olaf Tryggvasson. So how can we win a battle against a god's descendant?"

"But surely, if he's half human he can still be killed?"

"That's a point," Eric agreed.

Eddie thought to himself that if the wife of a Viking took a lover and got pregnant while her husband was away on a long raid, what a great excuse she could have by saying the father was the great god, Odin.

Eric interrupted Eddie's musing. "We'll assume your information is valid, and leave Osea Island. But before then we should have time to eat the feast kindly supplied by Ericsson and Agnar, don't you think?"

"I imagine so, Eric, and that would lift the men's morale before you move out."

"In that case I'd be honoured if you and your comrade will share the meal with us, and then accompany us on our journey. We'll let you off at Mersea Island, Colchester or Ipswich, whichever you like?"

"That would be good, Eric. I'm hungry already from smelling the hog cooking. But I'll have to consult Aefnoth about the sea journey as he's inclined to be seasick."

As Eddie feared, Aefnoth was not at all keen to go back on the sea. But Eddie argued, "Remember Aefnoth, we haven't accomplished our mission to get hold of a scope yet."

Reluctantly Aefnoth agreed. "Okay, I'll go then, as I want to please my father by getting a scope if I can. I just hope I shall feel better in a big longship."

The meal lived up to all expectations. The barbecued pork melted in their mouths. This was garnished with wild turnips and white carrots with black bread, followed by mead to drink. It was a feast indeed.

The Danes had lost one longship that had been burnt out and buried with their dead warriors. But they were now without half the rowing crews of their flotilla.

Eddie said, "Eric, if it helps, Aefnoth and I will row to make up the numbers. I'm experienced, although Aefnoth's a complete novice."

"That will help. Aefnoth's inexperience doesn't matter as we often use newly captured slaves to row when we've lost men to Valhalla. Also, on our biggest longship there are a few training benches that can accommodate two men.

"Is shortage of rowers often a problem?"

"Occasionally, but we usually start out with enough people for two rowing crews so they can alternate. That also allows us to still function if some of our warriors die or get injured. In any case, we're only going a short distance today and it shouldn't be long before we'll be able to use the sail. As the breeze is blowing from the south it's in the right direction for us to sail north towards Mersea Island once we get round the headland."

They boarded Eric's flagship that had thirty rowing benches each side. Most benches were singles but four were double benches,

227

making spaces for sixty four rowers in all. As the tide was in, it didn't take much pushing to launch the flat-bottomed longships into the water. Eddie could now understand why these comparatively lightweight craft were so useful to the raiding parties. They didn't have to row a small tender ashore, but could beach the longships directly onto dry land.

When the longships were launched, Eddie was pleased to see Sihtric was aboard, lying on a makeshift stretcher. He still looked deathly white, but at least he was still alive.

Eddie was seated next to Agnar while Aefnoth sat beside Ericsson on the opposite side of the ship.

Eddie now considered that his Romani tribe were more like the Vikings than the Saxons, because they were both travelling peoples and as the Romanies were descended from the ancient warrior classes of the Punjab in Northern India, fighting was in both tribes' blood.

He was concerned about what would happen to Maldon if the main Norwegian fleet reached them. As there were at least ninety longships, that would indicate around three to four thousand Vikings. That size of army would surely overrun the Maldon Burh by sheer weight of numbers.

Whatever the result, many would die or be enslaved. The prospect worried Eddie terribly. Kate would be in extreme danger and he could do nothing to protect her as he was leaving the area.

Twenty-One

Strong south-westerly winds pounded the Dengie Hundred. On the Blackwater Estuary the gale created waves high enough to break into rolling white caps. The sky was covered with dark clouds scudding at speed towards the north. Although it was June, warm clothing was needed by any humans foolish enough to leave their shelter.

The gale had created wind against tide conditions on the estuary. This, combined with treacherous side currents, made it madness to launch small craft.

Although the Danes' cooking fires on Osea Island were now abandoned, seemingly burnt-out logs were fanned and re-oxygenated by the gusting wind until eventually, the dying embers blazed and woodsmoke streamed across the island once more.

Possibly the only creatures to smell this smoke were a mother black rat and her half-grown litter as the rodents searched the erstwhile cooking areas for scraps of food dropped by the now departed Vikings.

Eric Greybeard had earlier sent two scout ships south towards Kent to search for signs of rival longships. Now, despite the buffeting west wind, the Danes' main seven longship flotilla was moving east with the tide. They'd left Osea Island on the Blackwater Estuary, heading away from the town of Maldon towards Mersea Island, east of Colchester. They had arranged to wait there for their scout ship's return and captain's reports.

As the Danish flotilla headed east, large waves smashed against the longships' side planking, and spray broke relentlessly over the low gunwales. At the same time, heavy rain hurled almost horizontally onboard, propelled by the now southerly wind. The resulting deluges soaked everyone on board. This included Eddie and Aefnoth, who were rowing in Eric Greybeard's large flagship.

At one point Eddie saw a Saxon farmer run from their view as (to him) potential predatory Vikings longships passed by him. Herring gulls followed the flotilla, some landing on the gunwales, screeching, their feathers ruffled by the gale's force.

Ericsson shouted instructions to Aefnoth, barely able to make himself heard above the whistling wind. "Lean forward, Aefnoth, catch the oar in the water at the same angle as the other rowers. Next, drag it through the water towards you and then extract it from the sea."

Eddie needed no instructions as he was already a proficient rower. He'd traversed the North Sea and the whole east coast of England when he was a rowing slave for the Norwegians.

Aefnoth still felt seasick. This, combined with his lack of rowing skills made him clash blades with the next rower. Eventually he had to be taken off rowing duties altogether, although he stubbornly stayed on the rowing bench, watching Ericsson pull the big oar.

The rest of the men fit enough to do so, rowed the longships the two miles to Bradwell. This was the point at which the Blackwater Estuary flowed into the North Sea. As they passed Bradwell's ancient Roman fort, Eddie saw smoke spewing out from a beacon.

Eddie watched as a big, square, woven wadmill sail was raised. He was relieved that now they'd turned north, the wind filled the sail, making the longship more stable and they could cease rowing. This reduced the sea spray and the rain had also stopped.

Aefnoth leaned over to Eddie's side of the ship. "Did you see my father's lookouts signalling at Bradwell? They were telling him that the Viking longships were leaving the area."

"How does Ealdorman Byrhtnoth know what the plumes of smoke mean?"

"That's easy. You can see this is white smoke, which means danger over. If longships enter the Blackwater, the lookouts dampen the straw and wood so the smoke is blacker, meaning hostiles approaching."

As the Danish longship flotilla was now heading north, the Essex mainland was on their left. Although they were well out to sea, Eddie could just make out movements on the land. At one point he spotted a Ceorl farmer ploughing his field using oxen. Groups of small farmers' huts could be seen every so often with smoke percolating through the thatched roofs. Occasionally, even at this distance, the barking of unseen dogs carried over the water as the animals warned their owners of suspicious strangers sailing past.

On the longship, Eddie was surprised to see two Danes in the bilges, constantly bailing out seawater.

"Why do they have to keep emptying water out, Agnar?"

"That's quite normal," Agnar replied, "as the planks are only held together with clenched iron nails. As well as water breaking over the sides, a lot more comes through gaps between the ships planks themselves. These ships are clinker built, meaning each hull plank overlaps the next. But nail holes and the movement of the sea allow leakage into the hull."

Eddie screwed up his face and slightly shook his head.

Agnar sensed that Eddie didn't fully understand, so he tried to reassure him. "It's all right though, as Norse law only regards a boat unseaworthy if it needs bailing out three times in two days."

"But what if it leaks more than that?"

"Well, Edward, we just assume the risk and bail harder. Sometimes when I'm the helmsmen, I can watch the longships' boarded sides flexing up to six inches from side to side as we battle through the waves."

Eddie gave another shake of his head and his eyes widened.

Meanwhile Aefnoth was white-faced, hanging over the gunwale and trying unsuccessfully to spew up the non-existent contents of his stomach.

Agnar sneered in distaste at Aefnoth's display of weakness. Then he told Eddie. "We do try to waterproof the hull by caulking it. That's covering the boards with moss, wool or fur that have been drenched with tar. However, this only helps a bit as the boards flex far too much to stop all the water getting in."

Eddie looked down to where the two guys were bailing and could see water running in as the boarding flexed. "Is there no way of making the longships stronger?"

"Not really, Edward. If the planks were stiff and rigid they would split and we would sink or be swamped. So what at first appears to be a weakness, their resilience is in fact the design's greatest strength, making our longships fast, sturdy and highly manoeuvrable."

As Agnar seemed friendlier now, Eddie asked him. "Are you a trader?"

Agnar nodded. "Yes, it's my next pleasure after fighting, drinking and sex."

"In that case, Agnar, would I be out of line to suggest a trade with you?"

"I'll always listen to trading suggestions."

"Okay. I believe you have four crystal lenses. Would you consider trading two of them for the return of your father's amulet?"

Agnar looked strangely at Eddie.

Eddie held his breath and sucked on his bottom lip, wondering if he'd said the wrong thing and blown his chances.

Agnar's facial muscles relaxed. "Do you realize how much that amulet's worth? It's solid silver with amber embellishments. It's also a very potent sacred pagan artefact. It's irreplaceable, you know?"

Eddie blew out his cheeks. "The value of anything is how much worth a person puts on it. I'm not of your pagan religion, so the amulet's only a beautiful example of art in silver and amber to me. But to you it's a magical talisman and heirloom."

Agnar pursed his lips thoughtfully. "Give me a few minutes to consider your offer." Then he walked over to the side of the longship, put his elbows on the gunwale and cupped his chin in his hands. Aefnoth was near to Agnar but neither acknowledged the other. Agnar was deep in thought and Aefnoth too unwell to care.

Eddie drummed the fingers of one hand on the rowing bench and bit the nails of the other. He coughed, nearly choked, and then stared up at the dark clouds.

When Agnar left the gunwale, Eddie felt his heart racing. Was that an angry expression on his face? The two men looked at each other and neither spoke for what, to Eddie, seemed an eternity.

"If I only had one crystal," Agnar began, "I wouldn't trade it. But as I've four, it's better for me to get my father's amulet back. So I accept your offer of a trade."

They shook hands and the items were exchanged. Agnar seemed pleased and said, "I'd wanted to keep the amulet when you offered it to me initially. But the potency of the oath was too strong. A trade, on the other hand, is a legitimate arrangement not connected to my oath in any way."

"I'm glad it worked out well for you, Agnar, as we should be friends now we've fought in a battle on the same side."

Later, Eddie found the big sickly Saxon. "Aefnoth, I've now got us the two crystals your father asked us to get so he can make them into a scope."

Aefnoth, retching violently, could only splutter. "Well done Edward," he managed.

Once the longships had the wind in their sails and the tide with them, the nine mile sea voyage was soon completed. The flotilla hove to just off Mersea Island. Eric didn't ground his fleet, but rafted them all up, with sea anchors down.

"This," he told Eddie, "is in case we have to sail away quickly.

"That's very sensible. Mind you, even though your ship raft is more stable, Aefnoth still looks ill."

"Yes he is very seasick so I'll get him taken to the beach by canoe. I suggest you go as well to look after him, as you're the only one who speaks his language. You can return later if all is well."

Ericsson energetically paddled Aefnoth and Eddie to the shore in a large canoe. He let them off on East Mersea's sandy beach. Then he chuckled as Aefnoth leapt ashore and collapsed onto the sand.

"I'll come back for you later if it's a false alarm," Ericsson told Eddie.

"Thanks for the transport, Ericsson; I'm afraid Aefnoth's no sailor."

Ericsson gave another laugh and waved dismissively at Aefnoth still lying flat out on the beach, and then rowed back to the flotilla.

At that moment, in his house in Maldon Burh, Ealdorman Byrhtnoth was giving Kate some more bad news. "Princess," he said, "my spies have informed me all the Viking longships have left the estuary."

Princess Catherine looked up anxiously into Byrhtnoth's eyes. "What does that mean for my fiancé and bodyguard?"

Byrhtnoth locked away. "I also have to inform you that as soon as the Vikings left Osea Island, Thegn Leofsunu and a troop of my best men crossed to the island but could find no trace of our two men. They are not on the island. Or at least, are not there alive."

The princess felt tears welling up in her eyes. She held her breath before asking, "What do you mean by not alive?"

The sounds of giggling from her girls outside the room impinged on the otherwise deathly quiet within.

Byrhtnoth stared at the serving girls through the adjoining doorway and grimaced. "Thegn Leofsunu reports two large barrows. Graves piled high with stones. However, without excavating them we don't know if my son, Aefnoth, and Edward the Tall are interred within them."

Princess Catherine's stomach churned and her heart raced. "Is there any way either could be alive?"

Byrhtnoth suddenly looked, to the princess, much older than his sixty plus years as his shoulders slumped and he shook his head. "There's not much hope, I'm afraid. They couldn't have escaped over the causeway, as I've had guards on the mainland side since they crossed onto the island. They report that nobody has come back from the island that way."

Princess Catherine's voice quivered as she asked, "Could they have swum to the mainland, or stolen a boat to escape?"

Byrhtnoth shook his head again. "Aefnoth cannot swim, though I don't know about your bodyguard. The Saxon families that fled the Vikings used all their boats to escape the invaders. That means there were only the Viking longships on the island."

Princess Catherine desperately tried to think of a way the two warriors could have survived. "Could they be on the Vikings' longships?"

Byrhtnoth nodded. "That's just possible, I suppose. But if they are, they will be chained to the oars, having been made rowing

233

slaves. There is the possibility that as an Eldor, the son of an Ealdorman, Aefnoth could be held for ransom. Your bodyguard, Edward, would have little chance of being worth a ransom at all."

It was a disconsolate princess who met her handmaidens at the door and trudged back to her own rooms. The girls gossiped among themselves about the boys who'd tried to get familiar with them while they waited outside the room. Kate registered that was the reason for their giggling. But she was far too pent up to admonish them.

Back on Mersea Island, Aefnoth still lay face down, digging his fingers into the sand. Trying to stop his mental world spinning, he rose to his feet unsteadily. Then, bent almost double, he staggered up the beach. When he could go no further he sat down on a fallen tree trunk with his head sunk between his wide-spread knees, retching.

The black rain clouds had dispersed and the sun was blazing down from an almost clear blue sky. Rooks cawed, some on the wing, others sitting on a massive intermingled snarl-up of twig nests. These made up a bewildering spread out rookery in the highest branches of a clump of elms just off the beach.

The cacophony of discordant rooks cawing was joined by two much larger members of the crow family, ravens. The bigger birds added their deeper voices to their cousins as they sat nearby on a rotting crab-apple tree.

The ravens watched the two men disdainfully as if they were hanging judges about to pass the ultimate sentence. To Eddie, these two-feet long, jet black ravens seemed sinister. He remembered what he'd been told about the ravens on Viking battle standards. The birds had their heads inclined, intently staring at the two men. Eddie shuddered. He had a premonition something was wrong, but what was it?

Eddie got the feeling Kate was thinking of him and as Aefnoth was still trying to recover, he resolved to try and contact his princess. He moved down the beach and sat on the sand in a deep depression that filled with water at high tide.

He concentrated his remote viewing on Kate and he could see her in her rooms. She had tears in her pretty eyes and looked glum. His revenant spirit put its arm around her and sent a psychic message to her to cheer up. She couldn't see him but sensed his presence. She understood he was not dead but safe. He tried to tell her where he was but she hadn't enough remote psychic experience to read the transmission. However, she did get a picture in her mind's eye of a hot, sandy beach and she felt happy again.

Kate didn't know why or how she knew Eddie was safe, but she started to sing happily to herself. Edith heard her and told the other two girls, "Our Princess isn't sad any more, she's cheerful again. I don't know what changed her mood so quickly, but I want some."

Eddie's psyche was back on the Mersea beach. He looked up to see how Aefnoth was doing, but he was asleep in the sun. He decided to leave him to it in the hope he'd feel better after his rest.

He actually had plenty of time to spare for once. It had been a hectic few days and now he knew Kate was alright, he wanted to see how his siblings were doing out in Denmark. So for the second time that day, he lay on his cloak and concentrated.

Again he used his seventh sense to transcend time and space as he targeted the Danish farm he hoped his Lavengro family was still living on. He used his human psychic ability and protocols to reach out to them.

It was summer in the middle of the day, so he didn't find any of them in the hut. He mentally moved around the farm target using his co-ordinated remote viewing.

He found his brother Fero working in the water meadows, cutting grass with a scythe and a billhook. Olga and Tipi, his elder sisters, were stacking hay, eight sheaths at a time, into stooks, forming them into pyramid shapes to dry it out. They weren't alone; several young Danes were with them. An oxen cart was being loaded with dried hay by a big blond guy and a buxom girl.

But where were the littlies, Mimsy and Delis, his younger sisters? He concentrated and found both pre-teens splashing about in the water of the fiord with several Danish children of about the same age.

Eddie was reassured. They all seemed to be well integrated with the Danish farmer's family. They looked well fed and healthy. He moved closer to Fero, the only other member of his family who was psychic.

Fero sensed he was there and put down his scythe. *Eddie is that you?*

Eddie answered, *Yes, brother. I see the family is looking well.*

They are. The farmer treats us all fairly and we are comfortable. What are you doing now?

Eddie told him a bit about his adventures.

Fero said, *Trust you to get a good billet guarding a beautiful princess. Don't leave it so long next time coming to see us. I'll tell the girls you are all right. I can feel you fading now. See you again, big brother.*

Eddie instantly returned to the sand of Mersea Island. He thought about their present position. He doubted he could get Aefnoth back on a ship if his life depended on it. Therefore he considered his best bet was to encourage him to talk, in the hope it would take his mind off his malaise.

Eddie asked him, "Aefnoth, could you tell me why there is a Royal Mint in such a small coastal town as Maldon? Isn't this dangerous?"

Aefnoth spat out some sputum and took a swig of water from the earthenware bottle Ericsson had left for them. Then, looking pensive, he said, "Sure, King Edward established the mint at Maldon after building the fortified Burh. You see, King Aethelred only has mints in towns protected by forts or burhs. Colchester, Maldon and Horndon on the Hill, are the three in Essex."

"But why have mints in small towns at all?"

"Well Edward, you should remember Maldon's the second biggest town in Essex after Colchester. Think what would happen if the King kept it all near his palace in London. Raiders could concentrate their forces and constantly besiege that city. In fact there could be an all-out invasion. A successful encroachment could either bankrupt the country or even take it over. By splitting the silver and coinage up into many smaller mints they are less of a magnet for raids."

Eddie scratched his head, opened his hands and said, "I get the point."

"You see Edward, like us, the Vikings crave silver. They either collect it by tribute, a form of protection money to leave populations in peace, called the Danegeld, or they raid and pillage to get it. In Ireland they cut off the ears and slit the noses of anyone unwilling or unable to pay their Danegeld demands. That's why we call it paying through the nose."

Eddie gasped. "So where is the mint in the Burh, Aefnoth?

In the safest place, obviously, Eddie. In the keep, our last line of defence. The keep has its own well and is extra secure. There are only three men employed there, the Master of the King's Mint and two big guys that make the coins. They use a coin die to make them. A massive sledgehammer is crashed down onto the die, forcing the King's picture and words onto the new money. The Master keeps the records of coins minted. Then he locks them into a secure safe, which is bolted to the stone floor."

"Don't some that have been coined go missing occasionally, Aefnoth?"

"No way, Edward. The penalty is severe. A hand is cut off anyone who steals, or of any mint workers who allow this to happen."

After telling Eddie about the mint, Aefnoth had to sit down again as he felt unwell once more. Eddie left him alone to recover and went for yet another walk.

He remembered what Prior Esmond had told him about the henge stones on Mersea Island and his own remote viewing visit. He recalled what Esmond had told him about variable north poles and about the Druid priests and their strange ceremonies.

His mind felt like a psychic whirlpool. He had swirls of consciousness. He envisaged strange phenomena that his extrasensory faculties allowed him to access. He sensed rather than knew what was happening at that very moment. He could see and feel that in that very circle of stone monoliths stood a dozen very tall, white-robed druids or priests of some ancient race or religion. In the middle of the stone circle was a marginally smaller black-robed female figure. The Druidess, sharman or wizard threw a handful of seeming nothingness into the sky.

The white-robed Druids raised their hands in the air and hummed one continuous deep note that brought extreme pain into Eddie's brain. Near the female sharman a tall, thin figure materialized and the Druids' humming stopped. The ghostly apparition that had appeared didn't wear a robe but appeared to be dressed like an Inuit, a Yupic or Eskimo from one of the northern tribes that Eddie had been told about by his mother when he was a boy. The spectre wore a white and beige coloured sealskin coat and dark furry trousers. Thigh-length sealskin boots completed its apparent clothing. The spectre's head and hands were translucent and it had white hair and large pink eyes.

The potent being sent out its thought patterns to the surrounding priests and Eddie. It gave them the message, *The lay lines are active, see that the rest of the stratagem is enacted.* The Druids and the Sharman bowed before the apparition, which then melted away.

Eddie's mind was confused by all this and the next moment he was shaking on the beach, near to Aefnoth.

After Aefnoth and Eddie had been on the beach for several hours with the sun beating down, they'd both relaxed a bit. Aefnoth's stomach was feeling more settled so they examined the crystals that Eddie had traded with Agnar. Both used them to scrutinize some fossilized shells embedded in the rocks, using the lenses' magnifying qualities.

"Edward, I'm of noble birth, having been educated in the best Monastery schools in the land. But I've never even heard of anything as extraordinary as these crystals. I'd assumed our Saxon culture was the most sophisticated there was. I'm perturbed to find that the pagans know more about anything. On this expedition I've learnt many things about this other race that my upbringing has not prepared me for."

"I know just what you mean, Aefnoth, and we've also both discovered from the Vikings' sagas it's what they believe in that makes them so daring in battle. Not worrying about dying, as they are convinced its time is predetermined, and the reward is to go to Valhalla. If you could instil this behaviourism in your Saxon warriors, they would be as intrepid as the Vikings. Less hesitancy could give your army the edge."

"You're a very unusual person, Edward. I don't know how you knew that the Norwegians were coming. I wasn't convinced you found out from those runes you threw. I studied runes in the Monastic school. The ones you threw didn't foretell a waterborne attack. Now you say more Norwegians are arriving. We haven't seen any yet, but you seem certain you're right. What's going on? Is this your behaviourism malarkey?"

Eddie laughed. "You're intelligent, Aefnoth. As I told you, I'm a Romani warrior. My race tells fortunes and some of us can sense imminent dangers. But I couldn't tell Eric that the warning just came from my mind. He wouldn't have believed me, would he?"

"I understand that. But tell me, Edward, what do you sense is going to happen now?"

Eddie was tempted to answer in encouraging terms. But instead he said what he felt. "If I'm right and it is Prince Olaf Tryggvasson's fleet, I feel doom in the air. Fear, pain and death coming soon... to me in particular, and then to you and the Burh."

Eddie scanned the scene before him. The Danish longships were silhouetted against the background of Point Clear and Lee over Sands, with the open North Sea stretching to the horizon behind them. This all seemed illusory, completely unreal.

Two jet black Ravens flew down and stared at the two men malevolently. Eddie wondered if his real nightmare was about to begin.

Twenty-Two

The bright sun shimmered on the wind-tossed sea surrounding Mersea Island. Waves broke rhythmically onto the sandy, rock-strewn beach. The black clouds that had covered the sky and deposited so much rain on the Essex coast earlier had retreated. Now the heavens were blue and the few clouds at altitude had been shredded by the high winds into a picturesque herringbone effect.

In the adjacent trees the rooks laboriously circled their rookery, fighting the still powerful, gusty wind. Two ravens stood on a crab apple tree branch as if they were on sentry duty. Both birds had their heads to one side, observing the two humans on the beach. Eddie, the Romani warrior, sensed an aura of hostility emanating from the great black creatures.

Sheltered from the wind by an extensive sand dune, the two men sweltered on what in more peaceful times would have been a utopian locality.

Eldor Aefnoth sweated, perspiration running from his forehead into his eyes. Eddie took his voluminous Viking-style shirt off and then lay down on the damp, compacted sand that had so recently been vacated by the retreating tide.

Aefnoth had stopped feeling seasick, but his stomach muscles were still sore. Eddie got up and walked along the water's edge, inhaling the ozone and seaweed augmented by the fragrances of flowering plants floating on the strong breeze. He recognized the scents of rock-roses and broom.

He bent and picked several green stems of the yellow-flowered marsh samphire. This sea plant resembled skinny green asparagus. The thin, salty sprigs crunched as he ate them, their solid stems and liquid content slaking his thirst and hunger in one go. Eddie remembered eating samphire plants in the salads made by his Romani family.

Handing Aefnoth a sprig, he suggested, "Try this samphire stem, it will revive you."

Aefnoth did so, but wasn't keen. "My stomach is not ready for such a salty plant. But I'll try it again later when I feel better."

Aefnoth paddled in the shallow pools while Eddie searched for more edible plants growing on the saltings.

Without warning Aefnoth pointed to the south then shouted excitably, "Edward, look in the distance! Two sails coming this way."

Eddie's gaze followed Aefnoth's pointing finger. "You're right. I can just see them on the horizon." Eddie hoped these were Eric's scout ships returning. He prayed they brought good news.

In an attempt to check what ships they were, Eddie peered through one of the crystals held out at arms length. Unfortunately, using just one lens in isolation didn't work. It obviously needed a pair of lenses correctly adjusted and restricted in a tube to create the magnifying effect he was hoping for.

The pair of ravens took off from their perch on the crab apple tree and circled the two men, cawing excitedly. The huge black crows dived towards the humans then swooped up again, eventually settling onto the sand barely fifty yards away. The birds' black eyes studied them.

Eddie shuddered, sensing naked hostility emanating from the birds, as if they were jailers watching dangerous prisoners. He could see a lookout using a scope on Eric's big longship. A few minutes later there were sudden frantic movements on the Danish longships. The raft started to separate and individual ships drifted north with the tide. Sails were unfurled and filled with the powerful offshore southerly wind.

Eddie stared at the two ships he assumed were the Danish scout ships, now nearing Eric's main fleet. On the Danish newcomer's masts blowing in the wind, blood red pennants had replaced the pure white ones on the two ships. Eddie sensed these new pennants and the main fleet's reaction must indicate danger.

Sure enough, a few minutes later Aefnoth pointed to the south again. "Look, Eddie, behind the two ships. Right to the horizon the sea is covered by a huge fleet of longships. There are too many for me to count."

"I see them, Aefnoth. I presume they're Norwegian or the Danes wouldn't have sailed off so urgently."

As the chasing fleet came nearer, Eddie could see black, axe-shaped, raven banners flying from their masts. These were indeed the Norwegians.

Mesmerized, Aefnoth and Eddie stood and watched as the mammoth fleet bore down on the two Danish scout ships. The whole horizon to the south seemed filled with longships' sails. Eddie thought that to a casual observer it must have seemed a magnificent sight, but he could feel the aura of menace surrounding the huge Norwegian navy.

The Danes were vastly outnumbered and Eric had taken his only possible course and fled with his flotilla. Although the newcomers were moving fast, it was apparent that Eric's scope had given him enough warning to get under way in time. The gap between the rival fleets was holding constant; the Norwegian longships weren't making up any leeway.

Aefnoth and Eddie stood enthralled as the mass of ships passed Mersea Island. But this proved to have been pure stupidity, as two of the Norwegian vessels turned towards them. Eddie was shocked when the two ravens flew from their position on the island to the approaching longships and landed on board the largest one.

Eddie shouted to Aefnoth, "We've been seen! We must run and hide now."

But Aefnoth would have none of it. He bellowed towards the Norwegians on the longships, "I'm a Saxon noble. I'll stay and fight you all." With that he drew his sword, waved it in the air and screamed at the Norwegian Vikings, "Come on, you pirates! I'll send many of you to your Valhalla."

For their part, several bear and wolf skin-coated berserkers could be seen standing in the two longships' prows, waving weapons and bellowing abuse back.

Soon arrows were landing in showers on the beach around the two men.

Eddie shouted, "For God's sake Aefnoth, I know you're fearless, but we must carry out your father's orders and get these lenses back to him."

Aefnoth looked at Eddie, his eyes staring in anger. Then his face changed to one of resignation and he said, "You're right, of course. We must obey my father's orders."

They turned and ran towards the undergrowth, arrows still falling around them. This wasn't a second too soon as the first Vikings, berserkers, were already ashore, splashing through the shallows in hot pursuit.

Aefnoth and Eddie ran as fast as they could from the beach towards the woods. When Eddie thought he was far enough away, he stopped. Then he surreptitiously hid the leather pouch containing the lenses in a hole in the rotting base of an old oak tree.

Eddie saw Aefnoth reach the woods and rushed after him. Unfortunately, by stopping he'd made what turned out to be a disastrous miscalculation. Suddenly, Eddie was cut off and then confronted by two massive berserkers.

He ran to the right, his stomach knotting up. But he was cut off by more Vikings. No matter where he turned, there was an enemy. No gaps at all, he was surrounded.

Drawing his sword, Eddie swung it in an arc around his head, trying to clear himself an escape route. But he had no chance and was knocked to the floor by a berserker's thrown cudgel. He expected to be killed there and then. But his captors had other orders so he was only punched, before his wrists were bound behind him.

Being kicked repeatedly, Eddie was propelled towards a rickety rowing boat. Not a word had been spoken until, with a curse aimed at him, he was thrown into the boat and ferried to a huge longship.

Eddie hoped Aefnoth had got away. At least he'd be able to tell Kate what had happened to him. Sinking his head into his chest, Eddie wondered why he'd been so stupid, stopping to hide the lenses even though they were one of the main reasons for the expedition. He knew whatever these heathens did to him wouldn't be good. Eddie was certain he'd be tortured, then butchered or enslaved. Either option wasn't a pleasant prospect.

Within a few minutes the rowing boat pulled alongside the biggest longship Eddie had ever set eyes on. He was hauled roughly and unceremoniously aboard the massive vessel.

A pale-skinned, hunch-backed Viking whom the others addressed as Heimdall, stood by Eddie. The crooked-backed giant's knife was held against his captive's throat, daring him to attempt to escape. Heimdall had lost his front teeth and his nose had been broken and reset at an odd angle to his other features.

Eddie blinked in disbelief. Sitting on a rail by the mast were two ravens. These birds were not shackled and were ripping pieces of flesh from the carcass of a dead hare. Eddie wondered if these were the same birds he and Aefnoth had seen watching them on the beach.

Abruptly, both ravens took flight and flew at Eddie, pecking at his face. Eddie forced his head onto his chest and closed his eyes. The birds' strong beaks pecked the top of his head, drawing blood. As his hands were tied, he couldn't knock them off. Eventually they stopped their attack and flew back to the mast to continue gorging themselves on rancid hare.

Eddie 'knew' the ravens held a secret to do with him. Psychically he sensed they recognised and hated him. There was something of great importance that he had forgotten. He could feel it was there in the back of his mind… it was something to do with the Druids.

Heimdall sniggered. "So you've met Thought and Memory, Odin's raven companions. They fly through the world and bring our chief god, Odin, news. Now meet Ravener and Greed." With that, he pushed Eddie against a wooden cage at the stern. Two massive, slavering wolves threw themselves at the bars, trying to get at him. The animal's eyes were blood red. Eddie could feel their breath on his neck and sensed they were full of hatred and antagonism towards him.

Heimdall saw Eddie pull away from the wolves and looked at him with utter contempt. "Dane, you halfman," Heimdall cursed.

Eddie knew the Viking was insinuating that he was effeminate and a coward.

"You've been introduced to Odin's raven and wolf companions. Now meet Odin's earthly son."

In front of Eddie a gigantic figure appeared. He was over seven feet tall. At least twenty stone of solid muscle. The giant's brawn and potency was emphasized by the sinews, tendons and raised blood vessels that stood out from his bare torso. Every feature of this monstrous being accentuated his sheer masculine strength and power.

The big man slapped Eddie across the face. Even with the monster just using the flat of his hand, Eddie was hit so hard it felt as if his nose was broken. He suspected that if this giant punched him with his knuckles at full force he could kill him with one blow.

The massive Viking roared at Eddie in a deep bass voice. "I am Prince Olaf Tryggvasson of Norway, son of the great god, Odin, and the half brother of the thunder god, Thor. You've met my father's companions, his wolves and the ravens who warned us of your presence, plus your celestial guard." Tryggvasson then gestured at Eddie's captor. "You've met Heimdall, the god of perception and observation, the watcher."

Heimdall screwed his face up, his eyes closed. He took a deep breath and looked away as if embarrassed. Tryggvasson laughed at Heimdall's discomfort. Then Tryggvasson moved forward until his face was so close that Eddie could smell the garlic on his breath. The giant demanded from Eddie, "You will now tell me how many of you cowardly Danes there are in this area."

Eddie's face reddened but he didn't back away. "There are many less than your great fleet and army. But there's a much larger force on its way that will outnumber you."

"I don't believe you," Tryggvasson snapped. "There is no bigger Danish force near here. If there were any longships they'd only be full of Swedish halfmen."

Heimdall sniggered, but was met with an icy stare from Tryggvasson. Eddie watched Heimdall slope off, assuming he didn't want to feel the wrath of his monstrous leader.

Tryggvasson spoke sharply again to Eddie. "How, by the thousand shamans of Hel, do you know our Norwegian language, Dane?"

Eddie answered in a low voice, anxious not to annoy Tryggvasson, "I'm not a Dane I'm a Romani warrior as you can see by my dark skin colouring. I've had dealings with your great Norwegian nation before, that's why I speak your language."

Tryggvasson wasn't interested and made as if to hit Eddie again. Eddie held his stance, meeting Olaf's eyes without showing a hint of the fear he felt. Olaf Tryggvasson held back his blow.

The giant seemed confused by Eddie's openly defiant stance. He was used to his own massive physique alone being enough to terrify lesser men. Tryggvasson had come to expect awe and dread, not arrogance and pride in others he confronted. His face reddened and his cheek muscles twitched. This was a challenge to his masculinity that he admired in some ways. He knew he could just kill this inferior being, but was curious to see how much torture the foreigner could endure before his pride broke and he begged to be put out of his misery.

Eddie was scared but he had always stood up to bullies knowing they got their satisfaction from seeing smaller, weaker victims squirm. He had developed a strategy for appearing calm; he thought about fishing, of all things. In his mind he went through the process of laying out his equipment, checking his nets and fishing lines, his hooks and poles.

Though his heart was pumping faster, he was able to control his breathing and facial expression. He aimed to exhibit the false appearance of calm rather than challenge. In his mind he thought about checking for holes in his fishing nets and mending them.

Tryggvasson tried to verbally demoralise Eddie by saying, "I'll decide your fate later, Dane. I may strip your flesh from your body bit by bit and let you watch as we feed it to the fish. Or supply you to my father Odin's wolves, Ravener and Greed, to devour. Then again I may make you a galley slave and whip you daily till your skin has been completely flayed off and then have Heimdall rub salt in your wounds for the rest of what will be your very short life."

All the time Tryggvasson tried to intimidate him, Eddie held the big man's gaze as he thought about cutting a new fishing pole from the coppice and preparing it for use.

The veins of Tryggvasson's face began to pulsate and one side of his mouth twitched. He shook his head, turned on his heel and strode off, laughing. He looked back, curling his lips with a pernicious expression that made Eddie's blood run cold, though he didn't give Tryggvasson the satisfaction of realizing he'd finally got to him. His mind was concentrating on hammering out a new fish hook.

Eddie was secured to the mast by chains and with one last kick from Heimdall, he was left to consider his fate. He concentrated on how he mended his fishing canoe.

The rowing was suspended on the huge longship as the sails filled with the strong winds. The Norwegian oarsmen started to move about and several came to the mast and took turns to punch and verbally abuse Eddie. He slumped to the deck, bloodied and bruised, but still pretending defiance. In his mind he was winding his hemp thread fishing line onto a spindle.

Later Eddie was released from his chains and pulled towards the stern. Heimdall sneered. "You've little time to live now, Dane. We'll watch with amusement as you depart this life in anguish. When the Valkyries, the choosers of the slain, select those who will die in battle and collect the fallen for Valhalla, you'll not be one of them. For you it will be just the pain and ignominy of oblivion as the squalid halfman you are."

Two Vikings held Eddie while another removed his chains then used hemp ropes to bind his feet and retie his hands behind his back. Eddie forced his limbs apart slightly while the knots were tied. This was in the hope that if he was left alone he may be able to slip out of his bonds. But he knew he was clutching at straws.

Olaf Tryggvasson towered above Eddie again, shouting menacingly, "Tell me, Dane, how did Eric Greybeard know my brave heroes were coming to attack him in the dark on Osea Island? How was he able to free our raft? Did he have allies? Speak. If you don't give me satisfactory answers immediately, you'll be flayed alive now."

Eddie knew he had to say something or be slowly skinned and left to die in absolute agony. "Your flotilla leader was drunk," he answered. "All your men were singing raucously. No wonder Eric knew your warriors were there. With all that carousing, only a fool would have been surprised."

"You're a liar, Dane!" Tryggvasson shouted at Eddie.

"You weren't there, or you wouldn't have allowed it to happen," Eddie replied. "Consider, my lord, as your men outnumbered the Danes two to one, how could your highly trained warriors have been beaten back? Except if your men were drunk or drugged?"

"This can't be true, insolent dog," Olaf screamed at Eddie. "My men of Norway wouldn't risk drinking alcohol before a battle."

"If it wasn't alcohol, perhaps they'd taken magic mushrooms to give them courage."

Tryggvasson's facial veins swelled with blood and his visage contorted into a maniacal mask of violent fury. With his face a few inches from Eddie's own, Olaf roared, "How did they release our longship raft then, Dane?"

Eddie concentrated on his memories of a successful fishing expedition when he'd caught several dogfish and a skate. "I don't know. But perhaps your men were so drunk they hadn't secured the sea anchors properly?"

Olaf Tryggvasson was purple in the face and shaking. "If that was so, I'll have my flotilla commander killed. But you'll die with him as the Danish halfman coward you are."

Without warning, Tryggvasson punched Eddie in the chest. The blow was so powerful the Romani was lifted off his feet and he hit the ship's side. His skull struck the planking with such concussive power he was stunned.

His ribs were broken yet again, this time from the potency of Olaf's punch. Each breath was agony. Every intake of air felt like knives piercing his chest wall. Eddie's ribs had been broken before, but he'd never withstood such brute force. He tried to ignore the agony and terror by remembering the days when he collected oysters and clams for the family's meal.

Olaf Tryggvasson roared at him, "I will beat the truth out of you, halfman. Then I may prolong your agony for years, torturing you every day till your mind breaks."

Tryggvasson gave orders to a crewman who hung signal pennants from the mast. A while later, another massive Viking climbed aboard Olaf's flagship.

Tryggvasson shouted at the other huge man, "Bragi, like me, your father was the great god, Odin. You are named after the god of storytellers and poets. But you may have told one story too many."

Bragi was as tall as Olaf with massive biceps and a huge muscular chest. He had a cleft palate, deep wounds across both eyes and his huge hands and feet were double the size of Eddie's.

"This Saxon captive has told me you were drunk at the Osea Island battle," Olaf Tryggvasson stated. "That was why you failed to win the battle against a force half your flotilla's size. Do you deny it?"

Bragi stood to his full height, puffed out his chest, and then replied in an arrogant nasal twang, "No way, Olaf. This Danish captive lies. He's a disciple of Surt, the destroyer god who leads the fire giants to Hel."

Olaf Tryggvasson stared closely into Bragi's defiant blue eyes with their red-flecked irises. "I know you, Bragi. You love alcohol even more than sex with your ten wives. You are intoxicated more than you are sober. This is not the first time you've let me down, but it will be your last."

Eddie thought his hastily concocted explanation had struck lucky this time, putting doubts in Olaf's mind about his flotilla commander. Not that he expected it would do him any good. He was surely still doomed. He again focused on fixing his fishing gear to stop him panicking.

He watched as the row between Tryggvasson and Bragi, his flotilla commander, became more heated. Tryggvasson shoved Bragi, who retaliated by jostling his commander-in-chief. Propelled by Bragi's elbow, Tryggvasson slipped and fell against the longship's mast. Eddie could see this was a blatant challenge to Olaf's authority by Bragi. It was gross subordination that Tryggvasson couldn't tolerate in front of his crew.

Tryggvasson swung a mighty blow at Bragi, who ducked beneath his superior's swing. Bragi retaliated by kicking out at Tryggvasson, his foot making contact with Olaf's kneecap.

Tryggvasson screamed, "You'll die for that mutinous act, Bragi."

Eddie's Romani intuition told him the flotilla commander welcomed this opportunity to attempt to usurp Tryggvasson's position and take power for himself. Eddie also suspected that Tryggvasson, on the other hand, had been waiting for the chance to discipline his rebellious and openly disobedient number two, and that what he had made up about the flotilla commander's drunkenness was merely the catalyst which had reopened an already simmering feud between the two mighty warriors.

By now the two giants were wrestling, kicking and punching each other, becoming more and more violent. Bragi tried to gouge one of Olaf's eyes out and Tryggvasson stopped him by elbowing the flotilla commander in his windpipe.

The fight escalated to the point where both men drew swords. They slashed at each other. In the tight confines of the ship the two combatants weren't the only ones in danger. Everybody else pulled back, well out of sword range.

Swords clashed and the two men closed until each was holding the other's sword arm to stop his rival's blades making contact. Both of the giants' muscles bulged and sinews stood out as they strained to achieve physical dominance.

Eddie looked on in wonder, knowing that either could beat him to a pulp, even if his limbs were free.

Bragi yelled, "I'm number two in the fleet but should be number one as you, Tryggvasson, are a fraud and not the son of a god at all."

Olaf nodded, bawling, "Now we get the truth, Bragi. You're a traitor to all of Norway as well as to me. You were indeed drunk, yet again, at the Osea Island battle. You led so many fellow Vikings to Valhalla, without winning a battle against a Danish party half your size. You're a disgrace to our father, the great god, Odin. You'll not leave this, Odin's, flagship alive."

At the Maldon Burh, Princess Catherine and her girls stood at the parapet of the watch tower. Kate shook her head as she looked upstream towards Osea Island. She had come to terms with the likelihood that Edward was still in danger. Then she started to tremble as she thought she saw a black-robed figure in the trees below. She felt this ghostly apparition was trying to contact her. Then, suddenly, she knew that both Aefnoth and Eddie were alive... at least for now.

Her mind cleared and her handmaidens heard her laugh for the first time in days. Kate said to them, "Come on girls, lets get some food and a drink of mead."

Edith turned to Alfthrith and Bretwalda. "Our princess is suddenly chirpy again. Do you think she knows something we don't?"

Alfthrith replied, "Royalty know many things we don't, Edith."

"Don't worry about it, girls," Bretwalda chipped in. "She's happy again, so we will all have an easier time for a while. Enjoy it."

On the big longship, Heimdall, who was supposed to be guarding Eddie was, like all the other Vikings, absorbed with the fight between Olaf and Bragi. Thus, nobody was watching the tightly trussed Eddie.

Although bound hand and foot, Eddie took his opportunity and managed to roll and drag himself upwards over the gunwales. Then, with difficulty, he forced his pinioned body up until he hung, bent at the waist, halfway over the side. This wouldn't help him, of course. He knew that if he fell into the sea the restraining ropes would tighten and he would drown within seconds. But even that would be better than having to endure the prolonged, agonizing torture of being flayed or skinned alive.

The Viking chiefs' fight continued until eventually Olaf's greater strength overcame his opponent. Tryggvasson freed his dagger from his belt and plunged it repeatedly into Bragi's body. Bragi slumped to the deck, arterial blood spurting in all directions.

Olaf Tryggvasson bellowed, "You men see what happens to cowards who let me down! Let that be a lesson to you all. I'll not tolerate rebellious behaviour." He grasped and swung his great two-handed sword around his head and gave a bloodcurdling victory roar.

By then Eddie had edged himself forward until he was almost wholly over the gunwales of the ship. But he was scared to move any more as he knew it would instigate his own death by drowning. He cursed his own stupidity. How could he have ever thought he was a warrior? He was only a young Romani youth and a stupid one at that.

Olaf Tryggvasson concluded his victory celebrations and then looked round, remembering his captive. When he saw Eddie hanging over the gunwale Tryggvasson roared, "Kill the bastard Dane! Cut slices of flesh from his living body; make his last moments agonising."

A throwing axe dug into the wood close to Eddie's hip and Olaf's men were almost upon him.

Desperately, Eddie closed his eyes and launched himself towards the water. A berserker's hand grabbed at Eddie's clothes, but his shirt tore and the Romani fell into the sea.

Eddie was sinking and unable to move his limbs because of the ropes holding them tight. Panic and desperation made Eddie try to wrench his wrists from the bonds. But it was no use. The hemp ropes had already painfully tightened from immersion in the seawater.

He plummeted deeper into the darkening depths, his lungs bursting. He was fighting the sheer horror of saltwater asphyxiation, the hopeless dread of drowning. But it was all no use. He gave up the impossible struggle and let himself drift to oblivion.

Twenty-Three

It would have been a hot June day but for the strong south wind. The blue sky and streaky clouds at high altitude made the aspect distinctly pleasing to the eye. In the North Sea, the high tide and strong wind piled up swells until they broke. The sunshine on the collapsing breakers created streamers of white fluorescence in the green-blue of the saltwater.

A colony of seals fished in the shallower water near Mersea Island in Essex. On this island a single Saxon, Eldor Aefnoth, was perched precariously in the higher branches of a huge oak tree. He scanned the island and ocean, trying to locate his expedition partner, Edward, concluding he had probably been killed or at least captured by the Vikings.

A few miles downstream, Eddie had taken one last breath before deliberately throwing himself into the North Sea from Olaf Tryggvasson's flagship. As he was bound hand and foot he knew he had little chance of survival. Reluctantly he'd accepted drowning as a preferable final expiration to being flayed alive or otherwise tortured to death.

In a split second he was immersed and frantically fighting to free himself from his bonds. But this had only resulted in him plunging to such a depth that the water pressure was crushing his eyes and ears. With his oxygen, energy and all hope gone, Eddie's struggles ceased and he resigned himself to his fate.

To his surprise, instead of his lifeless body sinking to the seabed, his intrinsic buoyancy floated him towards the surface. As his head emerged from the water, he gasped a mouthful of life-sustaining air before going under once more. Aware that his situation was still extremely perilous, he desperately wriggled his trunk to try to reach the life preserving oxygen once more. But this was self-defeating; it just made him sink even deeper.

Forcing himself to relax, he allowed his natural buoyancy to float him to the surface again. Attempting to take a deeper breath this time, he swallowed some of the revolting brine. Then he choked as he tried to expel it underwater, coughing up his stomach contents and bile as he was gut-wrenchingly sick.

Eddie floated to the surface and inhaled more carefully. Seeing the blue sky once more gave him courage. By not moving a muscle, he found he could literally just go with the flow and breathe as the opportunity occurred.

After floating to the surface spasmodically and taking a breath of air each time, Eddie was able to glance round. Over the white caps, he could see the flagship of Olaf Tryggvasson, the Norwegian Viking chief, in the distance.

Just above the longship, two ravens flew in circles over the sea as if searching for something. Eventually they seemed satisfied and swooped down and settled on the crosspiece of the ship's mast. Luckily, the powerful tide had swept Eddie away from the Vikings and Tryggvasson's pet ravens.

Involuntarily, Eddie bobbed up and down slowly like a half saturated cork, inhaling when he surfaced and exhaling when he sank. He found the whole process disagreeable as seawater and rotting seaweed brushed his face and foul-tasting flotsam entered his unprotected mouth as he gasped for life sustaining air.

It got worse when he saw a vast red swarm of lion's mane jellyfish coming straight at him. He twisted around, but he knew there was no way of avoiding it and multiple long, fine tentacles wrapped around his naked skin, stinging him. He felt as if his head, hands and exposed back had been dragged through a bed of intensely painful, super-powerful nettles. His whole face was burning with the most excruciating agony. This was far worse than the broken ribs; even his eyeballs hurt. He didn't want to die this way, in anguish.

Through his acute pain, Eddie realized he wouldn't be able to sustain this precarious way of inflating his lungs for much longer. With his limbs still firmly tied, he hadn't a chance of survival. He again tried to force his arms out of the bonds, but if anything, they had tightened even more.

He just concentrated on staying alive. As the alternative was death, he had no choice. He knew he was becoming weaker from swallowing and choking on salt water. Soon he would have to give up the struggle to live, accepting his inevitable destiny and demise as his strength deteriorated.

But… was he dreaming? What seemed to Eddie to be a miracle was taking place. He felt once, then again, his feet dragging across and into… soft, slimy mud? Despite his body's exhaustion and his mental semi-stupor, a glimmer of hope lifted his spirits from the depths of despair.

He reasoned the tide must be going out and by chance he'd drifted with the currents into more shallow water. He must be near land. He looked around and sure enough, there were trees in the distance.

After what seemed like an eternity, Eddie's feet embedded into soft mud and he was able to stay in one place. Now at least he could breathe constantly with his head above the water. As the tide ebbed he allowed himself to believe that he might survive after all.

When the water had subsided enough, Eddie was able to sit in the mud. Then, despite the bonds holding his arms behind his back and his legs together, he wriggled snake-like across the slime towards the nearest shore line.

A family of seals was out on the mud bank, watching him with wide-eyed curiosity. Eventually he squirmed completely out of the water. But he wasn't lying on the firm mud that was supporting the seals near the sandy beach. He was stuck fast in its stinking, slimy, clinging cousin. Frustratingly, he was so near but so far from safety.

Most of the tidal water had gone. But the viscous mud was incapable of fully supporting his weight. Eddie had heard of quicksand but not of quickmud that this effectively was. He was gradually sinking into it, his whole body trapped by its adhesive suction. To add insult to injury, crabs nipped him and shrimps tickled his skin as they strove to get back to flowing water.

The more Eddie tried to escape the mud's grip, the deeper he was engulfed in the mire. By lying still, the natural buoyancy that had kept him afloat in the water allowed him to semi-float on the soft silt. Just enough for him to breathe, but even this was becoming increasingly painful and difficult.

Eddie couldn't believe his bad fortune. He'd survived the deep seawater. But now was stuck fast in this disgusting primeval sediment. He realized with shock that he would either be suffocated by the foul, black, sludge, or imprisoned in its grip to be drowned by the next incoming tide.

He grimaced, cursing as he lay forlornly on his side. He was managing to breathe, but his bonds still left him unable to move his limbs. The jellyfish stings were excruciatingly painful. His eyes were so swollen from the venom he was hardly able to open them and could only see though a red mist from one eye.

Even that wasn't the end of his problems. His saturated bonds were cutting mercilessly into his wrists and ankles. This was stemming the supply of blood to his feet and hands, giving him pins and needles. Far worse was the terrible, agonizing cramping in his calves. It felt as if these muscles were detaching themselves from his legs and trying to escape through his very skin. His body's agonies were unbearable and there was no way he could release himself from this horrific torture.

Eddie was in serious pain and distress, sinking deeper into the slippery mire with every second. The tide was already flowing back. Muddy wavelets pervaded his nose and mouth as each surge swept over the mud bank. He was again forced to accept despair at the inevitability of his impending demise.

He couldn't believe his fate could get worse, but it did. Several gulls and crows attacked him as he lay immobile, enveloped in the mud. He felt the sharp pecks and smelt his own blood from the birds' assaults. He heard the birds cawing and screeching. In the circumstances, they sounded like harbingers of doom.

Perhaps the birds were prematurely classing his body as carrion and would eat him alive? He turned his head away and painfully closed his jellyfish-stung, swollen eyes, realizing they'd be vulnerable to the scavenging birds.

He tasted his own vomit in his mouth but there was no way to clear it. Though he coughed and spat, the sick taste and stench wouldn't leave him. Now he was lying in an almost comatose state. Only his cramping limbs and the intense pain from the jellyfish stings were keeping him conscious.

Vaguely, as if dreaming, he thought he felt hands on his swollen feet. Forcing his inflamed eyes open slightly, he realized it was true. Dragging him from what would have been his certain grave was his mission partner, Aefnoth.

"Edward! Thank God I've found you," Aefnoth exclaimed. "I'd given you up for dead."

Eddie was so weak he couldn't answer, just managing a half smile.

Aefnoth was only able to drag Eddie's supine form along the mud, unable to lift his extra weight as his own legs plunged deeply into the black sludge. Popping, squelching sounds accompanied each laboured effort to release one of his legs from the sludge's powerful suction.

Eddie's saviour managed to drag him from his erstwhile muddy tomb, finally pulling him onto the sandy beach. His heart and lungs were still pounding from his efforts, but at last he was able to stop. He collapsed, coughing and wheezing from his supreme exertions.

They both lay on the shore covered in foul black sediment.

Eventually, Aefnoth recovered and cut Eddie's bonds as he lay on the sand. Eddie's ankles and wrists were red raw and still cramping painfully from their previous confinements. As his blood flow returned, his agony was increased while his body tried to return to equilibrium.

Eddie gasped out, "I'm so grateful, Aefnoth, and I owe you one."

"You are welcome, Edward, but it was a close thing. I was just about to give up looking for you when I wondered what the gulls and crows were making so much fuss about in the mud. It was a good job they did."

Eddie lay on the sand in the hot sun until a semblance of strength and mental balance returned. Then Aefnoth helped him to a pool where they both washed as much mud off as possible.

Eddie's wrists and ankles were chafed and bleeding. This was an unwelcome legacy of the constant rubbing from the rope restraints that had confined his limbs for so long. His face, hands and back were covered in striped rashes from the mass of jellyfish stings.

Now the mud was gone, Aefnoth noticed the rashes and Eddie's red, swollen eyes. "How did you get those strange wounds, Edward? Were you whipped?"

"No, it wasn't whips; this was inflicted by a swarm of large jellyfish."

"I've seen the creatures washed up on the beach, and even eaten some cooked with a meal," Aefnoth remarked, "but I never knew they could cause such wounds."

Eventually, Eddie recovered sufficiently to tell Aefnoth the story of what had happened to him after he'd been captured. Aefnoth was wide-eyed and wouldn't have believed it if he hadn't seen the rope bindings.

Eddie staggered into the woods until he found the old rotting oak tree and recovered the crystals.

Standing on the earth walls of the Maldon Burh, Ealdorman Byrhtnoth spoke to Princess Catherine. "I must inform you, Princess, my spies at the mouth of the estuary have spotted yet another Viking fleet."

"Were these allied to the original ones that camped on Osea Island, Lord Byrhtnoth?"

"My men consider not, princess. As the longships were flying raven pennants, they were more likely to be affiliates of the ones that attacked the Danes before."

"What do raven pennants signify, Lord Byrhtnoth?"

Byrhtnoth clenched his teeth. "I believe they're the war pennants of Prince Olaf Tryggvasson, the Norwegian tyrant. The most disturbing thing is the size of this new fleet. My men estimate there could have been up to a hundred longships."

Kate's hands fled to her mouth in horror. "Are they coming this way?"

"No, thank God. They seemed to be in pursuit of the other flotilla. That means they're heading in the direction of Colchester and Ipswich. However, they could return quite easily. The reason I'm telling you this is to urge you to leave now while you can. I will have you escorted back to the King's palace in London.

Kate's face reddened. "I appreciate your concern, my Lord Byrhtnoth, but I feel I am part of this town of Maldon's community now. That's despite my fiancé being missing for the moment. In any case, when he returns I should be here to greet him."

"That's well spoken, your highness, and Aefnoth will appreciate your courage. But bear in mind, should we be attacked by the Vikings it will be too late to spare troops for your escort duties. You'd be trapped here with us."

"So be it, my lord. I'll throw my hand in with you in the Maldon garrison.

Byrhtnoth beamed. He bowed and kissed the back of the princess's hand.

Kate returned to her room accompanied by her girls. Edith whispered to the other two handmaidens, "Our lovely princess seems sad again; probably missing her fiancé, Aefnoth."

On Mersea Island, Aefnoth pointed out to sea. "Look, Edward, the Norwegians have gone and the Danish longships returned. Eric Greybeard's canoe is coming here."

"When we get back to the Burh I should teach you to speak the Vikings' languages, Aefnoth."

Aefnoth grinned. "Well, perhaps a few of the vilest Viking curses I could use in battle anyway."

Ericsson pulled the canoe out of the water. Then he and his father Eric Greybeard joined Aefnoth and Eddie.

"I don't know how you did it, Edward," Greybeard said, "but you were right again. There was indeed a great Norwegian battle fleet coming our way, so we had to leave in a hurry. It would have been reckless, if not suicidal, to take on such an armada. I was sorry we had to abandon you two, but there was no time to pick you up."

Eric and Ericsson were both looking askance at the striped red weals on Eddie's bare skin and his red chafed wrists. Ericsson looked as if he were about to ask how Eddie had sustained such odd wounds, but Eric put a hand on his son's shoulder and shook his head.

Eddie was relieved, not wanting to admit how stupid he'd been, allowing himself to be captured by Tryggvasson. So he assured Eric, "You did the right thing, guys, and thankfully came back this way."

Eric then sent Ericsson to get Eddie a replacement shirt from his longship to replace his torn one. He also told him to bring a spare sword and dagger as he noticed Eddie had lost his own in some way. Neither Viking queried how he had misplaced them.

Eric smiled knowingly. "Edward, I think you have some way of getting information without the runes' help? Perhaps you're a holy man or magician?"

"I'm neither holy nor magical, as I can only predict some things." Eddie answered. "Like you, I'm guided by the Druids."

"I also don't think you're German, or even Saxon, Edward. Not that it matters, as you saved our lives. However, I'm curious to know more about you.

"You're right again, Eric. I'll tell you about myself. I am from the Romani tribe. We're descended from the ancient warrior classes that lived in the Punjab in the mountains of Northern India. That's in Asia. Our whole warrior nation left India in the seventh century as we'd been cut off from our homeland by the hordes of Islam, a great warrior religion."

Eric looked astonished. Then Ericsson returned with the spare shirt for Eddie, and a sword and dagger with scabbard and sheath to hold them in. Eddie thanked the two men for their thoughtfulness, put the new shirt on and adjusted the scabbard and sheath to fit. The garment was a bit on the large side and he had to roll up the sleeves at the cuffs.

Ericsson told Eddie, "Those were all owned by one of our brave warriors who went to Valhalla in the Osea Island battle. I'm sure he would have wanted our blood brother to have them."

With that, Ericsson walked away and Eddie continued telling his story to Eric. "My ancestors crossed the Himalayas and followed the Silk Road west to the Caspian Sea. Then via the Caucasus range to Armenia, and on to the Byzantine Empire. For nearly three hundred years my entire nation has been dispersing across the known world."

Aefnoth and Ericsson were throwing rocks at sea birds. One rock landed near Eric and Eddie, splashing them.

"That's fascinating, Edward," Eric said, giving Ericsson a dirty look.

"We're a free people. Although being warriors, we've moved around the known world without trying to take anyone's land by force. Many Romanies are now integrated into local societies, where they live in peace."

"How does your tribe earn its keep in new territories?"

"It should be remembered that Romanies are warriors, and many fight as mercenaries for local warlords or kings. We are also farmers, smiths, carpenters, musicians and fortune-tellers."

"I see. How do your people tell fortunes?"

"We read palms, divining knowledge through crystal ball readings and a myriad of other ways."

"Is that how you knew the Norwegians were coming, Edward?"

"No. That was what I call remote viewing. However, the psychic system is similar. Nevertheless, I doubt you would have believed me without my runic subterfuge, so it was necessary."

Eric nodded confirmation. "You are right. I would not have accepted what you said without your play acting. But then we would have all been killed. Thank Loki, our god of the ego and brain, for your guile. Now, what about these crystal balls you talked of, Edward?"

"We're master craftsmen in our own right, so we are able to make them from the base crystal rocks that we mine ourselves. In fact, it was probably a Romani craftsman who made the crystals your father traded for in Constantinople, Eric. Many of our crystal master craftsmen settled there while moving through Byzantine. Ali Espigatt is an eastern Romani name, you see."

"Now that's interesting, Edward. But how do you come to understand our runic language?"

"That's because my mother taught the runes to me when I was young in Germany. So it seems the Norse and Romani races are similar in many respects. There is of course one big difference; while your nation are brilliant seamen, the Romani come from a land-locked area of the mountains of India, and have no nautical tradition. Thus, we Romani rove the land instead of the seaways."

Aefnoth and Ericsson had moved on to wrestling now. Both being big, strong men, they were throwing each other around and cursing in their respective languages.

Eric commented, "Edward, it's surprising how well Aefnoth and Ericsson are getting on together considering they can't talk to each other."

"True, but they're both warriors and have fought on the same side in battle. That creates strong comradeship; after all we're blood brothers now."

"You say you're a Romani but I've heard your nation called Gypsies. Which is correct?"

"Being called Gypsies was not of our choosing. When we first came to Europe we were confused with the dark-skinned traders from Egypt. They were called Gyptians, so gypsy is an abbreviation of that word."

Now Aefnoth and Ericsson were seeing who could throw their javelins farthest along the sandy beach.

"Now I realize your Idrottir is very long indeed," Eric said.

Eddie scratched his head. "Eric, I don't know what an Idrottir is. Can you explain?"

"Yes, a person's Idrottir can be defined as a list of his life's expertise. This can be any skill he has, for example, fighting, academic, athletic or craft skills."

Eddie still looked puzzled. "How do you rate anyone's Idrottir?

"We believe each person has a price fixed at birth. This is called a Ret. When he is born, a freeman's Ret is worth two marks of silver, while a noble may be worth six marks. However, every person can increase their Ret's worth, by learning or acquiring skills."

"Eric, this may seem a silly question. But what good does it do anyone to build up a high Ret value?"

"Well, if a chieftain or King hears of a person with exceptional Ret, or special aptitudes, he'd want to employ that man in his service and would reward him accordingly. So if a man has many skills, especially fighting ones, he can increase his personal Ret to the extent that he can attract his own followers. It's even possible that in this way a slave can become a freeman, and then perhaps even a powerful leader himself. In addition, if he is murdered or dies in battle, the Ret worth is the compensation that must be given to the next of kin by the killer or the Lord he was fighting for."

"I get it. That sounds like a great way for a leader's followers to strive to learn more skills."

"Quite so, Edward."

Aefnoth and Ericsson walked back with arms around each other's shoulders as if they'd been mates forever.

"Now, Edward, we really must return to our longship to get some sleep before sailing tomorrow. Remember we're blood brothers and we will come to your assistance should you need us."

"Yes, Eric. We must also go to Maldon to warn them about Tryggvasson's fleet."

"I can't offer you two a lift south to your homes in Maldon," Eric said, "as we are going north to Ipswich. I've arranged to meet up with some other Danes we know. But we will return to camp on Mersea Island afterwards, so if you need help let us know. Edward, my brother, I bid you farewell. We will meet again if it's Odin's will."

The two men parted with a mutual two-hands-to-forearms shake and Eddie said, "Goodbye, my brave friend."

Before they left, Ericsson brought over two stone flagons of beer and a cloth bag of food for Eddie and Aefnoth.

Ericsson gave his new pal, Aefnoth, a fraternal hug. Then he paddled the canoe and his father, Eric, back to their longship.

"Well Edward, when I came here, I hated all Vikings," Aefnoth said. "But I've learned that some of them, like Ericsson, are okay after all. However, I'm glad I don't have to go on their longships again. It made me so ill. But we must get back to Maldon Burh with the crystal lenses as soon as we can. Have you any idea which way to go?"

"I believe there's a causeway at the other side of this island, Aefnoth, so you shouldn't have to take to the sea again."

"I am so glad about that, Edward. Any idea what route we should take to get to this causeway?"

"The problem is whether to go straight across the island through the scrub, or to go around the coast?"

"I've been told that the island's about three to five miles across and about fourteen miles round. So to go either way round the beach could be seven miles, more or less, depending where the causeway is situated."

"That's true, but there'd be no vegetation or scrubland to slow us down? Plus I've no idea who lives on the island, or if they'd be friendly or warlike?"

"You are probably right, Edward, but I want to get back to Maldon as quickly as possible to warn my father about the Norwegians. So let's go across and risk it."

"Okay. But don't forget we're dressed as Vikings, so we might not initially be welcomed by Saxons if we are seen."

Aefnoth and Eddie climbed up the slope from the beach and worked their way across the scrubland in a westerly direction. The ground was hard and they soon reached the woods.

Suddenly, a deer shot out from the undergrowth in front of them. Who was most startled, the buck or the two men, was debatable.

Both laughed and Aefnoth said, "That's shows how much our nerves are on edge, Edward."

Eddie waved an arm in the air. "That's not surprising after what we've just been through, is it?"

"I agree, but we must press on now."

After they'd moved inland for about half a mile, the undergrowth became so thick they needed their swords to clear a path.

"Perhaps this route wasn't such a good idea after all," Aefnoth conceded."

However, it wasn't animals or humans, but artefacts that caught their attention next. When they emerged into a clearing, there was the circle of standing stones. Eddie recognized them as the ones he'd visited with the Norwegians and by remote viewing.

Aefnoth looked at them in wonder. "Edward, I'd been told by Prior Esmond these may have been set up by the Druids thousands of years ago."

"Yes. Esmond told me about the stone circle as well, Aefnoth. They're certainly impressive."

Slowly, from nowhere it seemed, a strange apparition appeared. It was a tall, white-robed figure, dressed like some form of priest. The figure vanished and then reappeared, if it were the same one. But now it was standing beside an eight foot rock behind them.

Aefnoth, spooked by the strange figure, drew his sword and held it in front of him defensively. He whispered to Eddie, "By Saint Cedd, what's that?"

"It might be a Druid priest," Eddie whispered back.

On closer inspection, Eddie noticed the figure's white robe reached to the ground, had a cowl covering the facial area, and its voluminous sleeves were clasped together. Not a fraction of skin was showing.

"This is very strange," Eddie said. But there was no answer. Aefnoth seemed frozen with his sword still held out in front of him, like a statue.

Before Eddie could go to Aefnoth to try to snap him out of it, the white-robed figure glided nearer.

It was at least eight feet tall and painfully thin. As the cowl was lifted by exceptionally thin white hands, Eddie was stunned. The being looked as if it were androgynous. Anyway, he couldn't make out its sex.

It seemed very young, like an extremely tall ten-year-old. He, she or it had the white hair and pink eyes of an albino. With its skin seemingly translucent, light seemed to be going right through it.

What was this apparition? What did it want with them?

Twenty-Four

Mersea, the largest North Essex Island, was situated eight miles east of Colchester and sixteen miles north of Maldcn. It was only sparsely inhabited due to the thick forestation and the frequency of visits from armed insurgents. Invaders landed there on their way to attack Colchester, the largest Essex town, or while passing along the coast. Colchester, like Maldon, had one of the King's mints full of silver within its fortified Burh.

While Eddie and Aefnoth were crossing the island they'd reached a large circle of stone monoliths. Mysteriously, a tall figure in a white robe had materialized near them. The androgynous essence turned in Eddie's direction.

At that moment, for Eddie, all the woodland sensations seemed to have been suspended. It was as if the three existences floated somewhere or everywhere in the cosmos.

Aefnoth seemed frozen in time, still holding his sword out protectively.

Without movement, the white-robed entity communicated, *Edward Lavengro, you have done well, as ordained.*

Eddie sensed this message. It was not speech, as such; not sound, sight or smell, but more like celestial bells ringing. The message was in a range that he could feel through his very skin.

Then without warning the sounds returned; a pigeon cooed as it landed on the ground near them. Lapwings, starlings and sparrows flew about chirping, but none entered the space occupied by the prehistoric megalithic stone circle.

Aefnoth snapped out of his soporific trance, glared oddly at his own drawn sword and, looking bewildered, replaced it in its scabbard.

"Edward, why are we wasting time? We must get back to Maldon."

"It's all right the white figure's gone now."

Aefnoth looked puzzled. "What white figure do you mean?"

Eddie presumed that only he had seen the strange manifestation, or Aefnoth's memory of the last few minutes had been wiped.

"We must go this way, west, towards the trail over there." He walked towards the position he'd been directed.

"What trail? I can't see one."

Aefnoth was right. No trail was apparent, just scrubland. It seemed as if he'd been dreaming after all.

However, when they reached the stunted trees there was a trail, its entrance hidden behind thorny blackberry bushes. As it was the only break in the undergrowth, they followed it even though it took them in what seemed to be the wrong direction.

When this trail ended abruptly they both drew their swords and, slashing down the briars and undergrowth, worked their way west. Eddie, being a Romani, knew how to keep to his direction in wooded areas. He checked the mosses, which always grew on the north facing side of the tree trunks. Without this, it would be easy to roam in circles.

Eddie picked some early blackberries from the briars and Aefnoth plucked up a young puffball. They sat for a while to consume the beer, meat and bread provided by Ericsson, accompanied by thin slices of the raw puffball. It was pure white all through and had an earthy, mushroom flavour. They followed this with the blackberries.

Now sated, they continued slashing through the undergrowth towards the west. The ground was rather boggy, with strong scents from the bracken, heather and gorse bushes. Eddie picked a handful of the yellow gorse flowers; getting many thorn pricks in the process. As they walked, they ate the coconut-flavoured flowers like children consume treats.

The bright sun shining through wavering branches created intermittent shadows alternating with blinding sunshine. Energetically, the two men slashed at the undergrowth with their swords. Then, dazzled by a shaft of brilliant sunlight, they stumbled into a clearing where Norsemen were felling trees.

The men ran towards Eddie and Aefnoth, wielding their woodcutting axes. Eddie refrained from hailing the attackers in case he chose the wrong language. Instead they both slowly and deliberately held out their swords and placed them on the ground, holding up their bare hands, open palmed, to show they were no longer holding arms and had surrendered.

With their axes still raised menacingly, the Scandinavians encircled the pair. Without talking, the men picked up the swords and removed the pair's daggers from their sheaths. Then they forced them past a herd of goats and some chickens, into their house through a narrow entry passage.

The leader of their captors spoke to them in Danish. "Who are you? What are you doing, arriving armed on our land? Did you intend to rob us?"

Eddie replied quietly in Danish. "My friends, we mean you no harm. We're scouting the land for Eric Greybeard and heading for the causeway to the mainland."

With that, the Danish leader visibly relaxed. Looking askance at the red jellyfish weals on Eddie's face and hands he said, "I know of Eric Greybeard. He's a brave fighter. My name's Tyr, you're both welcome, please eat with us."

The food was hard bread and buttermilk and was surprisingly filling. Tyr was a tall, angular man in his forties with blond hair and a beard streaked with grey.

Eddie had been in many buildings like this one in Denmark, but Aefnoth hadn't seen its like. Its overturned boat shape with a paved porch, a large main room and two separate bedrooms fascinated him. There was a dairy and even a sweating room.

Aefnoth examined how the house was built. It was of two-layer wooden construction, with the gap between the layers earth-filled and the roof covered with turf.

Eddie explained, "The use of earth in this way makes this dwelling cosy in cold winters and cool in the heat of the summer." He noticed the Danes had many Saxon artefacts, suggesting they were probably traders.

When they had rested, Tyr said, "I'll send my son Tyrsson to guide you to the causeway as this forest is daunting if you don't know the way."

Eddie thanked their host, and the ten-year-old boy led them into the woods.

Tyrsson, who was a gangly boy with curly blond hair, said, "The causeway joining Mersea Island to the mainland is known as the Strood in these parts."

Even with Tyrsson's guidance, the winding and interconnecting paths still took around two hours to cover. When they arrived at the Strood the tide was low enough to cross, but was already running in.

Tyrsson told them, "You must cross over the Strood to Peldon immediately as in a few minutes the depth and strength of the tide will be too dangerous."

Eddie smiled. "Farewell, Tyrsson. We appreciate your help." He gave him one of his silver coins supplied by Ealdorman Byrhtnoth. Tyrsson grinned shyly, looking at the coin with excitement, and then wished them well.

Signalling goodbye to Tyrsson, both men started to cross the natural mud and sand strood crossing. The boy had been right; they were only just in time, having to splash through surging seawater that was already over their ankles.

When they reached the mainland shore, Aefnoth said, "Thank goodness for that, Edward. Water still scares me. As you know, I can't swim."

"I must try to teach you to swim sometime, Aefnoth."

The burly Saxon didn't look enthusiastic about Eddie's offer. Looking dubiously at the rising seawater, he changed the subject. "Now our problem is that we're dressed as Vikings. It would be tragic if we were attacked by our own side."

"Yes. We must be careful. You are more likely to be recognized, so you should lead now, Aefnoth."

Warily, they moved towards Peldon village, travelling west despite Maldon being south of the Strood. They had to do this, as Aefnoth was aware that saltwater inlets barred their path in the southerly direction. There was also a reasonable bridleway to the west until they reached the end of the Thornfleet inlet.

Bypassing the inlet, they passed several farms and Aefnoth said, "I suggest we try to borrow horses from one of these homesteads."

"I agree, Aefnoth. If not, it will be dark before we get to Maldon."

Two of the farms were single hides but the third was larger, with several substantial buildings and many horses and cattle in the fields. Despite their cautious approach, a skinny youth saw them and ran off.

In no time at all, five armed men came towards the pair, not looking at all friendly.

"Here we go again," Aefnoth exclaimed. They placed all their weapons in an exaggerated fashion on the ground for the second time that day. As Eddie put his sword and dagger down he saw and smelt the horse and cow dung lying all round. He also noted the many circular growths of horse mushrooms in amongst the numerous molehills.

When the farmers were near enough, Aefnoth held his empty hands aloft and shouted in Saxon, "Hold friends! I'm Eldor Aefnoth, the son of Ealdorman Byrhtnoth from Maldon."

This had a quietening effect but the men's weapons were still in evidence until Aefnoth was recognized.

The older man said, "I'm Edgar, a Ceorl who fought in your father's select fyrd armies. Edgar was a ruddy-faced farmer of medium height. He was powerfully built, balding, with a scraggy beard and red calloused hands. His three sons Abel, Ben and Edmoss, looked like their father but were much taller and had masses of straggly blond hair.

Aefnoth replied, "Yes, I recognize you, Edgar, and your sons. We've been on my father's business. Now we'd like to borrow horses so that we can return quickly with important news to Maldon Burh. That's if you can spare them?"

"I'll be happy to help you, Eldor Aefnoth. I'm going to Maldon market in a few days, so I can retrieve my horses from the Burh's stables then. It will take a while for my sons to catch and prepare the horses. In the meantime my wife, Mary, will prepare you a meal."

Mary, a short, attractive, rather chubby lady in her forties, gave them barley beer, open-fire toasted bread, and freshly picked horse mushrooms baked with melted goats cheese. The smell of the food was so overpowering and the taste so palatable, Eddie consumed four portions. Aefnoth ate even more.

"Thank you, mistress Mary," Eddie said. "Your food's delicious."

Mary smiled. "You're very welcome. The mushrooms grow free in the meadows and we make our own bread and cheese, and the beer is brewed in this kitchen. I like to see men with such good appetites."

Edgar, who was also eating with them, had news. "Eldor Aefnoth, I've seen a vast fleet of Viking longships heading down the river Colne towards Colchester. Will you please pass this on to your father, Ealderman Byrhtnoth?"

"Thank you, Edgar. I certainly will. That's very interesting information. Call to see my father or me when you pick up your horses and you will be rewarded."

Replete and rested, Aefnoth mounted a strong horse and Eddie climbed onto the back of a sturdy pony. Then, waving farewell, they rode off towards Maldon.

Along the way they smelt the smoke of many fires, some with food cooking, but very few people. The ones they did spot gave them dubious looks and scuttled away. This was most probably because the pair was still in Viking dress.

Passing the end of Salcott Channel and the Tollesbury Fleet meant they could go as straight south as the bridle paths would allow towards Maldon. Later they made their way via Goldhanger to Mill Beach, then to Heybridge and up the steep, cobbled Maldon Hill to the fortified Burh.

Aefnoth told Eddie, almost apologetically, "I'd better do most of the talking from now on."

Eddie agreed.

When they arrived at the Burh they dismounted at the stables and handed over Edgar's horses to Rayhald, a young groom.

Aefnoth said to the boy, "A Ceorl called Edgar will call for these horses in a few days. See that they're stabled, fed and watered till then?"

The stable lad touched his forelock and led the animals away.

After entering Ealdorman Byrhtnoth's quarters, they sat by the fireplace. The fire was set with kindling and logs ready to be lit, should it turn cold. Eddie could smell the aromatic pine logs and even a smoky ambience from previous blazes.

Byrhtnoth entered the room. "Welcome back, both of you. I'd been perturbed by your long absence. Please excuse me, Edward the Tall, if I take my son away to get an initial report from him."

Eddie nodded his acceptance.

Byrhtnoth put his arm round Aefnoth's shoulders and led him into his inner sanctum.

Eddie mused that although he explained what the Vikings had said to Aefnoth it was only the bare bones. Only he himself knew it all, so he should really be with Aefnoth to explain what had happened on the island.

However, he could understand Byrhtnoth wanting to speak to his own son in the first instance. In addition, Aefnoth was an Eldor and had been in charge of the expedition. Eddie himself would have to give Byrhtnoth any extra information later if any gaps became apparent.

Eddie waited in the outer hall looking at the large, dark paintings of Byrhtnoth's father, Ealdorman Byrhthelm, and King Aethelred. He knew these emphasized how wealthy Byrhtnoth was. While they had been away, Aefnoth had told him there were few paintings of that size in the country and that, apart from those in the King's palace, paintings were usually restricted to church wall coverings.

Aefnoth had also said that the few artists who existed were monks that illuminated religious books. In fact the recently deceased Prior David had painted these portraits. He'd painted them in return for the grant of the income from several farms to fund Beeleigh Priory in perpetuity.

After ten minutes, the two noblemen returned to the outer hall. Ealdorman Byrhtnoth addressed Eddie. "You've done well, Edward the Tall."

Eddie bowed his head. "Thank you, my lord. Your son is undoubtedly a great warrior. He saved my life more than once."

Byrhtnoth looked at his son proudly.

Eddie continued, "I have something for you." He handed Byrhtnoth the crystal lenses. "These can be adapted for use as a scope."

"Thank you, Edward the Tall. Your mission is accomplished. Get yourself some food now, and then rest. You will be rewarded for obtaining the crystals when my son has given me the full details."

Eddie was keen to see Kate, so he reported back to her quarters, but she wasn't in her outer rooms. Alfthrith, her handmaiden, was there.

"Princess Catherine is having her bath in the back room by the fire." She winked sexily. "You could do with me bathing you before you see the princess. You don't smell too fresh, Edward."

"You are right, Alfthrith. I've been living and sleeping in these Viking clothes for ages. They do niff. I'll go now to wash and change my clothes, and then report for my princess's bodyguard duties tomorrow."

But before he had time to do this, Kate appeared, wearing just a wrap. To Eddie she looked absolutely gorgeous and smelt clean and perfumed. This made him feel even more smelly and inadequate.

"So you're back, Edward the Tall," Kate said. "I'm pleased. Ealdorman Byrhtnoth sent a messenger to tell me my fiancé and you had returned safely. We'd heard there was a big battle on Osea Island. I thought you'd been killed, especially after Ealdorman Byrhtnoth's search party failed to find you two after the Vikings had left."

"I'd just gone for a trip in a Viking longship, my lady."

Kate put a finger to her lips. "Please don't forget I prefer you to call me Kate when we're not in the company of other nobles."

Eddie's face reddened. "I'm sorry, Kate. I'll try to remember in future."

Kate gave Eddie a sweet smile. "What do you mean, just gone for a trip in a Viking longship? That sounds pretty dangerous to me."

"It's a long story, Kate."

"Well, I want to hear all about your trip sometime. But at the moment, from your dishevelled appearance you look as if you need to clean up. Also, you'll want to get yourself a meal and some sleep. I'll see you tomorrow with the Ealdorman. Please report here for your bodyguard duties after that. Then you can tell me all about your adventures."

While Kate was talking, Eddie couldn't stop himself staring at the beautiful princess. Her huge, powder blue eyes kept him spellbound. Then he noticed Kate's cheeks begin to colour a pleasing shade of pink. He spoke quickly, not wanting to upset her. "Yes, my... Kate, I will do as you say immediately."

Eddie walked away past the handmaidens in the vestibule. As he passed them he heard the sound of giggling and then Edith's squeaky voice whispering, "He fancies the princess, anyone can see that."

That evening, Eddie had an all-over wash with tallow soap, and a shave and haircut. This was followed by a night of sound, relaxed sleep. The next morning, after a change of clothes and a good breakfast, he felt respectable once more.

A short while later, he was summoned to the great hall for another audience with Ealdorman Byrhtnoth. Eddie had expected to be discussing their recent mission with just the Ealdorman. However, to his surprise there was quite a large group already present.

As well as Ealdorman Byrhtnoth, there was his wife, Lady Aelfflead, their son Eldor Aefnoth, Princess Catherine, Eldor Godric, three Thegns: Wulfstan, Maccus and Aelfhere, as well as Prior Esmond.

Byrhtnoth addressed Eddie. "Edward the Tall, I have examined the crystals you call lenses. They're one of the greatest wonders I have ever come across. My son has demonstrated the uses they can be put to. I can see they could be of great military significance to us."

Godric snorted in a derisive way, holding his nose as if detecting a bad smell from Eddie's direction.

Byrhtnoth ignored the rude interruption and continued speaking to Eddie. "You are a most unusual young man. You told me yesterday that my son saved you twice. What you didn't say was that you had already saved his life in the Osea Island battle."

Eddie didn't know where to look and shuffled his feet in embarrassment.

"You also did what none of us could have done, by gaining the trust of the Danes. To think that two of my warriors fought in a battle on the side of Danish Vikings is incredible. And if this wasn't enough, to have persuaded the Danish Vikings to give you such wonders as the crystal lenses into the bargain, shows exceptional aptitude and initiative."

While Byrhtnoth was speaking, Eldor Godric leered at Kate. Eldor Aefnoth swiftly moved next to Godric and stamped on his left foot. As both were of the same rank, and Aefnoth was much the bigger man, Godric couldn't retaliate. He just jumped around on one leg for a while, making pained faces and grunting.

Byrhtnoth had seen both incidents and looked amused, but continued to address Eddie. "My son tells me you also read their runes and divined the future accurately from them. Some may consider this to be blasphemous behaviour, dealing with pagan rites, but Prior Esmord has persuaded me that you are of exceptional intellect."

Eddie could see that Eldor Godric's ugly face was contorted and very red, emphasizing his terrible acne. His lips quivered and the degenerate's hands were bunched tightly into fists with his arms crossed over his chest.

Eddie noticed that the despicable creature now had an outbreak of boils all round his neck and chin and a sty on each of his close-set, piggy eyes. Godric stared at Eddie with obvious and unsuppressed hatred.

Thegn Wulfstan, Byrhtnoth's nephew, caused a diversion by sneezing violently, excusing himself to the rest of the gathering.

Byrhtnoth waited for Wulfstan to recover and then resumed. "Edward the Tall, because you have given excellent service, I have decided to award you four more hides of land adjoining the two already owned by you in Maylandsea. There's a good hall on the main farm that I've used myself on occasions.

"This extra property makes up your land ownership to six hides. This entitles you to a higher social status; in fact it confers on you the rank of Thegn. You will be given your own warhorse, chain mail and full kit of weapons from my armoury. Go to see Thegn Maccus tomorrow and he will guide you on the best available."

Thegn Maccus waved his three-fingered right hand, indicating that he'd noted the appointment and instructions.

Eddie said, "Thank you, my Lord. I'll do my best to serve you well."

With that, Godric moved towards Ealdorman Byrhtnoth, obsequiously bending his head forward. "But sire," he protested. "This shouldn't happen. This man's no Saxon. We don't want foreigners in the higher echelons of our army, do we? My two brothers have noble blood and should be promoted rather than this wretch. This man speaks the Norse languages, therefore he must be a Viking spy."

Ealdorman Byrhtnoth answered the Eldor with, "Go away, Godric. It will be better if you listen to what I say in future." Then he dismissed the inadequate noble with a sweep of his hand.

Byrhtnoth addressed Eddie again. "However, Edward the Tall, as you don't come from this area, I would like you to spend some more time with the good Prior so that he can help you to understand more about us, and we may even learn from you."

"I'll do your bidding with pleasure, my Lord" Eddie replied.

The Ealdorman continued. "My son has given me the report that Prince Olaf Tryggvasson's Norwegian Viking fleet is heading towards Colchester. They will almost certainly attack our brothers. For us in Maldon, it means we have some respite, although our gallant allies at Colchester will, I am sorry to say, have a terrible fight on their hands.

"I suggest, Edward the Tall, you visit your new properties in Maylandsea for a break, in case we're assaulted after Colchester. I would appreciate your help in any fight and I will need you particularly because of your linguistic talents. I shall send you a messenger if we're in imminent danger of being invaded."

Prior Esmond handed Eddie a signed scroll giving him ownership, and the detailed plans of his new property.

"I thank you, Ealdorman Byrhtnoth, for your generosity," Eddie said. "I should also inform you that the Danish Viking leader, Eric Greybeard, gave me his oath that he won't attack Maldon or anywhere in the Blackwater Estuary. So at least that takes his Danish Vikings out of our defensive reckoning."

"That's excellent news, young man."

"There's more, my Lord Byrhtnoth. Eric Greybeard also agreed to form an allegiance with us. In fact, he has made your son, Eldor Aefnoth, and myself his blood brothers because we fought alongside him in the battle on Osea Island. He informed me that if his Danes are nearby and Prince Olaf Tryggvasson's Norwegians attack Maldon Burh, he will offer his warriors to fight alongside us as they are his enemies as well."

The Ealdorman clasped Eddie's hands in both of his large strong palms. "I knew I'd made the right decision, making you my new Thegn. For these brilliant coups you have just informed me of, I wish to present you with a slave of either sex."

Eddie felt tempted to ask Byrhtnoth for a pretty female slave who could bathe him and ease his frustrations. But thoughts of Kate changed his mind, so he asked, "Lord Byrhtnoth, May I have Ecceard, the blacksmith slave?"

"Ecceard is a good choice, Edward. He has great skills that will be useful to you. He is yours."

"My Lord Byrhtnoth, I'm not comfortable with the basis of slavery, having so recently having been one. May I crave your indulgence for me to have him freed from his slavery? Then use him as my Ceorl freeman instead?"

The Ealdorman seemed slightly bewildered by Eddie's second request. "I'm surprised you want him freed from slavery, but if that's what you require it shall be done."

This was just too much for Godric, who was now purple with rage. He made a last disparaging rude gesture at Eddie and stormed out of the great hall, swearing under his breath.

Byrhtnoth sent a servant to bring Ecceard to the hall. While they waited,

Ruth and Sibyrht, the two middle-aged serving women, supplied goblets of wine to all present.

When Ecceard arrived, looking puzzled, Byrhtnoth spoke to him, "Ecceard, you have worked well in my household. This has been noted by my new Thegn, Edward the Tall." He swept his right hand towards Eddie, indicating his presence.

Ecceard looked across at Eddie with his mouth hanging open.

"As Thegn Edward the Tall has requested it, I have transferred you into his service. No doubt you'll be pleased that he's also decided to free you from your slavery."

Ecceard beamed and clasped Eddie's hands with his own, calloused and burned as they were.

"Prior Esmond, will you please perform Ecceard's freeing ceremony here and now," Byrhtnoth commanded.

"Certainly, sire, I have a spare official citation in my pack." Esmond used his quill to personalize it in Ecceard's name and within minutes, the ceremony had been completed. Byrhtnoth, Eddie and Esmond duly signed Ecceard's manumission document. Ecceard was now a freeman Ceorl once more.

Byrhtnoth then spoke to him. "Go with Thegn Edward the Tall tomorrow to get your Seax knife from the armoury as the token of your freedom."

The next morning Eddie went to the armoury with Ecceard to meet with Thegn Maccus. Firstly they let Ecceard, the new freeman, pick out a Scramaseaxe, or Seax knife, as it was commonly known. Ecceard picked out one about thirty inches long, more of a sword really. He told them he'd chosen it because he'd made it himself and it was one of his best blacksmithing efforts.

Eddie told Ecceard, "I want you to accompany me to my new farms in Maylandsea. You can move your family there. I'll provide you with a house and if you're willing, you can look after the estate for me."

"I gratefully accept, Thegn Edward the Tall. I won't let you down," Ecceard said with a broad smile.

"I'm pleased the arrangements suit you, Ecceard. Go back to your family now and give them the good news. Oh, and just call me Edward. After all, you knew me when we were both slaves"

When Ecceard had gone, Thegn Maccus fitted Eddie with his new suit of chain mail. He was surprised by the weight he would have to carry if he wore it. He'd have to decide on the conditions before deciding to lug it around. While in close combat it could save his life, but it would also make him less mobile, and to wear it anywhere near water that he could fall into could be lethal.

Maccus noticed the look of concern on Eddie's face and said reassuringly, "Chain mail armour is heavy, but you must remember you will usually only wear it on horseback or in battle. Oh, by the way, you're to go to see Aelfwold, our veteran stable master. He'll find you a sturdy warhorse. Try your chain mail on when you ride. It will seem strange, but the armour's essential when danger threatens."

Next, Maccus picked out a sword for Eddie. He told him it had been traded from the Germanic Frankish workshops. Eddie noted it was engraved with Ulfbert, the name of one of the world's best master sword makers. Both edges were razor sharp and it had a sharpened point. He then sorted out a good, stout, thrusting spear and five lighter javelins.

While Eddie was trying out the power of various bows, a very pretty blonde girl appeared with a plate of food and some wine for Maccus.

"This is my daughter, Athelflaed," Maccus said. Eddie recognized her name and could well see why Aefnoth was besotted with her. He guessed she was less than five feet tall. She had a slim figure and regular facial features that were set off by her almost constant smile. The girl had all round charisma and was obviously bright and intelligent.

Athelflaed blushed at the visual attention Eddie was paying her. She curtsied and said, "I've heard a lot about you sir, and all good."

Eddie smelt a heady rose flower perfume on Athelflaed that was in keeping with her overt glamour. Her tiny hand was soft but reddened, probably by doing many chores.

Athelflaed said, "I must go now, I have work to do at home." Then she walked off down the passageway, swinging her hips.

Eddie watched her go, thinking what a pretty girl she was.

Maccus laughed. "I see you approve of my daughter. She can cook, sew and brew beer and will make a good wife one day soon, I trust.

I'd hoped she would marry Ealdorman Byrhtnoth's son Aefnoth. There had been an understanding to that effect. But King Aethelred has decided Aefnoth should marry his daughter, Princess Catherine, and it would be unwise to disagree with our sovereign."

Eddie looked concerned. "I sympathize."

Maccus turned to Eddie. "You're not married are you? Athelflaed could bear you many children and be a useful companion. She's pining for Aefnoth, so it would be better for her to marry someone else, as that cannot now be."

"She's beautiful Maccus, but with a battle coming, getting married is not on my mind at the moment."

Eddie felt honoured that this was the second father who had offered him his own daughter for a wife. Both Emma and Athelflaed were beautiful and either would make him a good life partner. But he had lost his heart to a lady he had no chance of marrying... a princess he called Kate.

Apart from that, if after Colchester the Norwegians attacked Maldon, the Saxons would be greatly outnumbered by far more experienced Viking fighters. He'd witnessed Vikings and berserkers fight and seen their sheer ferocity in battle. In addition, he'd met the giant Olaf Tryggvasson once and never wanted to again.

In fact, the future didn't look auspicious for the town. That also left Kate and him in an extremely perilous position indeed.

Twenty-Five

On the Blackwater Estuary two small Saxon fishing boats sailed towards the North Sea, the yellow ochre sails contrasting with the blues and greens of the waves and sky. Seals and seagulls followed in the crafts' wakes.

Early in the morning Eddie reported to Kate at her rooms in the Burh for his bodyguard duties.

The princess said jauntily, "Congratulations on your well deserved promotion to the rank of Thegn; not bad for a scruffy Romani gypsy boy. Do you wish to leave my service as bodyguard and set up your own war party now you have your aristocratic status?"

Eddie replied, a little too eagerly, "No way, Kate, if you will accept a Thegn as your bodyguard?"

Kate smiled demurely. "That's in order then, my new Thegn protector. I'd be interested in learning more about your Romani race at some time. I'll tell you when."

Kate's cat, Bodi, slinked into the room and when she saw Eddie talking to Kate, she ran up to vie for her mistress's attention. The wild cat got her way as her mistress picked up the feisty feline and stroked her.

"I hear Ealdorman Byrhtnoth has advised my Thegn bodyguard to visit his new lands," Kate began. "I've not been to Maylandsea since being captured by the Vikings and rescued by you. I would like to return to thank the Maylandsea priest, Pastor John, for his bravery and help. Could I prevail on you to accommodate me and my girls for a few days in your new hall?"

Eddie's heart leapt. A delighted grin spread across his face as he spluttered, "Yes, yes, certainly. I... I'd be honoured, Kate."

With a shake of her head, Kate continued, "The problem is, Ealdorman Byrhtnoth may object because the Vikings are marauding along the coast. As I'm a princess, I would again be a prime kidnap target for the Norse Invaders."

Eddie was apprehensive that his fantasies about him and Kate getting together would come to nothing. "I'm sure Ealdorman Byrhtnoth will allow you to go if you ask, Kate? After all, we could soon return to the Burh if there's danger?"

"I think you're right. And it would be great to get away for a while, Edward."

At that moment, Charley, Kate's fat black tomcat, sinuously loped in and rubbed against Eddie's legs. The Romani suspected the cat did so because Kate was holding his rival, Bodi.

"You boys stick together, I see," Kate said with a grin as both cats purred contentedly.

When Kate released Eddie from his bodyguard duties he wandered back towards his room at the other side of the Burh. He had a spring in his step but was desperately keen to be alone with this alluring princess. Feeling relaxed and safe within the Burh's fortifications, he casually wandered into an area of deep shadow cast by the Burh's lofty escarpments.

His reverie was abruptly shattered by an attacker's arm violently encircling his neck in a tight stranglehold. In the same instant, a second assailant's boot crashed into the young Romani's guts. This had obviously been a well-synchronised, planned attack.

Eddie retched, involuntary muscular spasms attempting to eject his stomach contents but, with his captor's right bicep crushing his gullet, unable to do so. Eddie was choking on his own vomit.

Maniacal guffawing mocked the young Romani's futile attempts to throw up and break free from his captor. Eddie recognised Eldor Godric's peculiar eerie voice as the degenerate noble cackled, "So, foreigner, you thought you could usurp my brother's noble born right to improved personal status? Dead men hold no rank, so when your lifeless body is found in the Burh cesspit at least one of my brothers will be awarded your undeserved elevation."

"That's quite right Godric, you tell him before I break his dirty Gyppo neck," Godwine simpered in his high, feminine tone. Then, tightening his arm around Eddie's windpipe he thrust his own pock-marked face close to Eddie's cheek.

As the young Romani recoiled from the stench of Godwine's blackened, decayed teeth, a shaft of light revealed that Godwig, the third of the depraved brothers was standing immediately in front of him. Eddie realized it must have been he who had kicked him.

With the sun now blinding his attackers, Eddie took the opportunity to smash the metal tipped heel of his boot backwards and upwards into Godwine's crotch. Emitting an animalistic shriek at this instantly disabling agony, Godwine had no choice but to release Eddie's neck before crumpling, face distorted, onto the hard dirt, hands cradling his genitals.

Eddie gulped a lungful of air and seizing his chance while the brothers were distracted, attempted to get away. Unfortunately, Godwig threw out a leg and tripped him up, foiling his escape.

275

Eddie's chest hit the ground instantly and, with nothing to cushion his fall, he experienced sharp pains as his ribs cracked. However, this setback only intensified his determination to break free. With one supporting arm across his chest to negate the agony, he again attempted to stagger away. But this was not possible because now Godwig and Godric barred his exit with drawn swords. The sun glinted on the brothers' blades as they swung them savagely at Eddie. He realized that, unarmed as he was, unless a miracle happened he'd be cut to bits; he must duck or die. Closing his eyes, he steeled himself to make one last escape effort.

Fortunately for Eddie, his miracle did arrive before he was minced by the scything arks of the brothers' lethal swords. He heard Eldor Aefnoth's voice barking out an order restraining the attackers.

Opening his eyes, he saw that several of Ealdoman Byrhtnoth's elite Huscarls had already disarmed Godric and his brothers. Eldor Aefnoth then instructed Senior Thegn Uhtred, the Huscarls' commander, to throw the brothers into the dungeons to await their punishment for attacking a recently promoted officer in the Saxon army. Using brute force, the Huscarls dragged Eddie's three attackers away, despite Eldor Godric's protestations that they didn't have the authority to do so because of his superior hereditary nobleman status.

After Eddie's assailants had been removed, Aefnoth assisted his Romani friend to his feet and into the nearby kitchens.

"Thank you once again," Eddie gasped, still struggling to regain his breath and composure. However, his Romani instinct detected that Aefnoth had some even more pressing concern on his mind. His inherited intuitive powers were seldom wrong and again this proved to be so.

Aefnoth wiped his brow, rested his right, leather-booted leg on the solid oak canteen bench and spoke to Eddie of his worries.

"A Colchester resident returning home after a trading trip saw a massive Viking fleet attack the town and came here to warn us," he began. "He informed my father, Ealdoman Byrhtnoth, and me that they were under attack from Norse invaders. He told us Longships had arrived via the Colne River estuary and burnt all Colchester's Saxon fleet of ships at the Hythe harbour before they could put to sea. Then some of the Viking longships sailed further along the estuary and secured Colchester's North Bridge. The Colchester man suspected that the Vikings did this to discourage any Saxon reinforcements coming from the countryside and crossing the wide Colne estuary." Aefnoth's face was flushed and his brow furrowed with anxiety.

Eddie gasped. "That's terrible news! What do you think the Vikings' tactics will be after that?"

"The main Viking army led by Olaf Tryggvasson is already laying siege to the city's defences," Aefnoth answered. "As long as they keep their discipline our Colchester allies should be able to hold out almost indefinitely. That's because their garrison is protected by high and strong stonewalls completely surrounding the main Burh. Additionally they have an inner keep that is a full castle in itself; this also has thick stonewalls and was built by the Roman occupying forces as the Temple of Claudius many years ago.

"Unfortunately we can't send help from here, as it would leave the Maldon Burh and our own local inhabitants vulnerable. After all we are only a short sea journey away by the Vikings fast longships. Thus the Vikings may attack us next to try and plunder the King's silver in our mint. They have already ransacked several other coastal towns."

"What should I do in these new circumstances, Aefnoth?"

"I suggest, Edward, that you carry on with the visit to inspect your new hides and farm buildings. It may be the last chance you'll get for a while. Princess Catherine has indicated her wish to accompany you with her handmaidens. By all means escort her there."

Aefnoth winked conspiratorially at Eddie. "You see, I'm going to spend as much time as possible with Athelflaed, my lover, while she's away," he whispered. "Between you and me, after having a heart to heart talk with my father, he has agreed that my arranged marriage to Princess Catherine need not go ahead. We have never loved each other but would, of course, do our duty and marry if our respective fathers required it. Furthermore my father tells me he understands that King Aethelred is not insistent on the marriage. The Ealdoman is well aware our alliance was only offered as a reward for his loyalty and bravery in battle as the King's premier general. Thus my father believes the king will acquiesce if he requests that this engagement is put aside."

Eddie listened to this revelation from his friend with avid interest.

"I understand fully your reluctance to abandon Athelflaed," he said. "I met her recently and as well as being beautiful she has a wonderful disposition. She will make you a fine wife."

Aefnoth smiled knowingly, realizing that although Eddie was sincere in his good wishes, he looked somewhat bewildered and was probably assessing his own chances with the princess. He wasn't mistaken, as he found when his friend spoke again.

"Aefnoth, I have to admit that I, among many others, am attracted to the princess. Of course, I would never have betrayed your trust in me by moving above my station. Though now you have confided your intentions to me..." Eddie looked at the floor and then lifted his gaze slightly to judge Aefnoth's demeanour. Ascertaining that his mood was still friendly, he continued.

"I realize I could have no ambition in that direction. After all, I was only a slave in her service until quite recently."

Both sides of Aefnoth's mouth curled slightly upwards, not so much in a smile but more in recognition that he understood what Eddie was really angling to hear.

The Eldor replied in a benevolent tone. "On the contrary, Edward, you are now ranked as a nobleman in your own right and not only that, but also promoted for your feats of arms – your bravery and strategic battle planning. You should understand this carries a higher status with the King than any hereditary title.

"Think about it: being a monarch is an extremely hazardous position. Foreign powers, his own relatives and many English highborn nobles would like to usurp his supreme social status. Remember, King Aethelred only ascended to his position of sovereign after the murder of his half brother and predecessor, King Edward. Who murdered the teenage king is conjecture, although it is rumoured it was a close relative of the present king. Thus the king is desperately keen to gather as many self-motivated heroes as he can into his wider service – warriors like you who are able to make and carry out battle plans under duress.

"King Aethelred is well aware some hereditary nobles are worse than useless. You will understand this from your recent encounter with Eldor Godric and his brothers. Sons of heroes don't always follow in their gallant fathers' footsteps. As for Eldor Godric and his brothers, I will petition my father the Ealdoman to have all three either executed or banished from England; either way you shouldn't be bothered with them again"

Aefnoth then hurried off to discuss defensive strategies with his father, Ealdoman Byrhtnoth, and his senior advisors.

Eddie remained sitting in the canteen eating bread and spit-roasted pork washed down with a flagon of red wine for his midday lunch. Despite the enticing aroma of the pork, he still ruminated on the current situation. Now that Aefnoth had encouraged him to escort Kate to his new home there was less reason not to do so. Although Ealdoman Byrhtnoth could veto this, he resolved to try to grasp the nettle while he could. He finished his meal and exited via the heavy defensive oak door. He was immediately struck by the dramatic deterioration of the weather. Black clouds now masked the sun, with swirling, cumulonimbus storm clouds massing on the horizon. Eddie nodded his head, reflecting that this sudden squall coincided with the darker mood of most locals after the worrying news from Colchester.

Still deep in thought, Eddie wandered through the gloom towards Kate's quarters. He sensed rather than saw that the unearthly beings in priestly garb were with him. As he turned his head he noticed a flickering vision of a being in a white monk's habit. His mind received a message directly from the insubstantial entity. The spirit or whatever it was told him, 'Do not be afraid to discuss what is consuming most of your waking moments. You are longing for Kate. Be assured you and Princess Catherine will eventually be as one. I will guide you on how to handle your approach to her.'

Eddie asked out loud, "But who are you all?"

'We are your guardians from the spirit world. We are everywhere but only a few exceptional beings like your mother, yourself and one or two other Romanies per generation can sense us. You have no need to be afraid; always accept us for what we are, your helpers. We will never cause you harm, as you are one of the elite mortals.'

Eddie wanted to know more but the essence had gone. He was not afraid any more, but felt happy and reassured. He was now certain that with his guardians' help he could win Kate's favour and resolved to do just that.

As he reached Kate's quarters he was determined to conceal his chest pains from his princess. A small fire crackled in the centre of the vast store hearth. The fire's sweet scent and lack of smoke indicated that it was fuelled by rosewood. A large blackened kettle, suspended above the curling red and yellow flames, steamed merrily.

Kate was alone for once, except for Bodi, her cat. She looked radiant, dressed in a beige flax linen gown that reached to the floor. It had decorative hand-stitched blue and green flowers across the bodice. She did a twirl.

"Do you like this, Edward? I embroidered it myself."

Eddie looked her up and down; taking in the way her lightweight gown clung to her slim figure. Her allure was further enhanced in Eddie's eyes by long blonde ringlets that flowed past her waist.

Eddies breathing quickened, "You look fabulous in it, Kate, and your workmanship's superb."

Kate smiled coquettishly, and then screwed up her face. "You see, Edward, we ladies of the royal court are only expected to do genteel, noblewomen's things like needlework. Then marry and become brood mares to extend the royal lineage or die in the attempt." She sighed deeply.

"What would you prefer to be doing, then, Kate?"

She paused, sucking pensively on her bottom lip. "I'd like to have the satisfaction of achieving adventurous projects like my brothers. Go on far away campaigns, get to meet and understand other races."

Eddie hesitated and then said, softly, "Well I'm from another race and you said you'd like to find out more about us Romanies. If you come with me on my trip to my new properties at Maylandsea, perhaps I could enlighten you?"

She smiled flirtatiously, opening her big powder blue eyes even wider as she realized Eddie's dark pupils were revealing a look of pure admiration. He was captivated. Then, realizing that as a princess looking at a commoner she was acting far too provocatively, she lowered her gaze demurely.

"Okay, I'll try to persuade the Ealdorman to allow me to go with you."

"That would be wonderful, Kate."

"Edward," she said softly, keeping her eyes averted, "Aefnoth has just informed me that he has told you our engagement is likely to be put aside if my father the King agrees. Between you and me, my dad, even though he is King, is really a tame pussycat who dotes on me, his youngest daughter. Thus I am certain I can talk him round to my way of thinking. Aefnoth is a great guy but I soon realized his heart was with Athelflaed. I don't blame him; she is gorgeous."

She finally looked him in the eye. "I am only telling you this to explain why I need to get away from Maldon for a while... to give him space."

Eddie's heart was fluttering, but he realized he had to be careful; the princess's affections were not to be trifled with, so he merely nodded his head in understanding.

Kate spoke again, now in a lighter tone. "When I was a girl, Edward, a Romani lady told my fortune and she was right. One day I'll let you know what she said, but not now. Can you tell fortunes?"

"Yes, to a degree."

Kate's eyes widened again. "Really? Will you teach me how to do it?"

Eddie would do anything for Kate, especially after such a look. He gawped stupidly, mouth open, but quickly recovered his composure.

"I'll try, but it's only for those who have the gift It's not a science that can be taught to anyone." He noticed Kate's downcast eyes and the look of disappointment on her beautiful face.

Thinking quickly he said, "However, my senses tell me you may have an innate capacity in this very area. After all, I was able to use my remote viewing to reach you from Mersea Island. If I'm right and you have this special aptitude, I'll help you develop it."

Kate's sucked on her perfect teeth as if confused, and then a knowing grin spread over her exquisite countenance. She twitched her elegant nose then gushed excitedly "I've often had feelings that things are going to happen, and then they do. But I've dismissed them as coincidences. I want you to bring out what you explained as my psychic qualities—"

"You need to reach outside of the possibilities defined by natural laws, Kate."

The princess's face showed curiosity and she leaned towards him to learn more.

Emboldened and excited by Kate's closeness, Eddie lowered his voice to what he hoped was a more masculine tone and suggested, "I may be able to help you to develop an ability to use mental telepathy. To send and receive communications with others of thoughts, feelings and even desires."

Kate's face lit up. She licked her lips and her hands moved as if to physically grasp the ideas out of the ether. "Yes Edward," she breathed. "That's the type of excitement I've longed for since childhood. When can we start?"

Eddie began to sweat and his hands trembled. "We'd have to study it alone together for a long time?" He held his breath as he watched her facial expressions, partly in excited anticipation of her reaction and also to minimise the acute pain from his cracked ribs.

Kate in turn studied his face. He was indeed handsome, in fact very dishy. She would enjoy being alone with this Romani boy even though he wasn't of a noble bloodline. Knowing she wasn't going to be married off at any time soon, a trip away with the young hunky Edward would be a chance to break out from her privileged but rather tedious princess existence.

Eddie had been staring closely at Kate, devouring her fine facial features. He'd realized long ago that he was madly in love with her. But life and the Saxon class system were so unfair.

Kate eventually broke off from her personal reverie. "I've decided to come with you whatever the Ealdorman says. After all, I am a princess so I outrank him. Can you tell me something about fortune-telling to be getting on with, Edward?"

Eddie gasped with excitement, but then calmed himself as his ribs revolted. "Okay, let's try developing your mental telepathy. Stare into my eyes and try reading what I'm thinking about now. Reach into my very thoughts."

Kate put Bodi down and glided up closely to Eddie until their faces were almost touching. She breathed in shallow draughts and her heart drummed rapidly as her powder blue eyes stared into his, which she likened to warm mahogany.

She blushed. "I can read your mind, Edward. You think I'm pretty and want to kiss me. Am I right?"

"Dead on, Kate. You see, you can read minds already."

At that precise moment the dark clouds passed over and blinding sunlight streamed through the window portal, illuminating the lovers. If they had looked up they would have detected an indistinct translucent figure in a white monk's cowl, hovering paternally over them. But they only had eyes for each other.

Slowly Kate leaned forward and, slightly parting her full red lips, lightly kissed Eddie on the mouth. They melted into each other's arms.

Kate's lips were so soft; Eddie felt he was in heaven. Her arms drew him to her. He could feel her breasts and her heart beating rapidly through her thin gown against his chest. He inhaled her fine perfume. Even the pains from his damaged ribs were welcome as an indicator of his closeness to his precious and perfect love.

Kate swooned in Eddie's young, strong, manly arms. This was indeed the boy of her girlhood dreams, who the Romani lady fortune-teller had predicted would come to her. They would spend the next few weeks alone in each other's arms, away from the town and all its inherent complications.

She snuggled closer to him. With all doubts forgotten, both were convinced they would be together indefinitely and this exquisite sensation would go on forever...

Author's Notes / General Note:

Historians have made assumptions on sites, dates and locations for battles in Essex during the late 10th century. However, these have not been validated by artefact finds.

There are few corroboratory records from this era and little detail in the ones that do exist. The Liber Eliensis starkly reports as follows: 'In AD 987 Byrhtnoth met them with an armed force and killed nearly all of them on the bridge.' But met whom? On what bridge and on what date? How long was the battle and what were the numbers of combatants, injuries and fatalities? Most of the poem, *The Battle of Maldon* survives. But was this recorded by an eyewitness or commissioned afterwards by the leader's wife? Furthermore, some of this novel's characters existed, but in name only. Thus all reference to battles and the characters' actions and pronouncements in this novel are fictional.

The heroine, Princess Catherine/Kate:

King Aethelred married three times and had many children. Their names were all recorded except for one 'mysterious princess' who provides the basis for this novel's heroine, Princess Catherine/Kate, although it's unlikely the time line was exactly compatible.

The hero, Edward the Tall/Eddie:

Edward the Tall did exist and was indeed a hero. The poem *The Battle of Maldon* reports that after the death of the Saxon leader and mass desertions, Edward the Tall heroically led the vastly outnumbered Huscarls in a near suicidal counter attack on the Viking lines, thus saving the town.

Furthermore, DNA testing on skeletons in East Anglia indicates that Romanis were present around the time line of this novel. As this warrior tribe fought as mercenaries, it is possible Edward the Tall was indeed Roman.

The villains:

The poem *The Battle of Maldon* states that Eldor Godric and his brothers, Godwine and Godwig, deserted the battlefield after stealing their leaders' distinctive horses. This triggered a general desertion by the amateur men-at-arms, leaving the few professional warriors vastly outnumbered, which could have led to the loss of Maldon.

Olaf Tryggvasson (later King of Norway) was reputed to be the leader of one of the huge Viking longship fleets marauding along England's eastern coastline during this novel's time line.

Viking Telescopes:

History books suggest telescopes were invented in the 16th century. However, the Gotland Fornsal crystal lenses in Visby date from more than a millennium ago, making it feasible the Vikings did have telescopes in the tenth century.

Modern/Saxon Place Names:

Modern Saxon

Althorn Ale ThornAln
Asheldham Haintunic
Benfleet Beamfleot
Blackwater (Estuary)Panta or Pante (Estuary)
Burnham Burneham
Bradwell Othona (Roman fort)
Chelmsford Ceomaers Ford Chelmeresfort
Colchester Colne Ceaster
Colecestra
Colonia - Camulodunum
Creeksea Cricksea
Fambridge Fanbruge
Maldon Maeldun/ Melduna/ Maeldune
Maylandsea Malanda
Mersea Island Mersey/Meresig
Mundon Munduna
Heybridge Tidwoldington
Ipswich Gyppeswick
Latchingdon Laecedune
London Lundene
Londinium
Peldon Piltondone
Purleigh Purlai
Prittlewell Prittewella
Steeple Steola
St Peters Chapel St Peters Chapel
Rochford Rochfort
Tillingham Tili
Witham Witham
Northy Island Northy Island
Osea Island Osea Island
Temple of Claudius Temple of Claudius

This novel was intentionally written in modern day English and
using current place names. For interest the modern names are listed
above with their Saxon equivalents. Many, like Colchester and
Chelmsford, also had earlier names, including Roman ones. Anglo-

Saxon place names had no harmony so it will be possible to find variant speelings to the ones shown.

Maldon = Maeldun/Melduna/Maeldune.

The Saxon names also meant the hill marked with a cross.

There is a wonderful bronze statue of Byrhtnoth by John Doubleday situated at the end of Maldon Prom walk in Promenade Park. Follow Byrhtnoth's gaze and you can see Northy Island where it is believed the Viking armies camped and to its right is the causeway that they crossed to do battle. In Maldon high street there is an earlier statue of Byrhtnoth on All Saints Church. In addition The Maeldune Heritage Centre houses an amazing 42-foot embroidery, created to mark the 1000th anniversary of the battle.

St Peters Chapel, Bradwell on Sea, built in 654 AD by St. Cedd, is used for Christian services to this day. It is signposted and can be visited most days.

The Temple of Claudius is in Colchester's Castle Park. It is now a wonderful museum covering every era from the local Stone Age Clactonian tribe onwards. It is well worth a visit as are the remaining town/castle stonewalls dotted around.

Maylandsea = Malanda: Mailanda, the modern village has been built beside Lawling Creek. This was where, at the time of this novel, Byrhtnoth's wife Aelfflead owned farming lands.

Breinigsville, PA USA
17 March 2011
257879BV00001B/10/P